More Praise for *Crocodilopolis*

"A darkly intoxicating novel, at once mythic and wickedly contemporary . . . Here is a writer in full command of his world, delivering a ferocious meditation on masculinity, legacy, and national myth through an audacious, unforgettable book."

—Ocean Vuong, *New York Times* bestselling author of *The Emperor of Gladness* and *On Earth We're Briefly Gorgeous*

"The tales John Manuel Arias spins are as gripping as they are stunningly written. A natural-born storyteller of the highest order."

—Justin Torres, National Book Award–winning author of *Blackouts*

"In this beautiful novel, Arias creates a journey both mythic and necessary in the here and now. There is destiny, there is beauty, there is loss. In Arias's work there is life in all its epic and intimate glory."

—Nana Kwame Adjei-Brenyah, National Book Award finalist and author of *Chain-Gang All-Stars*

"The wonderful John Manuel Arias is bequeathing us—and Latine literature as a whole—his wildly imaginative second novel, *Crocodilopolis*. It's a high-octane cocktail of obsession, fraternal revenge, Costa Rican politics, and yes, crocodiles. Lots of crocodiles. What could go wrong? Read this romp of a tale to find out!"

—Cristina García, author of *Vanishing Maps*

"A lush, ambitious take on Cain and Abel intertwined with the rich history of Costa Rica."

—Silvia Moreno-Garcia, *New York Times* bestselling author of *Mexican Gothic* and *The Bewitching*

"A Costa Rican dynasty's lust for power drives this lush and suspenseful saga . . . Arias remains in control to the very end of this un-put-downable novel."

—*Publishers Weekly* (starred review)

"Arias offers a blood-soaked family drama that invites reflection on both Costa Rican and contemporary U.S. politics. 'Costa Rica is its own myth,' he suggests, in a brief poetic aside. 'Costa Rica is Costa Rica,' suggests another."

—*Booklist*

Praise for *Where There Was Fire*

"When poets write novels, you just know they'll be good ones."

—*Good Morning America*

"A haunting, operatic saga of family, history, and place. *Where There Was Fire* beautifully braids love, lust, magic, and the destructive power of man to wondrous and, at times, heartbreaking effect. Arias has created an utterly original, unforgettable tale of family that will sear a place in the reader's soul."

—Xochitl Gonzalez, *New York Times* bestselling author of *Last Night in Brooklyn*

"*Where There Was Fire* reads as if enchanted by the spirit of an ancient and generous storyteller. How privileged we are to read of this memorable family! It is an astonishing debut novel, written in prose so atmospheric and poetic that I gasped too many times to count. *Where There Was Fire* quite literally took my breath away."

—Kali Fajardo-Anstine, American Book Award winner and bestselling author of *Woman of Light* and *Sabrina & Corina*

"An arresting tale of love, regret, and redemption. John Manuel Arias offers a searing look into the legacy of American agribusiness in Costa Rica and masterfully tells the story of a family fighting to put itself back together in the wake of unimaginable loss. As poetic as it is powerful, *Where There Was Fire* burns with rage and grief, and most of all, hope."

—Jenny Tinghui Zhang, author of *Four Treasures of the Sky*

"A sweeping portrait of a Costa Rican family that has the energy of a speeding train. Each sentence that John Manuel Arias writes carries the juice of great gossip, the lyricism of a favorite poem, and the blood of forgotten history. I will never forget this book."

—Melissa Lozada-Oliva, author of *Dreaming of You*

"John Manuel Arias weaves an ambitious story that exposes the costs of corporate greed while revealing the power of personal agency and the enduring bonds of family. This is a book you'll want to read again and again."

—Cleyvis Natera, author of *The Grand Paloma Resort* and *Neruda on the Park*

"This novel showcases its author's lyrical gifts and deep, personal knowledge of Costa Rican history and agribusiness. In scintillating prose, John Manuel Arias, who is also a poet, tells the story of a family rent apart by the ruthless banana industry and a deadly fire that impacts multiple generations."

—*San Francisco Chronicle*

"Every page is a master class in how to wrap a reader inside of a book. Simply put, this book will make you want to reread it just to spend more time with the writing."

—Debutiful

"Vivid and rich." —Lupita Aquino, @Lupita.Reads

Crocodilopolis

BY THE SAME AUTHOR

Where There Was Fire

Crocodilopolis

A Novel

John Manuel Arias

BLOOMSBURY PUBLISHING
NEW YORK • LONDON • OXFORD • NEW DELHI • SYDNEY

BLOOMSBURY PUBLISHING
Bloomsbury Publishing Inc.
1359 Broadway, New York, NY 10018, USA
50 Bedford Square, London, WC1B 3DP, UK
Bloomsbury Publishing Ireland Limited,
29 Earlsfort Terrace, Dublin 2, D02 AY28, Ireland

First published in the United States in 2026

ISBN: HB: 978-1-63973-843-4; EBOOK: 978-1-63973-844-1

Library of Congress Cataloging-in-Publication Data is available

2 4 6 8 10 9 7 5 3 1

Typesetting by Six Red Marbles India
Printed in the United States by Lakeside Book Company

For Megan,
There's no one else I'd rather bicker with
for the rest of our lives

Behold, the hope of him is in vain . . .
He beholdeth all high things:
He is a king over all the children of pride.

JOB 41:34

Set . . . this is thy brother here . . .
Who is made to endure and to live
So that he may punish thee.

THE PYRAMID TEXTS, 173

Crocodilopolis

Costa Rica is home to millions of beasts as beautiful and ancient as sin. Like resplendent demons before the arrival of Man, they are winged, fanged, taloned, barbed, and cloaked in a desperation to survive until the very end. One creature, the American crocodile (Crocodylus acutus), is one of its most unforgiving executioners. Its own myth. Bulls can reach lengths of twenty feet and weigh up to 2,000 pounds. With eighty teeth the size and sharpness of splintered bone, they ambush prey, dragging it from the river's edge to drown. They are paler than other crocodilians, so at night, their leathery scales and spikes reflect light like moon rocks. In recent years, tourists have crowded on bridges overlooking the Tárcoles River—Costa Rica's most polluted waterway—tossing scared, flapping chickens to witness the crocodiles frenzy over an easy meal. Sometimes, their hunger confuses them, and they rip bitter pieces from each other. The more sinister specimens wait until a fool comes for a closer look. It is said that the bite-force of Crocodylus acutus is the most powerful of all living animal species. One can snap its jaws shut with almost two tons of force, and the pressure from each individual tooth (all eighty of them, the size and sharpness of splintered bone) can reach up to 350,000 pounds per square inch. The most unfortunate for quarry: crocodiles are unable to chew. Without cheeks, they can only swallow chunks of meat that fit into their jagged mouths. This means that with larger prey—say, the size of cattle or that of humans—they must perform what is known as the "death roll." Biting down (with almost two tons of force), and using the friction of the murky water and their own body weight (2,000 pounds in some cases), they roll, over and over, until bones are smashed, joints are disjointed, and sizeable, swallow-able pieces are torn away. As always, nature is the mother of cruel invention. In Costa Rica, the aggressiveness of the American crocodile eclipses that of all other nations in the Western Hemisphere.

2011

Seth Oreamundo stepped into his two-bedroom apartment, and without the slightest greeting to or from his wife, he began watering his tropical plants. Many had grown from clippings he'd snuck into the United States through Customs ten years ago, bundled in moist paper towels, their budding white roots readier to take to this country than he'd ever been. Other specimens arrived later, from gardening websites in reinforced seed packets, or in thick, *Fragile*-stamped boxes. Horticultural enthusiasts protect their plants above all else. Recently, Seth had become one of these fanatics: in the mornings, acknowledging his glories before his wife or even their son; playing the mirabilis sultry hits from Smooth Jazz 105.9 WASH-FM at dusk. The longer Seth and his family spent here in D.C., the deeper Seth receded into the nostalgia his flora exuded like nectar. If he closed his eyes tight and inhaled the perfume from the potted hibiscus, purple-yellow orchids, and crowned birds of paradise, he would be home again. If only he could go back. How he longed to return to Costa Rica.

A decade now of this droll American existence, of the capital's dense, slicing winters and lush, lively springs. Summer blanketed with overwhelming sun and humidity, then fall's fresh alleviation. A cycle not unlike his moods. His wife, Nieves, called him hot and cold. Hot when they made love or he made her laugh, cold when he ignored her existence. An unfortunate habit of receding into himself. A silence louder than anything else in the world.

While Seth kept quiet and tended to his forest, in the kitchen Nieves hovered over her stew as a chemist does her greatest discovery. Her frameless spectacles safety goggles, the tongs she wielded like those meant to cradle a beaker of radioactive material. White earphones dangled from her ears, blasting the Zombies and Soda Stereo from her lime-green iPod Mini. She danced as she added the chopped beef short ribs, then the yuca and plantains in compulsory order. Nieves was making olla de carne, which, if entered into a yet-to-be-organized international competition, would surely bring home a ribbon of winning color. In truth, Nieves didn't long for Costa Rica as Seth did—she had always preferred the United States (she was half gringa, after all)—but she pitied her husband, and so out of that pity she made home for him in pots of picadillo and skillets of gallo pinto and other traditional dishes. Nieves thought that if she could occupy his tongue, it would bring some sort of peace to his mind. But there was no such thing as peace for an exiled man. Seth was stuck here in the United States. And she was stuck here with him, ladling comfort, reducing her pity until it resembled something digestible.

Locally, Nieves was known as an undiscovered gastronomic genius, a restaurant-less Michelin-starred chef. Neighbors commissioned her for cajetas and puddings, tacos and chifrijos. And she wasn't one to let a good thing go to waste. If her food was truly *that* good, she might as well monetize her talent and share it with the world. So, over the years, she gathered family recipes and documented them on legal pads strewn about the apartment, hoping to compile them in a cookbook that would land her a show on Food Network. In lucid dreams, she sautéed elbow to elbow with Ina Garten in her elegant Hamptons home, teaching the master chef Costa Rica's culinary delights. In one special dream, she tickled the Barefoot Contessa's nose with a sprig of culantro and kissed her softly. It was a dream she would keep secret from Seth. The widening gap between Seth and Nieves was filled with these harmless secrets, like biodegradable trash in a landfill. Eventually decomposing over time, but in the moment: obvious, plentiful, rotten.

Another of Seth's own secrets he would toss into the void between them was his outing today. In the early afternoon, he entered the Costa Rican Embassy on S Street after no less than twenty minutes of anxious self-deliberation at its gate. The secretary at the front desk, on a personal phone call, froze at the sight of him, her mouth hung open like a pitcher plant. Seth could smell her stale morning coffee breath from where he stood. She, on the other hand, grimaced as if inhaling gasoline fumes.

"Darling," Seth said, reading her nameplate. Her haircut must have been more expensive than her white satin blouse. She blinked fast.

"Señor Oreamundo," she replied. "¿To what do I owe this pleasure?" It seemed hatred wasn't enough for her to dispense with respect.

"I'd like to speak with Ignacio."

"He's not here, I'm afraid. The ambassador stepped out for lunch a few moments ago."

"I don't think so," Seth said. "I've been waiting outside."

"He—he went out the back. He was on his way to his favorite pupusería."

Just then, Seth and the secretary heard guffawing from behind the closed door of the ambassador's office. A laugh as large as Ignacio's belly. Again, the secretary froze. It seemed she was neither old enough nor experienced enough to lie to a politician, ex or otherwise.

"I'll let myself in," Seth said coolly.

"Señor, I don't think that's the best—"

Seth ignored her and entered the office, where he found Ignacio reclining precariously in a too-small black leather chair.

"You seem to be as cheerful as ever, Ignacio," Seth said.

"I thought I heard your voice. But then I thought to myself, '¿Do ghosts visit this early in the day?' ¿How have you been, old friend?" Ignacio swiveled in his seat, exchanging his view of the tree line for the disconcerting sight of Seth's dramatically aged face.

"Spare me the bullshit, please. We're both too far on in our years for niceties," Seth answered.

"We're in politics, you and I. ¿Isn't that what we do?"

Ignacio gestured for Seth to take a seat. The metal folding chair in front of Ignacio's desk creaked beneath him, reminding Seth of how cheap Ignacio could be. The cheapest bastard in the world, cutting every possible corner, but flaunting gold rings on every finger. Hypocrisy in Costa Rica is as abundant as coffee, or bananas, or tourists.

"Tell me, Seth, ¿to what do I owe this pleasant visit from an old friend?"

Seth had fantasized about this moment—the aplomb with which he'd stride into Ignacio's office like a man come back from Everest. As if exile were a peak to be conquered, a frigid loneliness to impress others upon retelling. And like a wide-eyed admirer blowing steam from his cocoa, Ignacio would grant Seth's any desire. But Seth couldn't summon his victory speech. Banishment hadn't been a test to be passed, or a feat to be applauded, but a life sentence to be appealed.

"I want a visa. I want to return" was all Seth could say.

"¿Just yours? ¿What about one for Nieves and for your son?"

"They're happy here, but I'm not. I want to go home."

Seth spoke with the desperation of a frightened child, and Ignacio grimaced, as if he'd also just inhaled gasoline fumes.

"Please," Seth said.

"I didn't know the Oreamundo brothers were capable of begging. It's most unattractive, I must say."

"Ignacio . . ." If Seth could uproot himself from the chair, he'd plant himself before Ignacio, kiss his every ring with exaggerated sounds. He'd remind Ignacio of their history—the hotels and whores; the lurid parties and furtive lunches; the arsenal of secrets balanced precariously upon the tongue like knives.

"Fine, Seth," Ignacio finally said. "I'll grant you this: I can give you a week's visa. That'll be enough time to play in the forest, watch a sunset or two, visit your parents' graves. The last thing anyone wants is for you to return for good. That's the most I can do. I don't want to lose my position, not even for an old friend."

Seth agreed to Ignacio's exiguous proposal, but not without Ignacio first subjugating him to the humiliation of small talk—if the years had been kind; if Seth had ever gotten used to the cold, and snow, and ice that flecks December hair; if the tap water tasted odd last week—idiocies Ignacio extracted from Seth like teeth. And when it was over, Seth stood, but faltered for a moment. He was to pick up the visa in two weeks' time, Ignacio explained. They did not shake hands when Seth left. Darling, the secretary, covered her nose as he passed.

Smells haunt like specters.

* * *

After the embassy, Seth found himself wandering the streets aimlessly in the late April sun. All these years he'd survived this exile—dethroned, tossed on the first plane out of Costa Rica; dropped here in the U.S. like cargo, like jetsam. Seth had once been powerful, he wanted to explain to passersby. He wanted to grab their cheeks, gaze into their eyes, and allow his history to swallow them like it had swallowed him. The past and its insatiable gullet. Before his cramped apartment, before Kalorama and its wealthy, tree-lined streets, before even the United States, Seth had been somebody. Not this forgotten, green-thumbed ghost. He'd been director of Costa Rica's national petroleum refinery. He'd lived a lavish, oil-slicked life. But Osario, his younger brother, had taken all of that away. Sure, brothers have their little rivalries, but Osario had taken it too far. He'd yanked Seth from paradise and tossed him into this purgatory; at times, sweat-stained from his incessant meandering, Seth was convinced he was paying the price in hell.

Heading north, he crossed the Calvert Street bridge, gripping every mint-green bar so that he wouldn't jump. He felt like an animal in a cage, staring out over the empty space between Rock Creek Park's canopy and the uninterrupted sky, wanting nothing more than to fill its expanse with his body. If he could just slither through the bars and hurl himself toward the horizon, the overwhelming void would no longer exist.

He managed to reach the opposite end of the bridge. At the busy mouth of Calvert Street, the famous mural of Marilyn Monroe stared down at him, her lips like the bulbous petals of a rare flower, sensuous eyes begging to be filled. Inhabited, occupied by another. And just as the infinite void between canopy and sky had urged Seth to expand, so, too, did her gaze implore his body to engorge and explode, until all the universe was him, and him alone.

Seth couldn't remember how he'd wound up back home. But there he was, watering his tropical plants, debating on whether to inform Nieves of the ambassador's deal. He knew that if he did tell her, she'd try to persuade him to stay, if only to avoid a second round of humiliation. But Seth had to return. He had to satisfy the urges within himself that had, at first, boiled like the stock for Nieves's stews, and then, for the last ten years, simmered quietly—a slurry of nostalgia and spite that bubbled at the top of his skull; that would continue bubbling until Seth could extinguish the blue-hot flame of anger that fed it.

From that flame appeared his younger brother, handsome, and dapper, and cruel. It was as if the ambassador's very mention of Osario summoned his memory, and he accused Seth of rot. As Seth pruned dangling pothos and dipped his fingers into dirt to check humidity, he accused Osario of betrayal. How easy it was to blame an echo. Seth had always preferred one-sided arguments.

At six on the dot, their ten-year-old, Andrés, returned from his after-school program, and the family of three sat down to eat in silence. Their TV trays lonely boats in a dysfunctional sea. Seth turned on Animal Planet, and as they slurped the delicious olla de carne, they watched in awe as a menagerie of beasts mauled those who didn't seem to think Darwinian theory applied to humans.

"It's either out of ignorance or arrogance that humanity assumes we are above the food chain," Seth said philosophically to his wife and son, who ignored him. "As if art, or music, or language could save us from the natural order of things. Nature is the Devil's playground, after all."

It was then that Fate played a cruel trick on Seth. On a segment titled "Untamed & Uncut," a twenty-something Thai boy antagonized a Siamese crocodile for applause. Surrounded by a pool, in front of a studio audience, the young man, clad in a vinyl purple vest and matching shorts, tapped the crocodile's snout, eliciting a rise out of the gulping crowd. The show's narrator introduced the circus act as *Sawatdi*, the Thai word for "farewell," as ominous music played beneath his voice-over (to Americans, violins spell doom). When the young man balanced his whole arm between the crocodile's jaws, they unexpectedly snapped shut. Hard and lightning-fast—from hand to shoulder. Then, to the horror of the Thai audience, the American narrator, and Seth and his family watching at home, the crocodile began to roll. *The death roll*, it was called. An aptly chosen name because the boy's arm twisted like licorice. Bones popped through flesh, blood splattering the wet concrete stage. Andrés vomited, and Nieves rushed to him. She howled at Seth to turn off the program as she put her son's dizzy head to her bosom, but Seth didn't—*couldn't*—hear or heed her. A sly grin had cut across his face. The expression of a playwright who had just stumbled upon his story's climax.

"That's right," he whispered. "Just like *that* time."

A buried memory sprang forth and sat right next to Seth on the couch. It pressed Seth's thumb to the remote, replayed the footage for him. It was true—many years ago, at fifteen, Seth *had* witnessed a horrendous spectacle just like this. But the victim had been a woman in the river Tárcoles. In the memory, Osario stood chest-high next to Seth, the young brothers frozen, feet nursed on by the greedy mud of the riverbank. Seth remembered frantic splashing, the flash of pink water, and Osario's shallow breaths. Back then, they'd watched a nightmare, but seeing it now on the television, the whole thing seemed almost artistic: the crocodile's expert pliés, innumerable pirouettes. The old memory birthed a new idea. In Seth's mind, Osario was no longer next to him on the riverbank. Instead, what Seth saw now—what had sliced that grin across his face—was his younger brother splashing in the water. Succumbing to the laughing, reptilian night.

THE OLD KINGDOM

1910–1985 C.E.

MENES

1910

They didn't know it at the time, but the Oreamundo brothers witnessed their fate the day they saw a giant crab coiled up in a giant viper's grip. When they returned to their family's mansion from the forest, no one believed them—a scene that horrible, that incredulous, was a thing of fiction, not beholding. What was a crab doing so high up in the mountains? What kind of viper couldn't be ripped apart by its pincers? And why didn't the two cosmic beasts abandon their battle to devour the boys? But they swore, those two Oreamundo brothers, until their faces turned to eggplant skin, that a crab, red and black and deep purple, had lain entangled in mortal combat with a viper twice its size. A claw to either scaly end; poisonous fangs digging into slick, marbled eyes. It was biblical, they screamed to their parents at the dinner table that night. The maids flanking the table whispered to no one in particular, *¿What do children know of the Bible?*

Despite the disbelief they inspired that day, the two brothers had a point. They had indeed witnessed something epic. Not a premonition, exactly, but a promise from a far more ancient past. The struggle on the forest floor had already played out for many millennia. It was a warning. Or better yet, a preview.

This is your destiny, it whispered to them. Fangs and claws, blood and all.

As destiny would have it, Seth and Osario had been born of royal blood. That is, as royal as blood in Costa Rica can get. Their unnaturally common ancestor was a man named Otilio Oreamundo, the latest in a long line of oligarchs turned politicians: heir to a dynasty with deep pockets and a sophisticated palate for power.

One president begat another president, who begat their grandfather Otilio, born the day the city of Cartago crumbled from the ground up. Otilio's mother had thought this was how every birth was supposed to happen: the earth caught in convulsive sympathy for her efforts. His father, having just taken his first presidential oath, left his infant and sweating wife to address the disaster victims, and till and reap the rubble for his voter base. Later, by government decree, Cartago would be rebuilt with stone, not with the poor man's adobe, so Otilio's father led by example, designing a spectacular limestone mansion in the center of his sprawling coffee latifundio outside the holy city. Many years later, Otilio would comment to the sparrows how closely Seth's childhood resembled his own: the gullet of the elegant mansion cool on even oven-hot days; a mother's swimming lullaby netted by high ceilings; the unrelenting aroma of roasting beans. Decades before his grandsons' feet shivered from the gelid marble floors, Otilio marched upon them like an arctic explorer. His mother ran honey through his blond hair, kissed the lids of his blue eyes. She was beautiful, worldly, and educated. Instead of *king* she called him *pharaoh*. Instead of the New Testament, she read to him from the Old. He possessed a sun-reaching, heaven-stepping greatness, she said. So ancient and worthy it preceded the written word. Even the spoken word. Perhaps even His word.

Otilio would compartmentalize his childhood memories by his father's presidential terms. Four-year pockets of joy and tragedy. Galas, dinners. Death, and more death. Otilio swore he remembered the violent tremor of his birth, the soreness of milk-wailing, and even the first time he noticed that green had different shades—coffee bushes, their leaves and unripe berries; oases of rainforest studding the manicured plantation; the mansion's jade gabled roof; and then his first sibling: stillborn, slick with sick-green muck. After the first death, the curse wouldn't stop. More siblings came whenever his parents could cool their grief long enough to conjoin. But every time, another would be born, so another would die, and his parents would separate like mourning islands, leaving Otilio upon the tumultuous waves of his solitude. Two sisters succumbed to cholera at the same time in the same bed; the middle boy was squashed beneath an ox and its cart on a Sunday; the youngest got lost forever in the woods. On and on, again and again, a cruel cycle of lovemaking and gravedigging. Eventually, when Otilio played with his siblings, it was with the detached love of a child who knows he will outgrow his toys. By the age of ten, he'd become aware of his own fate to move forward, and that death aimed to freeze the rest with glassy eyes and plastic-cool flesh. Over the years, his mother molded her heartache into worship: she returned to her original creation and convinced herself and Otilio that he'd survived because he was special. It was the yellow hair she stroked, the irises she looked into like reflective pools, the skin she couldn't discern from his milk baths—all signs of his genetic and biblical favor. It was his siblings' black hair, dark eyes, and tan complexions that had condemned them. *Death creeps in the shadows, but it balks at the glory of the light.*

An only child again at thirteen, it was clear that Otilio was meant to be his father's successor. The thick, drowning tedium of studies plagued Otilio's memories of his father's second term. The mansion's hallways swelled with forensics and elocution lessons, while its library rivaled that of the capital's. And at all hours of the night, Otilio could be heard reciting texts in his sleep. His childhood home became a university for one.

"Power does not come accidentally," his mother replied to Otilio's loneliness. He'd complained of his studies, questioned their worth in the scheme of things. "Power is an organ some are born with. It grows, becomes stronger. It can flex like an arm, or supply like a heart. Those like your father . . ." She paused, thumbed down her son's eyebrow. "Like you, are inheritors of power. You have no choice but to nourish it, nurture it. Like a desperate lung or a gluttonous throat, it will crave, my child."

"I didn't ask for this," Otilio said. "I didn't wish for kidneys or a spleen, ¿so how could I have wished for this? Maybe I could cut it out. ¿Where, Mother, where can I cut? I'm trapped in these walls to satisfy my father."

"You were born with the soul of a libertine," his mother answered. Her tone wasn't to mock or patronize, but Otilio felt the earth open up from under him. "But you weren't born to bohemians. Your destiny was written the moment your forefathers ruled this land. Perhaps even before then. Power does not come accidentally, my son."

Otilio, mustached and handsome, arrived in New York City the day after his father's third inauguration. He hadn't realized that the metropolis wasn't black-and-white like in the movies—neon signs overpowered the snowy sky and charcoal buildings; sun-bright pinks, reds, and unnatural greens blanketed the brumal heads of bustling passersby. They beckoned Otilio to shops, nightclubs, restaurants, and theaters. The mountains of Cartago couldn't compare to the Empire State, or the fact that a coin dropped could split a person in two. His law school buddies at Columbia University took him to the Morocco, where bootleggers supplied alcohol as rare and sharp as arsenic. At parties, he rubbed elbows with other heirs—of fortunes, eventual cabinet positions—tailoring his network as an orb-weaver does its rain-flecked web. A waiting, careful nature that would serve Otilio throughout his career. Many at Columbia thought Otilio as white as them. An immigrant from Spain or Germany, his features a vestige of the Visigoths. At first, he corrected them, with a charming smile around the consonants of his homeland, but when he received lukewarm responses and invitations dwindled, he began the charade as Prussian-born. He went by Otto, and though he never quite mastered the accent, his locks of fool's gold became a ticket to every function. How titillating it was to belong to somewhere other than his home, his parents. How sweet it was to be someone else for a while.

But one day between classes, on the wintry university steps, a man slightly older than Otilio approached him.

"You're not German, even though you look it," the man said. He lit a cigarette, the warmest thing for miles. "You're Costa Rican. Like me."

"I don't know what one does when they're found out," Otilio said. "I suppose I should ask the sleuth's name. Holmes?"

"Max." The man smiled and switched to Spanish. "I only noticed because I'm *both*. Parents of noble German blood, but I was born to the same land as you. There's nothing wrong with being from there."

"¿No?"

"No," the man named Max answered. The wind receded his hairline and smoked his cigarette for him. "It's enough that your hair is blond, your eyes blue. Superiority shines bright in the darkness of this world. Your pride is not misplaced, at least not completely."

Five years Otilio's senior, Max was a graduate of Columbia's engineering program and now an employee at the German embassy. Otilio gravitated to him like a sapling to the sun. What comfort it gave him to speak his own language, to reminisce over their shared culture and education. Sometimes nostalgia would overcome him, and Otilio would crave the tortillas the mansion maids would make, but Max exclaimed they were Indians' food. Savage little pancakes, he scoffed. Nothing like true Teutonic gastronomy. At these and similar comments, Otilio kept quiet. They were small enough compared with the compliments Max supplied: Otilio's intelligence, savvy, skin—men like him were meant to rule Costa Rica. The world, even. That's what was going on in Europe, Max reported cheerfully, contrasting what the headlines warned. Max filled a brother-shaped hole in Otilio's heart, sometimes reminding him of death's overreaching pattern, but then his mother's words would elbow his anxiety aside: *Death balks at the glory of the light.*

It was on a steaming day in July of '34 when Max invited Otilio to a midnight gathering. Max led them to an empty alleyway where a steel door moaned open, revealing a large man who asked something in German and to which Max replied with a solitary, unintelligible word. They entered and headed down steep stairs to a sweltering basement alleviated only by an overworked ceiling fan. Dozens of men sat in wooden chairs, their blond heads swaying animatedly like a field of threshed wheat. Max sat them both near the back and shooshed Otilio with a grin before he could ask what the hell they were doing here. A man older than the rest of the crowd stepped onto a low stage. Behind him, an American flag danced lazily next to another flag: scarlet, sealed in its center with a white disk and a series of odd black lines. A broken-armed cross. Otilio had seen it before in the papers.

His chair scraped the concrete floor, and sixty eyes homed in. Their blue beckoned Otilio to sit; they judged him, encouraged him to stay, to hear them out, to think about it; open himself up to convincing, to logic, because it was inevitable that he would come to the same conclusion, tread the same path forward; it was destiny, the organ he'd been born with, the features his mother and Max held in such esteem; it was nature, God-given, an honor to lead this world into the next. But Otilio shook off Max's grip and disappeared up the stairs, out into the alley, where two tramps were fighting over a scrap of food. Otilio's soles seemed to melt on the asphalt, steps sticky, laborious. Max hadn't followed him, so he trudged alone in the streets. Otilio faced his open palms, let the moonlight reveal his fingerprints, his love lines. The whiteness of his hands frightened him, so he clenched them into fists. He promised himself he'd never see Max again.

The president who succeeded Otilio's father in 1936 carried himself like a lion: the majestic gait, a pride indistinguishable from destruction. He was soft-spoken until he wasn't, bloodthirsty within the cage of the presidential palace. At the tail end of his father's final term, Otilio had been assigned a high-ranking administrative position in the Department of Public Works. Developing a country out of stone was not dissimilar to developing it out of power, his father said. In fifteen years Otilio would take up where his family had left off—the world would think *Oreamundo* was another word for *utopia*.

And since returning to Costa Rica the year before, Otilio had also been falling in love with a German woman he'd known from childhood, her father a longtime exporter of the Oreamundo's coffee to Europe. Every day, Beatriz dressed as different orchids—a delicate lady slipper, a white nun; skirts like holy week and showers of silver, gold, and evergreen. She'd bloomed into womanhood, a damsel always in season, who spritzed the perfect amount of perfume. Notes to attract far-off men, and subtler ones to keep Otilio close. After many superficial trysts in New York, it refreshed him to come home to find someone who'd known him before his studies, before politics and his inheritance. Beatriz challenged Otilio's beliefs, claimed independence of his schedule and needs, and wouldn't let her maids wash the dishes or skip vacations. Many times, he invited her to come live at his family's mansion—they'd start a family of their own and remind the corridors of children's footsteps. But she was a woman concerned with timing, like a flower that waits for the optimal position of the sun to unfurl herself.

It was 1938 when Otilio saw him again: Max in a three-piece, sitting at his former boss's desk, empty for six months. Max had become gaunt, cheeks of carved-out canyons, precipices beneath his eyes.

"I want to apologize," Max said.

"It was jarring," Otilio answered. "One needs a warning for that kind of thing."

"It's hard to accept the truth."

"¿Is that why you're here? ¿Has our president accepted the *truth*?"

"You could say that," Max answered, clicking his lighter like a metronome. Keeping time of their conversation, a disconcerting rhythm Otilio wished to interrupt with a chair. "We're grown-ups," he continued. "I bear no ill will, and hope you don't either. You'll see the light. You'll see."

Lying next to Beatriz that night, Otilio turned to her unconscious body and asked what she thought. How much she knew, how much she believed. How far did *her* pride go? As far as red flags with sharp, black objects? Had orchids the capacity to hate? To preach of borders and pogrom? The darkness pressed down upon him like an answer, or at the very least her shirking the question. He shifted onto his back, hypnotized by the four blades of the ceiling fan, in their movement crooked like the talons of an eagle. How far could *his* pride go? What about blue and yellow—streaks in lapis, sunrise and cloudless sky, gold sifted from rivers—barbed the heart, readied a gun?

"Power," Beatriz whispered in her sleep, then let out a soft, liquid whimper.

While war in Europe loomed, Max drove Otilio mad with new public works projects. Blueprints, schematics, permits, contracts, quotas, and charcoal sketches littered his desk. When jigsawed together, others would have seen the vision of a master, a man with his sights on the future—but that future was what troubled Otilio and made him wiggle the department out of permits, draw up contracts clumsy with clauses. Otilio put Max's designs together into a beautiful, modern, organized, and sophisticated world. A world he wanted no part of.

The day Otilio decided to quit his position and finally rid himself of Max, he sipped expensive whisky for courage. The president's term was over; he'd lost to a communist. Better, Otilio thought. Germany had recently invaded Poland, and Max had convinced the president to bar any fleeing Polacks from landing ashore. Next would be the Jews, then any Nicaraguan who thought to cross the San Juan River. Otilio had been attending secret meetings with a man named Pepe, a descendant of Catalonia who feared Costa Rica's fermenting fascism. Otilio had been feeding him whatever information his lowly public works position allotted him. The man was short, fierce, and unbending in his beliefs. With the intensity of his stare, one would have thought that fire burned blue. *The election was between a dictator and a Nazi*, the man, Pepe, had declared. *Who won was not the lesser of the evils, but the easier to deal with.*

Max was hunched over his desk, scribbling furiously, when Otilio opened the door to his office. The curtains were drawn, and the darkness was dank with anxiety. A solitary desk lamp illuminated Max's projects like an opened treasure chest, Max the hovering discoverer. He'd not acknowledged Otilio. Pushed to the end of the desk was a series of photographs of a bizarre building Otilio had never seen, in various stages of construction.

"¿Is that a temple?" Otilio couldn't help but ask.

Max didn't lift his head from his notes. "Something like that," he answered.

"¿Here?"

"Yes."

It seemed that Max didn't care if Otilio studied the structure for pre-Columbian glyphs. Otilio prepared himself for a finding, the prospect of a revelatory excavation. But no Indigenous tribe had ever used this style of architecture. It was more Egyptian than anything, Otilio thought. A shrine to some god or some king.

"That's right," Max gloated. "A gift for a victorious conqueror."

"This is *your* design," Otilio muttered. Slabs upon a dozen columns, fat and segmented like worms. Through a climbing, angular courtyard, elegant steps ascended knolls to the opening of a bastardized temple. Atop its pyramidal steeple, a long animal angled its snout open, in song or reptilian ululation. "¿When did you do this? I never signed off on this project."

Max ignored Otilio's bureaucracy. He hadn't the need to assert his position. "You'll come around, Otilio," Max said. "It's begun, and no one can stop it. This is a world made for you, my friend. For your wife." He lifted his head and flashed him a kind, sinister smile. "For your children," he said. "And your children's children."

Leaving the office, Otilio vowed to never step foot in politics again. Government was for those with bones to pick or morals to betray. He hadn't the stomach for it anymore. Costa Rica was caught between two warring leviathans now. Rows of snapping jaws from the north and from the east. This country was such a small meal, Otilio wanted to tell the rulers of the world. A snack, really. A meager drink of water in relation to other lands with advantages. Costa Rica had no need for nights of glass (though its own version would come soon enough). Otilio took refuge within Beatriz, whom he proposed to on her birthday. He would trade power for her, gladly. He performed surgery on his instinct and tried to transplant other organs that would make him a good person. For her, he longed to be good. But history has a talent for foiling men's plans, their best intentions.

The road to hell, and all of that.

Deep into the muck of war, the world powers were insatiable for coffee. Kaffee, one called it; the other, a cup of joe. It was as necessary on battlefields as it was at the breakfast table. Coffee led armies to victory, and both sides refused to lose it. To the Allies and to the Axis, Costa Rica was but a field of beans, so the Costa Rican government was confronted with a very American ultimatum: continue exporting to the east, and lose all loans and funding. Deciding over a mug of tea, the president chose sides.

Across Costa Rica, Germans awoke to midnight raids, especially those with ties to coffee—oligarchs, producers, exporters—and were corralled into the center of the capital for processing. The secret police came for Beatriz in their marriage bed on the Oreamundo plantation. She was sent to a camp the government had built for Germans they didn't deport (Otilio would eventually hear that Max was shipped off to the state of Texas—to a city made of glass). The news of the German solution spread throughout the country, and it would become local legend that the moment Costa Rica declared war on the Third Reich, the great Führer spun his globe three times, searching suspiciously for somewhere he'd never heard of. When he zoomed in, he mistook Costa Rica for a fly's shit stuck to the map and tried to wipe it away. It was said he laughed in his wolf's lair, a flabbergasted, uncontrollable guffaw that crossed the ocean on a westward breeze.

Sympathizers and innocents, women, children, and the barely German spent the next four years in the government's concentration camp. Otilio visited Beatriz every day. He beseeched old colleagues, demanded an audience with the president, and even wrote to Franklin Delano, all to no avail. Trembling from rage most nights, Otilio was crushed by his powerlessness—the first time he'd ever felt the sensation. At the end of his rope, he dug within himself, feeling around for the organ he'd shut down with sheer will. Then, it beat for the first time in years. A stir at first. A tremor. Then the thunder of a war drum, audible through his chest. He burst into the newsroom of *El Cartaginés*, demanding a weekly column in which he could relay the squalid conditions of the camp. Until the war ended, Otilio would sit with his wife, interview children, describe the acidity of their hunger, the fantasies for regular baths, the wish for a place without lice mistaken for grains of rice.

Initially, his column did little to move public opinion, so his frustrated organ began pumping hatred throughout Otilio's body. He tried a different strategy to galvanize Costa Rica's white population and sounded the alarm of genocide—how blond hair, regardless of nationality, would be sheared from the fatherland. Blue eyes scooped out and tossed to the dirt like handfuls of water. Costa Rica was committing its own type of extermination, one that could eventually affect people like himself and those he passed by on the street. The whites of Otilio's palms no longer frightened him; he let them pour his spite onto the front page for years. The citizenry finally answered his call and kept a river of letters flowing into the newsroom in support of his column. One day, a letter from Texas arrived, no return address.

Welcome, Otilio, was the only text on the stark, white page.

By the time the Second Great War had ended, and Beatriz was finally released from the camp, Otilio was a changed man. He'd become conspiratorial and cruel, hosting secret meetings at the Oreamundo plantation with men of different nationalities, including old Pepe, who greeted Beatriz with curt kindness. She skirted past her husband when he walked through the corridors, at night reading and rereading his four years of columns in an attempt to isolate when he'd lost himself to this bitterness. Beatriz considered leaving, but she remembered the man who had never left her side, even when this evil had taken hold of him. She wondered what someone like him would want, what type of affection could cure him. An heir, is what he told her. Not a baby, or a child, but one to inherit something he intended to pass down through her. If it would make her life livable, she'd oblige her husband. Her own birth had brought her parents back together—a child performing miracles for a marriage wasn't totally unheard-of.

Nine months later, Otilio laid eyes on two morning figures. One large, the other small. One familiar, the other foreign. The latter squirming, cooing. The former still as a slab on her bed. The old midwife apologized to the father for having performed both birth and death at the same time. A mark against her record, for which she wouldn't charge. She muttered something about King Solomon as she handed Otilio his baby, daylight through the window cutting the child in two. The midwife asked its name. Otilio couldn't answer. She pinched open the baby's knees with her index finger and thumb and grunted. From the almanac within her bag, she scraped out a name. Today was the feast of San Gilberto, and a good enough moniker as any for a cheerful boy. *Brilliant arrow*, she read. Otilio fixed his eyes on the child as if he were cradling a murderous weapon. It had the gall to giggle, its victim a meter away. It reached for Otilio's mustache, but he curled Beatriz's arms into a bassinet and laid the baby there. The cooling corpse of his beloved wife possessed more love than he ever could for this child. He would raise it, he told Beatriz, but only because he had to.

Otilio's grief quickly turned its sights to power. Dirtied its hands with it. He attended fundraisers and political functions alone, in black suits with black ties and obsidian rings on every finger. He used his father's connections like fishing line, hooked the right friends and snagged the right allies—those who would serve his eventual goal to become president, and those who could sell his family's coffee at higher prices. With allies came enemies, whom Otilio crushed with acumen and greed. He evolved his birthright into an empire, growing the Oreamundo plantation like a newly christened country. Otilio bought land and people, but every night was haunted by dreams of his dead wife, and every day by the face of his son who had killed her.

Otilio's only spiritual consolation came from brothels, from brunette women with blue eyes and blonde arm hair. He took them with or without a yes from their lips, bribed the madame if they complained, or had them silenced if they promised to go to reporters. Otilio kept his reputation clean and soiled the lives of others. But there was one brothel worker he treated gently, a Nicaraguan night maid named Casandra, who always wiped up the floorboards after he left. For years he left tips where only she would find them cleaning. She was young, barely out of her teenage years when Otilio finally propositioned her, the night before the election meant to leave him president. He wanted to enter that day victoriously, he said. She would be his prize, a trophy he'd take into the presidential palace, he promised. He needed a new wife, a woman to stand next to him in the newspaper photographs, even if journalists would mistake her for his daughter. He wrapped up Casandra's hopes with a bow. And so she let him take her in that room, whose walls closed in on them like a trap. But when it was over, he left with no ceremony. No kiss, or pat, or hand to escort her to his royal blue Talbot-Lago. He'd consumed her like a rare dish and realized he had no taste for seconds.

But Otilio was denied his presidency the next day. Before he could clear his throat and approach the podium, the communist opposition called foul play and ballot tampering and blocked his party from entering Congress, which prompted Otilio's old political ally, Pepe, to enact his plan of civil war on the conservative parties. For two months, bullet-riddled bodies of countrymen lay in the streets. Brother grappled with brother on their parents' farms, and blood flowed like rainwater in the gutters. Otilio's political career was over, only intensifying his rancor and hatred for everyone around him.

GIZA

1948

He didn't know it at the time, but Otilio had sired a girl. A slick baby with a head full of hair Casandra bore on Christmas that year. She'd spent Nochebuena chugging rompope between contractions, drunk and merry despite a child out of wedlock. The madame became Casandra's midwife, and the brothel women brought boiled towels to wipe her forehead of sweat and private parts of blood. They sanitized the baby girl, slapped her ass for a shrieked confession of life, received the placenta with the care of a twin, and crowded around Casandra and her newborn like a manger of animals. *A good night, indeed*, the madame said. *¿Do you know who the father is?*

Casandra knew because Otilio was the only man she'd ever lain with. *He had good aim*, the madame said, grinning. When asked if she would go to him, Casandra shook her head no. If he'd been callous enough to manipulate and abandon her, he'd have no heart for a child. She wouldn't subject her new daughter to cruelty—the world would give her plenty of that. She'd raise the baby by herself, introduce her to a world full of women who would love her. *¿What will you name her?* the madame asked. Casandra looked to the Christmas sky, its pink dawn dewy as birth. *Cielos*, Casandra said. María Cielos.

Unlike Otilio, Casandra fought with herself not to resent her child—it bore no sin of its conception. Casandra would hate the memory of Otilio by itself, compartmentalize his whetted flesh and smug expression, his jolts, and heaves, and bad breath. As María Cielos grew into an effervescent little girl, Casandra convinced others her daughter's blonde hair and careful lips belonged to her grandmother, a Basque. The brothel women drowned María Cielos in love; they fashioned themselves into a village inside that house of sweat and moans. The bordello took on the air of a convent, nuns replaced by prostitutes, led by the madame who saw no difference between herself and a mother superior, and whose center of worship was not the Virgin but María Cielos. All favor and money went to her: expensive dresses, personal tutors, a phonograph for her favorite boleros. They raised María Cielos as the best of them.

Ten years after her encounter with Otilio, Casandra found a husband for herself. A tall, handsome Jamaican who'd reluctantly followed his older brother to the brothel and sat in the parlor twiddling his thumbs. He was unbelievably shy when Casandra entered the room to grab a rag drying by the fireplace. She stopped, and he stood. She smiled, and so did he. She asked his name. Michael, he answered. He asked hers. Embers crackled and sweat pooled between their collarbones. The silence burned. They made love on Casandra's bed. He inhaled her rosemary oil and iris perfume and called her a garden. They married months later, and Michael adopted María Cielos with the same tenderness the bordello women had provided.

As a young man, Michael had worked for the slaving banana trade in the south. It would take him years to admit to Casandra the exact number of limbs he'd seen fall to the dry dirt—fingers and the hands they were attached to relieved from the man like ripe fruit. These memories crowded his mind, and in the act of retelling he harvested them so that they wouldn't litter his heart and rot. His older brother, Alex, had eventually introduced him to a man named Garvey, a visionary with a fleet, sailing to nations of men who looked like Michael, who dreamed of returning to where their ancestors had been stolen from. He organized events for Garvey, parading through the hamlets of the Western Hemisphere like a prophet. It was a good gig, Michael together with his siblings under the banner of unifying the past with a promising future. But Garvey was jailed and exiled to Jamaica, leaving his followers to splinter. Michael and his siblings kept up their own chapter, but they, too, would drift apart for their own reasons. The trip to the brothel was to heal Michael's heart from their organization's final meeting. Casandra appeared from the shadows with lips and bandages; she was a woman who promised a different kind of future.

To support their new family, Michael and Casandra opened a shop, selling wood furniture to the capital's white, wealthy elite. María Cielos grew up polishing table legs and armoires; sanding, nailing, and varnishing; haggling prices with vinegar-hearted aristocrats. Despite Michael's initial years of questions and María Cielos's own curiosities, Casandra never revealed the true father. To settle the dispute, Casandra claimed that her first husband had fallen victim to an oxcart, run over and left for dead. Sometimes the story described a drunk, other times the Devil (*¿Why not both?* Michael asked once, sarcastically). But Otilio's memory would still scratch its way into her psyche when she looked upon her daughter, and Casandra's mind would fight it off with a broom. She had an idyllic life in that furniture shop, with her devoted husband and radiant daughter who was budding into a flower of a girl. Delicate, soft-hearted. A girl boys arrived to pick.

One boy, tall, tan, and fleece-haired, took special interest in María Cielos. Casandra and Michael chaperoned as he paid their daughter monthly visits. His hands never left his lap, though they knew he wanted to do nothing more than grab her everywhere. He swallowed persistent saliva and spoke often of his family's coffee latifundio, though he never mentioned anyone by name. The aroma of roasted beans exuded from his linen suits, so that every time he arrived to court her, María Cielos grew unreasonably excited, either from his presence or from the secondhand caffeine. Even long after he was gone, and Casandra brushed her horse-straight hair, María Cielos's heart beat with the ferocity of a hummingbird's wings.

Deep into the courtship, María Cielos's aunt Ola arrived at the furniture shop. A dozen bangles heralded her return, her skin scented with a new oud or oil she'd bought on her travels. Like Michael and their brother Alex, Ola had once worked for the man named Garvey, assisting his wife in her duties to the organization. Whenever Ola appeared at the shop, she would kick off her heels, recline like a king on a customer's chaise lounge, and recount to María Cielos tales of the latest exotic lands: a kilometer-long train in India, immortal priests in Jerusalem, ruins of libraries across the African continent, or Caribbean islands with hidden, healing waters. Michael would greet his older sister with a masculine hug, and Casandra would rush to clean her hands of varnish and rock back and forth in Ola's embrace. When Ola had finished her adventure stories, Michael revealed a bottle of rum, and they'd reminisce about their childhood in Limón. The pristine beaches, their parents' sternness, teachers who tried beating English out of them. It was complicated, Ola giggled. But seeing Michael out in the ocean next to where they were born, she'd say, was worth anything the world threw at them.

María Cielos loved to cook with her aunt. In the glow of kitchen fire, she admired Ola's yellow dresses, a wise adaptation to her turmeric obsession. Her aunt treated dishes like potions, an exaggerated, spellbinding process. Besides the jazz tunes and calypsos Ola hummed over the crackling stove, the kitchen swelled with María Cielos's laughter. Ola had taught her everything and fantasized about opening a restaurant with her niece as her sous-chef, their food and dancing a local attraction to keep them in business long after they were gone. Preparing dinners was also a way for María Cielos to ask her aunt for advice that, over the years, evolved with her maturation. At first, María Cielos wished to know what presents to beg for on birthdays, then how to deal with her parents' fussing about studies. Now she sought counsel about the young, fleece-haired boy who arrived to court her once a month.

"¿Is he handsome?" was the first thing Ola asked. María Cielos lowered into a nod, the stretch of a smile cramping her cheeks. "That's the most important thing." Her aunt winked. "My favorite foundation for a courtship is a handsome boy. ¿What animals crowd your stomach when you see him?"

María Cielos closed her eyes and waited for the familiar flapping in her belly. "Albatrosses," she said.

"Well I'll be damned," Ola said, cradling María Cielos's chin with a delicate, bony finger. "I don't need to check your love lines or read your leaves to tell you it's meant to be. ¿What counsel do you need from me?" she asked skeptically.

"¿What will it become?" María Cielos asked innocently. "Our love. Its longevity. Density. Whether it will grow spikes or soften like a ball."

"That habit of overintellectualizing," Ola said, smiling. "Not a bad habit, but not the best in this type of situation. Let's see . . ." Ola paced about the kitchen, removing pots from flames, plopping diced onions into her mouth like gumdrops. "First, I must see him," Ola decided. "Allow me three months so that I may study his aura. His energy that disperses throughout this house. Inspecting a relationship's prospect is like checking the veracity of a diamond.

Some boys' love reflects, others' refracts. Some will shatter quickly like glass, and others can withstand hellfire."

With that, María Cielos introduced the boy to her aunt and sat back as his heart raced from finding himself beneath the gaze of the great and powerful Ola. María Cielos was forbidden to ask what Ola thought, what her aunt's hunch spelled out like cards. Not until after the boy's third monthly visit did Ola shuttle María Cielos into the kitchen to whisper cryptically, "There's only one way to be completely sure, my beloved. A Lakota man taught me this."

So María Cielos wasn't to eat that night's delicious dinner. In fact, she couldn't eat for the next few days. Underneath her parents' noses, María Cielos was to fast until her mind entered a strange euphoria, so that her hunger nibbled away at what kept her earthly mind separated from the spiritual realm. On the fourth night after their conversation, Ola stole María Cielos away, driving them up the side of a mountain to a clearing. In its center stood a ceiba tree, back-straight as a proud man. There was no moon, so Ola built a fire. Embers danced up to the leaves like lazy bugs. María Cielos stared through the flames at her aunt, who was muttering, eyes shut. She waited for her aunt's cue, but Ola didn't speak to her, even an hour after they'd arrived. But something within María Cielos told her not to break the crackling silence. Instead, she allowed the bonfire to take hold of her, lap up the moisture from her eyes. The world blurred to orange, then black.

A horizon emerged from the new darkness. Shifting, languid. María Cielos realized she was in a river. Night-stained, flowing all around her, its current soothing music. A fingernail of moon rocked upon the water. She noticed a shadow standing beyond her, on the riverbank. The shadow was a figure whose shoulders were those of a man. Hunched at first, then pulled back to attention. Past him, closer to her in the water, two arms flailed, surrounded by muscular, giddy tails that slapped a spray into the air. The arms belonged to another man being devoured, while the shadow of the first looked on from the shore. From him erupted sudden laughter. A joyous, victorious chant. Then it felt as though María Cielos was crawling out of the water onto the bank, toward him on her belly. The man turned to look down at her. Dimples punctuated his smile like parentheses, his eyes were slits of pale blue moonlight, and malice pushed his heavy brow forward. María Cielos screamed and didn't stop screaming. The hum of the river washed away, the splashing and laughter faded back into the loud flames, and Ola's cries snapped María Cielos out of it.

María Cielos's throat was rubbed raw by the time she could balance herself in the car. Ola begged her forgiveness the whole ride back, but she couldn't lift her forehead from the cool window or separate her jaws into words. They arrived home, and as María Cielos lumbered back to her room, her parents confronted Ola: violent screams and accusations, doors slamming, a motor running until it disappeared. Even when María Cielos's hunger abated and she awoke the next day good as new and asked of Ola's whereabouts, still she saw the figure on the riverbank in every shadow. A year later, when the boy, Gilberto, finally proposed, she could hear that terrible splashing. But without her beloved aunt around to interpret, María Cielos couldn't decipher its meaning. So she let it fade from her imagination just as easily as it had emerged from the dark waters of it.

Gilberto's father arrived at the furniture shop in a sleek, black Chrysler to offer his son's hand in marriage. Michael greeted him at the door, impressed by the man's expensive, European clothes. Michael brought him to the back of the shop where Casandra was punching numbers, and when she saw the man, her blood ran with cold lead. A familiar twitch scratched at her womb as she lay eyes on Otilio Oreamundo. His face carved open by wrinkles, back hunching beneath the weight of all that he had ever done. But his mouth, its sly, pointed ends and quivering lips, was exactly the same as that night. He, too, froze, but with a politician's quickness he introduced himself cheerfully.

It took Casandra forty-three seconds to extend her hand and reciprocate a greeting. The sudden humiliation within her became murderous. The first six seconds, she imagined all the ways in which she could kill him right then and there: with the fountain pen in her hand, the hardwood chair on which she sat, her own nails freshly painted and filed into razors. The following ten seconds, she analyzed her options: react negatively and reveal her life's greatest shame; play along, then corner Otilio later and threaten to castrate him while he slept; or third, accept life's cruel joke with a defeated sense of absurd humor. Hatred clouded the following sixteen seconds, so, later, Casandra couldn't remember what horrible, malicious, and inventive thoughts entered her brain. And at the last second, she decided to wait. She would convince Michael afterward that the boy, Gilberto, wasn't the correct suitor for their daughter. Casandra didn't care if María Cielos would reproach her and berate her for her perceived jealousy. Casandra would protect her child from incest and preserve the reality she'd created all these years at the same time. Her own mother had taught her that a proud woman never reveals her dirty laundry, so Casandra extended her hand to Otilio but didn't let him kiss it.

That night, before she could find her chance to convince Michael, Casandra was overcome by exhaustion and dreamt of a desert. She looked upon the dunes through the shifting eyes of different animals—a mangy jackal, an Anubis baboon, an elegant Nubian bustard, a buzzard of every shade of black. With these morphing bodies she prowled burning sands, scrounging for water, devouring smaller species to satiate her thirst with their blood. She came upon a sphinx with her mother's face, eyes torn out by cannonballs. Beyond it lay a pristine oasis, crowded by colorful birds, humans, and their dromedary companions. Casandra dipped her beak, her snout, her lips, or her maw into the pool to drink but couldn't. The water spilled through her mouth, refusing to enter her gullet. She even tossed herself into the oasis, but still no water could satiate her.

Casandra awoke scratching at her throat out of unbearable thirst. Michael lay next to her, as still as a stone in the dark. She stumbled to the kitchen freezer and gulped down ice that melted immediately in her mouth. The rest of the house was cool and dry. Casandra decided to break the news to María Cielos right then. She'd caress her hair and shoulders till she woke, speak softly, promise that rejecting Gilberto's proposal was for the best. But in her daughter's large, pitch room, Casandra saw an empty bed and the curtains fluttering from an unlatched window. A solitary candle burned in the corner opposite the doorway, and on the periphery of its light sat the shadow of a motionless man. Casandra didn't scream because she hadn't recognized Otilio at first.

"She snuck out," he said.

"¿What are you doing here?" Casandra replied when her eyes had focused. She ran her thumbs over her fingernails, which in the moment felt serrated.

"I was awake when she made it to my property and my son let her through the back door. I don't know why I drove here."

"But here you are."

"Here I am."

"I will stop it."

"It's already started," Otilio sighed. "There's nothing we can do to deny it."

"Get out before I start screaming," Casandra growled. Even if Michael was a heavy sleeper, he'd come running if she shrieked.

"I'll get out," Otilio said. "And yes, you will scream. ¿Haven't you noticed it yet?"

Casandra quieted her rage and inhaled. Varnish. She looked down. A slow wave of it licked her bare toes; slick, and cool, and pungent.

Without another word, Otilio knocked the candle over onto the floor, and the varnish ignited. The fire moved like quick, blue water through the darkness and gripped Casandra's nightgown. It enveloped her, stuck to her skin like a garment. She ran through the house to make it to the cistern out back; her wet footsteps set everything else aflame: fresh chairs and the primed oak walls, stacks of papers, the rugs. The fire made its way to a sleeping Michael, his lovely mind cradled by a dream. Casandra crumpled like a matchstick before she could reach the back door. She watched the world go bright, then dark. The smoke took her before the flames could. She'd hoped this moment would be gentle. She had prayed for it all her life.

Otilio's smile shined through blaze. His malice a pure, cerulean flame beyond the darkening, orange world.

≈≈≈

It was easy for Otilio to cover his tracks. When he returned to the Oreamundo mansion, he threw his smoke-stained clothes in the washroom to soak, scrubbed his hair and skin of the penetrating varnish, stayed awake until he saw María Cielos sneaking out, and offered her a ride back home. Smoke rose lazily into the dawn, and when María Cielos realized its source, she wailed, overpowering the sirens and hissing hoses. They scooped her parents from the pyre. *Ashes to ashes.* At the funeral, the priest tossed what had been their loving bodies into a grave big enough for two. *Dust to dust.*

Local tabloids blamed Casandra for the blaze. She'd lit the house herself, burned her husband alive for a possible affair or a bout of hysteria. The aristocrats were drawn to the gossip and began piecing together an imaginary scandal, poor Casandra the culprit and fire starter. Otilio fed the media frenzy, dropped anonymous morsels to hungry journalists. And like the idea of a doting patriarch, he invited María Cielos to live on the latifundio, to safely be courted by his son. Otilio's hatred for Gilberto condemned them both to an unspeakable sin. Casandra's spirit would sit at Otilio's bedside on moonlit nights, audience to his obvious and unreasonable rancor. Her ghostly skin charred, flickering like lit cigarette paper.

Gilberto and María Cielos conceived Seth the night of her parents' funeral. Gilberto had stroked María Cielos's back, her ass, then inched his fingers through the crevice between her legs as they stood at attention before the priest. In the dark, Gilberto threw María Cielos's sadness against a wall and replaced its vacuum with his hardened flesh. She cried out, and moaned, and sobbed from it all. A concoction of pain and primordial pleasure overtook her. Then it planted a disgusting seed in her belly, a pip that would eventually germinate into a child, who, at the age of forty-four, would murder his younger brother.

Whether Seth would be justified in doing so is still up for cosmic debate. The only sure thing is that Destiny is rather immune to justification. It does what it pleases, when it pleases, just as pain and pleasure do. Just as Man does. And as with all the primal things of which human hands are capable, Destiny is dramatic and arrogant. But most important, it's cyclical. A play performed again and again for millennia. And it's only by the end of its run that the new players realize, too late, the roles in which they have been unwittingly cast. And are soon to be recast.

Costa Rica is home to beasts as beautiful as
Man they are

the end
of

the river

they
wait for

prey the
size of

nature

2011

Seth Oreamundo immediately began hatching the plot to kill his brother like an egg. Or, one could say, the plot was hatching itself. A host of animal species (lizards, avians, crocodilians) develop an *egg tooth* to break free of their shelly sanctuary into the living, breathing world. This plan—his brother's end—was evolving its own tooth, tearing into the veiny membrane of Seth's brain. It did not beg to be born. It demanded it.

Seth and Nieves had had a fight last night, but not a marriage-ending one by any means. Nieves had the habit of coating Seth's bones in frost rather than pummeling him like a blizzard. She had become unbearably passive in that way. Sometimes he wanted her to take a knife to his throat or place his fingers delicately in the doorway to slam. He'd become tired of blaming himself for their fate—he wanted company, not an audience. With that frustration, Seth's temper flared, and he called her a name that would be tossed into the widening gap between them.

After turning off the Animal Planet program and putting Andrés to bed, Nieves confronted Seth, who was still glued to the television set, staring into it like a black mirror. How could he replay the clip when Andrés begged for him to stop? How could he ignore her as she cradled their son? Her mouth full of rage and motherly instinct? Seth couldn't answer her questions truthfully. There was no logical explanation as to why he'd just sat there, transfixed, disregarding his family. So he called Nieves a cowardly four-letter word to get her off his back, and they spent the night in separate rooms. Nieves fuming and tossing on their king-size bed; Seth with a throw pillow on the carpet, his ceramic pots of plants arranged in a protective oval around him.

Before either his wife or their son awoke, Seth decided to take one of his endless morning walks to clear his head. He stopped at different row houses on different side streets, peered through giant bay windows to admire rare African art or marble kitchen islands. Families crowded around flat-screens, news channels competing for breakfast like cereal brands (what is an anchor if not a corporate mascot?). This morning, everyone was jabbering about birth certificates—the president's, namely (yet again). Seth watched Donald Trump curl his thin pink mouth, explaining something, as if of great profundity, to an interviewer. He adjusted his silver tie and gloated. POSSIBLE GOP PRESIDENTIAL CANDIDATE, the lower third read. Seth couldn't help but chuckle. In Costa Rica, he'd worked with myriad idiots, Neanderthals, lunatics, tycoons, scammers, thieves, racists, fearmongers, evangelists, and every other evil in between. But he'd never met them all rolled up into one person. Seth's chuckle settled in a shudder. *Possible* was a horrifying word.

Leaving Kalorama, he slid like a dawn shadow onto a path toward Rock Creek Park. Power walkers basked in the cool, purple light. The sun had awoken fresh, if not a little groggy. April brought life teeming back to D.C.: cicadas hummed power ballads, birds yipped and pecked at undulating earthworms, leaves sprouted like positive thoughts, and Rock Creek babbled, clearing its mind of winter. Chanting *Om* as Seth strolled alongside.

Seth wondered if crocodiles had ever graced these waters. If a million years ago, this rocky creek had once been a grand river, filled to the brim with teeth. Perhaps it had downsized at some point, grown tired of the constant din of hunting, and wanted a demure, quieter life. So those crocodiles had to move south like birds. Packed up and moseyed out, down to Costa Rica, where they could tan, and swim, and slaughter in peace. The irony that Costa Rica would make one more violent. An irony that radiated from the creek's surface back onto Seth's straight face and hooded eyes. Osario appeared again, the image of him rippling in the current, face imprinted on the reflections of every passerby. His age depended on the person—a child Osario frolicked, and Seth wanted to embrace him; a man in his thirties dodged Seth, and his fist took aim at the water. More than a dozen expressions of his younger brother—those he'd loved, others he wanted to twist with his fingers. Seth wished for snapping jaws to spring forth from the creek and devour the memory.

A jogger's *On your right!* snapped Seth out of his trance.

He'd double back and visit the bank where Nieves didn't know he had an account of his own. They did have a joint checking, however, in which they both deposited money from odd jobs—Nieves's delicious desserts and Seth's salaries from short stints in offices. He never stayed at a job very long. Now that Google had allowed co-workers to stalk and search without hindrance or shame, Seth was afraid he'd be found out. His mug shot in Costa Rican newspapers, history splayed out for all the gringos to see. No, he jumped from position to position about every six months. But he liked these chances at a new beginning. He was waiting for the one that felt like it was on his own terms.

The new bank teller was rude at first, but after checking his savings, she wasn't. The hundred thousand dollars reflected in her eyeglasses had been slowly siphoned from offshore accounts, hoarded for the past ten years from his career at RECOPE in Costa Rica. Oil had provided him a nest egg, even in exile. Until Ignacio the ambassador finished preparing his visa, Seth would withdraw the daily limit until he had enough to complete his mission in Costa Rica. Money for the plane ticket, car rental, hotel, and other, miscellaneous expenses an accountant would have trouble deciphering. While he counted the cash at the bank threshold, Seth wondered if travel agencies had Revenge packages. All-inclusive stays for brothers betrayed by brothers. Chloroform towelettes presented by polite hotel staff, pillow mints swapped out for tabs of cyanide. But that would be no good: allowing someone else to curate Osario's death. Seth had always been controlling, always meticulous. The Devil was in the details. And for this—for eliminating the brother who'd taken everything from him—Seth would gladly become the Devil.

SEPERMERU

1971

Seth had enjoyed exactly four years as the center of his own universe. On his family's two-hundred-hectare coffee plantation, the moment he was born, he was doted upon by his parents, his grandfather, Otilio, and even the workers. For those dwelling on the Oreamundo plantation, not even the beauty of spectacular sunsets over the province of Cartago or the gentle babbling of the volcanic springs could compare to the wonder of little Seth. When María Cielos roamed the grounds with him in hand or trotting behind her, the coffee pickers would abandon their work to fawn over the child. In fact, the first feeling Seth could remember was the soreness of his cheeks. Unnaturally chubby and round, the maids, and workers, and washerwomen would flock to his hesitant face to pinch off a piece. When he was old enough to run, María Cielos let him loose in the fields of coffee bushes. Hurtling over fat sacks of beans and dodging hard, waxy leaves and the promise of venomous snakes, Seth explored the expansiveness of the plantation, every day going farther and farther, until a picker or overseer would catch sight of him going too far and snatch him up to be returned. Seth pushed these boundaries whenever he could because he loved heading back to the hacienda on the oxcarts. The oxen reminded him of the huge beasts called dinosaurs that he had seen on a movie screen in San José's theater. The animals' heavy breathing, muscular backs, protruding horns, and musky, shit-stained smell fascinated him. Often, he would wrestle the reins from the driver, snapping them up and down for the beasts to go faster. But alas, their heavy bodies couldn't manage more than an elderly man's walking pace.

When Seth was old enough to ride, Otilio would take him on horseback beyond the plantation's barbed wire fences. With his grandson on his lap, Otilio introduced Seth to the prehistoric jungles surrounding Turrialba's volcanic hills, crossed rivers as wide as oceans, and even once stumbled upon a colorful orgy of macaws, writhing, feathered bodies tucked into the clay side of a mountain. Otilio taught Seth to identify tropical flora, pointing out the different sizes and shapes of leaves, their textures and medicinal uses. Otilio tended to Seth as he did the prized plants in his greenhouse; as the next rung in the ladder of his legacy, Otilio invested half his days to nourishing his grandson's mind. When they returned in the afternoons, Otilio began Seth's studies of arithmetic and philosophy, elocution and forensics. He was raising Seth to be a more accomplished politician than he himself had ever been. If Otilio started grooming his grandson early, he reasoned, the child could be the youngest president ever to be elected in the history of the hemisphere.

María Cielos, on the other hand, nourished her boy's spirit. Before bed, she read to him, brushed his curly hair, steeped herbal teas to settle his stomach. She snuck him cookies when Gilberto wasn't looking and spoiled him more than her parents had spoiled her. Every word Seth spoke fascinated her, as if his thoughts were the first of their kind. One night, as they looked up to watch galaxies spin and ripple, Seth spoke of God.

"Mamá."

"¿Yes, my king?"

"¿What form does God take?"

"Why, all forms, I think. He is everywhere, all-knowing and good."

"I believe he is light."

"¿Oh? ¿Why do you say that?"

"Like you said, Mamá. Light is everywhere. Light is all-knowing and good. From the stars, the moon, and the sun, and from fire, I feel warmth. It makes me feel better, ¿and could that be God? That which makes me feel better."

"I think you're right, my king. Light must be the medium He takes to visit us. To warm our spirits, as you say."

"¿So that we won't feel alone?"

"Yes. Because we're not. We're never alone."

"¿Will you always be with me, then?"

"Yes, my dear. I'll always be with you, to visit you as light does. When I leave this place, I will return to God, and I will take His form to come back and warm your spirit."

"¿Do you promise?"

"Of course. You are my king, my greatest and favorite creation."

Mothers do not mean to lie to their children. It is, in many ways, against their nature. But María Cielos was merely an idealist, as all young mothers are. She was fooled by her own love because love is an idea that exists only in the present moment. In the past: not anymore; in the future: undecided. But in the present, love is as sincere and transparent as possible. So what María Cielos didn't know yet (what Seth had sensed, which is why he asked her to promise) was that her love *could* reach new heights. When she thought she couldn't possibly love anything more than Seth, Osario was born. The most beautiful child María Cielos had ever laid eyes on. And what became her betrayal of Seth also became God's betrayal. If she could lie, so could He. The moment Osario was born on Seth's fourth birthday, Seth's universe shifted. No longer at its center, he would become but a satellite, slowly orbiting away until he became just another distant star of weak, cold light.

The week before Osario's birth, María Cielos looked as if a birthday clown had blown too much helium into her belly. Seth was afraid she would float to the ceiling and never come down. Every waking moment he clung to her leg, hoping his body weight would stop her from escaping into the atmosphere. María Cielos misinterpreted this as a big brother's natural excitement. Gilberto, sensing something was off with their son, didn't correct her misinterpretation. He often let María Cielos live in her own reality. But Gilberto's usually calm, quiet demeanor took on an air of anxiety, a restlessness that manifested in a shaking leg or twiddled thumbs. María Cielos again misunderstood, attributing his behavior to a father's natural excitement for a second son. Again, Gilberto didn't correct her.

That week, Don Pepe Figueres himself was staying at the Oreamundo latifundio. While yes, he, too, was ecstatic for the birth of his old friend's grandson, his visit was not one of amity. Don Pepe slept in a different guest room each night with one eye open, and when he was awake, both eyes darted with fear and anticipation. Don Pepe was barely into this third presidency when Ted Williamson, that first secretary to the U.S. ambassador, began running his mouth at a party, exclaiming that Don Pepe's time was almost up. *He won't last much longer*, he slurred, still unaccustomed to alcohol as potent as guaro. His Cuban wife (that conceited niece of a wealthy sugar baron) also ran her mouth like a boat's propeller, parroting her husband to anyone who would listen. *He won't last much longer*, she hiccupped to Otilio himself, ignorant of the fact that, even after all these years, he was still Don Pepe's right-hand man. But Don Pepe's camp didn't know that Williamson's position as first secretary was merely a cover—he had been appointed CIA chief of station, which meant that his threats were frighteningly real. It seemed the Americans were becoming wary of Don Pepe again (they had already tried to assassinate him *twice* in the 1950s, and apparently now again twenty years later). They sensed he was becoming too cozy with the Soviets. While, yes, Don Pepe explained to the U.S. ambassador, he had allowed the sale of ten million dollars' worth of coffee to the Russians, that gesture was no invitation for communism in Costa Rica. But those gringos, forever paranoid, would not believe him. They had already lost their sugar in Cuba, and goddamnit if they were going to sit idly by as they lost their morning joe.

The situation boiled over when a fisherman off the coast of Limón noticed a mysterious ship unloading long wooden boxes onto the dock—weapons, Don Pepe was convinced. The gringos were predictable in their attempts at coup d'états: rallying separatists, delivering arms, assassinating leaders, and instating a puppet president. Wash, rinse, repeat. So, as a precaution, the Guardia Civil secreted Don Pepe away to the Oreamundo plantation, where Otilio protected his friend with an armory of ancient rifles, and the agents of the Guardia Civil, perched in towering conifers, awaited a CIA attack.

Don Pepe took an instant liking to little Seth, and he and Otilio took turns plopping the child onto their laps and bucking their legs like broncos, or philosophizing about American neoliberalism and recounting chilling ghost stories from their childhoods. Even in his constant state of subdued panic, Don Pepe roamed the grounds with dignity, flashing his forehead high in case a bullet decided to greet him after breakfast. He, too, wandered with Seth through the coffee bushes, playing tag and riding the oxcarts back. He even offered to bake Seth's birthday cake, though, after two failed attempts, he decided to let the personal chef have a go at it. Seth would remember this week with both fondness and an aftertaste of spite—the beginning of the end, he decided. The silver lining lost in a cloud before the storm.

Predicting María Cielos's water breaking, Don Pepe summoned his sweet American wife from San José to make the arrangements for the doctor, the midwife, the nursery's decorator, and the priest to baptize the boy upon easing out of his mother. Up until the very last moment, María Cielos prepared the hacienda for Seth's birthday, unaware that birth would interrupt the party. It began the moment the room began singing, the harmonic notes turned to those of unimaginable pain, and the guests, reluctant to witness her being ripped apart by new life, exited in one fluid motion. Don Pepe, his wife, Otilio, Gilberto, the doctor, and the midwife rushed María Cielos to the master bedroom, forgetting Seth at the table on his fourth birthday.

The blue-and-white-striped candles burned for all nine hours of María Cielos's labor. Seth stared into the four flames, his mind wandering, searching for shade from some new, oppressive light that arrived in the form of the encouraging voices, the clotted screams of birth, the inspiring *Pushpushpush* from his parents' bedroom. Though Seth sought sanctuary from this tempest of agony and joy, he never found it. What found *him* was one of the Guardia Civil's officers—a sergeant or lieutenant, by his arrogance—who walked up to Seth and his cake and blew out the candles himself. Seth hadn't even made a wish.

"Too bad, kid," the officer snorted. "I guess I get a freebie. Thanks a lot."

Seth observed the ribbons of smoke, how they ebbed and flowed with his breathing. Some got in his eye, and he began to cry.

"Aww, don't sweat it, kid," the officer said apathetically. "Being a rich boy, you'll have plenty of birthdays and plenty of blessings. You've got bigger things to worry about now."

Seth stopped crying to listen closely. His eyes reflected the curiosity of innocence, and not having had a childhood himself, the officer struck at that innocence like a scorpion.

"That's right. You've got a brother now. ¿Don't you hear him? He's already been born."

Seth nodded. It was now that he heard a different screaming from the master bedroom, and along with it, laughter and cheering.

"*That's right*," the officer hissed. "As long as you're both alive, kid, everyone will love him more."

"¡That's not true!"

"Oh, ¿it isn't? Hmmm . . . I've seen it plenty of times, kid. The new baby comes along, and the old one just fades away. ¿You ever had a new toy?"

Reluctantly, Seth nodded.

"¿And what happened to your old toys?"

Seth looked down at his lap and shook his head. "I don't know," he said. But he did know. Of course he knew.

"Take it from me, kid. Just be ready for it."

The officer stood at attention when Don Pepe reentered the room. Perfectly erect, the officer stared down at Seth, whose world he had just shattered. Even after San José was deemed safe for Don Pepe to return, and his unit left the Oreamundo latifundio, the officer would gloat secretly, congratulating himself, for he had finally stood up for his impoverished, adolescent self.

Don Pepe led Seth from the table, the cake, and its blown-out candles to his mother's bed. The new baby slept soundly in María Cielos's arms, wrapped in a dripping blanket the color of pig skin. All around, the witnesses congratulated each other, fanned themselves, hummed. María Cielos looked to her firstborn and smiled. "Seth, this is your new brother, Osario. ¿Isn't he a wonderful birthday present?" The weakness of birth covered her face in a lovely, radiant gelatin. "¿Isn't he what you've always wanted?"

Seth Oreamundo, on his fourth birthday, did not answer his mother's ridiculous question. Everyone misconstrued the boy's silence for the shock of adoration, as this was their own reaction. But the truth was, the officer's words had summoned a beast with ragged teeth within Seth, and it had already started gnawing at his organs. His stomach somersaulted, his lungs shriveled, and his heart beat with the force of a man running. Only when María Cielos looked down at the newborn and called him "my king" did Seth finally react. His brow pushed forward in malice. His eyes became pale blue slits. Parentheses curled around Seth's mouth as he spat in the newborn's face.

The midwife, Don Pepe and his wife, Seth's father and grandfather, all stood frozen in panic, their bodies like ancient ruins. In the burning stillness, María Cielos would do something she'd immediately regret. Something that everyone in that room would regret on her behalf. Until that moment, she hadn't realized love was territorial. Her love, it seemed, chose sides, and María Cielos brought the back of her hand down hard across Seth's face. Her sapphire ring sliced her son across the lip. The drip-dripping of his blood filled the overwhelming silence, falling to the sheets like sand in an hourglass. Counting the seconds of hush. Of remorse and cooling anger. Realizing what she had just done, María Cielos fought herself to move, to rush to the aid of her first-born and hold his head to her heart. She wished to beg his forgiveness and relent only when he granted it. But even after everyone else had begun to fidget in their own skins, commanding her with their minds to do something, *anything*, María Cielos didn't coddle her son. Rather, she couldn't. Not anymore. Her unspeakable reaction had dug a gorge between them from which emanated an echo, clear and hollow. Its ringing declared María Cielos as Seth's *once-mother*. And by definition, a once-mother would never dare to console her once-son. Especially now, in front of her new child. Her new king. María Cielos left Seth with two scars that day. One he could touch with his fingers, and another he couldn't.

ABYDOS

1971

María Cielos awoke from yet another fever dream. Her body couldn't tolerate the furnace inside her belly, and she was plunged into a world from which she wished to escape with her life. She endured nightmares of a desert, wandering the sand naked, her flesh pouring salty water that dried and caked her white, cracked skin. Her feet sank into the sand, exchanged for smoldering coals. They bled, the blood turning immediately black, as magma does when it touches air: solid, leaving behind little islands as she trudged forward. Or backward. She didn't know anymore. But María Cielos found no oasis. Without an animal's instinct, she ambled aimlessly for eternity, until bouts of wheezing ripped her from her dreams. Her cough on the verge of whooping, her head a field of land mines. Every moment of consciousness a wrong step, an explosion. And still the furnace in her belly, using the desert's hot coals to feed itself. If only she could have mustered the strength to scream.

Osario's birth left María Cielos dying. An infection had erupted from within her womb, a rare complication from the afterbirth refusing to be born. It festered, the bag of nutrients that had fed the baby now a toxic sack. Her body lit itself and her dreams on fire. The doctor tried with forceps and a hook, his own fingers and a plunger, but the placenta stayed lodged within her, stubborn as a deep-rooted weed. Gilberto did not leave her side—not for a moment—watching his wife mummify on the bed they shared. He beseeched his father for advice, but Otilio answered, *Women are not safe to give birth around you.* Gilberto cried softly to himself at night, only when he was sure his family was asleep. Don Pepe stayed, too, despite the fact that San José was deemed safe for him to return to. He convinced Gilberto to write Ola, María Cielos's aunt, whom she hadn't spoken to since before her parents died. She'd healed popes and lamas, and even presidents who'd already received last rites. She was María Cielos's last hope. Gilberto was as desperate as a man who seeks warmth from the setting sun. He was unsure if Ola remembered him, or had even liked him. When he'd courted María Cielos, he watched Ola rearrange the furniture shop's layout in something she'd called feng shui. Vases here, not there; love seats and fainting sofas closer to walls to allow good energy's river to flow. *People, too, are obstacles of positive vibrations*, Ola had said to him. Her bangles seemed to float like icy rings about her wrists, her voice priestess-calm, warrior-steady. *I will remove any and all blockages.* After that, whenever Gilberto had seen Ola, he stood up straighter, spoke to her not of the weather but of new texts from his father's library. María Cielos once told him it was impossible not to try to impress Ola, because she was so aloof. When one had seen the entirety of this world and the next, people didn't inspire much awe. Gilberto took to writing the letter with care and profundity—he needed to impress Ola to bring her back.

The letter was delivered by the officer who had shattered Seth's world. He would play postman, *fine*, but the officer took his sweet time, indifferent as he was to María Cielos's worsening state. The normal hourlong trip from the Oreamundo plantation outside Cartago to San José took him six, almost seven hours to complete. First he went for a haircut, bragging to the barber about his exploits with Don Pepe's wife. Then he visited one of his many girlfriends, coming in less than thirty seconds and staying for two hours to berate her while he indulged in the labors of her cooking. Finally, after other random errands, he arrived at Ola's house on the northern outskirts of San José, a rickety concrete structure coated in fading, Popsicle-orange paint. The officer knocked sheepishly until Ola finally opened her front door. He avoided eye contact, having heard that her evil eye was the most dangerous in the hemisphere. He instead analyzed other, safer parts of her body: dark, taut skin covered with constellations of moles, the architecture of her bones, her bare feet, and her wrists that might have snapped if she held on to the letter too long. Anything to distract himself from her gaze.

Ola read the note with skepticism and an unmistakable melancholy. The officer swore he saw drops hit the dirt by the witch's feet and looked up at the sky for rain. When she was done, Ola packed a few things and climbed into the back seat of the officer's black Chrysler. The entire time she eyed him through the rearview mirror with an instantaneous and growing dislike of his energy. He kept his eyes on the road in front of them, this time speeding like a madman, wanting nothing more than to escape from Ola's sight.

Don Pepe greeted Ola at the latifundio's threshold. They exchanged warm salutations and kisses, their voices holding the timbre of old friendship and, to the trained ear, an undertone of shared sadness. "I miss Michael every day," Don Pepe said with a weak smile. "I tell Alex as often as I can."

"Yes." Ola spoke English Creole. "He tells me you still write him once a month, and I'm sure you see each other in the capital from time to time."

It was Alex who'd introduced Michael and Ola to Don Pepe, and as teenagers to the man named Garvey. They'd arrived home from a pleasant swim, dripping seawater and joy, only to find a strange portly man, no taller than Ola, at their kitchen table. His mustache gleamed and his eyes twinkled like black stars in his head. Two memories would stand out from that day: how immediately Garvey ignored Ola and how stunning his wife was, resting elegantly on their couch, touching tea to her smiling lips. When the men excused themselves to another room, Ola sat with Amy in awkward, admiring silence.

"Your brother tells us you write better than even the great poets," Amy said.

"Alex flatters me," Ola muttered, squeegeeing her arms and her bare legs with trembling hands.

"The world needs women with words. And if she can command them like waves upon the sea, there is nothing she can't accomplish." Amy blew away steam, sipped so royally from the chipped teacup Ola thought Amy was posing for Velázquez himself. "I'm not so bad with words, you know. I know their power, how they can get us back to our rightful place."

"Where is that?"

"Home," Amy answered. "Far away from here or even the island on which I was born, where the mothers of our mothers' mothers held court like kings. Those words your brother says flow through you are their prayers answering themselves. If you come with us, you can spread them far and wide and help lead our people back to where we belong."

Ola heard only half of what Amy said. It didn't matter where, but Ola would follow her to the ends of the earth, so she agreed without hesitation, and after Garvey emerged from the smoky room with her brothers, the three set upon the sea with their new mentors.

If she were honest, Ola had as few interactions with Garvey as she did freckles on her nose. He kept women (including his wife) at arm's length, which meant what hung between Alex and Michael's legs allowed them access into Garvey's entourage, gave them special privileges to opine, argue, and counsel. Ola would have been pricked with jealously if not for Amy's generous, doting tutelage. The women upon the ships of the Black Star Line smoked fat cigars in their own lush quarters, as fierce as any man too cowardly to sit opposite her in friendly debate. As Ola drafted Garvey's speeches, she listened intently to Amy's arguments, dismantling the white man's vision of the world—it was neither a geocentric nor a heliocentric model but a Eurocentric understanding of the universe that kept them from reaching cosmic truths. Resituating their focus on Africa and its rich history was the only way to any future in which they could find peace. Amy spoke of Tutankhamen's newly unearthed tomb, how quickly the whites studied the pharaoh's funerary mask for Caucasian features. *Egypt is in Africa*, Amy reminded. That day, she looked at Ola and said sternly, *Every pharaoh was Black. They looked like you and me, Theola. Never forget that. Train your heart's compass to lead you not north but to the center of this world.*

Ola followed Amy for fifteen years, during which she was allowed the space to explore the world beyond what others saw. Amy had heeded Ola's spot-on premonitions, witnessed her chatting afternoons away with wayfaring ghosts, and found her splayed out in bed, pupils missing from her eyes, while she astral projected to only God-knew-where, returning once with the Queen of England's crown. While Amy, Garvey, and Ola's brothers fought for the liberation of flesh and bone, it was up to Ola to light the way for their spirits. Ola spent more time away from her mentor, more time away from her brothers and Limón, spending years wandering the wilderness like Moses. She visited tribes from Burma to Kenya, studied with vodun priests, Yoruba medicine men, and famous santeros in the Cuban countryside. And even after Garvey's death and Amy's subsequent leadership of his organization, Ola continued tapping into these cultures as one taps into the different ley lines that connect all sacred places on earth.

But Ola's journeys brought no laudation from her brothers. They didn't care about ancient gods or rituals that still existed somewhere deep in their blood. After Don Pepe's war in 1948, Alex and Michael joined his efforts to create the scholastic, cultural, and economic incorporation of Limón and its people into the mestizo culture of greater Costa Rican society. And despite her brothers' attempts to include her, Ola ignored them to travel the globe in search of something that only she could see. They considered her sabbaticals nothing more than a woman's gallivanting. The feminine instinct to shirk hard work and the things that really mattered. But they were wrong. Men were always wrong about these types of things. Their lot lacked the divinity to truly connect the body and the soul. It was up to her, she answered to Michael's rebukes in his furniture shop. Her studies and travels were for the greater good.

But now, so many years later, kissing Don Pepe goodbye, Ola was no longer sure. The mansion grounds would promise to challenge everything she'd ever known to be true.

"Tía," María Cielos coughed when Ola entered the master bedroom. She had escaped another fever dream and was lucid enough to speak. "¿What are you doing here?"

"It was me," Gilberto confessed to his wife. He lay by María Cielos's side reading the morning's newspaper—current events and lottery numbers distracted him from the veins that bulged from his wife's neck like earthworms. "I apologize for not telling you, but it was my only option."

Ola leaned against the doorframe, suddenly dizzy. "You don't look well, child," she said.

"¿Is it that obvious? I guess someone who's dying always hopes they don't look like they're dying. But, ¿who am I to complain? I'm the luckiest woman in the world to have an aunt like you. It's been so long, tía . . ."

"Quite lucky." Ola smiled.

With only a few more hours of sunlight, Ola declined to meet the boys just yet and instead roamed the latifundio alone in search of healing herbs. For many years, Ola had been known as *the* curandera, healing the capital's elite for hefty prices, which they paid gladly. The rich get sick, and doctors can do only so much for them. But they will pay whatever is required to live long enough to enjoy the very last drop of their money. And so, it was with their desperate, greedy funding that Ola had continued to travel the globe, praying under the moon on white mountains and holding her breath beneath sacred lakes.

Despite her thin, aging limbs, Ola climbed the trunk of a eucalyptus for its waxy leaves, scrounged the forest floor for mint and skullcap. With every uproot, memories surfaced, delicate as herbs or stubborn and bitter as weeds. She remembered the night of María Cielos's vision—how Ola had done everything the Lakota man had taught her. She'd lit the fire with wet leaves and soft branches, let its flames rise a meter before beginning the prayer. She'd re-created the ritual to a tee. But as Ola wiped thick yuca clean, she wondered if she'd misremembered. If another shaman's words had bled into the Lakota's chant. Perhaps she'd mixed up ceremonies, and the fire that licked her niece's sweat had burned too high or too wet or too bright for a moonless night. Ola couldn't recall the prayer now. She was only trying to help her niece, she'd told her scolding brother upon their return to the furniture shop that morning. María Cielos had drifted past her parents, and Michael and Casandra let Ola have it. While Casandra interrogated, Michael cast a lifetime of stones: Ola's selfishness for coming back only when she wanted and leaving when it suited her; the irresponsibility of starving their daughter and stealing her away in the middle of the night. He berated Ola for abandoning their organization to go on some wild, cosmic goose chase. She'd not been searching but running from what truly mattered. She'd abandoned their people for phantoms, scouring the earth for a god that didn't exist.

Ola dug her fingers into the earth, gripped dirt as she had the steering wheel. The ground vibrated like a motor. Her younger brother, who looked like their father, had blocked the doorframe as she tried to see around him for a glance at María Cielos. If her niece reemerged and pleaded Ola's case, maybe Michael could forgive her. But Casandra had already given up, and Michael towered like a colossus over any future Ola had with her family. So she pulled out of the driveway without waving goodbye. She cursed him under her breath. But a year later, she smelled his embers on a morning breeze. When she arrived at the shop, the authorities were already scooping ashes into coffins, and María Cielos was nowhere to be found. Ola returned to her shack, planted the shivers of her heart in the garden, packed up her guilt, and plunged herself into the wilderness.

The first year she wandered the rainforests of Puntarenas, feeding off the fertile land, eventually venturing into the territory of the Brunka tribe, who taught her their medicinal secrets. With the elder shaman, she tried Reina de la Noche, its tea a powerful hallucinogen used to travel through time. In her visions, she saw poor Michael cremating on the bed, whistling to distract himself from the unbelievable pain. "He was like that," she told the shaman afterward. "He was the most positive of men, the happiest person I've ever met."

It was when Ola truly learned to harness the tea's power that she was able to graduate from episodes of the past to those of the future. In one session that left her hollering and weeping on the forest floor, she witnessed a pair of twins gut each other, braid their intestines, and squeeze each other's organs as one does a pump. It took the whole village to calm her down. She vowed to never leave the present again. The past was too painful, the future too frightening. After that, she returned home to San José, where she became a shut-in, her only human contact with her older brother, Alex. He'd been the only one of the three siblings to remain in politics and was now a congressman. Between government meetings, he dropped groceries and eloquent letters on Ola's doorstep once a week. She read them by candlelight, sobbing from the beauty of his language and the sheer amount of love imprinted in every handwritten sentence. Every period was a kiss she wouldn't let him give her, every gorgeous Creole phrase an invocation of their younger brother, whom they both missed every waking moment and still, sometimes, in their dreams.

Her inventory of healing herbs complete, Ola transformed the mansion's kitchen into an alchemist's laboratory. The stiff metal that had surrounded her heart all these years melted away, of which she distilled its finest and most valuable ores: the eternal adoration for her late brother, the rediscovered connection with her niece, and the prospect of this new home, this new life, and a family she could finally call her own.

In just three days, the placenta slithered out of María Cielos with the gait of a slug. The teas Ola concocted massaged it out, their potency like that of chemotherapy without its harmful side effects. And three days after that, María Cielos could walk again and even dance weakly to the old calypsos with her beloved aunt.

María Cielos returned her attention to her newborn Osario, pouring whatever energy her body could muster into adoring him like nothing and no one she ever had before. And when she wasn't coddling the new baby, Ola cradled it with one skinny arm. With the other, she continued to brew medicine that would fortify her niece's strength.

As the house refocused on the baby Osario's needs, Seth kept to himself and to the shadows. Ola tried her best to interact with him, but he shuddered at the very prospect of a woman's touch. She relented until he was ready. While María Cielos and Gilberto obsessed over the baby, Otilio took charge of caring for Seth. He bathed him, fed him, brushed his curly blond hair, and still took him horseback riding. Despite these small kindnesses, Seth did not speak to anyone for over a month. Otilio and Ola understood. Trying to care for the child became a catalyst for their new, unlikely friendship. In passing they discussed what Seth required, what they could do to coax his voice out of him. Eventually this led to platonic midnight dates during which they'd linger at the dinner table, a pile of dirty dishes and memories between them. One night, as María Cielos and Gilberto slept with Osario between them, Otilio and Ola shared a bottle of rum.

"They call it sibling rivalry, ¿don't they?" Ola said after shivering from her fourth shot. Her yellow dress radiated like another candle.

"That's right," Otilio said. "Something so simple as jealousy has the power to eclipse the heart. It's incredible what we humans feel, especially as children."

"Michael and I started life around the same time." Ola smirked. "Our mother couldn't remember who was born first. Even if Alex was older, he was too young to know for sure, and our father was a fisherman—he took stock of snappers and corvina, not kids. As long as our mouths were fed, he didn't care who'd said *Papa* first. But it was me. I remember it."

"¿Being born?"

"Yes. I don't recall the sight of it, but I can still hear every sound. The midwife's muttering, my mother's agony. I told my parents so. But they said all births happen that way—none stand out from the others.

"Michael swore he was older, but he couldn't prove it. That drove him mad for a time. He teased me, pulled my hair, swam out farther into the surf than my arms could take me. I would see him floating there on the waves and wish the sea was a bed on which to lie next to him. When we grew out of that bickering, he would tow me out on a soft wood board and float on his back, arms out like a savior. If the light hit him just right, I would cry."

"A child's tears are saltier than an ocean," Otilio simpered. "My mother told me that once."

"¿Were you an only child?"

"I was." He licked his fingers of some spilled rum. "Then I wasn't. And then I was again." To Ola's perplexed expression, he said, "I was the oldest. And my siblings were born, one by one. And then they died, one by one, until I was an only child again."

"That's cruel," Ola answered. The cherry of her cigar coruscated, dimmed.

"More affection for me," he chuckled.

"You don't mean that, Don Otilio."

"No," he said, interlacing his fingers, squishing his flesh between his rings. "I suppose I don't mean that."

"You must understand your grandson, then. Alone at first, now not alone anymore."

"Hopefully not alone again," Otilio said. The rum had polished his eyes. The world was blurred, bright. Ola redistributed her weight in the armchair, then chirped. Seth had stepped out from the hallway's shadow, his face shifting in the flickering candlelight. He held a stuffed bear and his blue blanket. Words escaped for the first time.

"Tito . . . tía . . . I'm scared."

"Come here, child," Ola said. She wrapped her arms around Seth.

"¿Did you have a nightmare?" Otilio asked, scooting his chair closer. "¿Another?" he offered Ola, grasping the neck of the bottle.

"Of course," she answered. "Seth, ¿what are you scared of?"

"My parents don't love me anymore," he said. A matter of fact, as all children's observations are.

"Don't say something so horrible, child," Ola replied. She and Otilio exchanged awkward glances. There is nothing that makes adults more uncomfortable than the truth from the mouth of a child.

"It's definitely not true," Otilio encouraged. "Your mother and father have just been presented a new gift from God. And something so special as a newborn needs the most love possible, or it will grow up to be mean and bitter. This is vital in his development. And you, too, must play a part, Seth. You must love him with all your heart. And he, in turn, will love you back with his. Your parents will eventually redistribute their love. It's a passing phenomenon, my boy. ¿Do you understand?"

Seth nodded. Ola sensed the officer's face cut into Seth's mind. Eyes lit up with malice, slimy lips curling around Seth's greatest insecurities. She tightened her arms around him and whispered Michael's favorite song, "Zancudo con dengue."

Seth's eyelids became leaden; his hands twitched, swatting a buzzing mosquito from his body. Ola felt his heart slow, and she rested her chin on his head as he drifted off to sleep. Otilio poured her another shot, and they sat together in the candlelight, Ola still whispering the gay calypso that reminded her of home. Of the beach, and the humid, tepid days of ocean air. Of her sweet brother Michael, floating off on the placid sea. A wide smile across his wet, beautiful face.

Costa Rica is home to *beautiful*
demons

the
most unforgiving *can*
weigh *teeth*
from the

moon

the most powerful
can

swallow

humans they perform what is known as

nature

2011

Seth and his son walked north along Connecticut Avenue, dodging a homeless man who held open the door of a McDonald's and blew chapped-lipped kisses to would-be altruists, his yellow McD's cup a jingling purse with fewer coins inside it than on the ground around him. Seth and Andrés both ordered Happy Meals, though Seth was too giddy to feel hungry. Spring break had just started, and Seth took the opportunity to spend this new free time with Andrés. He did so seldomly; not because he didn't like his son, but because he didn't trust Andrés's kind nature. It wasn't that the boy was soft, but he did dimple at harsh words: from teachers, from Seth himself. Seth wanted to toughen him up, make him impervious to the world. But who was he kidding? Seth had no spine to speak of.

Father and son finished their meals, dodged the homeless man again as they left, and continued north, ogling all the elegant apartment buildings: limestone, art deco structures that housed D.C.'s burgeoning rich.

"How many people do you think live in this one?" Seth asked, pointing up toward a building that, from this angle, blocked out the sky.

"More than a hundred," Andrés said, his Oreamundo blood confident in his veins.

"Two hundred, I'd say."

"Three hundred."

"A million," Seth said, laughing. He lifted Andrés and plopped him onto his shoulders. The two bucked down the gum-littered avenue until they reached the disappointing western gate of D.C.'s National Zoo, flanked by two black lions, which Andrés later mused must have been plucked from the MGM logo and spray-painted. A concrete zoo sign stood surrounded by flower beds. Bamboo shoots shot up from every direction along the path. Despite the sincere happiness Seth felt at the prospect of spending the entire day with his son, he had ulterior motives for suggesting the zoo. Motives that would eventually configure themselves into a plot. A plot that would eventually fashion itself into fratricide. For a moment, Seth thought it a shame that Andrés would never have the opportunity to meet his only uncle. But at the brick entrance to the reptile house, with its turquoise Stegosaurus mosaic drifting overhead, Seth resigned himself. Not everyone can have what they want. Or need.

The reptile house proved muggy but at least unperturbed by the body heat of other zoo-goers—odd, given that school had just let out. Seth and Andrés were alone. Seth moved slowly only to appease the incessant curiosity of his son, who floated like a helium balloon losing air, asking too many questions, stopping at every glass enclosure to gawp at leaf-tailed geckos, still as mice in traps; a lime-colored caiman lizard who, like a tanning housewife, kept close to the heat lamp; snake-necked turtles, snapping turtles, those ubiquitous ones with tiger stripes. Who could have thought Seth was capable of such patience? But Seth wasn't Seth in this moment. He was imagining what it might be like to be one of those crocodiles he had researched the night before, hunger throbbing just below the surface of the water. Eyes visible, but nothing else. Seth was on the hunt for a specific species. The one from all those years ago—the river crocodile that had pounced from the water to devour a woman in front of him and Osario.

"Papá," Andrés said, breaking Seth out of his trance. "Look at that one!"

Seth feasted his eyes on a gharial that in turn feasted on a soft-shelled turtle still trying to swim away from its executioner's elongated snout. This gigantic crocodilian took on the banal, menacing charm of a mosquito.

According to the fading sign: *300–550 lbs . . . 16 feet long on a good day . . .*

"No, this isn't the one," Seth said.

"What? Which one?" Andrés asked.

"It has to be as white as this one's belly."

The turtle's blood dribbled down the underside of the gharial's scales like soda spilled between kitchen tiles.

"Is it that one?" Andrés was pointing to a larger enclosure with cerulean water and plastic palms blanketing the cheap concrete.

"The Cuban crocodile . . ." Seth read. "No, not this one, idiot."

Before Seth even realized what he'd whispered to his son, Andrés bolted away, sobbing. But Seth didn't budge. This Cuban was indeed the wrong species, but its anatomy was similar to the crocodile from his memory. Half the size, but with osteoderms as arrogant as horns, teeth like formations in a cave, and the aura of the Devil. Seth smushed his face to the bulletproof glass and leered deep into the crocodile's eyes, his reflection in the slits of them.

They were close enough to notice a family resemblance, close enough for Seth to bond with such a murderous beast. *Beast, beast, beast, beast, beast*, Seth thought. The satisfying perfection of kin.

Outside the reptile house, Seth found Andrés waist-high with a man who patted him on the head, rustling his hair like a fiend. Grinning with the lurid expression of victory. Without thinking, Seth snatched the man by the collar and forced their gazes to meet. The man's reflection in the slits of Seth's eyes. Without having to utter a whimper, the pervert ran like quarry out of sight. Rather than pursuing, Seth kneeled down to comfort his son, but Andrés took a step back, far enough that Seth couldn't reach him anymore. And in the mirrors of his son's eyes, Seth no longer saw himself. This plot to kill Osario would morph Seth into something unrecognizable. And Andrés, with his pure, innocent instinct, had just witnessed Seth's first transformation.

WADJET

1979

The day the Oreamundo brothers witnessed the crab coiled up in a viper's grip had been their birthday (Seth's twelfth and Osario's eighth). That day, Anastazio Somoza robbed his country blind. On his way out of Nicaragua, the overthrown dictator prepared his father's and brother's caskets, lining them with crushed purple velvet, the crushed will of his supporters, and about 115,000,000 dollars. No one knew if he had stuffed his family's bodies with the cash or hidden it in secret compartments in the pinewood, but one thing was certain: when the Sandinistas took Managua, they found less than 3 percent of that amount in the national treasury. Somoza flew to Miami with a pleased smile on his face. A banished man, but richer than his own country had ever been, and perhaps, ever would be.

Hundreds of kilometers south in Costa Rica, the sky was cloudy over the Oreamundo plantation. Brisk, breezy, licked with mist. The surrounding rainforest flourished in the gray light, and everyone in attendance wore long sleeves. The hacienda was abuzz with birthday preparations. Balloons and cake and guests, and alcohol for the adults. María Cielos chatted with Ola in Limonese creole, while the maids scrubbed the floors. Otilio fed his morning coffee a small bottle of whisky. Gilberto, the controlling DJ that he was, chose a specific order of vinyls to be played at the party. Bossa nova to set the mood, followed by boleros, then "disco" records that had just arrived from the United

States: a music unexpectedly delicious to dance to, but only once the children went to bed.

The Oreamundo brothers and four friends escaped the party and ventured into the forest. Sibling rivalry guiding their limbs into the dense underbrush, seeing who could go farther than the other. The fellowship was composed of the Oreamundo brothers, the Mendez twins, and the Villarreal sisters. As the oldest of the six, naturally Seth took the lead, though he was fought at every turn by Osario. Despite their four-year age difference, Osario had grown at an impressive rate, and he stood almost as tall as his older brother and was just as intelligent. Upon introduction, new acquaintances assumed that they were fraternal twins, though one (the opinion was evenly divided and fervently argued) was more handsome than the other. Osario, the vainer of the two, surmised that it was him. So, through the forest, Seth and Osario walked side by side, leading the group like a snake with two belligerent heads, snapping at each other, looking for every fork in the path as an excuse to bicker and throw light jabs.

The twins, Jesús and Miguel, followed closely behind with the air of a young married couple. Their hands always interlocked, one resting his head on the other's shoulder at stops. The aristocratic circle with which their parents surrounded themselves found the twins unnaturally feminine. They sashayed through the forest, picking delicate flowers, presenting them to each other. It was as if they had sundered from one feminine egg, and a masculine gene was supplemented as an afterthought. It seemed these two children were made up of one spirit, so perfect was their synchronicity. Their parents, unsure of what to do, left them to their own devices, neither encouraging their behavior nor reprimanding it. The twins, in their later years, would thank them for it.

Towing far behind, the Villarreal sisters crept along the path as Snow White had in her Disney biopic, anticipating horrible monsters between the webs of dead branches. At every turn they shrieked in unison, causing the Oreamundo brothers to roll their eyes.

"If you're gonna be scared the whole time," Osario shouted, "¡Turn back now! ¡There's no need for girly girls on this trip!"

Isa (Marisa Villarreal) answered Osario with a howl: *a-rooooooooo, ar-ar-arooooo!* Besides Seth, she was the only one confident enough to go toe-to-toe with Osario's personality. "¡I'm only pretending to be scared so that Nieves doesn't feel alone!"

"¡Hey!" Nieves said, popping her sister on the shoulder. "I'm older than you. Show me some respect."

Nieves, eleven years old, and Isa, nine, were the daughters of an American diplomat and his Costa Rican–born socialite wife. Having fallen in love with the country and his lover's perfume, their father recanted his role as a gringo neoliberal and dedicated every waking hour to Costa Rica's betterment. As an activist, he had been on the front lines when the aluminum company ALCOA arrived to begin mining operations. He instigated university students and supplied them with rocks from his backyard. His wife fortified the protestors with coffee and crackers. And yet, even with their radical ideas, they still integrated easily into high society, which is to say, their political compass pointed one direction and their personal lives pointed in the opposite. They raised Isa and Nieves with the annoying altruism of a gringo who falls for a Latin American, and the oppugnant snobbery of a Latin American who falls for a gringo. Noses held high but hands open, giving.

Periodically, Seth and Nieves met each other's gazes, but for most of the journey, they were mired in their own anxieties—Nieves huffing from sweat and unfamiliar bugs, and Seth from having to cover his crotch with the sweater tied around his waist. These involuntary erections had been plaguing him the past year, manifesting at the most inopportune moments—witnessing the slit of a maid's uniform, or after dreams of a distant cousin he'd met years ago. Once, as he watched his grandfather step out of the shower. Seth trudged on ahead until the erection dissipated, overcompensating by yelling for the group to keep up.

"¿Where are we going?" Osario asked, in a rare display of not-knowing-everything.

"To the falls. Tito took me once on horseback."

"¿What's there?" shouted Isa.

"¡Macaws! ¡A rainbow of them!"

"¡Slow down, Seth!" The Mendez twins moaned, their little patent-leather shoes smushing through viscous mud and bugs, brittle stones, and littered orchids.

When Nieves caught up to Seth, he studied her face, her shoulders peeking out from her dress through miniature holes. So many, the fabric looked like lace.

"¿What happened?" Seth asked.

"Oh," Nieves said, pulling the fabric from her chest to inspect. "I like caterpillars."

Seth again studied her face, her shoulders.

"I think they're cute. I collect them from the garden. They're green and brown and yellow. I collect them and keep them under my bed because I want butterflies flying around my room. I love butterflies."

Again, distrust and intrigue flashed in Seth's eyes.

"But they always turn out to be moths. They crawl out of their little cocoons and eat my dolls' clothes and mine. My mother spanks me for it." Nieves lifted up her dress just enough to reveal a golden, pulsing blob on the back of her thigh.

"But no matter how many times, I still hope they'll hatch into butterflies."

"I want to give you butterflies every day," Seth said. Even he was surprised by this sudden confidence. "That one," he said, pointing to a blue morpho suspended from a furry vine, iridescent as tropical water in a photograph. "Or that one." Seth held out his palm. On it landed a glass wing butterfly. He turned to Nieves to show it to her, and through its fluttering windows, he could see her face brighten into a sun.

The Oreamundo brothers would be the only two of this motley group who would remember the two fantastic, horrifying beasts they encountered that day. Seth and Osario would recount the memory decades later to their wives, Nieves and Isa, respectively, over random dinners or splayed out in the dark, in hopes of jolting them into corroboration. Seth tried to jog Nieves's memory a few times a year, baring his teeth like singular fangs, fashioning his calloused hands into claws that he clamped around Nieves's temples. Perhaps if he could shoot the memory through his fingers like electricity, it would resurface in her mind. But her only reaction would be a chilled kiss to his forehead. Condescending, but refreshing nonetheless. Osario's narration to Isa would be punctuated by deep, swelling breaths. He would bring it up only two or three times during their marriage, describing the memory with the detail of a film: the primordial ceibas strangled by the vines; the familiar butterflies with majestic wings that Nieves once hoped would hatch in her room; the stinky mud; the waterfall's childlike hum; the cool; the breeze; the static.

That day, as boys, and without the slightest doubt in their minds, they saw a gargantuan crab coiled up in a gargantuan viper's grip. Behind the monsters, the turquoise dish of water beat with a pulse. Overwhelmed by the scene, Seth and Osario both compartmentalized the details. First, the colors. Of the crab: purple throughout its shell, black globular eyes, legs like a series of carrots whittled into killing instruments. Of the viper: scales of every shade of green, as if an artist had dabbed each scute with a patient brush, and its eyes like the rings their grandfather wore. Second, the brothers focused on movement, then sound. Vibrations from each creature—the slowly tightening body of the snake, a single muscle with one instinct. Bubbles screamed from the crab's feathery mouthparts, only slightly louder than the waterfall. A steady, whispered pop. Exoskeleton crushed makes a distinct sound—not unlike a roach beneath a boot—thick calcium snapping, revealing the frightened meat inside. A harsh, mewling crack. Then the brothers heard gasps cupped in hands. The Mendez twins were the first to run. The squash of frantic feet through clay. Nieves pulled Isa away, and they ran too. But Seth and Osario stood their ground. Without looking at each other, they plummeted into a fraternal competition to see who could witness the carnage the longest. Men confront horror head-on—that is what the last five thousand years of civilization had taught them. They were two little boys with something to prove. To the crab, to the viper. To each other, and to themselves.

By the time Seth and Osario returned to the hacienda, the other children were gone. And standing on the barren veranda, the adults looked on with pale, petrified faces. Otilio rushed to whisk Seth away, as did Ola to Osario, before Gilberto and María Cielos had the opportunity to hammer their faces with a parent's worry. The brothers were thrown into separate rooms to confess.

"Seth," Otilio said in the master bedroom. "¿Where were you all?"

"Osario," Ola ground her teeth like a pestle and mortar. She sat down next to the fireplace in the parlor. "¿Where were you all?"

The mosquito netting in the bedroom flapped like a dress. "In the woods," Seth answered his grandfather.

An ember singed the parlor's carpet. "In the woods," Osario said to his aunt.

"¿What scared the other children so bad?" both Otilio and Ola asked, from opposite ends of the mansion.

"A snake."

"A crab."

"A crab."

"A snake."

Both brothers dove into their retellings as if they'd rehearsed it together. As they would with their wives later in life, they fashioned their limbs into the limbs and nonlimbs of the beasts. Osario threw shadow puppets on the walls, Seth wrestled with himself on the floor. They both entered an ecstatic state, eyes like clean eggs in their skulls. Otilio and Ola escaped their respective chambers. They met in the center of the corridor, in the center of the mansion, where María Cielos and Gilberto stood swaying, trying to calm their fuming.

At dinner, the members of the family sat as far from each other as possible. The plated vegetables stewed in their own discomfort. The prime rib was a leathery bootstrap. Slices of birthday cake stiffened from neglect. Still, the two brothers shouted their story, at everyone this time, completing each other's frantic sentences, which made the adults shift in their seats. The boys concluded that what they had seen was biblical.

And the maids flanking the table whispered to no one in particular, *¿What do children know of the Bible?*

MAAT

1980

If Catholics (practicing or not) were to acknowledge the existence of lesser gods—not counting the polytheistic nature of saints—and assign those divine talents to earthly individuals, Osario Oreamundo would have easily and unanimously been ordained the God of Mischief. Like Anansi, or Loki, or the great Coyote of the Navajo, Osario's pranks were exquisitely planned. And with a child's sense of humor, embarrassment was, above all else, his specialty. Without whoopee cushions (and without knowing that they even existed), he'd put the base of his palms to his pursed lips and blow out whenever anyone sat in their seat. He misplaced cups, and plates, and pots; rearranged the innards of dressers, whole rooms, and once, his father's study. He threw his voice, pinched bottoms, feigned seizures. Though always nonviolent, as he aged, his pranks took on more menacing airs—the Oreamundo latifundio lost a string of maids, for example. Osario had perfected his technique of fashioning dolls out of straw and cloth. He snipped the hair of the maids as they slept soundly in their quarters, and he left said dolls in the centers of doorways, with curly, lopsided wigs and dozens of pins like porcupine needles. That was enough for packed bags and wisps of the domestics hailing oxcarts at the front gate.

And, like all families of a trickster, the Oreamundos suffered. Most of all, Seth, who felt obligated to stand watch while Osario executed his remorseless jokes. The anxiety of always needing to cover for his little brother kept him up at night as images of crueler tricks intruded before bed. Seth regularly devised excuses for those missing cups, and plates, and pots. He re-rearranged the innards of dressers, rooms, and their father's study. Anything to protect Osario's buttocks from the hard, open palms of Ola, then María Cielos, and lastly, Gilberto, standing in a conga line of punishment.

Eventually, after the tale of the crab and the viper had disappeared from the mansion, Isa and Nieves began to visit again. These playdates steadily curbed Osario's pranks because he quickly realized that he'd met his match in Isa, who had her own affinity for trickery. After the girls had gone home, Osario would notice his toys placed in too-high places, so he'd be forced to beg for help from the vengeful maids, who would suddenly go deaf and limp. Isa snipped his own hair when he wasn't looking, and pasted it onto his own dolls, and left those dolls, with their own hides of porcupine quills, in his doorway. The house of adults caught on that Isa was the only one who could best Osario at his own game, and they begged the girls' parents for weekly visits. After just two months, the mansion grew calm again. The God of Mischief dethroned.

The oncoming rainy season extended these dates into sojourns, the mountain roads impossible to traverse during storms. Mudslides buried highways and shifted the foundations of new hotels that came crashing down the sides of mountains, their concierges, room service, and presidential suites all included. And if the rain lingered too long, it dug and filled a moat all around the Oreamundo plantation. The more time Seth and Nieves spent together over the next year, the deeper his affection grew. Besides the uncontrollable erections while imagining her bathing or peeling off her moth-holed dresses, his attraction manifested in heart palpitations and pools of sweat from his palms. It was as if her very presence forced Seth to undergo puberty. He employed any tactic he could to separate her from everyone else, just so he could inhale the scent from her hair. Wrapped in her gossamer nightgown, she would hum whatever song her American father featured that week on his record player. She never knew the lyrics, so Seth made them up for her, building a melody from scratch with Nieves's off-tune accompaniment. She peered into the kitchen as Ola cooked with María Cielos, asking specifics of techniques and recipes. While Isa torpedoed into the Oreamundo mansion, Nieves swept in like a cool breeze, calming everyone's nerves, especially Seth, who sat in the snow of her.

Osario noticed his brother's fondness immediately, and his jokes were endless. The jeering grew serrated and tugged at Seth's brain until he'd threaten his little brother with pummeling while he slept. A nine-year-old couldn't understand the logistics of a thirteen-year-old's body. Its goings-on. Hormones pinballing; a brand-new, itchy skin of shame. Seth wished to escape himself and his brother, who would only let up when adults moseyed by, glancing adoringly at Osario before continuing on their merry way. Every day, Osario discovered new buttons that adolescence acned in Seth. Launch codes, self-destruct sequences. All with the smile of a war hawk at his presidential desk.

A year after the crab and the snake, the entire family sat down to read. Isa and Nieves had left that morning; Seth had thrown up butterflies into the toilet bowl all afternoon. For dinner, instead of sitting at the dining room table, the Oreamundos found their way into the drawing room. Osario sat on María Cielos's lap; Seth plopped himself on the red Afghan rug. The adults sat snugly in large leather recliners. Forks scratched the china, adding an eerie rhythm to the story about to be told. Gilberto volunteered to be tonight's lector, but Otilio waved him off and began the thick epic of *Beowulf* already balanced in his steady hand. When asked of mead by the boys, Gilberto pointed to his tumbler of whisky; when asked of singing lodges, Ola began to hum. Otilio continued despite these footnotes and childproof explanations, telling the tall tale of a Norse hero locked in combat with a monster. A monster who hated laughter and chanting, celebration and feasting. Beowulf was a man—a demigod—of whose likeness the boys had never encountered in person. They inspected their father and grandfather for brawn: none. For bravery: unlikely. So, it was up to their imaginations to conjure such a giant, masculine man, capable of slaying, capable of doing what was right, even if death itself were just another evil to vanquish.

"It sounds biblical," the boys whispered. Yet again the two brothers were right, and the adults all took note between two sips of scotch. Otilio continued.

Till the monster stirred, that demon, that fiend
Grendel who haunted the moors, the wild
Marshes, and made his home in a hell.
He was spawned in that slime
Of Cain, murderous creatures banished

By God, punished forever for the crime
Of Abel's death.

At the monster's hideous description, the brothers exchanged glances. Had what they'd seen in the forest a year ago been kin to Grendel? Had he obsidian claws, or fangs of blood and bone? No, this monster was human somehow. They imagined him with legs, and toes, and calves that strained when he jumped to avoid Beowulf's sword. This Grendel—human, they were convinced now—was capable of envy. And they knew that because animals are mindless, they kill without intent, so that meant that because Grendel was a man, and an envious one at that, his killing was considered murder.

Grendel's hatred began,
The monster relished his savage war
Keeping the bloody feud
Alive, seeking no peace, offering
No truce, accepting no settlement, no price
In gold or land, and paying the living
For one crime only with another.

Osario went to sit next to Seth, and wrapped an arm around him. The adults interpreted this as a younger brother showing affection to his elder brother, as if their roles were switched. They all knew Seth was a sensitive boy, and maybe Osario was finally beginning to see that.

Out of earshot of the adults, Osario whispered to Seth, "You're Grendel," then promptly lifted himself up again and went back to María Cielos, who beamed with a mother's love. Her favorite had shown kindness to the one who was not her favorite. If this beautiful, darling boy was capable of such compassion, perhaps she could find it within herself to resurrect her own.

Seth watched his younger brother sit in the lap of their mother. He touched the scar on his lip, from the day Osario was born, from the ring still on María Cielos's finger. His brow grew heavy, and his pale blue eyes stretched to slits. Otilio paused his narration and looked at Ola, who frowned and checked her wristwatch.

"It's not magic. It's alchemy," Ola said to Seth beneath a cloudless sky. When dinner had settled in their stomachs, she led him out of the mansion to an open field she'd been to before. They were alone, and the whites of her eyes shone as bright as the full moon, suspended just above the eastern canopies. Seth sat next to her, their backs to a ceiba, its giant, ancient roots armrests. "Feel the tree breathe in the moonlight," she said. "Feel it hum. The Brunka taught me to listen. They told me no matter how quiet, all trees have breath. The moonbeams calm them. Not in a bewitching sense, but in an alchemical reaction. Life is the elixir, and wood is the element from which it flows."

The maids in the house called Ola a witch, which didn't much bother her, because they skirted their eyes when she passed. They had taken an instant and insistent dislike to her because Ola did not clean, and she'd proclaimed as much from the moment she'd stepped into the house to save María Cielos nine years ago.

Don't be fooled by my skin, girls, Ola had said. *I don't wash dishes or mop, and don't expect me to.* They had indeed looked at Ola's dark skin and assumed she was the new nanny, and for a while they grumbled that she was even if she didn't know it. But to their dismay, María Cielos never demanded anything of Ola, nor did Gilberto ask any favors. Furthermore, Ola and Don Otilio spoke like equals. The maids, white as starch, returned to their shared quarters to gossip about the Black woman who'd traded her sweeping broom for one that could fly.

While Otilio educated the Oreamundo brothers with history lessons and philosophy, Ola introduced them to literature and spiritual tomes. Poetry, novels, the Book of the Dead. She made sure to balance their intellects with their spirits. She was indeed an alchemist, manipulating the boys' minds into something of greater value and brilliance.

Ola lit a black candle. "You've seen monsters," she said to Seth. "With your brother. I, too, have seen them."

"¿Where?" Seth asked.

"In visions and dreams. Those beasts emerge from earth, or water, or from fire in a forest, and writhe, and scream, and crack each other in two."

"But ours wasn't a vision. We weren't imagining it."

"No, of course not. I can see in your eyes and those of your brother that that serpent and crustacean planned to tear the world asunder. That is why I have lit this candle and shown you the sky tonight. The black yin of the wax, the white yang of the distant moonstone: life and the protection of it."

"¿Why haven't you invited Osario? ¿Doesn't he need protection too?"

"Yes, he does. But you must be the one to protect him, Seth. It is you who has the power to make sure no harm befalls him. ¿Do you understand?"

Ola's thoughts returned to the vision from her time in the wilderness: the twins. Gashes in their bellies into which the other squeezed intestines as one does a pump. She knew now that their faces reflected those of her nephews. Perhaps this ritual could negate their eventual fate. This was indeed a spell of protection, but one to protect Osario *from* Seth. As the candle burned down to the wick and the moon climbed to the center of the sky, Ola hoped that she had the power to influence the future.

They returned to a silent mansion. No snores or scurrying geckos. Seth crossed a long cay of moonlight back into his room. He hugged Ola's waist good night. Her body shivered. "It is cold," Seth said lovingly, and shut the door.

Walking down the lonely corridor, Ola wished to sob. There *was* an emptiness in Seth's touch. It took all of her self-control not to recoil whenever he tried to hold her hand or lean against her shoulder. Seth's skin as cool as scutes, intentions submerged somewhere she couldn't exactly see. In her darkened bathroom, Ola untied her hair scarf, draped it on the towel rod. Her earrings and bangles clinked on the porcelain sink top. She undressed and filled the bath with cold water and salt. With three quick breaths, she immersed herself, shocking as an Icelandic lake. She let her muscles tense into iron, her lungs shrink down to beans in her chest. Ola needed to feel as if she were dying. The powerful chill of the grave. The salt fought her sinking, her wish to drown. At the bottom of the tub, she exhaled in a scream until she couldn't anymore, the bubbles from her nostrils a violent boiling. When Ola finally broke the surface of the bath, the water was hot. Steam rippled. She grabbed her towel to dry her sweat.

Back in her bedroom, Ola noticed a figure on her bed. A familiar shape—slender, with curves like hills, others like pointed mountains. "María Cielos," Ola whispered. "¿You've come to lie with your aunt?"

"Like the old days," María Cielos said, turning to Ola as she rested on the comfortable mattress. Her niece's breath smelled of cardamom and berries.

Ola didn't face her as she adjusted her head on the pillow. Instead she stared at the ceiling and asked what the matter was.

"You took my son out into the night."

"I cannot deny that."

"¿For one of your rituals?"

Ola grunted. In was an odd sensation being interrogated in one's own bed—not the first time, as her ex-fiancée had done as much their first night together. Nor would it be the last, as death is a fan of exit interviews. Ola grew spines against her niece but kept her voice sanguine. "Their story of the beasts," she said, "worried me."

"¿So you believed them?"

"Of course I did. Only a fool doesn't heed the forest."

"I suppose. Tell me, Ola, ¿what kind of ritual did you subject him to?"

"¿Are you feeling protective of him, María?"

"Always," María Cielos answered coolly.

"¿Did that include the day of Osario's birth?"

María Cielos shot up, and Ola felt the covers next to her pull and scrunch. She prepared for a blow to her cheek but felt only the gust from her niece collapsing back onto the bed.

"¿Do you remember that night, tía?"

"¿Which of the many?"

"The night of the ceiba. The last time I'd seen you."

Ola bit her lip. Of course she remembered.

"You were silent beyond the bonfire's flames when the world went dark, then suddenly everything burned bright black," María Cielos began. Ola turned to her niece, whose eyes were glassy in her recollecting. "I woke up somewhere else. I emerged from something warm and tight and fell onto something that scratched my skin. First, I searched for you, but I was alone on a bed of reeds and mud. It was a nest, I realized. Past its safety, the night was alive with music. Croaks, a river, predators and prey, and loudest: my belly, begging. I couldn't quiet it—I was so hungry from being born. So I dipped into the water in search of food. I found a school of tadpoles, sleeping together in a cloud. I slurped them up, one by one, sibling by sibling. I continued downstream, gobbling down anything that looked appetizing. The more I consumed, the larger I grew, and the river overflowed its banks from my size. I swam farther to where there was more room. I picked off colorful birds and those with muted colors; unsuspecting snakes, basilisks, and anything else that could flap or squirm deliciously inside me. I grew, and I grew, but I was still an empty vessel of pure appetite. I stalked the murk and muck, jumped out at anything arrogant enough to move a muscle before me. I was born without cheeks, so I swallowed whole. Then I found prey so large I was forced to dance. I spun and ripped away valuable things. And for a while, I admit, I was sated. I thought I would wake back up to the flames, to your chant, but then a new hunger poured into me, so I dove into a stronger current. There, the water was black. It stank of sludge and poultry, and every bite coated my maw with something slick and viscous. Unsatisfied, I followed a floating fingernail of moon to a bank, where laughter and wailing broke the stillness. Beyond me, in the water, a dozen tails and two arms thwacked mist into the air. But on the sole-sucking mud, there was a man caught in knee-slapping, bottle-sloshing laughter. I wondered to myself if prey that feels pleasure could bring me pleasure. If joy seasons the meat the same way fear does. So I hauled my body out of the water, felt the humid breeze travel through my scutes like musical chords. The world muttered something I finally understood: murder was a language, and I was fluent. Before I took the man in my jaws, he looked down to face me. And even though I'd never seen him before, I somehow recognized his dimples, and his blue eyes, and the brow that weighs heavy when he gets angry." María Cielos screamed as she had the night of her vision, her syllables uncontrollable, her cries sure to wake the entire mansion.

"I saw the same man's expression in my firstborn the day I birthed Osario. Like a fool I called Seth over to the bed to admire his new brother, but he might as well have been on the banks of that river. Once he spit, I knew what he was capable of, and that's why I struck him. That's why I cannot stand the sight of him."

Ola didn't bother convincing María Cielos that her vision wasn't real, because she believed it too. They wept together on the darkened bed because what else was there to do? If something is seen, it cannot be changed. If it is written, it is impossible to erase. The future was not a phenomenon to be stopped, but a convergence, like barreling full speed into a brick wall. The two women didn't hear the bedroom door shut and footsteps pattering away on the moonlit marble.

CROCODILOPOLIS

1981

At the beginning of August, Otilio took Seth on a riding trip. Intended to last only the day, they took cold-cut sandwiches and a canteen of water to share. Otilio's eyes carried dark crescents beneath them. It was more often now that Seth saw his grandfather's ribs poking out like scythes whenever he shaved his face or trimmed his chest hair. On the dirt roads and trails, pilgrims going in the opposite direction passed by in droves, or all alone if they were too slow to keep up with their group. It was almost the day of the Virgin of Los Ángeles—the celebration of the country's patron saint, whose statuette called out to believers. As Mecca attracted Muslims, so, too, did the Virgin attract Costa Ricans (Catholic, traditionalist, and skeptic alike). A few even hobbled on their knees all the way to the Basilica of Cartago, her sanctuary. Otilio, too, seemed to be called by something. Seth had expected this trip to be about Nieves, his budding love for her. A grandfatherly pep talk. Otilio had made comments, elbowed him like a buddy, flashed Seth masculine grins. But for most of the ride, Otilio stayed silent atop his horse, commenting only about new constructions on once-empty lots.

Otilio had never taken Seth to this part of the province. The emerald mountains he was used to were dyed deep blue, and he wished he'd brought a sweater, despite the noon sun. Birds sang different songs here; trees had traded in leaves for pines; and even the architecture of houses was different—lower structures with gabled roofs, painted cheerier colors. Creams, goldenrods, and warm, inviting browns. Seth felt transported to another end of the earth, some European grassland he'd seen in movies. *The Sound of Music* came to mind. Otilio made no acknowledgment of their change of scenery. His horse was on a buried track leading higher into the countryside. A secret place, perhaps. Somewhere new that would bring Seth and his grandfather even closer together. Watching Osario with their parents, Seth knew that if Otilio ever died, he'd be alone. He wondered if his grandfather knew that too.

Otilio dismounted at the edge of a dense thicket. So did Seth. His grandfather unsheathed a machete from his saddle and hacked a pathway through, with great thrusts and grunts. After a few minutes, they emerged from the other side, wet from condensation and sap. Then Seth saw it. It made him stop suddenly in the soft earth. Otilio trudged ahead, toward a great temple. A structure of slabs upon a dozen columns, fat and segmented like worms. The stone was sand-pale, parts of it stained by endless rains. Seth trailed behind Otilio up an overgrown path of laid bricks. The closer Seth got, the more the structure intimidated him, as much for its intricacy as its decay. History had been unkind to it. Its facade was perhaps a hundred meters long; the left end had caved in, a forest replacing the roof. Vines and orchids exploited cracks in columns. Seth imagined this is what a body endured upon life's abandonment of it: the majestic violence of nature's reclaiming. Before following Otilio into the building, Seth looked up at the tip of the temple's pyramid, on which a crocodile gaped its maw to swallow the sun. Above the doorway: a brick labeled *1939*.

"He built this behind my back," Otilio's voice said.

"¿Who, grandfather?" Seth tried to calibrate his vision to the sudden darkness. Otilio's wandering shadow eclipsed distant pillars of light pouring from holes in the roof.

"The north end holds a barracks. Dozens of rooms, with bunks and wooden chairs. Rotten now. Enough space for a hundred soldiers. ¿Feel that draft? Vents latticed every few meters above us. Was probably meant to keep them cool for when they arrived. A comfort to offset the tropics. No emperor likes to sweat." Otilio seemed to be talking to himself and to the light-pillars he approached like a butler. "We're standing in the grand hall. It's too dark to notice, but the ceiling is six meters high. The pyramid, hollow. Watch your step—the chandelier fell ages ago." Seth looked down at stars of glass on the black floor. "Here there would have been velvet chaises. A full bar on this wall. Animal heads above it. I saw the schematics, his sketches. Down that corridor, the kitchen. And there"—Otilio paused; Seth squinted, peering through a hallway that led to a dozen tree trunks: the left wing of the temple—"there would have been the emperor's quarters. Stunning, from the drawings. Palatial. Knowing him, he'd been hoping the conqueror would stay here, get acquainted with the country, make it his summer home. We're lucky they lost the war." Otilio's shadow had moved to the bright doorway. Looking again through the corridor to the left wing, Seth thought he saw a figure behind one of the trees. He approached the mouth to inspect but saw no man or ghost, just a white hand of sunlight palming a trunk. Seth exited the temple after his grandfather. "Here he would have given his victory speech. The Western Hemisphere, his. This land, this country, its people, all his. I do not know why men want power." His grandfather turned back to face him. "¿Why do you want power, Seth?"

Seth recoiled at his grandfather's voice, honed into an accusation. Power, Seth thought. What did Otilio mean? Seth pushed down his childish instinct to cry, and straightened up his back.

"You're lying, Grandfather," Seth said. "You know exactly why."

"Good boy," Otilio said, smirking, and descended the stone path being swallowed by the earth.

At three A.M., Seth found himself underneath his bed, staring up at the wooden planks holding his mattress in place. The entire mansion was quiet, so he held his breath, imagining the black space above him as a screen on which played images of Nieves removing articles of clothing. The soft parts of her revealed by the holes those blessed moths had nibbled away. He gripped his penis, its head and hood, and rubbed it as one applies chalk to a pool cue. The sensation like being tickled and pricked with needles at the same time. Images of his grandfather, bathroom-naked—a scant towel barely clinging to his waist, the outline of his penis almost as low as his knees—forced their way into his mind, so that Nieves and Otilio stood side by side, ignoring each other as each embraced the nakedness of their own bodies. Every part as forbidden as the other's. Each sight a new throbbing vein that Seth clutched, and pressed, and pulled. He felt overwhelming shame despite his inability to let up. As if shame were a deep-bellied glass, and ecstasy a sweet drink filled to its chipped rim. If

Seth drank, he'd cut his mouth. But pleasure's smell, its syrup and burning, filled him as he sipped and finished, so that he, too, became a deep-bellied vessel of shame.

Seth finished without knowing what finishing meant. Even underneath the shadow of the bed, he saw what had been released from him was white and sticky as moonlight. Sleep overtook him then, the cool floorboards his pillow until morning, when he was jolted awake by his mother's frantic knocking, her hollering through the door. Her tongue clanging in her mouth like a funeral bell.

Seth unlocked and opened his door to find that his mother was no longer there. Rather, her shadow curled its finger, beckoning Seth to his grandfather's bedroom, whose door had been swung open. Inside, Seth found a frozen scene, a medieval painting he'd once seen—royalty caught in their own despair. Osario had shrunk and curled against the aged armoire; Ola smoked the stub of a cigarette that, once time resumed, would burn her fingers; his father held his mother back from shaking his grandfather's body awake. Otilio lay dead on the soft, still sheets. No one turned to acknowledge Seth's entrance. He tried moving as slowly as possible because with every step, time resumed. It sped up as his realization did. The only man in the world Seth trusted had been whisked out of his body by a midnight stroke, a truth made apparent by the red pools surrounding Otilio's pupils. Like a careful hummingbird, Seth hovered about the room, consoling the members of his household. He picked up his little brother for a few moments, pressing their chests together, allowing their hearts to pound against each other like fists on opposite sides of a locked door. He kissed Ola's arms, which smelled of sweat and soot. She emerged from herself for a moment to fake a smile, then sank back into the part within herself where she was drowning. Seth released his father's grip from María Cielos's elbows and wrapped his arms around the trunk of his chest. And to his mother, Seth rubbed her back as she floated over Otilio's body like a bridge going nowhere, connecting nothing but grief on either side of her.

One by one, they left the room to make calls, or refill tumblers, or vomit into the pristine toilet bowl of the guest bathroom. Seth was left alone with his grandfather's body, which, after eight hours on such a humid morning, had already begun to decompose beneath the skin. Seth couldn't help but think it was his fault, that some divine cruelty was punishing him for releasing himself in such a shameful way underneath his bed. That pleasure is always answered with consequence.

He went to Otilio's closet to pick out a suit, a pressed button-down, a presidential-looking tie, and wingtips he knew had been his grandfather's favorites. Because Otilio had died so early in the day, the funeral would be at noon.

Seth stripped the body.

What was left of his grandfather lay as naked as what had played out on the screen of his closed eyes last night. He had imagined it perfectly, despite having never seen what existed below his grandfather's belly button down to the knees.

Seth dressed the body.

First the underwear, then the socks. He lifted the legs to slip on the navy-blue trousers, lifted the torso to fasten the white shirt, then the blazer. He buttoned as quickly as he could as panic began to set in. He tied the red tie with trembling hands. By then, Seth was performing his task blinded by tears. He didn't realize he'd been screeching until Ola wrapped her arms around his face. Again, sweat and soot, soothing the axe-like pain that hacked at every part of him. Seth finished lacing the chestnut leather shoes before following Ola out onto the veranda, where she offered him his first cigarette, which he smoked with wincing, liberating puffs.

No one in the house remembered the hours between discovering Otilio's body and the funeral. Somehow arrangements were made—a nursery of flowers surrounded a coffin of shined cherrywood; Otilio's stoic portrait stood on an uneasy easel; eulogies were prepared; and guests from every corner of the country filled the local church's pews, lit by a midday sun through the stained glass. It was a stifling, quiet service. No one but María Cielos wailed. Gilberto took to the podium to deliver what everyone expected to be inspiring words about his father, but instead he slurred and swayed. He'd drunk his way through the top shelf of the liquor cabinet. He'd filled a basin within himself that from then on would beg for daily filling. Instead of fond anecdotes, Gilberto exhumed childhood traumas at the hands of his father, who had been a womanizing monster, a manipulator of the grandest sorts, and who had claimed Gilberto as his son only to torture him. Gilberto confessed in a series of grunts and shrieks, even as two pallbearers tried to tear him away from the lectern, that his father hated most of those in attendance. He looked out at the faces of everyone in the front rows and slung Otilio's gossip just as a child hurls stones with a sling. By the time his gaze reached Don Pepe, whose glacier-bright eyes homed in on Gilberto with an unbearable malice, the pallbearers had successfully thrown Gilberto out of his own father's funeral. Not long after, Don Pepe stood at the rim of his friend's sarcophagus and whispered a question: was even half of what he'd heard true?

Costa Rica is home to

Man they are

executioners

they ambush the

River

their

hunger

is said

to

chew Without cheeks

This means

they

are

cruel

2011

Seth carried on with his life as though he weren't preparing to murder his younger brother.

He eventually apologized to Nieves for calling her that cowardly four-letter name and made love to her twice a day.

He watered his tropical plants. Fed them fertilizer, watched them bloom. The glories at sunrise, marigolds at noon, the queen of the night from sunset until four A.M.

He fixed the sink of its drip.

He helped Andrés with his math workbooks. Multiplication that week. With threes turning into nines, morphing into more difficult eighty-ones. *With nines you just add forward, then once you reach forty-five, reverse the placement.* Zero-nine, one-eight, two-seven, three-six, four-five; then five-four, six-three, seven-two, eight-one, nine-zero. Multiplication was just going forward, then backward. Andrés was smart, a quick learner, and absorbed Seth's lesson. (The next week, his teacher would reproach him: *That's not how it's done in Common Core.*)

Seth continued his daily walks. He stalked the mural of Marilyn Monroe. He never knew how he always wound up at home afterward. It was a week of blanks and glitches, losses of memory.

He researched crocodiles.

He googled his own name in the private browser because Nieves had forbidden it. A man's past is his greatest threat. More dangerous than prostate cancer, a careless bus driver, or the prospect of Nieves's eventual temper. An exciting episode of *Snapped*.

Seth found articles from the year of his exile. Archived, grainy scans from the Costa Rican tabloids. He didn't need to google Osario's name because it showed up in every search of his own. Seth sat there, surrounded by the blotchy ink of the past.

He smelled a river of oil.

He tasted it in the back of his throat.

He saw, through tears, a rainbow shining on its surface.

He rubbed his fingers together, slick from saturated memory.

He listened gleefully to the sloshing, crocodilian bodies in that infernal river of oil.

AKHENATEN

1981

The day before his body went stiff with death, Otilio called Gilberto into his room to confess his greatest sin. After Gilberto watched his father's mouth crust with cruelty, then indifference, he went straight to the liquor cabinet to mix no less than four types of alcohol into a poison that would spread to everyone else in the Oreamundo household for years to come.

Gilberto had always hated his father. For one, Gilberto had never met his mother. Otilio had never said who she was or where she'd gone, so Gilberto had survived his entire life without a bosom on which to rest his head, and he'd never had anyone but maids to feed him, clothe him, and bathe his limbs, who did so out of duty, not affection. Their labor was an ugly excuse for the love he had always craved. Second, his father womanized women who cared nothing for Gilberto, or for his innocence. They'd stroll through the mansion's corridors in the middle of the night, dressed only in sweat, admiring the paintings on the walls, deciding which ones to burgle. Gilberto could always hear their sopping footsteps, a steady drip-dripping, and the rapping of their long, goading fingernails at his door. Third, and perhaps most significantly, he knew his father hated him, and though Otilio never expressed his disdain outright, his rejection glowed like a candle from across a darkened room.

What made matters even worse was that Otilio showed his grandsons more affection than he ever showed Gilberto. He'd staked his claim to Seth immediately, marking him as his own heir, a boy worthy of his guidance and coddling. Every time Gilberto saw Seth sitting on Otilio's lap or accompanying him on horseback into the jungle, he flew into a silent rage, which is why, when María Cielos had sliced open Seth's lip with her ring, Gilberto giggled (not loudly, but with such sincere pleasure it frightened him).

Gilberto was surprised when Otilio summoned him into his room that morning. Otilio asked that he close the door and offered Gilberto a cigar. The sheer curtains danced with a gust of maybe-rain. Sparrows crowded on the terra-cotta tiles outside the sliding glass door. Otilio curled his mouth into a sinner's smirk and confessed. At first with cruelty, then indifference. Otilio explained that when he stepped into that furniture shop to meet María Cielos all those years ago, he'd immediately recognized her mother, Casandra, as the woman he'd taken on the wet floorboards of a brothel. A man like him knew when he'd impregnated a woman, Otilio said. Powerful men never missed. Otilio saw María Cielos for the first time that day, and her face instantly reminded him of his own sister. He coughed, tapping his cigar like a pen running dry.

Otilio didn't need to be explicit. Merely the implication was enough for Gilberto to drop his own cigar onto the rocking chair, singeing a clean hole in the leather. Gilberto stumbled out of the room while his father tossed his morning bread to the sparrows that hopped with a glee that would never return to the mansion.

Everyone in the house had already been living with the consequences of Otilio's many secret sins, but now, following his death, Gilberto took it upon himself to continue his father's legacy. He transformed into a drunken bank teller, doling out punishment like withdrawn cash. Each reproach and abuse as valuable to him as bills and coins.

After being thrown out of his father's funeral, Gilberto sealed Otilio's room with concrete. When the blocks were plastered and painted over with three coats of paint, Gilberto hung a thick-framed painting on the new wall, as if erasing Otilio's memory was as easy as decorating over it. The window to the bedroom and sliding glass door were also sealed. Inside, Otilio's odors would ferment until the wing's eventual demolition. His cologne and smoke, the stench that permeated the sheets, pillow covers, and mattress from his time spent rotting on the bed. Gilberto had chosen the most effective way to completely erase one's memory for good: through the elimination of smell. As Man's oldest sense, smell reaches deeper than the others into the reptilian brain. As long as the olfactory receptors shoot their lightning, the dead never truly die.

Once the mansion was scentless and quiet, Gilberto took to the bottle without distraction. Only alcohol could stop him from looking upon María Cielos with disgust—inspecting her features for signs of his own, gazing so deeply into his mirror reflection that it was impossible not to detect a family resemblance. Alcohol numbed the part of him that now deemed life impossible. Abhorrent, an abomination. But the bottle could not occupy both of his hands. It could not stop one from tightening into a hammer.

As with most drunks, Gilberto eventually found religion. God, it seemed (though He'd never admit it) is a bartender. With a shot comes a crucifix across the chest. A glass of wine is His son's blood. And the goodness of a man's heart comes pouring out when his tongue is slicked at a bar, leaning over on a stool to whisper the praises of whoever's in earshot. Because what is godlier than loving thy neighbor?

Gilberto, the alcoholic evangelical. The doler-out of his father's bitterness, betrayal, belligerence, and bile.

Gilberto, who found the Holy Ghost in his liquor cabinet and would leave his boys cowering underneath their beds, watching his shadow connect to María Cielos's by fist and face.

Gilberto, the cliché, blithely unaware that his newfound calling was neither unique nor especially inventive.

After sealing off his father's room, Gilberto went about transforming the mansion into the abode of a true Christian. He sold every French vase, all the mahogany furniture, the china, silverware, and María Cielos's jewels: any surplus of wealth, anything that might indicate more than his family's fair share. God rewarded the soul, not the corridors of a palace. Gilberto learned the Bible, cover to cover. He became a man full of verses and roamed the latifundio communing with the God of the Old Testament. The vengeful one. The deluge-bringer, garden-ejector, plague-provider, salt-pillar-turner: the wrathful, unreasonable, impossible-to-negotiate-with God. And so his punishments grew meaner. What he learned from the Lord was the art of control. Fear, manipulation, consequences for disobeying the rules he made up as he went along (Exodus 20:3).

Next on Gilberto's list was Ola's expulsion, and it took only a year for him to have her chased out of the house. While he had stripped the master bedroom and the boys' rooms of only their riches, he gutted Ola's completely. What he left was a mattress, a quilt, and a crucifix opposite the lonely window on the south-facing wall. He auctioned off Ola's treasures to the lowest bidder while she was in San José visiting her property, inspecting its wood for reported termites. After fumigating her house, both physically and spiritually, Ola made her way back to the Oreamundo plantation, where it looked as though the mansion had been the victim of an art heist. She ran to the parlor, where she heard ice clinking in a glass. Gilberto sat in the only remaining leather chair, counting cash, a whisky in hand. When Ola peered into her own bedroom, its nakedness embarrassed her. She couldn't help but weep just as María Cielos and the boys had done in the library, where hundreds of books sat in mountains on the floor because their cases had been sold right out from under them.

Even still, she stayed.

When Gilberto realized Ola's resilience, he decided to creep into María Cielos's mind like an instinct. He invited her to drink with him and reconstructed the joyful bits of their marriage before Otilio's death. He caressed the bruises he'd splotched on her. Spoke her name to every goose bump. He convinced her with the sweetness of a husband, and when her guard was down, he flicked his fingers at her insecurities, one by one. He turned their marriage-worth of pillow talks against María Cielos and undermined her relationship with her beloved aunt. For example, how in her childhood, Ola had come back only when it was convenient for her. She'd abandoned her own family to tour the globe, to pursue nonsense, and left María Cielos to the strictness of her parents. Gilberto twisted Michael and Casandra's conventional disciplining into abuse, and Ola's absence as neglect. María Cielos could have been saved, but all Ola did was give her nightmares, *¿remember?* That terror beneath the ceiba . . . How irresponsible for an aunt to subject her niece to a soul-devouring vision. Leaving María Cielos to fend for herself in her dreams. Suffering until she screamed, and kept screaming. And what did Ola do? She left. Again. Pulled her car out of the driveway and didn't come back for five years. Ola's love for María Cielos was as capricious as the wind that shooed her sail to the ends of the earth. It was only a matter of time that she would leave. *Again*, Gilberto said. She would abandon María Cielos when she needed her aunt most. *Again*. He repeated it—*again, again, again*—as a cutler passes a blade over the spinning whetstone for the cleanest cut. Then he handed that blade to María Cielos, to sever ties with Ola herself.

Ola stayed on for as long as she did because she was the only person standing between Gilberto and the complete emotional domination of his family. Turning their mansion into a desert was merely the first step in Gilberto's plan, a way to strip them of their defenses. The stark property now resembled a prison more than a home. Ola began pleading weekly with María Cielos to leave Gilberto and save them, but most of all, the boys. They were at an impressionable age. If the masculinity they witnessed was violent, they would surely mimic that malice for the rest of their lives.

"We'll open a restaurant," she said to her niece. "We'll move to Limón, where we are from. We'll live by the beach, and the boys will fall in love with the ocean as your father did. We'll eat well and feed all who pass by. They'll talk for years and years about our food. From all over the world, hungry people will come to see us, and eat, and stay long enough to try every dish on the menu."

One day, her niece finally offered Ola a definitive answer.

"Leave," María Cielos said bluntly.

"¿What, my love?"

"Get out."

"But I don't understand—"

"You've done enough damage."

Ola couldn't believe what she was hearing. Seth and Osario, who were pressing their ears to the other side of the door, couldn't believe what they were hearing either.

Ola stared into her niece's face and did not recognize it anymore. All its features had changed—her cheekbones were uneven now, her eyes sunken. Her lips were no longer painted, her ears bare of their rings; her collarbones, wrists, and fingers were all naked, so it was impossible to distract oneself from María Cielos's horrible transformation.

"All of this is your fault," María Cielos said. "Leave."

"I won't."

"Leave, Ola."

"I can't."

"If you don't leave, I will cut you."

"Please, child. Please don't do this."

But Ola saw Gilberto's face burned into María Cielos's eyes. Despite Ola's attempts to protect her family from his possession, she'd failed. She'd known this day would eventually come, but she'd wished it would be later—years later, a decade later—so that she'd be able to watch the boys grow into handsome men. But Gilberto had won, and Ola had lost. Everything. Again.

Ola had nothing to pack, so without hesitation or preparation she walked through the fields into the forest, her yellow dress a bright flower disappearing into the underbrush. She didn't say goodbye to Seth or Osario, who watched her leave. She marched with such resignation the brothers thought they could catch up with her. But they got lost in the unrelenting labyrinth of coffee. Instead what they found was Gilberto on his knees, setting fire to one of the bushes, watching, in a trance, as it burned.

Unable to manage business ventures now that he was a full-time zealot, Gilberto leased the fertile land to foreign coffee manufacturers. They came with their state-of-the-art drying and roasting facilities, so consequently, many workers—even those who had been born on the property—were laid off. The laborers' sudden poverty brought them closer to God—and, incidentally, closer to the new church Gilberto had founded. Teach a man to pray, and he'll be blessed for a day. Teach a man to preach, and he'll be blessed for life. Something like that.

Gilberto's evangelical congregation angered the local Catholic diocese, as their Sunday offerings now flooded the Oreamundo plantation. But rather than react hastily, the bishops of Cartago lay in wait, expecting this new preacher, bastard son of a politician, to bungle it somehow. Butcher a sermon, or anger the wrong god. But the flock of laborers came to Gilberto because the evangelical form of worship excited them. Instead of the quiet, solemn kneeling and sitting, sitting and standing, Gilberto brought in musicians who praised through melodies. In the majority of his homilies, Gilberto admitted to his own alcoholism (but not to beating his wife), and this candidness attracted hordes of congregants. No one had known sinning was such an epidemic. If a preacher man could discover God at the bottom of a glass, theoretically one could find Him under his mistress's sheets, or deep in her mother's purse. These Sunday sinners, of course, judged loudest.

In the vacuum left by Otilio and Ola, a new cast of characters set up shop at the Oreamundo mansion. A regular at Gilberto's services was a sweaty Arkansas-born man named Thomas who oversaw the coffee roasting. He had learned Spanish by reading the Bible, though his accent betrayed his origins; no one had ever heard the language spoken with a southern twang before. Seth and Osario marveled at Thomas's ability to turn red, either from the sun or from sudden spells of intense emotion. He resembled a lobster. Boiled, cracked, buttered up.

A woman named Esmeralda took up cleaning and cooking for the family, since they couldn't afford maids anymore. She materialized one night, as if sent by God as a joke, a duster in one hand and a bottomless pack of cigarettes in the other. The spotless mansion took on the miasma of a grimy bar in the slums. Esmeralda also brought with her a hacking cough that the boys mimicked silently whenever they heard it. There was a musicality in the mucus, only appreciated when heard in the perfect acoustics of the empty halls. Of the chorus of new squatters, the boys weren't bothered by Esmeralda's presence in the slightest—loud and eventful as it was—as she'd arrived with a repertoire of surprisingly tasty family recipes. All memorized, luckily, because her continuous diet of tobacco had robbed her of her taste buds.

María Cielos watched these marauders and thought back to the bordello in which she had been raised. The men and women who had seasoned her childhood like a too-spiced, odd-tasting dish. How her mother thought it appropriate to raise a young girl in a whorehouse was beyond her. But staring at the starkness of her home, its walls stripped bare, antiques and furniture long gone, she remembered the store's worth of toys the women brought home to her. Long before her sons, before Gilberto, and even before Michael's unconditional love, the men in María Cielos's life had been johns and random businessmen who mistook the brothel for a proper establishment. One would have assumed them to be degenerates, but those men had treated María Cielos with unexpected affection and a child-size chivalry. She was a little lady who happened to be raised by prostitutes. Some customers even considered bringing her home to meet their wives. But these interlopers at the Oreamundo mansion paid her no mind. She was no little lady, nor the lady of her own estate anymore. Just a bystander who didn't even really love her sons. How could she? They were old enough to defend her now—Seth especially—and strong enough because they were men. She'd raised two little cowards without sufficient balls to confront their father when he took to her body. To Osario, she could give the benefit of the doubt. Perhaps an eleven-year-old was not a knight in shining armor, come to vanquish the land of evildoers. But Seth. If he had the potential to whet his eyes into slits and watch on—*laugh* at, even—as another man succumbed to the jaws of beasts, he could certainly intervene right now to save her. But her sons did nothing, and the cold-blooded congregants continued their invasion of her home.

A year before the Baptism, a man named Johnny Díaz traveled from a small town in Guanacaste south to the Oreamundo plantation. He'd heard from a grifter buddy that there was a newborn congregation just waiting for a manager. The boys noticed him one Sunday sitting near the back row, patting his gargantuan neck with a hand towel, which, upon closer inspection, belonged to their bathroom. Seth and Osario watched him as one did—and should—a reptile. With fascination, disgust, and the overwhelming instinct to run.

If any government entity or scientific institution were to finally (and fairly) classify Man as an invasive species, Johnny Díaz, with his shellacked hair, gold rings, and kind, doting eyes, would be photographed and printed as the textbook example. With all the makings of a demon and a used car salesman, Johnny sashayed over to Gilberto after his lively sermon, took his hand, kissed his knuckles, and convinced Gilberto to entrust him with all the books.

"I've been sent by God," Johnny exclaimed. "He called me from my village, plucked me from my lucrative job in lumber, and guided me to your doorstep. It was a miracle."

At the word *miracle*, Gilberto couldn't help but sign over his soul. For one so desperate to believe as Gilberto, any mention of the miraculous was as good as the light that leads to the jaws of an angler fish.

The Baptism happened on a hot, evil evening in 1983. Seth was now almost sixteen, and Osario almost twelve. They were as close as they had ever been (and ever would be), thanks to the monstrousness of their father. Seth tended to Osario's bruises with frozen steaks and, to distract from the pain, recounted stories of their grandfather. Osario made Seth's bed and washed his clothes when María Cielos would lock herself in her room for days on end. The brothers had quickly realized all they had in this world was each other. By then, Johnny Díaz had built himself a bungalow next to the mansion with embezzled church funds and had spent the last year turning Gilberto's calling into an actual, profitable scheme. Just days before the Baptism, Johnny had been on the phone with a representative from Canal 7 who promised she would talk to her producer about giving Gilberto a show on Tuesday evenings. Not ideal for the Christian viewership, but an evangelical preacher will take whatever time slot is offered.

Seth had grown into a muscular teenager thanks to the meat-heavy-hand of Esmeralda's cooking. He'd become a swatch of colors—the fleece-blond curls of his childhood darkened to ochre, while his arm and budding chest hairs retained the golden sheen that also flecked his emerging auburn mustache. Specks of green in his blue eyes had widened like continents in an ocean. By contrast, the stress of daily life had stunted Osario's growth. Finally, he looked his age. Bird-chested, lanky limbed. An eleven-year-old in an eleven-year-old's body. His personality, however, kept its courage, which is to say, Osario regarded himself as a grown man.

On this hot, evil evening in 1983, the brothers stood beneath a huge tent, by the back row of metal folding chairs that sank into the mud. Johnny Díaz had convinced Gilberto to become a traveling preacher. Every week they moseyed into a different canton, where, in villages near waterways, Gilberto performed waterside baptisms. Lakes, ponds, watering holes. Tonight, Johnny Díaz had chosen a spot in Capulín along the serpentine body of the Tárcoles River. Hours before, he'd paraded through the local roads, shouting an abridged series of the gospel, which Gilberto would present unabridged for as long as his bottle of guaro would allow him. He was surprisingly lucid for a drunk. In fact, the alcohol energized his sermons, and by now he had become legitimately famous.

A massive congregation crowded on the banks of the Tárcoles River, where mangrove trees undulated in a cool breeze that disturbed the water just enough so that one couldn't notice the huge reptilian bodies beneath the surface. Gilberto had situated his pulpit uncomfortably close to the shore, and many who lived there in Capulín shifted in their seats, unsure if they should inform Gilberto of his present danger. In the end, though, they said nothing, choosing instead to believe the preacher knew he was risking life and limb to preach the word of God.

In truth, Johnny Díaz hadn't a clue about the crocodile infestation, and Gilberto was too drunk to care. They'd positioned the tent at the river's edge for the sake of convenience alone: Gilberto did not wish to walk very far when it came time to perform the baptisms. The Oreamundo brothers, forced on the road with their father, passed out programs to the arriving congregants and rested near the back as their father prattled on, flicking Bible verses with a guaro-slicked tongue.

"Seth, I'm thirsty."

"It is hot. I'm thirsty too."

"¿Can we go get something to drink?"

"Yes, let's be fast, though, because it's getting dark. I don't want to trip on any roots. Osario, say 'excuse me' to people when you pass."

"Excuse me, sir."

"Be careful with the pole going out—you remember what happened last time."

"I swear I didn't mean to knock it down."

"It was funny, though. The whole tent came crashing on everyone's heads."

"It wasn't funny to me, Seth."

"Yeah, I guess it wasn't. Father really let you have it. ¿Do you still have the bruise on your ass?"

"I can't see it anymore, but I can still feel it."

"Keep up, Osario. We've got to hurry."

"I miss Mom."

"She's home, we'll see her soon."

"It's been months."

"Weeks, Osario."

"Well, it feels like months."

"You are younger, so time is different for you."

"Yeah, right. Don't act so much older."

"Four years is a lot."

"Yeah, right, Seth."

"It is."

"Yeah, right."

"Oh, look, there's a vendor."

"¡Coconuts!"

"¿You want one?"

"¡Yes!"

"Go on up and ask."

"¡A big one, sir!"

"Say please, Osario."

"Please, Osario."

"I'm gonna kick your ass. Sir, two please."

"Look at the machete, Seth."

"I can see it."

"Look how he hacks into it."

"I can see it."

"You're no fun."

"Here, take yours, Osario. ¿How much, sir? Okay, here you go. Drink a little, but then we've got to run back. The trees look really dark, and in five minutes we won't even be able to see each other."

Following the beacon of the tent's harsh string lights, Seth and Osario trekked back through the overgrown path. Their father was still preaching over the hiccupping electric generator. His sermon was nearing its end, and the brothers watched their father's spittle soar in all directions. The believers in the front rows neglected to dodge it, for a preacher's spit was as good as holy water. Gilberto's back was still to the river. At his final word, the crowd stood and applauded so loudly it echoed in the forest. Birds startled awake and flew away from their cozy branches. Darkness and humidity closed in around the tent and its inhabitants. Tonight, the brothers felt uneasy when their father offered the worshippers the service of a baptism. After any other sermon, a long line would stretch past the glow of the tent, but tonight, all the worshippers stayed put in their seats, with the exception of one giddy woman who approached the pulpit. Gilberto and Johnny Díaz exchanged nervous glances. But the show must go on. It seemed neither questioned for very long why the locals didn't need a christening. Perhaps this woman (who'd taken three buses from the capital just to get here) truly was the only sinner in need of saving.

Gilberto and the woman donned white frocks, and when he led her to the shore, the crowd left their seats to take a step back. But Seth and Osario took a cautious step forward, their bodies drawing nearer to the water.

At first, everything went according to plan. Waist-deep in the water, Gilberto began a hymn. In one hand, he gripped his Bible like a bottle, and with the other he cradled the back of the woman's neck, ready to dunk her, to let her sins wash away and be carried off by the current. Gilberto recited a verse.

> *Jesus stood up and cried out, "If anyone thirsts, let him come to me and drink. Whoever believes in me, out of his heart will flow rivers of living water."*

Just the brothers and their father noticed every detail of what happened next. They alone could tell the precise change in the color of the water, the immediate red flooding the blue-brown. The rest of the congregation heard only the splashing and Gilberto's sudden yelp. The jaws emerged out of the water first: the playful grin of the crocodile as it closed around the woman's peaceful face. She had shut her eyes in preparation for absolution, but when she opened them again, it wouldn't be to the darkness of the night but that of the creature's gullet. Gilberto caught his horrified reflection in the crocodile's eyes before it began pirouettes around the woman's head. The brothers heard a pop, a quick tear. When it was done, when the water had regained its composure, and the crowd was so silent they could hear the ocean breathing ten kilometers away, Gilberto returned to shore with the woman's body, and the woman's body alone.

APOPHIS

1985

Gilberto barely wriggled out of a prison sentence. The prosecutors threw any and all charges at him—public drunkenness, criminal negligence, involuntary manslaughter—whatever might stick. The Catholic diocese secretly footed the prosecutors' bill, but in all honesty, it was overkill because they'd gotten exactly what they'd wanted in the first place: Gilberto could no longer preach. This bastard who slurred the gospel couldn't steal their congregants anymore because the flock had turned on its shepherd. Once the churchgoers at the Oreamundo plantation caught wind of Gilberto's actions, they set fire to the church. It burned with the Will of God, they said. All that survived the inferno were the crisp, black frames of unfolded metal chairs, still organized in neat rows for a laity of faithful ghosts awaiting Sunday service.

Seth and Osario sealed the memory of the Baptism away as if it were the tomb of a tyrant king. Teeth, and pop, and red became too much for their adolescent brains to handle. Just as insistent archaeologists are cursed for disturbing a pharaoh's pyramid, so would the brothers be cursed for unearthing the nightmare of the crocodile. Their minds laid booby traps—walls that closed in, pits of spikes, snakes—so that neither would be foolish enough to go digging within his own memory.

The only upside was that the Oreamundo plantation was finally rid of Johnny Díaz. The night of the Baptism, he cut through the darkness, back to wherever he'd sprouted like a weed—the imaginary home where his family, community, and lucrative career in lumber allegedly awaited his prodigal return. To pay for his defense, Gilberto had to sell the rest of the latifundio to the coffee companies, who timbered and bulldozed every tree until they reached the edges of the huge property. Now an ocean of coffee bushes flowed all around for hectares. Another facility was built and the usual piquant aroma of roasting beans turned into a penetrating stench, saturating their clothes, their hair, and their bedding. They'd been robbed of the lush vista and their olfactory senses.

As the latifundio became a barren field of coffee production, the brothers sought refuge in each other. Seth took charge of Osario's studies, and as Otilio had once drilled arithmetic and philosophy, elocution and forensics into Seth, he, in turn, now guided Osario through these valleys of knowledge. From Aristotle to Thomas Jefferson, Galileo to Einstein, Seth offered up all he knew. The brothers would stay up for hours on end, reading from the mountains of books whose shelves had been sold right out from under them. Education provided a blueprint for escape—a university far away would save the two Oreamundo brothers from the fate of their father. But what children do not know is that fate is clever and sly. All roads eventually lead to its hand.

Two years later, Seth sat with his back to the wall that used to be the doorway to his grandfather's bedroom. His vertebrae fit perfectly into the grooves of the cinderblocks painted emerald green. Outside, a Christmas breeze huffed the dirt, pelting the north side of the mansion. Osario was probably in the parlor with their parents, chatting about the towering size of the pine tree, the warmth of the fireplace, or the lights dangling from strings along the walls and in wreaths like fireflies. Their mother had made rompope on the stove: emulsified the egg yolks, poured in the cream and vanilla, flecked in cinnamon. Most important, she imparted it with a little dark rum for their father, who still partook, even if he'd mostly calmed down. María Cielos and Gilberto were sleeping in the same bed again. They visited neighbors who worked for the coffee conglomerates, and even showed glimpses of affection—reluctant pecks, interlocking of fingers for seconds at a time. The pendulum of their marriage was swinging back to its original position, with María Cielos seemingly in control of its momentum, its replacement. There was an agency in her Seth hadn't seen since before his grandfather died. It had led her to become softer with Osario too. This warming up must be a gradual phenomenon, Seth thought. It was well worth waiting his turn to receive it.

"Seth," Osario said. He'd turned the corner without Seth having noticed.

"¿Hm?" Seth snapped out of his blank stare.

"¿Are you ready to go?"

"I just need to brush my teeth. ¿What time will the girls get here?"

"They said six o'clock."

Osario helped Seth up from the cold marble. Osario was barefoot and could barely stand the chill, so he was surprised Seth could sit there for hours without shivering. This had turned into a weekly ritual: Seth with his back to that wall. Osario didn't have a clear memory of their grandfather, more than four years dead now. With every passing birthday, Osario felt as though he'd survived a decade. He didn't know what he'd do without his older brother.

Osario walked into the kitchen and kissed their mother on the cheek. He was tall enough to wrap his arms lovingly around her shoulders, and she kissed his skin. María Cielos showed him affection again, which brought him a dull, stinging regret because her interactions with Seth were frigid and apathetic. But Osario couldn't comment on her behavior; he didn't know how to broach the topic or even how to express himself. So he handled his mother's affection with both gratitude and guilt. Two orbs of equal mass in either hand, to be dropped from a tower to test the theory of gravity.

The girls would be here soon. The Villarreal sisters, whom neither Seth nor Osario had seen in years. Isa had phoned yesterday, wishing them a peaceful Nochebuena, and invited them to go to the Festival at Zapote in San José. The brothers had never been, so Osario accepted without hesitation. He longed for fun and for relationships outside his family. And coincidentally he had begun dreaming about Isa, imagining what she would be like after all this time, how she might have been growing into a woman just as he was growing into a man. He donned a leather jacket because he thought he would look cool. And he did. He did look cool, like those rockers on MTV. Seth, however, kept on his bulky sweater and corduroy slacks. Not cool. Not in the slightest.

At six o'clock, the sun had fully set, and the brothers made their way down the driveway to the gate of the latifundio. On the other side of the high, iron-barred fence, the brothers looked back to the mansion as if they'd made a break for it. They expected sirens and dogs barking, sudden whirling lights. But all the property was silent, except for the wind. Their mother had weakly approved of the outing, and their father was nowhere to be found.

The Villarreal sisters pulled up in a banana yellow Corvette convertible. Osario had never seen one up close, and he turned to Seth, who had snapped out of his mood upon the mere sight of the garish car and the two beautiful sisters inside it. Seth smiled at Nieves with a confidence that impressed Osario. The smile of a leading man. Osario, naturally competitive, gave Isa the same smile as she moved from the passenger's side to the back of the sports car, patting the seat next to her. Osario unzipped his jacket and puffed out his chest, but alas, Isa intimidated Osario as she always had. She had a way of looking into the deepest parts of him: the raw, trembling truth that lies inside all men, no matter their age.

Nieves interlocked her fingers with Seth's, guided his shy hand to change gears. His heart raced as fast as the car. From a cassette, she blasted European cold wave, American New Wave, and punk rock. It was a sight—that banana yellow Corvette hurtling through the dark dirt roads, blaring the Smiths and the Ramones. Nieves yelled over the music, and all three passengers listened to her story of what the sisters had been up to over the last few years.

"Our parents split," she said with an odd accent now. "And we moved to the United States with our dad. He was a diplomat, ¿remember?"

The two brothers nodded. Isa bopped her head to the electric guitar, half listening.

"We ended up in D.C., the capital there."

Both Seth and Osario had seen D.C. in the photographs of a guidebook. The gleaming white monuments, the gleaming white people with their suits and democracy.

"We ended up in a really nice part of the city: Georgetown, overlooking this canal. On the other side of our condo was the Potomac River—you can't imagine how dirty it is.

"Polluted," Nieves added. "Sometimes they find two-headed fish."

Seth laughed, and Osario looked to Isa, who cracked a smile and shook her head.

"Liar," she whispered.

"Anyway," Nieves continued. "We ended up at this school where everyone's parents are foreigners. Children of ambassadors from Guyana and Argentina, the World Bank, the IMF, international architects—you name it, their kids turned their noses up at us."

"Fuck the elite," Isa said. "The bourgeoise."

Osario remembered clearly that the mother of the Villarreal sisters had inherited ore mines throughout Central America. She'd told him once on a playdate over at their own mansion, Nieves and Isa eating caviar with their fingers. She'd turned to Osario and said it out of the blue, and for no reason other than the hypothetical of María Cielos asking him later.

"Everyone, shut up," Nieves interrupted herself.

"Turn it up," Isa interrupted her sister's interruption of herself.

"Hypnotized" by Fleetwood Mac reverberated from the speakers, and its beat took all four teenagers out of themselves and into another world. Nieves closed her eyes for a moment, and Osario thought they'd crash.

They arrived at the Festival at Zapote, now in its fifteenth year of operation. Before, the festival had hopped like an indecisive frog for over a hundred years, moving from city to canton, canton to park, and now park to the huge clearing here at Zapote, where a wooden colosseum emerged like a celestial body orbited by food stands, novelty vendors, and a county fair. It was perhaps the brightest spectacle in San José, and the four teenagers parked the Corvette, secured its convertible roof, and followed the neon glow of the towering Ferris wheel like Polaris.

Christmas cheer was thick in the air as they walked into the fairgrounds. Isa on Osario's arm, Nieves on Seth's. The sisters were much more confident than the brothers. They were forward and unapologetic, had probably picked up that trait in the United States. They'd been back in Costa Rica for only six months, and they often clashed with their mother over their brash comportment and quick retorts to her commands. The American fashion sense had also followed them back home, and every Costa Rican who passed looked at the sisters as if they were asylum escapees. In the U.S. their clothes were all the rage, but here, their fashion sense enraged the conservative conventions of muted dresses that went past the knee, and the understated heels just comfortable enough to walk in.

Nieves wore a high ponytail of crimped, still-wet hair, her eyeshadow an electric blue set to the highest voltage: her outfit was somewhere between Material Girl and a Jazzercise class. Isa, being two years younger, didn't yet have the boldness of her sister, but she, too, wore colors as bright as the amusement rides—a white sweater overpowered by pinks, greens, yellows, and other colors previously undocumented. Her high-waisted jeans accentuated her midsection. The boys, however, were not embarrassed. They remembered the sisters from when they were all children. Seth hid a budding erection, and Osario's crotch joined in the shameful, uncomfortable reflex. The couples paired off. They would meet back at the entrance of the bullring in an hour, giving them enough time to explore the fairgrounds at their own leisure—and yes, enough time to explore each other. At a crossroads, Isa and Osario went left toward the rides and Seth and Nieves right toward the food stands.

Isa grabbed Osario's hand and put his arm around the small of her back. He could feel the sensual mechanics of her walking. He rambled nervously as they meandered, noting which rides they should ride later when the lines were shorter. The girls hadn't engaged the brothers about their lives at all during the trip, but now Isa broached the topic, and out came Osario's story like water from a busted dam. He asked if she remembered his grandfather. She did. He died, Osario said, and Isa gave him a condolent frown. Then she removed his hand from her hip and squeezed it gently. He continued, explaining that their father had swallowed the liquor cabinet and become a preacher. They'd traveled the country with him, performing dramatic baptisms in bodies of dirty water. He did not mention the Baptism at the Tárcoles River because he did not remember it. It was a blank, he said: the reason why his father stopped giving sermons and his wood church crumpled to matchsticks. After that, Isa did not ask any further questions. Osario's bizarre and tragic tale had knocked her mind clear; she was void of language, unable to completely connect such horrible events to the boy she'd loved since they were children.

They stopped at the noisy bumper cars, and Isa pulled Osario aside. Her hands latched onto his biceps, clad in his leather jacket, and in her mind, she tried to heal him with a kiss—that's how it worked in movies, after all. Osario, for his part, had never shared a kiss with anyone before. His only thought was the fear of mimicking a fish gasping for air. The bumper car drivers, both children and adults, stopped and clapped, and parents and family members watching from the sidelines began to cheer. *Long live young love.*

After the kiss and more walking, Osario and Isa made it to the entrance of the bullring, where Seth held one of Nieves's hands as the other balanced a corncob between her chomping teeth. They paid one thousand colones and made their way to the newly painted wooden bleachers of the arena, a huge circle of dust and bull droppings. Not Roman by any means, but large enough for thirty occupants to run for their lives away from a bull with horns as long as a man's arm. More audience members trickled in until the stands held over two hundred cheering fans. Some rooted for the bull, while others hoped their sister wouldn't be left a widow. Goring was the name of the game, but *light* goring. Hopefully not enough to stain the earth.

After a short announcement from the loudspeakers, the enclosed bull run began, with participants hurdling over the walls to escape certain death. The animal kicked up dirt with its front hooves, dove and charged, tried its best to give a good show. When the beast was tired, cowboys on horseback circled the bull as it traipsed the periphery of the ring, twirling their lassos around its horns to lead it back to the paddock. A job well done.

Seth was reminded of the gargantuan oxen of his childhood, the shit-stained smell of their lumbering, the sweaty reins he'd snatch cheerfully from the cart driver. The memory brought him back to the time before Osario entered his universe: the life Seth had been so happy to live as its center. Turning to his little brother, who smiled back at him, shame washed over Seth, and so he shifted his focus back to Nieves, who had finished her corn and moved on to a lukewarm beer that he stole sips from, either from the flimsy plastic cup or directly from her lips.

After three more runs, punctuated by exciting, short-lived bull riding, the rodeo was over, and the four made it out of the arena, still clinging to the adrenaline as if they themselves had run with the bulls. Now that the beer and corn had settled in their stomachs, they decided to try their luck with the rides. They would brave them, empty their pockets of coins, and live this night as if it were their first, and their last.

First, the couples climbed into the bumper cars, the sisters behind each wheel, the brothers their anxious and eager passengers. The rivalry between Nieves and Isa revealed itself, and perhaps this attraction shouldn't have been first, because the four had whiplash by the time they stumbled out and on to the next: a Tilt-A-Whirl, which was kinder on their necks. They rode it twice, becoming addicted to the pull of centrifugal force. Next, the carousel and its rainbow coalition of horses; then the death trap that was the roller coaster, a creaking steel-and-two-by-four monstrosity. Seth felt his stomach turn inside out but refused to let Nieves see him vomit.

He'd become more comfortable with Nieves—he squeezed her hand back, caressed her shoulders, even found their lips fused for minutes at a time. He felt at home next to her because she treated him as the center of the universe. He, too, treated her as such. Her style, her nerve, her poise, infatuated him. No longer was she the shy little girl who hatched moths beneath her bed. She had become the butterfly she always wanted.

They purposefully strayed from Osario and Isa and wandered into the shadows behind two carnival games—clowns shot up by water guns, ring-clinked fishbowls—and lay on the dirt together against soft, heavy sacks of unknown contents. The teens turned face-to-face, chest to chest, and kissed harder than they had the whole night. Something animalistic possessed their limbs: an awkward, newborn beast. Reaching, grabbing, and stroking all the wrong places.

It didn't matter because somehow their fumbling was in sync. Seth unzipped his corduroys and Nieves pulled down her neon tights just enough. They made love. Or at least a teenager's idea of it. Seth finished fast, but not too fast as to disappoint Nieves. She had done it once before with a boy at a house party, but not with this electricity. Seth's unsure, horrified look in the glow of the carnival games endeared her.

When Nieves finally spoke, Seth couldn't hear her over the fishbowls or the water guns setting off gay alarms. It didn't matter because there was nothing she could say that could ruin this moment. Seth would replay it throughout their marriage, dubbing his own words over what she might have actually confessed that night, panting, splayed on the hard ground next to him. He never asked her, either. It didn't matter because he was happy.

Seth and Nieves regrouped with Osario and Isa at the line for the huge Ferris wheel. Isa studied her sister's face, then focused her full, obvious attention on Seth, who darted his eyes away.

"Merry Christmas, indeed," Isa said, and left it at that. Osario didn't catch on—his gaze stayed glued to a fistfight that had broken out. A crowd formed and bets pooled. Isa yanked Osario by his jacket and pulled him onto the swinging seat.

The larger man fell to the skinnier one after a swift punch.

"Knockout," Nieves laughed. "It's our turn, Seth."

"Ladies first," Seth said. He climbed in after her, and the bored attendant half-heartedly buckled them in. Nieves glared at him as he moved on, and locked the bar into place herself.

"We could've died," she said.

"I would've caught you," Seth said.

Nieves blushed. Such a corny line in the United States would have had her scanning for an exit, but coming from Seth, who'd never kissed anyone before, it was sweet. Romantic, even. Perhaps it was the language, she thought. Yes, Spanish added some deep poetry to pickup lines. But Nieves couldn't ignore Seth's sincerity. It was like he was still twelve years old.

"You're seventeen, ¿right, Seth?"

"Eighteen."

"¿Are you going to get your degree?"

"I want to. In what subject, I don't know. But I want to get out of here."

"You and me both. I hate it here."

"But you just got back."

"The second our plane touched down, I got nauseated. Not from the flight either," Nieves said after Seth opened his mouth to chime in. "There's nothing like it over there, Seth. It's fast, and there are so many different kinds of people. Museums and galleries, and no one is riding a horse down the street. They're so behind here. Nothing has changed since I left."

"But look down there," Seth said. The Ferris wheel had stopped, and the two were at the top of the world. Seth pointed out expensive cars and passersby in sophisticated clothes below. Their eyes drank in the pulsing ocean that was the Central Valley. The lights from every house and building, every new skyscraper and lamppost were like bioluminescent plankton caught in a wave. From this height, surrounded without escape, Nieves could finally grasp some modicum of the capital's beauty, its progress.

"You can't change my mind, Seth," she said.

"I'm not trying to." He smiled back. The Ferris wheel started again. The glorious vista would soon be shared by another couple in intense contemplation.

Nieves turned to Seth with eyes so full of determination, he shuddered.

"Come with me," she said.

"¿What?"

"Come back to D.C. with me. I'll help you get into a good college, and I'll show you around, introduce you to my friends, perfect your English. It's wonderful over there."

"But I can't, Nieves. You know I can't."

They both looked forward to Osario and Isa, joyfully swinging in their seat. Despite the slick leather jacket, Osario laughed like a boy. To the untrained eye, his outward confidence would peg him as much older, but when really studied, when his cheeks reddened from giggling or his voice cracked like a green, slender branch, one could see clearly that Osario was still just a kid.

"You know I can't leave," Seth repeated.

"I know," Nieves said. "You're right."

The trip back in the banana yellow Corvette convertible wasn't as raucous as the first, but still blessed by rock 'n' roll. This time, emerging bands from Argentina and Britain, and more B-52's and Nacha Pop. The darkened forests along the dirt roads welcomed this injection of youth. Vagrants, ambling back home from a Christmas party or a bar, wanted so badly for the car to hit the brakes so they could ask what song was playing. Again, Nieves held Seth's hand on the gearshift, letting him feel the different speeds and patterns. Their purpose. Isa and Osario had dozed off in the back. It was past their bedtime.

Arriving at the gate of the Oreamundo property, Nieves begged to enter to greet María Cielos, whom neither she nor her sister had seen in years. Isa awoke with a cranky slur, argued against it, her warm mattress beckoning. Seth and Osario looked at each other.

"Our parents are probably asleep," they said. They were too embarrassed for any outsider to see how far the mansion and their family had fallen. It would be a shock for the sisters to behold the rotten innards of such a gorgeous house.

"I'll call you tomorrow," Seth said, and kissed Nieves. He pressed his forehead to hers. "I promise."

The sisters sped off into the night, a fleeting neon echo. The brothers smiled and opened the gate as quietly as possible. They didn't know exactly what time it was, but they knew it was late enough to incur wrath. The brothers could hear the weak, smoldering embers in the fireplace, the hypnotic hum of the cheap Christmas lights. They shed their beer-sticky shoes, tiptoeing to their respective rooms. Seth hugged Osario, whose exhausted body was swaying.

"I love you, little brother."

"You stink," Osario chuckled.

"Go to bed, idiot."

Seth climbed into his bed but didn't sleep the whole night. Periodically he'd put his hand to his crotch in disbelief. Was this too early an age to lose his virginity? Inversely, what if he had waited in agony for ages? Had he finished too quickly? Had Nieves enjoyed it? It looked like she'd enjoyed it. But he wasn't sure, and he surely wouldn't ask her. Should he ask her? When? Just bring it up randomly, or the next time they did it? Would there be a next time? His thoughts spiraled into insecurity, and then ecstasy again.

Otilio visited his grandson that night in the darkness, dressed in the same navy suit he'd been buried in. Seth had done it. He had accomplished what men should all accomplish—a little later than he had, but still at a respectable age. However, Otilio had made love to only one woman. After Beatriz, he'd only ever taken it, like fruit from a stand. But the children had made love there at Zapote, and grandfather looked on with pride and affection at this shy, sensitive boy who didn't deserve this present reality, or his eventual fate, in which Otilio had had a heavy hand. The dead can see what's coming. He begged his grandson with his dirt-filled mouth to cling to this night, to this feeling, as if it were an oasis in destiny's barren, unforgiving past. But alas, the dead can't warn the living. The true curse of dying is having sight but not speech.

Seth was startled awake by his mother's cries. Screams, thumps, knuckles. Osario was already at his doorway. The two brothers ran to the parlor, and in the gray-pink light of dawn, their mother winced at the despicable, towering frame of their father. From what Seth could tell, María Cielos had let the fire die out, and the mansion had fallen to frigid temperatures. The pendulum of their marriage had swung out of his mother's control. And if it went back to the way it was, Seth would never get his chance of seeing the light return to his mother's eyes when she looked upon him.

The taste of happiness from last night injected bravery into Seth's veins—he knew now that his life wasn't normal. That this reality was unacceptable. Seth caught his father's next blow by his wrist. He was strong enough now to challenge Gilberto. Strong enough to change all of this. Seth landed a haymaker in his father's chest, knocking him to the floor. Cowardice and momentary pride painted Gilberto's face. He tried to rise, but Seth threw his foot down onto his throat. Seth could end it all right now. He could set his family free, and they could begin reconstructing. The threat of their father's all-consuming shadow would flee into the corners of their memory. Seth looked to Osario, who nodded. So Seth transferred all of his body weight into his right heel, willing it into an anvil.

Gilberto's eyes looked past Seth, to María Cielos, who prepared a fire poker like a baseball bat. She swung, hard onto Seth's back. A home run.

Seth yelped, crashed onto the cold, stone floor. Something in his back was broken. Something else had been torn. He curled up in pain, felt as if the iron still cut into him.

"Don't touch him, you son of a bitch," María Cielos hissed.

Seth had seen this look of hatred before. His eyes darted to Osario, who was staring down at a pool growing around his own feet.

"You're a curse," María Cielos said to Seth. "You brought misfortune to our lives."

Seth regained his breath and sat up, disbelief radiating from every cell in his body.

"Get out, you mongrel," she continued. "You beast."

Seth could stand again. He faltered for a moment but balanced himself. The muscles in his legs involuntarily tightened, prepared to sprint. Seth burst out of the mansion's door, past the black iron gate, following the rising sun to Nieves's house.

Osario, fixing his broken attention to the surrounding room, saw only their mother crouched over their father on the ground, dabbing his sweaty face with a handkerchief. Seth was gone. Osario ran about the house, desperately calling out for his older brother.

"¡Seth!" he yelled. "¡Seth! ¡Seth! ¡Seth!"

THE MIDDLE KINGDOM

1986–2011 C.E.

2011

Nieves put on an old Blue Magic record and examined Seth's splendid tropical flora. She wanted to see what the big deal was. He'd gone out on another hours-long walk to God knows where, and Andrés was back at school after spring break. This rare time alone in the apartment was better than therapy. Accompanying Nieves was a beer that froze her slender palm, which she periodically touched to her forehead. It was hot for a late-April day. Too hot, she thought, so she opened the window and sneezed. With spring came allergies, so she gulped down her beer to coat her throat against the pollen. A girlfriend had introduced Nieves to this particular ale: Magic Hat #9, light and fragrant as balancing a rose petal on the tongue. She squeezed a slice of tangy blood orange into the mouth of the bottle, shoved the rind down the neck, and leaned against the radiator with her back to the window, letting the lazy breeze cool her. To her right, the morning glories had closed up shop for the day. The queen of the night wouldn't open until sundown. Only the marigolds were in full bloom, but they ignored Nieves and instead looked to the sun for companionship. With a pair of shears from the kitchen table she relieved one of its head. It was a random act of cruelty, so she put it behind her ear. In a mirror across the room she looked beautiful with that orange flower in her hair.

What *happened* to me? she thought. She'd been so spunky before all of this, before returning here to D.C. ten years ago. Long ago, a flower in her hair would have been some ironic commentary on patriarchal beauty standards, but now she'd become so bored she chopped a flower from its stem out of infantile spite and, in repentance, stuck it in her hair to admire how its petals softened her face. God, she'd become some Waspy housewife in a two-bedroom co-op apartment by Woodley Park. She cooked, and cleaned, and did yoga in Lululemon pants that left red marks on her thighs. Whereas in her youth she had rejected her name, now she embodied it. Serene, gentle. Passive to any sort of wind or cold front. Even her obsession with home cooking—*why?* She'd been a successful restaurateur back in Costa Rica. And her culinary career here hadn't been so bad. But she'd abandoned it all after just a few years, and for what? For her family, she reasoned. Her toddler who needed attention and her husband who'd lost himself. So, to make up for it, she returned to the recipes her mother had hammered into her and documented them on legal pads strewn about the apartment in preparation for a *cooking show*? Who *was* she?

Seth's wife.

Andrés's mother.

She'd let herself fall into this Marianismo trap.

Willingly, which disgusted her. How could she turn around, see the prints of the barefoot-in-the-kitchen women who came before her, and go *backward*? She accused Seth in her mind: turned on him, blamed him for everything (which would be fair, honestly). But she, too, shared responsibility for this. She didn't have to follow him here. But she loved him. She'd always loved him.

For Nieves to stop feeling sorry for herself, she allotted five minutes to feel sorry for her husband. He'd begun falling into his moods again. Depressions and a revisiting reticence that frightened her. A bubbling, violent quiet that broke only in arguments or when he stubbed his toe. Seth would never hit her, she knew that, but sometimes it was as if he were an exotic pet, and she, his irresponsible owner. And when she was eventually mauled, those who knew them would say, *What did she think was going to happen?*

It didn't anger Nieves that Seth was keeping secrets from her. She preferred not being privy to *everything*. To know one's husband completely struck her as unfortunate and unwise. One should be aware of, at most, 70 percent of a man's thoughts. The remaining thirty would surely send a woman straight to a divorce lawyer for the quickest settlement, then the cheapest flight to the farthest country away. No, for their entire marriage Seth had revealed about 58 percent of himself, and that was a perfect number for Nieves. Just enough to win at a game show, but not so much as to flee and change her identity.

The five minutes were up, so she made her way in front of the new flat-screen TV, turned on the *Yogalosophy* DVD, and stretched into upward dogs and downward ones until the beer in her belly begged her to stop. Nieves went into the bedroom, sat on Seth's disheveled side of the bed, and began to masturbate. But she was interrupted by the ringing landline on the night table. Nieves sighed, pulled up her Lululemons, and answered the unrelenting phone shaped like a hamburger—a novelty Seth gave her last year for their anniversary as a prank, now in full employment, because their cordless broke two months ago.

"Hello?"

The line was quiet long enough for Nieves to get annoyed.

"Look," she said. "Whatever you're selling, I've already got three."

"Nieves."

"¿Isa?" Nieves said after pausing.

"That's right. It's me."

"¿What are you doing calling here?"

"I—"

"¿What if Seth had picked up the phone?"

"I wanted to take the chance."

Nieves sat up. She was holding a hamburger to her face, talking to her little sister whom she hadn't spoken to in a decade. "I'm sorry for snapping," she said.

"No, you're fine. I understand. I thought about you. Horacio saw a picture of us, and he asked, and it made me so sad."

Nieves was strong in situations like these. She could muster up a smile even if it felt like all four chambers of her heart were collapsing.

"¡Horacio! Baby boy," Nieves said. "¿How old is he now?"

Silence answered the ridiculous question. Nieves imagined the look on Isa's face. To be ebullient in this moment was to be cruel. Nieves's flippancy a quick barrier between herself and her sister, like pressing an elevator door closed to someone running to catch it.

"He's ten," Isa replied weakly.

"Just like my Andrés," Nieves said.

"Yes, I know. I sent Andrés a card for his birthday."

"Oh, that's a pity," Nieves said. "Never got it."

The birthday card from Costa Rica was hidden away with nine others in a shoebox, either in the bedroom closet or the foyer's. Nieves changed the subject.

"¿Is Horacio tall?"

"He's getting there. We think he'll grow taller than Osario."

Nieves winced at that name.

"Just like my Andrés. He's already the tallest in his class."

"¿And how is he?"

"Oh, he's fine. Just fine. Well, sometimes he gets into trouble," Nieves admitted. "Boys will be boys. You know how it is."

Boys will be boys.

Brothers will be brothers.

Brothers will betray brothers.

You know how it is.

"Isa, I've got to go make lunch. Seth will be starving when he gets home."

"Yes, of course."

"Look," Nieves said in a moment of tenderness. "Take care, sis."

"Thank you. I love you."

"You, too, sis," Nieves said, and hung up the hamburger. She shot up, wanting to rip the telephone from the wall, hurl it out the window. Exiting the bedroom, she was confronted by Seth's tropical flora—the only witnesses to the call from her little sister. Nieves was too dizzy to fell the forest with her bare hands, so instead, she paced. How could Isa have had the balls to call her? Out of the blue, and with a tone as if nothing had happened. As if she didn't know the part she had played in Seth's exile. The only greater sin than a brother betraying his brother is a sister's betrayal of hers. If given the chance, Nieves would cram Seth's flowers into Isa's mouth. Shove them down until her sister's throat was a garden.

She faced the marigolds again. Seth would return soon to water them. With the kitchen shears, she resumed the decapitations, every ruffled, orange blossom a phone call she never made to her sister over the years—to reproach, to confide in, to berate, interrogate, commiserate with; to talk about old times, to compare husbands, their idiocies and idiosyncrasies, or the dishes they didn't wash or the litany of ejaculations, premature. She handled the pruning belligerently, littering the window ledge with those orange heads, like bits of peel or fabric swatches for a new couch. And when Nieves was done, when she'd dialed all those calls in her mind, the plant lay bare, indistinguishable from any other.

The dead bolt unlatched. Seth entered the apartment in a better mood than when he had left. Nieves composed herself, ditched the shears, and snatched the warm beer from the window ledge to sip. Seth kissed her on the forehead. Noticing the yoga mat, he asked if she was an expert yet.

"Oh, you know I'm already pretty flexible," she said.

"Yes." Seth smiled and kissed her on the mouth this time.

"What's got you so happy?" she asked.

"I'm going away," Seth said.

Nieves studied his face, raised her eyebrows like a bridge. "Away to where, Seth?"

"West Virginia," he said proudly. "I saw an ad for a retreat in the Shenandoah. Meditative, some spiritual mumbo jumbo."

Nieves stopped herself from laughing.

"But I need it," he said sincerely. "You know I need it. I need to find some peace so you can be peaceful too."

Nieves crossed her arms, puckered her lips to the beer. "I guess you do need it," she said. "You've been kind of an asshole lately."

"I know," Seth said. "I'll come back to you with a weight off my chest."

A man with a weight off his chest, Nieves thought. Now, wouldn't that make a wonderful world.

"And the marigolds?" Seth gasped at the graveyard of orange ruffles.

"I tried to make a bouquet for the kitchen. I guess I'm not very good at it."

FIELD OF REEDS

1986

Nieves and Isa had arrived home from Zapote elated and exhausted. Isa was too tired to make it to her own bed and bunked with Nieves, whose breath smelled of corn and bleach. They didn't have the energy to process the night. They passed out and squirmed from time to time to pull the covers away from the sister who was hogging them.

At dawn, the house awoke to a frenzied knocking. The women thought it was an earthquake—Nieves jumped to toss Isa beneath the bed, their mother, Gloria, somersaulted into the bathtub, and Fulvia the maid threw one of the many rosaries around her bedpost against a wall, for which reason she didn't know. When they all realized it was just the door, a sigh of relief came in a chorus. An intruder was better managed than a quake because Gloria kept a shotgun beneath her pillow—she snatched it up to load and pointed it at the entranceway, only to find Seth Oreamundo drenched in stink and sweat, waiting for his breath to catch up to his body.

Nieves and Isa escorted him into the living room, where he collapsed. Gloria didn't let the shotgun down, not for a minute. Fulvia the maid, hurrying to the boy with a glass of fresh water, wondered what it was like to see life through the barrel of a 12-gauge. After her American husband divorced her, Gloria set a cardinal rule in the house: no man would ever make it past the foyer. Not a milkman, or a policeman, or a fireman, even if her house was being swallowed by flames. They brought nothing to women's lives but trouble and heartbreak. Their words were segments of a centipede, crawling in and out of women's ears. No, she'd have no male this far into her home.

"Get him out," Gloria said to her daughters.

"But, Mamá, look at him," Nieves said. She attended to Seth with hand towels.

"Mamá, please," Isa echoed.

Gloria hated it when her daughters tag teamed her. "It's loaded with bird shot," she answered.

"For the love of God, señora," Fulvia the maid said, downing the glass of water herself. "The least we can do is get an explanation out of him."

Gloria lowered her arms, and the four women waited on the sofa and a velvet lounge chair until Seth was startled awake by his own inhale. "¿Where am I?" he asked.

"You're in my house," Gloria answered.

"I'm sorry," Seth began. "I ran."

"¿From where?" Nieves asked.

"My house."

"¿Your house? That's fifteen kilometers."

Fulvia the maid touched her right hand to her forehead, her heart, and both shoulders.

"¿Why?" Gloria asked skeptically.

Seth motioned to his back, to which Nieves and Isa pulled up his sweater, revealing a bruise the length of a weapon. Gloria stood, placing the shotgun down for the first time since Seth had arrived and inspected what had caused her daughters and Fulvia the maid to cup their mouths with both hands.

"¿Who struck you with iron?" Gloria asked. The bruise changed colors as Seth breathed.

"My mother."

"María Cielos would never do that."

Seth turned his gaze up to her with a pain she'd seen only once, when her father kicked her childhood dog.

"Take him to the guest room, Fulvia."

"Right away."

"Isa, make coffee. Nieves, sit here with me."

Fulvia the maid took Seth to the guest room, Isa rushed to the kitchen, and Nieves sat down next to her mother just as she'd said. Gloria asked why the boy would come here of all places, and Nieves confessed what had happened the night before. As hardened as she was to the idea, Gloria asked if her daughter loved him. Nieves did. But Gloria replied that he couldn't stay. She gave Nieves the option of finding a solution on her own. Nieves was smart, and when the brain and heart work together, nothing was impossible. Nieves spoke after a while. She would call her father. Not on her phone, Gloria answered. She didn't even want that man's voice in her house.

Fulvia the maid drove Nieves to the nearest hamlet and its solitary pay phone where she could call her father, Dan, in D.C. Nieves barely had to beg to come back, and for Seth to accompany her. She timed it on her watch: only three minutes for her father to fold and promise two plane tickets in a month's time. They could stay with him indefinitely. Nieves thanked him ungraciously, hung up, and invited Fulvia for a few celebratory beers at the bar down the street. When they returned, Gloria's annoyance had steeped in the house; Isa shot rubber bands at the ceiling fan; Seth was sleeping and didn't wake up until New Year's Eve.

Gloria took that month to hammer her family's recipes into Nieves. She became an unforgiving chef because she had deemed her daughter too American. Culture was passed down through gastronomy, she said. Generations are defined by seasonings and techniques, and even if her daughter spent the rest of her life in the United States, her palate wouldn't soon forget where she came from. Gloria largely ignored Seth, who didn't much mind. He slept at the opposite end of the house from the women, so only Nieves and Fulvia the maid checked in on him. Isa had become quiet and resentful that her sister was leaving her for a boy. Three years until she was eighteen seemed like a long time, but Nieves promised it wasn't, and that she would be waiting at the airport when Isa was old enough to decide for herself.

The subject of Osario sent Seth into quiet spells, so it quickly became taboo. However, thoughts of his little brother became intrusive, and some days Seth felt as though he were a magnet being drawn back to his house. But Nieves helped curb the urge. She assured Seth that his little brother would survive. Survival, he answered, was the easy part.

Ronald Reagan was preparing to deliver his State of the Union address when Seth and Nieves deboarded their plane at Washington National Airport a month later. They'd arrived later than expected—the layover in Atlanta had been slow and viscous. Snippets of last year's address on CNN followed them throughout the airport, blaring on dangling televisions. At the baggage claim, the recording was almost finished, the president having concluded with Nicaragua: Soviets and Sandinistas, rebels and government repression. *We cannot play innocents abroad in a world that is not innocent*, he had proclaimed to a standing ovation. Good old American interventionism, but with a neon '80s twist. This year's address promised no difference of opinion.

Outside the airport, the February evening wasn't as bad as Seth and Nieves had expected, especially just weeks after a cold snap had frozen every state like cubes in a tray. Seth sighed and saw his breath for the first time in his life. "It's like—"

"Smoke." Nieves grinned.

"Right," Seth said, lips chapped already, so he couldn't smile too widely.

Nieves's father arrived in a black Crown Victoria. The license plate had more zeros than numbers, *Diplomat* stamped underneath the code.

"How was the trip, kids?" Nieves's father asked. He turned to his daughter in the passenger seat, and Seth quickly realized that when he spoke in English, he was just addressing her.

"¿How did it go?" he asked Seth through the rearview mirror.

"It was fine, sir. First time ever on a plane."

"No need to call me *sir*," he corrected. "My name is Dan."

"Yes, sir. I mean, Dan, sir."

Both Nieves and her father chuckled. Dan sped, skirting past other drivers itching to get back home.

"I'll never get over how polite Ticos are," Dan said.

"Oh, shut up, Dan." Nieves rolled her eyes.

"¿See?" Dan said, again to Seth's reflection. "You've never heard a child address her parent by first name, ¿right?"

"No, never," Seth admitted. He smushed his face to the glass as they crossed the Key Bridge over the Potomac River into Georgetown. His eyes drank in the skyline on the eastern horizon, the marble monuments that stood out from the night. The phallic Washington Monument blinked with two glowing red eyes. "I've read about them," Seth said, his breath splotching the window.

"We'll take you tomorrow. It's supposed to be nice weather. Finally."

"We're hungry, Dad. Do you have food?"

"Of course. I stocked up. I can predict these things, honey."

Dan's tone was affectionate, melancholic: that of a father who was losing his daughter—and losing her to the handsome boy in the back seat, which made it slightly worse, or slightly better depending on which position Dan would wake up in, or how bitter the percolator would make his coffee. The divorce had left his daughters rebellious. But he couldn't help but spoil them to the point of enabling. He smelled marijuana on Nieves's clothes and knew she was having sex. But he didn't want to lose her to Costa Rica, to their mother. Nieves had gone back in the first place because they'd gotten into an argument over curfew. But just after Christmas she'd phoned and asked him to let her return. More of a proclamation than a plea, because it depended on one condition: she could bring Seth back with her. Dan found it reasonable because he had always taken Seth's sensitivity as an indication he was gay. But now, passing through Georgetown on their way back to his condo, Dan sensed with all the fury in the world that Seth and Nieves had fucked. Paralyzed by a divorcé's desperation, he couldn't do anything about it.

An obelisk is a sunbeam petrified into stone. Millennia ago, transcriptions and hieroglyphs were etched onto these monuments, retelling harrowing tales to anyone unaware. Seth was fascinated that the Washington Monument was blank, its white limestone pristine, untouched. This was perhaps because all were well aware of George Washington's epic, and it wouldn't soon be forgotten. As the father of modern democracy, he was as close as a man could've gotten to a sun god.

On their tour of the National Mall, this monument was by far Seth's favorite. Despite February's chilled breath, he lay on the grass staring up at its point, which poked a microscopic hole in the sky. At first Nieves and her father watched Seth patronizingly—it was cute that he'd never marveled at something so tall before. But after their ears began to redden and their noses dripped clear drops, the novelty wore off. They lifted Seth from the grass and ferried him to the other sites: the Korean War Memorial, with its doomed soldiers reflected in mirrored slabs; the Vietnam War Memorial, descending the ramp into a crater of black, slick steles etched with names of the fallen, an American

Book of the Dead; and finally the Lincoln Memorial, climbing its steep steps to his statue, where some people kneeled as if receiving Communion.

Once spring settled in, Seth began what would become his peculiar walking habit. At whatever time of the day, Nieves would call out to him—for dinner, advice, lovemaking—only to be answered by the emptiness of the condo. At first, Seth ventured along the canals, the cobblestone streets of Georgetown, its cemeteries, and gaslit parks at dusk. And as he'd done in the coffee fields of his childhood, every day he went farther. He was completely alone when wandering the city, and by the time fall arrived and his classes at George Washington University commenced, he knew every corner and side street of Northwest D.C. Even the parts where people of his complexion were terrified to go.

GW accepted Seth on an international scholarship, and with the aid of ESL classes, he quickly dominated discussions in philosophy and political science courses. In his core curriculum classes, his accent and tanned skin gave him away immediately, and the fresh-out-of-prep-school Wasps taunted and confused him with English idioms and called him many-syllable insults to his face. The Black students rallied behind Seth and befriended him, provided him with verbal ammunition against the gringos (a word the whites especially hated).

Seth made two best friends at GW. The first, Deborah, a native of D.C.—fourth generation, her great-great-grandparents once southern sharecroppers turned florists, with a shop in Mount Pleasant. She and Seth bonded over horticulture, often roving miles in whatever cardinal direction, exchanging watering techniques, grooming tips, and fertilizer brands. Deborah sipped her coffee and closed her eyes to imagine all the tropical flora Seth described with vivid nostalgia, and she invited him to the flower shop, introduced him to her grandparents, who tended rare plants and picked out roses for Nieves. Seth's other best friend, Isaiah, had no interest in flowers—he'd seen so few, having been raised on the Lower East Side of Manhattan, and he didn't much care to learn about them now. Architecture, not botany, was his expertise. *D.C. is where the best architects come to do their worst work*, Isaiah said affectionately once, pointing out his favorite brutalist structures, art deco hotels, and even the ever-rampant classical style that reminded Isaiah of an ugly history Seth never truly understood until slowly and brutally explained.

Seth often invited Isaiah on his excursions with Deborah, but he never joined. The two had been an item at the beginning of summer, but they'd broken up by the Fourth of July because Deborah too-soon discovered Isaiah was a player. She mentioned the term in passing to Seth; Seth then innocently asked Isaiah what it meant, which sent him into a monthlong silent treatment of Deborah (or Debbie, as he had called her sweetly in his bed). And Seth was good enough to absorb Nieves into his new friend group—whereas most boyfriends exclude girlfriends to keep their lives separate, Seth took her to the concerts he'd been invited to, or to the bars they would have to sneak her into because she was seventeen and still in high school. By November, they'd all become as tight-knit as an ancestral quilt, settling into each other's idiosyncrasies and language barriers.

Thanksgiving came, and after separate dinners, Deborah and Isaiah arrived at the condo for drinks. The four friends raided Dan's cabinet of dark liquor, including a fifty-year-old bourbon given to him by the Bolivian ambassador. Since Seth had arrived, Nieves had noticed he often winced at his first two sips of alcohol. Jerked his head for a millisecond before gulping the liquor down as if trying to avoid the taste, but not the bite. Never the bite. However, when the whisky loosened his shoulders and tongue, he took to drinking with the special enjoyment of an alcoholic. But without the eventual bite of one. Never the bite.

When alcohol almost replaced his blood, Seth forgot most of his English. His sentences got shorter, and he would have to employ Nieves as his interpreter. But sometimes the power of translation couldn't curb cultural differences, and Nieves floundered the more offensive a comment became. Tonight, the word *Negro* floated out of Seth's mouth, and it immediately shut everyone up like a gunshot. Seth and Nieves quickly realized it had been the first time he said it in front of Deborah or Isaiah. The silence sobered them.

"I can explain," Nieves said. Deborah was eyeing the door and squeezing her glass so hard it could have shattered. "It's different there," Nieves explained. "In Costa Rica. It's normal."

"To call us Negro?"

"Y-yes," Nieves stuttered, reluctant to continue. She had been confident their friends would understand, but Deborah's disbelief threw Nieves into shame. She'd never considered it wrong. Odd, but never wrong.

"It's true. They do that," Isaiah chimed in.

"Who?" Deborah asked.

"Latins. I'm from Manhattan. The Puerto Ricans all call me Negro. It's cultural. They don't see it as wrong."

Nieves opened her mouth to correct that they were Costa Rican, not Puerto Rican, but stopped herself before making the situation worse.

"And you're okay with that?" Deborah asked Isaiah. Her hurt had transferred to him like a game of telephone.

"Don't shoot the messenger." Isaiah shrugged his shoulders. "I'm just telling you it's what they do."

"My aunt is Black," Seth interrupted. "She raised me."

It was the first Deborah and Isaiah had heard of it, and while it seemed like some desperate attempt to backpedal, they remembered who Seth had been to them all these months, and instead took it as a bridge with which to connect them on a deeper level.

"What is she like?" Deborah asked, swirling the ice in her glass. Her eyes eased, if still a little skeptical.

"Kind," Seth answered. "Another?"

"No, thanks," Isaiah said, eyeing his half-full glass. "Where is she?"

"I don't know," Seth said.

"What do you mean?"

Nieves shifted in her seat. She knew only morsels of what had happened back at the Oreamundo plantation, but even the scant details she had coaxed out of Seth were still hard to swallow. She debated changing the conversation.

"My mother kicked her out."

"Of the house?"

"Yeah."

Seth hung his head low.

"Well, who knew you were Black." Isaiah smiled. "That's welcome news to me."

Seth didn't correct that his mother had been adopted by Ola's brother. It had never mattered, and he decided it mattered even less in this conversation.

"Let's dance," Nieves said, her American half having grown tired of discussing race.

"Put on a record, baby," Isaiah said. He put a muscled, tattooed arm around Deborah.

"Fine," Deborah said.

They popped cassette mixtapes into the stereo, danced until their still-teenage knees tired, and each couple collapsed on the expensive Persian rug. Dan returned home drunk, and upon seeing the kids, happy and prostrate, snoring on his floor, he felt thankful.

Exxon Valdez could've been the name of a titular character in classic Spanish-language literature: Don Quixote, Pedro Páramo, Artemio Cruz, Exxon Valdez. Or perhaps the brother of coffee magnate Juan Valdez. Exxon, trailing behind Juan and his mule, Conchita, but instead of freshly harvested beans in sacks, drums of petroleum strapped to the haunches of his animal. That was a prospectively nightmarish smell: roasted coffee and crude oil. A smell only Seth could imagine if his past and future could meet like doomed lovers.

But *Exxon Valdez* was not a beloved literary protagonist or a relative of a corporate coffee mascot. It was a tanker, gigantic and frail as the *Titanic*, carrying a black hole of crude oil in its belly. A reef, not an iceberg, peeled open the *Exxon Valdez*. Petroleum, not passengers, spilled out into the frozen sea.

If Seth had taken that internship at Exxon's satellite office in D.C., he would have watched in horror as managers and lobbyists sprinted around the city like headless chickens. He could've interpreted the oil spill as a warning and said, *Oh, this is something I want to avoid. This is a scandal that is preventable not only logistically but politically.* But in 1989, Seth was interning at the International Monetary Fund, and the organization was instead concerned with corpulent loans to turmoiled Central American countries. Seth would graduate GW in June with a degree in political science and international relations. Until then, he sat in on semi-important financial meetings, copyedited materials for review, and fetched coffee for his boss, who crowded his desk with photos of his wife and two children: only a family man had the heart to calculate the perfect loan interest for an entire country, as if Nicaragua had applied for a mortgage at Wells Fargo, or Guatemala for a Pell Grant to attend Stanford.

After graduation, Seth would continue on his subconscious political path, landing a well-paying job at the Organization of American States. Dan was happy to provide Seth with all his connections because Seth made Nieves happy. She'd been trying her hand at different jobs and hobbies—waitressing, hairstyling, working as a barista at their local coffee shop—having finally landed on art history classes at GW and, on the weekends, a school of culinary arts in Alexandria. The couple eventually moved out of Dan's Georgetown condo and rented the one-bedroom atop Deborah's grandparents' flower shop in Mount Pleasant. They were kind landlords, and Seth and Nieves awoke to stunning bouquets outside their door every Sunday morning next to the *New York Times*. Deborah had moved to Manhattan with Isaiah. They worked in neighboring offices at the United Nations and visited D.C. every few months, staying in a studio next to Seth and Nieves.

Despite Seth's burgeoning career and this serene life surrounded on all sides by Nieves's cooking and music, he would still sometimes wake up in a cold sweat, the fire poker staining his back. Still the memory of María Cielos on the stone floor, Gilberto's throat beneath Seth's heel. The pool of urine flowing beyond Osario's feet. Seth had left him there. How many years would his little brother be able to withstand Gilberto if he transformed back into a beast? How many years would Osario look to Seth's empty bed, his abandoned sweaters and dull razor, and be reminded that his older brother had fled like a coward; that he hadn't looked back—not for a second—to save himself? Seth never phoned, never wrote, because deep down he knew any reconnection would call him back. Snatch him from this shiny new existence where the love of his life comforted him after nightmares with records, and where his work saved him from himself. Seth had abandoned and continued the abandonment. It wasn't just the initial act itself but its perpetuation that made him feel like a monster. Seth worked long hours to quiet his conscience and took those endless walks to distract himself from the fact that he had indeed done the worst thing an older brother could do to his younger: leave without bringing Osario with him.

BOOK OF THE DEAD

1986

The moment Seth escaped the Oreamundo mansion, it felt as if the property and those on it had righted themselves. As if in a collective exhale, a foreign entity had been expelled. Exorcised. Left bruised and exhausted on the stone floor, Gilberto and María Cielos started to laugh. Osario watched them in terror from his pool of urine and ran searching for Seth, because this all felt like a bad dream. Osario ransacked the mansion. He ripped away shower curtains, left dents in walls from slammed-open doors, flipped over mattresses, inspected every shadow dawn was evaporating. When the harsh reality had sunken in, Osario returned to the parlor, where his parents awaited him, sitting back-straight on the couch like office patients. He watched them watch him as he crossed the room. His urine had been cleaned, the fire restoked, burning cheerfully.

"We're relieved," María Cielos said.

Osario sat cross-legged on the floor. Dubious, terrified.

Gilberto looked lovingly at his wife. "It's like the house is full of fresh air," he said. "¿Don't you feel it, son? ¿Don't you feel that it's easier to breathe?"

Gilberto smiled, finally free of his father's favorite. María Cielos gleamed, finally free of the man on the riverbank.

Shock set into Osario's veins. His body tensed from what he'd witnessed, what he was witnessing happen right in front of him. Seth had left him with these people he no longer recognized.

"That's right," María Cielos sighed. "He left you."

"And I don't think he's coming back," Gilberto said. "Look around."

Osario looked around.

"He left you, my love," María Cielos repeated. "My king."

"¿How could he have done that?" Gilberto leaned in, craned his head so that Osario could hear his whisper. "It doesn't seem like he's coming back. I can't believe he did that to you."

The shock ebbed, and what now flowed into Osario's young body was rage. A tooth-numbing despair that made him want to sob and fire a gun. His mind raced: the only fact that remained was that his older brother had just abandoned him. Fled like a coward and didn't come back. He had left him here, all alone.

"You're not alone," María Cielos said sweetly. "You have us. You have always had us."

"It will be different," Gilberto said, caressing María Cielos's shoulder. "We'll be different; you'll see."

Gilberto had half the mansion demolished, including Otilio's room and the smells that lingered. With cash from the foreign coffee companies, Gilberto and María Cielos went about purchasing back all the furniture they had sold years ago. Before long, they'd reincarnated Osario's childhood home. They enrolled him in a prestigious private academy in the center of San José, named after some writer, or some priest or president. None of the students cared enough to ask. It was better to be honored by a monument, or a library, or at the very least a park bench: having a school dedicated in one's name is more tragic than being forgotten. Five or so nuns had been left over from the school's conversion from Catholic to secular. They'd come with the building, including Sister Octavia, who led physical education classes, and Mother Orquídea, who no longer wore a habit and allowed her hair to descend from her liberated head. The rest of the teachers were men. The school had become the first co-ed in the country. And everyone's parents were either newly liberal and didn't care or were too rich to have even noticed.

Somehow Osario assimilated seamlessly into adolescent social life. Sheer charisma exuded from him, and as deliriously as insects, his classmates surrounded him in an ever-constant cloud. They inquired about his childhood, and he retold the good or the exciting parts. They asked what he wanted to be when he grew up. *Remembered* is all he ever answered. The boys begged him to play soccer, while the girls squabbled to hold his hand. It felt natural, this attention. Osario drank in the endless stream of admiration and could not stop himself from drinking. Osario fashioned this admiration into scaffolding to rebuild himself after Seth's abandonment. It protected him from harm and the elements, from sadness or dreams that scratched him awake. Popularity saved him from imploding. Eventually (and expectedly) it turned the boy prideful. At times, depending on the light, Osario was a spitting image of his grandfather.

Puberty hit Osario with a blessed haymaker, hard and fast overnight. He grew tall, his muscles became as strong as woven iron, and hair sprouted on his body in perfect distribution. But he had none of the awkwardness of a high school teenager: no pimples to embarrass him, and his voice changed pitch as if tuned by a master musician. Adults had never seen anything like it. By many accounts, they'd never seen a more handsome boy, enough to stop grown men and women alike in their tracks.

Osario's sudden good looks coupled with his charm made him dangerous—that is, he could get away with anything. Every day until he was actually punished, he pushed the limits of this newfound immunity. Egged on by friends who smoked cigarettes in the hallways and pushed old women to the dirt, Osario's proclivity for mischief reawakened. But his pranks went through a quick and horrible evolution. A child lacks a certain type of cruelty—rather, he hasn't the level of intelligence it takes to be cruel. That was no longer the case for Osario. He loosened desk screws, laced food with laxatives, and once snuck out of class to the faculty parking lot and sliced the brake cables of a teacher he never liked. Luckily, the teacher crashed into a fruit stand before he could get onto the highway. Mangoes mangled in the grill, a banana plugged into the exhaust pipe. The police came to the school the next day to interrogate scores of students, with Osario as their number one suspect. But even the cops were ineffective against his ability to lie with effortless conviction, so another student—quiet, lonesome, bad at his studies—was pinned as the culprit and would serve five years in prison for attempted murder. Protective as vassals to a king, María Cielos and Gilberto shielded Osario from any consequences.

Any negative comment from instructors or visits from officers in the middle of the night only dug their soles deeper into the mud of their obsession.

As slippery as gods of mischief are, they're all eventually caught. And like his predecessors, Osario ultimately faced judgment. It came after a particularly heinous act. An accident, technically, but horrible enough to strip him of his impunity. One of Osario's classmates returned to Costa Rica from visiting family in Oklahoma with fireworks smuggled in a false compartment in his suitcase. He laid out the armory in neat rows, color-coded and organized by blast radius. Teenage eyes widened, mouths watered. The smell of gunpowder called out to them like a new, exciting friend.

The boys stole half-empty bottles from their fathers' liquor cabinets and drunkenly roamed San José one night, leaving a trail of smoke as they stumbled. They stuffed mailboxes with firecrackers, shot Roman candles at telephone poles and parakeet nests, dropped M-80s into gutters and felt the sidewalk burp beneath them. With only one cherry bomb, it was reserved for Osario, their ringleader. He found it a delicate device: round, red, delicious-looking enough to nibble at. But his friend assured him that the unassuming fruit he held was a grenade.

They arrived at the plaza in front of their school, sat at the rim of its concrete fountain and laughed. They recounted every detonation as if they were war memories. It was true, though—not in forty years had Costa Ricans heard something so close to warfare. Osario felt the pressure then of being the last to spark his firework, of closing out the show with a literal bang. He scrambled for matches in his pocket and lit the fuse. Looking up to the school windows, he considered hurling it through the glass but then turned his attention to a bench, next to which a stray dog sniffed and licked a bone.

Osario had just wanted to scare it. He'd wanted it to yelp and flee so that he and his friends could cackle at its cowardice. Osario rolled the cherry bomb like a bowling ball, gently so that it would stop a meter away, and the mutt would be spared from the blast. But Osario hadn't considered the incline of the plaza, so undetectable that the boys realized it only when the bomb kept rolling. Transfixed by its meal, the stray didn't notice at all. The cherry stopped right beneath its rumbling belly. Needless to say, the dog was destroyed.

The other boys escaped in all directions, while Osario didn't budge until the officers cuffed his wrists and banged his head against the hood of the police car. Watching the streetlamps on the way to the station, he wondered if someone would arrive to clean the splatter before tomorrow's classes.

Osario was young enough that he didn't receive jail time. The same lawyer who represented Gilberto after the Baptism convinced the judge that Osario's were the actions of a child. His intention had been to frighten, not annihilate. There was a fine line between prank and slaughter, he argued. And the judge, swayed into mercy, and creative in his punishment, sentenced Osario to one hundred hours of community service at the Simón Bolivar Zoo. It was to teach the boy the importance of natural life.

At first, Osario wasn't trusted to go near the mammals. The zookeepers didn't even allow him to grip the chain-link fence to watch the jaguar feast on raw meat, or the capuchins on papaya. He spent the first half of his community service cleaning the restrooms throughout the park, scrubbing and bleaching with his bare hands. The employees eventually found out why they were forced to work with him, so they treated him badly. They called him a dog behind his back, and one girl, a student at the university majoring in biology, wore a T-shirt printed with a picture of her own chow chow. Just as the judge had predicted, shame was more effective than jail time.

After fifty hours over the course of a year, Osario was allowed to feed the birds. Macaws hopped from tree to tree all around the zoo, the toucans housed behind mesh. Ambling peacocks pecked at Osario's shins for seeds, and sparrows watched him with sweet, pathetic expressions. Osario's supervisor Victor couldn't help but notice that the animals flocked to Osario with a trust not normally shown to humans. He'd heard the story of the dog and expected the boy to be some sort of psychopath, but according to the curassows who brushed against Osario's legs like cats, Osario wasn't capable of such a crime.

"Hey, kid," Victor said one day as he brushed the dreaded mane of the lion everybody called Bob. "¿Did you grow up around animals?"

Osario pushed his face to the chain-link enclosure, spoke through one of the gaps with puckered lips. "Not really, but sort of. The place where we live used to be surrounded by forests. I mean, there were animals, but none in the house."

"¿What kind?"

"Well, on the plantation we had horses, oxen. I've seen a cliff of macaws. Butterflies a lot of the time. A viper once," Osario remembered. "And a crab . . ."

"¿A crab? I didn't know you grew up by the ocean."

"No, in the mountains."

"¿What was it doing there?"

"Tangled up with a snake."

"You're lying."

"No, seriously. My brother and I saw it when we were hiking as kids."

"I didn't know you had a brother."

"Well . . . we were hiking, and it was our birthday."

"You're twins."

"No. I was born on his birthday. He was twelve, and I was eight, and we were hiking. We heard gurgling, and crunching like when you step on a roach. And we saw them, the two creatures locked onto each other. They didn't want to let go. They were huge, bigger than us."

"Okay, *now* you're lying."

"No, I'm not. I swear. The crab must have been a meter tall. The viper was so green you'd have thought it was a vine. But its eyes were as yellow and bright as the sun."

"¿What did you all do?" Victor had been resting his head on Bob's back, the lion purring like an alley cat.

"We couldn't move at first. Those beasts stopped to look at us. They abandoned killing each other to stare straight into our faces. We ran. We hurtled through that forest all the way home. No one believed us."

"I barely believe you, kid. It sounds like something out of the Bible."

"That's what we said."

The longer Osario spent with the animals and Victor's mentorship, the softer his demeanor became. He didn't seek out his former friends who smoked cigarettes in the hallways and pushed old women to the dirt. They were all eventually expelled, anyway. Osario excelled at his studies again, returned to being the charismatic, likable boy who was constantly asked what he wanted to be when he grew up. But Osario no longer answered with something so narcissistic as *Remembered*. Instead, he began to speak of saving the world.

After two years, Osario graduated from both high school and the Simón Bolivar Zoo. He enrolled in environmental studies classes at the University of Costa Rica and volunteered at a new animal sanctuary called Zoo Ave. There he met altruistic Americans and Costa Ricans who had worked in rainforest conservation for years. Yes, they were all a bit sanctimonious, but Osario didn't mind at all. In fact, he wanted to become one of these warriors. He learned that habitats were being stripped bare for fruit and livestock. Costa Rica's economy was destroying the land. He thought of his own father, who'd felled the rainforest surrounding the latifundio to pave the way for those American roasters. He thought of that endlessly monotonous vista of coffee.

Costa Rica had lost over 50 percent of its forests to industry. Ancient trees hewed and incinerated so that cattle could graze upon renewed pasture; species escorted into extinction; Indigenous communities pushed farther from their ancestral lands and forced onto reservations whose borders were drawn at the whim of the government. He became what the Americans proudly called a *tree hugger*, manacling himself to trunks to block bulldozers and men with axes. Osario took on leadership roles, learned English, organized protestors who marched with blue and green signs to the legislative assembly. They congested roads, sabotaged construction equipment and heavy machinery. Anything to save what rainforest the country had left. Anything, Osario thought, to save the world.

Costa Rica is home to

desperation

a fool
is *living*
with
the pressure from

mouths

Biting

2011

Juan Santamaría International Airport had changed drastically in the ten years since Seth was exiled. The passengers no longer had to deboard on a flimsy ladder; instead, they exited into a proper terminal. Seth rubbed his lumbar, his eyes, relearned to walk after so many hours sedentary, and struggled for a whole minute to wrap his earphones while balancing the falsified passport and Customs slip. He followed the garbling crowd of travelers mindlessly down ramps and stairs, through doorways, past intimidating exits. Seth felt like a sheep on its way to slaughter. Following and following until an executioner met him on the other side. With a swing and a slice, the story of Seth Oreamundo would be over. Heading straight into fate's trap without any struggle. But how would that be any different, he wanted to ask the ten-year-old trailing behind her mother. How much control had he *really* had all this time? He'd always been an animal stuck within the parameters of someone else's design. But the little girl might challenge him, ask *how* or *why*—if he knew he hadn't had any control, why couldn't he retake it now? If he was conscious of destiny, couldn't he just change it? Just turn around and fly back and abandon the whole fantasy of sacrificing Osario to the river? Why couldn't he just be a man and shut up; put up with it, or forget it, or swallow it until it became cancer? There were so many reasons, Seth wanted to scream. She wouldn't understand; she wasn't old enough. She wasn't a *man*. She didn't know what it was like. Neither she nor her mother could imagine clawing from the inside of themselves, desperate to escape the borders that confined them. That's what it was like being a man, he wanted to say: being an animal and having to pretend that he wasn't.

Seth arrived at the long line for Immigration and looked down at the falsified Costa Rican visa Ignacio the ambassador had provided, printed with another man's name. Ignacio had refused to leave any trace of his role in Seth's return. Along with the document, Ignacio handed Seth a matching identification card. Watermark, holographic details, and all. He'd been reborn as Paulo Sebastián Torres-Minor. Age forty-four, one hundred and eighty-four centimeters (that was generous of Ignacio), seventy-two kilos (the generosity continued), eyes brown, hair brown. But the identification number began with a 9, meaning he was born abroad. A sucker punch.

Mean-looking officers faked smiles to white men in Hawaiian shirts, whose translucent skin would glow red by the end of their trip. The officers didn't fake smiles when they motioned for Seth to go through. The agent behind the desk was a woman, so Seth turned on the charm, which she quickly turned off as if his ego were a light switch. Name, she demanded. Seth almost said his real name. She raised her eyebrow at his pause, but he caught himself and recited all the information printed on the visa that would get him past. The agent waved him along without looking. Seth had made it into Costa Rica unsuspected.

After baggage claim and Customs, he made it out of the airport and to the car rental, deciding on a slick, black Audi that reflected the blue mountains standing at attention on either side of the highway leading to San José. He parked in the lot outside of Hotel Del Rey, a glorified brothel for American tourists, and checked in, finally collapsing on the grimy bed. Its cheap sheets scratched his skin like grass. He tossed for a while, watched blades of dusk light slice the dirty walls. Unable to sleep, Seth reached into his backpack and pulled out a delicately folded piece of paper. On it was Osario's mobile number he'd gotten from the ambassador, and outside Seth's room was a pay phone.

BOOK OF THE DAY

1991

Seth and Nieves sat outside the Salvadoran restaurant Haydee's on Cinco de Mayo. Seth's co-workers at the Organization of American States had invited them for happy hour, having assumed that everyone from Latin America celebrated the holiday. Seth would have protested if not for the fact that Andrew and Dana were treating. The four friends lost count of the margarita pitchers and devoured enough chips to fill a corner store. Dusk fell, and Andrew caught a cab after vomiting in the gutter, and Dana wobbled her bike back to wherever she lived. Seth and Nieves leaned back in the metal chairs, grinding salt flakes in their teeth, admiring the first truly perfect evening of the year. Starlings began their nighttime chatter; bats spun like trapeze artists in the air.

Mount Pleasant was a changing neighborhood. Most of the new residents were Salvadorans fleeing the civil war. They were reticent, though cordial to Seth and Nieves. The rest of the neighbors were an even mix of Black and White. Experts attested that this had unwittingly made Mount Pleasant a social experiment: could the different races cohabitate? Could languages and cultures mesh, adapt, and transform into an ecosystem with the power to stave off implosion? For years the answer had been yes, but tonight, at seven on a Sunday, naysayers would be proved right.

A shot rang out, quieting the birds and the restaurant-goers. Its echo from five blocks away: a gun pointed blank to a chest. The gun provided by a Black rookie policewoman, the chest by a Salvadoran man in his thirties. He'd been handcuffed for public drunkenness. The officer, new on the force and untested with something so brutal and delicate as a gun, swore in later testimony that the man had brandished a hunting knife, despite his wrists restrained behind his back.

The flood came almost immediately. From all corners and sidewalks, Salvadorans rushed in the direction of the bang. Seth and Nieves were caught in the current.

"Nieves!" Seth yelled. They'd been separated.

"I'm fine!" Nieves yelled back. "Stand still!"

"What?"

"Do it!"

Seth did as she said, becoming a stone in river rapids, and as Nieves had seen in a movie, the charging mass reacted with the instinct of water, bypassing their still bodies. When the street was quiet again, Seth and Nieves decided to follow and inspect from the safety of the periphery of the scene. The growing crowd converged in a pool at the site, men and women alike brandishing their fists against the surging flow of officers who hit back, firing canisters of tear gas, swinging their batons in home runs.

"¿What happened?" Seth asked an older woman who wore an apron and hollered into the mass.

"¡They shot one of us!"

"¿Who?"

"¡The police! ¿Who else? Again and again, ¡they're always shooting! ¡Everywhere we go, they shoot!"

There in Mount Pleasant, a miniature civil war erupted, the Salvadorans reminded of why they had fled their homes in the first place. A man's chest blown open, the spark for an inferno of memories. The atrocities of the police knew no borders, no hemispheres, or whether one was in the First, Second, or Third World. There was no escaping the unholy union of badge and firearm. Rioters torched cars and storefronts, and Seth and Nieves ran home to hunker down, wheezing from the gas and smoke. Fire invaded Mount Pleasant like daylight. That night, the apartment window became a television set into which Seth and Nieves watched the riot unfold in high definition.

Nieves spent the whole next day cooking, preparing them for possibly weeks of rampage. If she could have painted their studio apartment's walls with lead, she would have.

"Help me board up the windows, Seth," Nieves said, a dozen nails balancing between her clenched teeth.

"I want to go out there," Seth answered. "I want to fight."

"Are you insane? Why the hell would you want to go out there?"

"Because they're killing us, Nieves."

"Killing whom, exactly?"

"Us."

"Be specific."

"Us. Central Americans."

Nieves laughed, which deeply offended Seth. A sudden, momentary rage demanded he hammer the nails in her mouth.

"They're killing Salvadorans, Seth. Not us. We're safe."

"But—"

"But nothing, Seth! You can't always group us in with them. We've never watched anyone get slain in the street! You can't possibly imagine that, and neither can I. Let them fight their own fight. It has nothing to do with us."

"But it's the right thing to do. We have to stand up for them."

"No, Seth. I don't believe you. Not for a second. You just want to light something on fire."

Seth turned away. He focused his attention out the window, to the riot police patrolling the dark streets, enforcing a new curfew. Nieves was right because Seth's fingers itched for a match.

"I've spent my whole life in a golden cage," he said. "We never wanted for anything back home. Maids and marble floors, and all the money in the world. And why? Just because I was lucky enough to be born? What makes me different from all those people down there? The right place at the right time? Destiny? Is this all random, or are some people meant to suffer, while others are fated for lives of luxury? For having grandfathers who own coffee and people?"

Seth had lowered to his knees, resting his chin on the window ledge. "I saw a peon once when I was very, very young. Osario wasn't even born yet. I recognized him from the plantation. He'd brought me back a few times from the fields when I wandered too far. He'd always been nice to me. I don't know how he'd managed to break into the house, but he was rummaging through the silver, stuffing utensils into his pockets, pricking his fingers on the forks. I don't even know if he saw me because he was doing it with such desperation. I just stood there, hypnotized. I didn't consider why he was stealing because I was envious of him. I'd never seen anyone want something so badly before. I wished to feel that—the willingness to risk everything for something that, to me, was insignificant. Like a spoon."

"You lacked other things, Seth."

"Anyone can lack love, Nieves. Like any other resource. You can sleep on a dirt floor and be unloved. In fact it is *because* you are unloved—by society, by the system—that you rest your head on the mud. My parents hated me, but aristocracy didn't. My genes didn't." Seth was staring at the reflection of his blond hair, dirtying with age, his eyes wide and dark blue. "The world was laid out to me in a paved, soft road. How is that fair?"

Nieves fiddled with the nails on the floor, organized them into shapes. "It's not," she said. "Fair. But you're not some revolutionary, Seth. You're not going to take a motorcycle down to Patagonia."

"But I can do *something*."

Nieves splayed out on the hardwood and closed her eyes. "If the city isn't razed to ashes by the end of the week, we can revisit this topic."

Seth's chin fell asleep on the window ledge; his knees cramped.

"What happened to the peon?" Nieves asked finally. "With the silverware?"

"I told my grandfather," Seth said. "And I never saw him again."

After four days, the dust settled. Seth and Nieves left the apartment to wander the morning roads of Mount Pleasant. Rubber-charred smoke ribboned into the air; an abandoned bus slept in the middle of the street; glass, and splintered wood, and pennies littered the sidewalks in a carpet. Seth returned to work, haunted by the smoky quiet of his neighborhood. Each evening that week he returned from downtown to the collective, lingering trauma. Hearts breaking in every apartment, the muffled cries of women who'd left horrors, only to be greeted by new, American ones. Even Nieves, with her even temper, was shaken. The couple discussed quietly over wine what to do. What future awaited them here in Mount Pleasant? If riots broke out again, would they flee, or do what was right and join their Central American siblings in their fight for justice? *Justice* was the word that plagued Seth that silent week.

With Nieves's blessing, Seth decided: he went to his boss at the OAS and asked to be transferred.

"Where?" she asked.

"To the Inter-American Court of Human Rights."

"But that's in Costa Rica."

Seth nodded. He was finally ready to go back.

Costa Rica is home to

the Tárcoles River

It is

the mother of *Costa Rica*

2011

With the careful obsession of a cartographer, Seth spent the week before his reunion with Osario exploring the one-hundred-and-eleven-kilometer serpentine basin of the Tárcoles River. The slick black Audi shone in the April sun like tar. His dark aviator sunglasses never left his face, even if it was cloudy and began to rain. He had no intention of being recognized, especially by those who still fought the bitter aftertaste of gasoline when downing a cup of water. Some days Seth wore a full pin-striped suit; other days, cargo shorts and a guayabera. He was either embarrassingly conspicuous or expertly inconspicuous, depending on the passersby. But in every town the populace came to the same consensus: Seth was most likely a secret agent on a much-needed vacation. James Bond with a Groupon.

Sitting on the hood of the expensive rental, the white bread of a ham sandwich stuck to the roof of his mouth, Seth waited for hours at different entrances to the river. While it was beautiful, and while he enjoyed the knotted mangroves and the pearl-feathered egrets, his mission was to scope out a perfect spot, both open and private, away from whatever hamlet of nosy residents. Through a dense thicket, perhaps, down to a wide shore undisturbed by foot traffic or fishing boats. Local butchers questioned why a man would purchase so many raw chicken bits, but inflation cut their curiosity short, because Seth paid with crisp dollars. Seth tossed those chicken parts to the placid water to see how many snouts and pairs of eyes peeked out from the river's surface. He eventually stumbled upon a place that checked all boxes—secluded, spacious, and teeming with crocodiles that held their maws agape for livers and drumsticks.

Deep below layers of viscous mud and stubborn oil, Osario's footsteps still followed Seth's to the bank. Still stopped a safe enough distance from the water, and still turned to run after witnessing what their father had been capable of. Of which Seth, holding a chicken carcass like a christened child, was finally capable.

On the other side of the country, a community held a funeral for a crocodile. In Siquirres, just kilometers from the Atlantic Ocean, dozens of local mourners paraded the taxidermy creature through the streets in a cart decorated with red ginger flowers. Women dabbed their eyes with tissues or their too-short shirtsleeves. Children marveled at the scales, as if they'd been buffed by a well-paid janitor. A fisherman—the Costa Rican Tarzan they called him—balanced next to the animal that had been his best friend for twenty years. He and his reptile companion had brought fame to this town. From all corners of the globe, nonbelievers and biological enthusiasts alike traveled to witness a simple man swim with a gigantic crocodile, turn it over, rub its belly like a dog, and kiss its snout without being devoured.

The relationship had begun with the secrecy of a love affair. After discovering the almost-slain animal on a riverbank, gunshot from a cattle farmer, the fisherman brought it home, smuggled the beast under his wife's nose. Nursing it back to health with affection and meat, the man learned ancient secrets the crocodile whispered through its teeth before falling asleep in each other's arms. Its strength returned, and the fisherman hid it in a nearby pond to steal midnight dates like two paramours in a Jacuzzi. His wife would ask why he was always drenched when he arrived home for dinner; she asked if there was another. An Olympic swimmer, or a mermaid. But he guarded his dalliance fiercely, savored the warm touch of cold scales.

It was inevitable that the fisherman's secret got out, but instead of committing him, the town dug a pool, fenced it in, and brought the man and the crocodile to perform their adoration for each other for all to see. The community took pride in the fact that here, in a pueblo sandwiched between two rivers and the expansive wilderness beyond, a cardinal rule of nature had been broken: predator and prey could coexist with the playful affection of kin.

Upon its recent death of natural causes, a sacred shrine was erected to the beast. In supple clouds of incense, neighbors grieved into a microphone, secured their palms to their scalps, sang popular ballads, and celebrated this unlikely, unique union of humanity and nature. The man in his loincloth—the Costa Rican Tarzan, they called him—wiped his teary eyes of smoke and grief, and glued his face to the crocodile's.

I'll never forget you.

BOOK OF THE NIGHT

1995

Seth checked into his less-than-desirable lodgings in downtown Port of Limón. His boss had been put up at a resort by the beach for the next two nights, while the company had booked Seth into a dingy hotel in the center of town, in the only room without hot water. Despite the dilapidation, the place was clean—the sink, the toilet, the sad kitchenette, all bleached and smooth as an egg. The sheets were stiff and scratchy from the sun, but if bunched up right, Seth was comfortable enough to nap. He did so for a short while before the company driver knocked three times in quick succession to transport him to the oil refinery ten kilometers away.

After witnessing the riot of Salvadorans in D.C., Seth had been transferred to the Inter-American Court of Human Rights as he'd asked. Part of him was happy to be back home in Costa Rica, and the morality satisfied him at first; gave him just enough of a high for a couple of years to stomach lowly administrative duties, petty procurement negotiations, and embarrassing development opportunities at galas. But his mission went stale as quickly as it takes coffee to cool on a countertop. With his new position's dismal pay, its frantic schedule, and the organization's bureaucratic obstacles, Seth quickly considered a career change. At a crowded bar one night, he eavesdropped on an older man complaining over the loud music to his lover—desperate for a protégé so he could finally retire. The man was the senior vice director of RECOPE, Costa Rica's national oil refinery.

Seth strolled over and introduced himself, and the vice director complimented Seth's tie and his ability to down whisky without wincing. It didn't take long for Seth to be offered the job, and after hearing the salary spill out of the senior vice director's mouth, Seth accepted on the spot, even if he knew nothing of oil production. He felt he was the type of person who could wing it.

It took only two years at RECOPE for Seth to steadily climb his way to the vice director position. Originally created by the Costa Rican government to combat the sweeping influence of the Seven Sisters—those powerful maidens of international petroleum production—the nationalized refinery proved lucrative and now extended from the Caribbean coast of Limón all the way to Puntarenas in the west, pipelines constellating silos that housed millions of barrels of oil. Initially Seth imagined he'd be overseeing rigs, watching black geysers shoot from the earth with the force of a rocket, but the job was painfully bureaucratic. A sluggish stamping of mountainous paper stacks and boring tours of refinery sites.

The tour today in Limón was routine. It began at the port itself, where a gargantuan tanker deposited its contents into a line of cylindrical trucks like a cafeteria lady serves impatient inmates. Seth's mind wandered from the tour to the turquoise ocean that fused to the sky on the horizon. He wished to walk to the end of the breakwater, taste the mist from crashing waves, but the guide hurried them along into cars to the refinery itself. There, a woman of above-average height who had worked for RECOPE for ten years gave the tour. She'd become the station manager after a decade of dedication, and Seth could tell from a furious glance that she knew he'd fallen into this job. But she did end up complimenting his tie. And if she would have seen him down a whisky without wincing, she'd have complimented him on that too.

The tour dragged on until dusk. Seth's boss was chauffeured to his resort in a limousine, while Seth was hauled back to the hotel in an '82 Honda Civic. Seth couldn't help but covet his boss's position—the harems it attracted, the convertibles it procured. Silver cars on silver platters. Losing himself didn't seem all that bad, especially cramped in the back of this clunky, creaking Civic. If he was promoted to *senior* vice director, Seth *could* live the life his grandfather had promised on their family mansion. Politics and power. Trying to roll down the broken window, Seth wondered what type of spiritual bartering it would take to achieve what Otilio had always wanted for him. What he secretly wanted for himself.

The driver would return tomorrow afternoon to take Seth back to San José. Trapped in his hotel room, Seth wondered what the hell he would do for the next eighteen hours here. Gas fumes had stitched themselves into his suit jacket, so he shed it, dunked it into the tub's freezing water to soak, and made himself instant coffee in a Styrofoam cup. The hotel's facade faced a public square, and beyond the room's drawn curtains, zanates skirted the vibrant grass in hoards, soaring away at passersby, landing again to gossip and peck at the dirt. One or two families barbecued in the golden hour, thick smoke reaching up to the tree line. A Malinche's blood orange flowers bloomed next to a Corteza's fine yellow ones—la Chingada and her conquistador, forever caught in an arboreal dance, accompanied by gay calypso blasting from portable stereos. Seth lay exhausted, drifted into slumber, lulled by the joyous ruckus outside. The noise and notes reminded him of Ola, her swaying hips and swift feet he balanced on as a child, learning to dance her people's dances. As his eyes fluttered to sleep, so did his hips in a dream.

Someone had set the alarm clock for midnight. Seth swung his fists and kicked at some sudden figure in the dark. He didn't know where he was, or why, or how he had even gotten there. When the adrenaline passed, and frustration set in, Seth sat upright on the bed, put his feet to the ground, grabbed a pillow, and screamed into it. He would never fall back asleep now. Not with his heart so far up in his throat.

The streetlamp lights beckoned Seth to the still-open window, where he stared out into the night. The one or two barbecuing families were long gone, had left just their garbage strewn on the lawn. Humidity and quiet loitered on street corners. Seth decided to take his chances and take a lap around the park. The terror of walking alone might clear his mind. He reasoned that another round of adrenaline would exhaust him right back to sleep.

Despite this being the center of town, most of the buildings and businesses sat abandoned. Some storefronts wore cracks from the earthquake four years ago, windows sporting boards like cheap sunglasses. At the end of the square, instead of about-facing, Seth turned left, toward another park, where trees grew tall and muscular. As he drew closer, Seth heard soft moaning and clapping, all in tandem like a muffled, holy chorus. He saw a handsome Black man leaning against a tree, sucking a cigarette. He wore flip-flops, baggy shorts, and a tight-fitting tank top that revealed a body designed by an artist. The man gestured with a grin and led Seth to where the streetlights couldn't penetrate. The holy chorus grew louder the deeper they ventured, and in a small, circular clearing, the man unbuttoned and pulled down his shorts to his knees. He smiled, waiting. As patient as a priest anticipating confession. And like a repentant sinner, Seth dropped to his knees and prayed to the man, until it was all finished, and the man kissed the semen from Seth's lips and left. Seth stayed, kneeling there alone in the sweaty dark, where some entombed wish had been dug up, cleared of dirt and shame, and enshrined.

The next morning, Seth ate breakfast at a café next to the hotel. He'd spent all morning with the bleached, berry-bitter taste still in his mouth. It ate into the lining of his cheeks, coated his gums in dew. He was almost disappointed the coffee and acidic pineapple would wash it away, but luckily, memory is better at savoring than the tongue. He looked at his leather watch. The chauffeur would be there in four hours to pick him up. San José was a drab option when compared with Limón. He wished to stay here, take a week off and explore the beaches and slice coconuts open with iron. But he was reminded of his and Nieves's second wedding anniversary on Friday. Sometimes he hated loving his wife. It was a bothersome, troublesome, tedious thing to love another. A decade of any relationship weighed on the soul: three years past the itch that tortured like a mosquito bite or a grandmother's knit sweater. It was because cells replaced themselves every seven years, a supermarket cashier had told him once. He'd first slept with Nieves a pancreas ago, fallen in love with her three pairs of lungs back. How many rounds of kidneys did their relationship have in them? How many hearts could he present her and still mean it?

With this cellular iteration of himself, he had no choice but to love her, and when all was said and done, Seth appreciated the chance. Nieves was still a spectacular person to be in love with. So he decided to go to the kilometers-away souvenir market and buy her a gift, and arrived after a humid, heavy trek, with stalactite-long sweat stains from his armpits. Behind the souvenir stands, Black women spoke Mekatelyu to each other, the Queen's English to American tourists, and Spanish to him. Their heads were wrapped in bright rainbow cloth, and the older women's earlobes drooped from gold earrings. Rasta men handled their stands with cool confidence, selling Jamaican flags and beanies to amateur gringo surfers. Seth spent longer than he should have exploring the market for a perfect gift for Nieves. He bought an item from every stand—a tiger's eye bracelet, a woven bag embroidered with her name, a glass shark figurine, a granite cutting board, a kerosene lantern decorated with ceramic frogs, and a fourteen-carat gold ring Seth suspected was fake. At the end of the bazaar, Seth planned to return half of the items and head back to the hotel, but out of the corner of his eye he noticed what he thought was Ola, carrying a skimp grocery bag toward a side street. Seth nearly dropped all the trinkets. It *was* Ola he had just seen. He ran to follow her.

Ola ambled trance-like, a robotic sashay, the bags in her hands not swinging, even though they should have been. Seth followed with a fifty-meter gap between them, periodically waiting behind objects—street signs, decrepit cars, opened garage gates—then jumping out in a sprint to catch up, which confused everyone he skirted past. Never before had they seen a man possessed by a lily-hopping duppy. He tailed her until he could hear the ocean. Close enough that if he'd stand still, he could count the waves. At the final corner, Seth turned, walked into a parade of dancers surrounding a metal stage, where a man dressed in a yellow Nigerian agbada sang. His sleeves billowed as he swayed, holding a microphone too close to his mouth, and belted a calypso Seth immediately recognized.

The choreography to "Zancudo con dengue" mimicked a bug's wings and vibrating body. The dancers twirled their arms in O's, peppered in some salsa steps, spun, and traded places with each other. Seth crossed the crowd to the white apartment building Ola had just entered, and hiked to the third floor, to the unit farthest back, whose door had been left ajar. Seth hesitated, and for a moment his foot couldn't cross the threshold, but when he did, he was stunned by the apartment's lush decor. From every corner grew palms, monsteras, birds of paradise, and snake plants. Wind chimes dripped from the ceilings, and in the tepid breeze their sound almost overpowered the music playing from the street.

Ola sat in an elaborate peacock chair, overlooking a realm that was undeniably hers, and Seth merely a subject approaching her throne for counsel.

"Ola," he whispered.

"Seth."

"You're here."

"I'm here."

"¿Where did you go?"

"Here, child. ¿Where else?" Ola was smiling now. "My lord, it is good to see you."

"I thought I'd never see you again."

"You never came looking for me." Ola grinned. Her playfulness activated a stabbing nostalgia in Seth, and he began to cry. "Oh my," she said. "I'm sorry, child."

"No, no, it's not you, I just . . . I've missed you so much."

"And I, you, Seth. Sit, please. Sit."

"¿Is this your home?"

"It used to be. I was raised on this land, but it was once a shack. It seems they developed it at some point."

"¿Was it painful?"

"¿Coming back to where I was born?"

"No, Ola. Leaving us."

"Unbelievably so, Seth. I don't think anything else has torn my soul asunder like that. But I felt I would die. I felt your parents would have killed me, and I couldn't die there. Not in that house."

"¿Did you think about us?"

"Every day."

"¿Did you ever think of coming back for us?"

"I want to say yes, but . . . no, Seth. I couldn't. You're older now, so you know I couldn't."

"I guess I must look older to you. You haven't aged at all."

"¿Is that right? Every woman wants to hear that."

"I'm serious. You're glowing."

"It's the plants. Their oxygen."

"I thought you'd died."

"Well . . . I left and trekked through that forest. Warm as a womb, the leaves so soft and kind. One doesn't die in a forest, Seth. If anything, you're reborn. Trees and vines welcome you back because they were once you and you them. From there I returned here, found this apartment. You can see the ocean from my balcony. Go on and look. My brothers and I swam in that very water. We raced on the sand and buried each other, skipped on the waves, and ate the foam like cotton candy. You can see one of them at dark, floating. I found him again. We've been reunited, so I float with him too. And there are so many others floating with him whom I don't even recognize. Maybe that's what death is."

"¿What?"

"Reuniting. When someone dies, they reunite with their loved ones. But those loved ones have already reunited with their own loved ones, ¿right? ¿So then do you just reunite with every single loved one of the ones you loved? Death is an infinite reuniting."

"I guess we'll know when we get there."

"That's true. Say, ¿don't you have to be somewhere?"

"Yes, you're right. ¿How did you know?"

"I always knew things I wasn't supposed to."

"I could never hide anything from you."

"Never. No one could."

"Well."

"Go, child, you'll be late."

Seth sat up from the sofa and motioned to embrace Ola, but she smiled in a way that stopped him from approaching. As if their gazes were sufficient affection. That, yes, she loved him, but touch, no matter how kind, would only deal pain to each other. Seth understood and kissed the air, which Ola returned. He left, descended the staircase, brushed his hands on the warm, whitewashed walls, weaved through the dancing crowd, and journeyed those humid kilometers back to the hotel, where the driver had been waiting, surprisingly patient, because Seth had left a good impression on him.

Ola walked out to her balcony and looked out at the horizon's smooth, latitudinal stage. Her grief dampened by the surf, and the wind, and the cars' frustrated honks at the impromptu street parade. Once night came, she'd revisit Michael. From the shore, because he would be too far out at sea to touch. She rested her bony arms on the concrete railing and exhaled.

Costa Rica is home to

American

tourists
Costa Rica's

an easy meal

for

them

The

aggressiveness of the American *eclipses that of all other nations*

2011

The night before Seth was to meet Osario at a lonely bar on the outskirts of Escazú, he spent a few hours sulking at Hotel Del Rey's cantina/casino. He wondered if there was an inn more infamous—the Overlook Hotel in *The Shining*, maybe, or the thundering hill of the Bates Motel—any place that raised an eyebrow as quickly, or caused a grin to unzip across a gringo's face. He was determined to drink as much as he could tonight to prepare his brain and liver for tomorrow, coating his arteries with alcohol, as if it were possible to build up an immunity. He wanted to prevent himself from getting too drunk in front of his younger brother. Seth would still have to drive the rental to the river, still have to remember every step in his ingenious scheme. He would need a clear head, so tonight he was building up a tolerance.

Girls with skirts shorter than his patience crowded the blackjack and roulette tables. They solicited sex from all the fat, pasty American bachelors and the more handsome ones cheating on their wives. Sunburn was as effective as catnip, so Seth had fewer girls float over to him. They expected colones to line his pockets, not dollars. They were smart about exchange rates. Well-versed in economics, accounting, international relations, and some (if asked) could give university-level seminars on existentialism.

One girl, intoxicated but speaking perfect English, swayed like seaweed in front of a gringo who balanced a pocket-size Nikon digital camera on his knee—breaking the rule of *No Recording*—fixed on her as she tried her best not to fall over in her seat. The American seemed to be interviewing her. Some sick video project. Seth, three meters away, couldn't tell what the girl was on. She slurred slightly. The scene disgusted him: this American humiliating her, baiting her with dollars, exploiting her. What was she supposed to do? The chance at money is better than no chance at all. Seth decided to intervene. With the flash of a wad of cash, he lured her away from the American, who smiled, as if thinking, *Yes, I got it. I got the shot.*

"Some of us are born to suffer," she said as Seth pulled her hard by the arm, which in her state didn't seem to bother her in the slightest.

"Up to my room," Seth said.

"¿How much?"

"One hundred dollars."

"Let's go."

"¿What's your name?" Seth asked the girl as he corralled her into his room.

"Sandía," she said.

"¿Like the fruit?"

She nodded her head. It looked so heavy it might snap off her neck.

"Well, I'm sure you're very sweet."

Sandía tried to kiss Seth when he sat on the bed next to her. Her mouth stunk of cherry, with an offensive, medicinal undernote. *Cough syrup. She's drunk on cough syrup.* Seth pushed her aside respectfully, and she toppled backward onto the hard mattress.

"I can't seem to get it right," Sandía said, the indecisiveness of sleep garbling her syllables. "I think sometimes, ¿was I really born for this type of life? I had a scholarship, you know. To the university. I wore nice dresses, down to my knees so the wind couldn't even pass through. I was just a good girl who met a bad guy. He's dead now, but I can't shake him. He worked here, so I started working here. *She works hard for her money . . .* ¿you remember that tune? Of course you do. It's true—I work hard. I'm as dedicated as a maid or an engineer. Women like me put their whole selves into their jobs. Because it's a job, you know. The world's oldest profession. It should be held in better esteem, in my humble opinion. We should have an executive lunch option and get Christmas bonuses. We put in more work than lawyers and garbagemen combined, and eat more shit and shame too. I could have been a lawyer. I could have spoken English like Hillary Clinton and argued like her husband on the stand. *I did not have sexual relations with* ... Yeah right. Men are always guilty, because power makes you all guilty. But a woman doesn't get into my profession for power. There's no ladder I'm climbing, no country I'm bombing to shatter any ceiling. I work hard, and I go home to my apartment that doesn't fit, and kick off my shoes that don't fit, and watch the travel channel. I want to travel. I want a life that takes me anywhere. I want to fly in a plane. No, I *want* a plane. But once you get that amount of money you lose yourself. No matter how much shit I have to eat, I'll never lose myself. Not even enough to kill my own brother."

"¿What did you say?" Seth said, whipping his head to her prostrate body. But Sandía was already asleep, turned over onto her stomach, snoring. "Jesus Christ," he muttered, rubbing his index and thumb to his forehead.

"I can't tell if you know exactly what you're talking about or if you're full of shit," Seth chuckled to Sandía's unconscious body. "*You'll never lose yourself.* Of course you will," he said to the nightstand, the Bible stashed in its drawer. "Happens to all of us. Even to me. From rich kid, to humanist, to oilman. You lose yourself or you find out what you were all along; you evolve or you return to what was fated for you. I wanted to help people like you. I guess I *did* help you tonight, but I used to want to do it systemically, not randomly in a dump like this. But you don't get anywhere in human rights. You starve just like the people you're trying to help.

"Then oil found me." Seth fought against exhaustion or shame bowing his chin to his chest. "And I found it. Chugged petroleum gladly, bathed in it. It greased everyone's palms and everyone's wallets, and I got to where I was destined to go. '¿Was I really born for this type of life?' you asked. Yes, little Sandía, you were. And I was born for mine. Like my grandfather before me: Otilio the coffee baron, Seth the oilman. Power will never corrupt *you*, that much is true, kid. Power launches people like me alone into the wilderness, and if you come back, you come back stronger. What one has paid for that power is always different. But just like you said, you work hard for your money."

Sandía let out a charming grunt. Then a snore, a lip smack, and a tender whimper. Seth's monologue dissipated from the room, and he considered calling Nieves. Not to confess this encounter, but to receive her blessing. She would celebrate his empathy for saving such a philosophical girl. If Nieves were here in Hotel Del Rey, she'd have done the same thing. *Saving someone.* Seth wished to cancel out tomorrow's sin with a good deed tonight. Sandía snored again. Seth would sleep on the floor to allow this girl to have a bed all to herself for a change. He pitied her. He pitied himself. He'd promised her one hundred, but pulled out two bills from his wallet. Perhaps that would allow her to take the week off. She could hitch a ride with a cousin to the beach, take a break from this cathouse and its clientele. Maybe she'd find a job there as a waitress or a boutique manager. As Seth drifted into sleep, he fantasized that this money would change her life, save her from this fate. But there was nothing that could save him from *his* fate. No amount of cash or kindness would persuade Seth to stop.

VALLEY OF THE KINGS

1998

The gated community of Villa Real was as strong as a magnet: its luxury either drew homebuyers in an inexplicable, hypnotic pull or violently repulsed anyone who couldn't afford it. There are those with ambition who crave decadence, and others who realize its hollowness and condemn it. This mountainside neighborhood grew mansions, studding the protected forest like overwhelming boulders. Villa Real overlooked the Central Valley, and at night, one could see San José's concave belly sparkle with lights. Prehistoric trees grew considerately outside properties or in between them, dividing these decadent abodes for privacy. The rich don't like others to know what they're up to. Elegant dinner parties, an orgy here or there, or human sacrifices, because how else could one amass so much money to buy multimillion-dollar properties? There in Villa Real lived presidents, tycoons, vacationing billionaires, wealthy heirs, corrupt government officials, and, more recently, Seth and Nieves.

Osario and Isa drove up from the dark, winding roads to the gates of Villa Real. There, two AR-15-armed guards sized up the couple's beat-up sedan and checked the visitors' list. The gated-community members called the guards Thing 1 and Thing 2, Dumb and Dumber, and, if Tuesday's guard was on watch: Dumbest.

"I'm Osario Oreamundo."

"You're Mr. Seth's relative," said the guard, chewing gum. He snapped it in his mouth like fingers.

"His brother."

"I didn't know he had a brother," said the second guard, lowering his gun.

"Sir, please just let us go through," Isa interrupted.

"Whatever," said both guards, and waved them along.

Two minutes up a perfectly paved road—something neither Osario nor Isa had ever experienced—the asphalt so smooth they were floating. Osario said that when they left Seth's house, he could fly them down. After an endless series of S's, they arrived at a spectacular gate not unlike the intricate iron bars of their own childhood home. Osario pressed a buzzer; it opened. They had to walk up the driveway, because three cars blocked their path to the doors. Osario and Isa wondered to each other if there were other guests invited, but it turned out that the Porsche, BMW, and Saab were all Seth's.

Nieves and Isa hugged in the mansion's foyer. They rocked each other in a giddy dance, from one shared foot to the other, skirting their heels on the lapis lazuli tiles, the floor like staring into one of those satellite images of the universe. All colors in waves and smoke. Nieves and Isa saw each other once a week, so they could finish each other's sentences and bickered as they had when they were girls. Seth and Nieves had bought the mansion six months ago, and this was the first time Isa had stepped foot in it, and when Seth entered, it was the first time either Osario or Isa had seen him since Christmas of 1985.

The four all noticed the startling differences between the brothers. Whereas Osario had decided to wear a sky-blue, ratty linen button-down, Seth wore a formal suit, his own shirt adorned with platinum cuff links, with a skinny tie comfortably around his collar. Osario's khakis faded in the white light from the crystal chandelier, while the black fabric from Seth's dress pants devoured it like antimatter. Osario wore flip-flops, hadn't even bothered to shave the tops of his toes. Seth stood firm in Ferragamos. What followed was a silence as uncomfortable as all of them had imagined. Both the sisters had discussed contingency plans beforehand—offer cocktails, compliment architecture, shout nostalgia—but all their preparations were washed away in the aching, humiliating quiet.

"Brother," Seth said.

"Brother," Osario replied.

"Thirteen years."

"An unlucky number."

"There's no such thing as luck or unluck. Just us."

"And our wives." Osario smiled. Slowly, warmth regained its footing in the room.

"¿Are we allowed to hug?"

"¿Are men allowed to hug?"

"¿Ladies?"

Nieves and Isa both nodded gravely as if Seth and Osario were bomb technicians tasked with defusing the explosives in each other's chests. A wrong comment, boom. Insults, wisecracks, and inappropriate memories lay tangled in a rainbow of wires, and the sisters couldn't help but shallow their breathing and force back the sweat on their foreheads. The brothers finally embraced, Seth more firmly than Osario as Osario's arms went suddenly limp right past Seth's rib cage. Tension wished with all its heart to return with a swift knock, but Nieves invited them all to the patio, where they could inhale the glorious night air of the mountainside.

After many drinks, Seth decided to give Isa a tour of the mansion. Osario and Nieves lay on comfortable lawn chairs, admiring the sky. "This reminds me of Ram Luna," Osario said, gulping down his second whisky. Neat, straight.

"Seth took us there last year for our anniversary," Nieves said. Osario offered her a cigarette. She accepted. She offered him another whisky. He declined, wanted to wait until dinner.

"It's kind of corny, that place," Osario said.

"It is, ¿isn't it?" Nieves admitted. She drank gin with graceful sips.

"But that view is spectacular. Just like the view you have right here. Just like the view—"

"On the Ferris wheel that time."

"Yes, exactly. I can't believe you remember."

"¿Who could forget that night? The lights, the music and noise, and the stink of those bulls. Magic."

"The first and last night of magic," Osario whispered. Nieves saw him regress, back into that shy, faux-arrogant boy who had looked back at his big brother on an amusement park ride, knowing deep down in his heart that Seth would leave him, abandon him in a room, in a house, in a country that at any moment could and wanted to tear him apart. "¿But who wants to speak of the past?" Osario said. "It seems like all of us are looking toward the future."

Seth led Isa from room to room of the mansion, and she asked him to describe every detail in an anxiety to keep the brothers separate for as long as possible. The moment Osario barely returned Seth's hug, she knew it had all been a mistake. She knew Osario better than anyone else. She'd reunited with him three years ago. A fledgling journalism school grad, she was covering a story in a rainforest, grotesque because of the insects. Isa hated being in places where she felt outnumbered. She'd gone about the camp interviewing volunteers who stared down bulldozers and men with axes. She asked around for their leader, and they pointed her to a remarkably sturdy tent. Inside, Osario briefed the top brass of volunteers for the coming battle. His feathered hair fell to his shoulders, black and shiny. Isa recognized him despite his scraggly beard and chapped lips. A handsome boy's eyes never change, especially those of the one whom she'd fallen in love with as a child. Isa donned a professional demeanor, unsure if Osario remembered her. But of course he did—he returned the professionalism until all his comrades and her cameraman left the tent. Then he plopped a stick of gum into one cheek, approached her in silence, and kissed her as she had kissed him all those years ago. It was a chemical reaction of returning, an explosive excitement of two atoms locking into place, creating a new element. The spark immediately intoxicated her, and Isa fainted. When she awoke, Osario was laughing, and she, too, laughed at how ridiculous and cliché it was to faint after kissing a man. But he kissed her again and gripped her temples so as to keep her awake this time. They became inseparable after that. Osario became her muse: a large percentage of her news stories covered him, creating his celebrity. Her reports painted him as humble, brave, altruistic, and unwavering in his dedication. A man hellbent on saving the world. Subconsciously, she was setting him up for his eventual political career, which had taken off last year as he'd entered the Ministry of the Environment and immediately took the helm of projects targeting deforestation. In just a few years, this path would put Osario and Seth at odds with each other on the political stage, because Seth was just a matter of time away from becoming director of RECOPE, with its petroleum interests and murky relationship with eco-sustainability, while Osario's ascension to Minister of the Environment was written in stone. They would eventually meet on the battlefield, one that scores of brothers throughout history knew well: blood-saturated, with limbs scattered in the dirt like seedlings. A place where nothing could grow, where nothing would ever grow. A wasteland of taking the sanctity of what brothers have. What they're always willing to give up to best the other.

"I'll show you the master bedroom," Seth said. "It's the final leg of the tour."

Isa thought they'd just entered a bungalow in the African savannah. The rest of the mansion was a bastardized mix of Mediterranean and Tudor—one would think the architect had been drunk, or a genius ahead of his time. But the bedroom was its own creation—the canopy bed, mosquito netting, bamboo blinds, earth-toned paints, and wicker furniture transported Isa. The cawing underbrush outside the window only added to the illusion, which disoriented her long enough for Seth to lay her down on the bed and mount her.

"You've become beautiful," he said. "I see you on the television."

"Seth, ¿what are you doing? Get off of me."

"I saw the way you looked at me downstairs. It's all right, they're outside chatting, and they'll have no idea."

Isa pushed against Seth's pecs with her ten fingernails, digging a tattoo that Nieves might find later. "I was only noticing how shamelessly you were holding your brother as if nothing happened."

Seth stepped back, leaving the barrier of mosquito netting between them.

"¿And what? ¿You want to betray your little brother again? ¿With me?"

Isa was using her journalist voice, enunciating every syllable as if reading a teleprompter written by someone with intimate knowledge of the story. It was a biting accusation, delivered so mechanically Seth could never mistake its meaning. There was no passion to mince her words: she'd called him a bastard, and there was no rebuttal.

Seth's eyes gleamed in the lamplight. He recomposed himself. "Well, Isa. ¿Shall we go down to dinner? Nieves slaved over a hot stove all day for you both."

Each brother held out his wife's seat at the dining room table. Chivalry, the first move in battle. Seth kissed Nieves's cheek with a slight glance toward Isa. Nieves had displayed a feast before the guests—so much food that the four barely had room for their plates or wineglasses.

"¿Shall I go through the menu?"

"Please," Osario said.

"Yes," Isa echoed. "Please do, sister."

"Well, we have traditional coconut rice and beans from Limón, chicken cordon bleu, roasted broccoli with garlic and lemon zest, bacon-wrapped scallops, a strawberry-arugula salad with a balsamic reduction, grilled octopus drizzled with California olive oil, and a chocolate flan for dessert."

"My God," Isa said.

"No wonder you don't have *four* cars," Osario chuckled. "You must have spent a fortune on this dinner."

Nieves laughed, but Seth did not.

"Nieves is going to open a restaurant," Seth said coolly, biting into one of the scallops with his front teeth. "My job gave me a bonus, and I decided to invest in a place in Escazú."

"¡Seth! ¡It was supposed to be a surprise!" Nieves huffed.

"There is indeed money in oil," Osario murmured.

"¿What was that?" Seth said.

"Well, this is the tasting menu." Nieves cut off her husband. She had the speed of an American housewife, able to defuse awkwardness with tedious conversation. "It's going to be spectacular, completely exclusive. All these ingredients are organic and sourced, grown, and raised right here in Costa Rica. ¿Can't you taste how fresh everything is?"

"Yes," Osario admitted. "It's still fresh."

"You'll have to do a news report on it, little sister," Nieves said, fiddling with arugula stuck in her teeth.

"Yes, I must. ¿What's the name going to be?"

"It won't have one," Nieves answered proudly.

"¿What do you mean?" Isa asked, almost laughing at her sister.

"It's going to be so exclusive it won't need a name. You won't be able to find it unless you're a VIP," Seth said.

"So, then, ¿wouldn't a news story defeat the purpose?" Osario said, unintentionally sarcastic.

"Huh . . . maybe you're right."

Tension nestled in its own seat at the dinner table. Made conversation with itself in the pockets of quiet, complimented the food, stole bites from everyone's plates. The sisters had been unwittingly roped into the brothers' war, and whereas before they had been an unshakable pair, next to their lovers, their camaraderie was shaken.

"You smelled of oranges when you walked in," Nieves said to Osario.

"I noticed it too," Seth added. "It reminded me of the orange oil Mother used to drop into her lotion."

"That's the first time I've heard you speak of Mother," Osario said, as nonchalantly as if accusing someone of insider trading. "You haven't asked how our parents are."

"I haven't been invited to a funeral yet, so I know they're still alive. That's all there is to know, really."

"I suppose you're right, Seth. No, they're not dead."

"Yet."

"Yet."

"The oranges," Nieves reintroduced the topic. "Delicious. One of my favorite notes. Perhaps I'll add a dish that features it to my menu."

"I just got back from Guanacaste this morning. Me and some professors from Princeton were conducting an experiment," Osario said.

"¿An orange experiment?" Seth asked.

"Yes. We convinced Del Oro to donate peels and pulp left over from their juice production so that we could carpet the earth where there was once a teeming forest."

"I like that juice. We have a carton in the fridge. ¿And what will your experiment prove?" Nieves asked.

"Our hypothesis is that the compost will feed the ground enough nutrients for a new forest to grow. You know, since it was murdered."

"¿A forest can be murdered?" Seth smirked.

"Indeed, it can. RECOPE has proved itself to be this country's butcher of trees."

"¿Pardon?"

"You heard me. That forest died because your company ripped it up so that you could bury a pipeline right under it. You all somehow convinced the ministry that the land beneath forests isn't technically protected, so you ripped out roots that were older than we are and laid metal that pumps petroleum underneath."

"That petroleum quenches the thirst of our country," Seth said. "¿Or did you forget that? This world runs on oil whether you like it or not."

"Necessity is always the excuse for people like you."

"¿People like me?"

"Yes. Like you. Look around at this mansion, your three cars, this feast. The only necessity is the insatiability of your wallet. I can't even imagine what kinds of kickbacks you're getting."

"Ah ha . . ." Seth said. "That's what this is really about."

Seth had been presented his first opportunity to counterattack.

"¿You want to talk about kickbacks, little brother? They're coming from your bosses."

"¿What did you say?"

"You heard me. ¿You think the little law they passed was for Mother Earth?"

Seth spoke of the Forest Act of '96. A trailblazing idea on paper: the government could subsidize income for farmers who preserved the forests on their property—instead of felling trees to make room for grazing cattle or coffee bushes, these farmers received monthly benefits for the government repatriation of their land.

"No, little brother. That law's for the government to take *away* rights to the land. I didn't think you'd turn into such a romantic. The act only protects what's above the ground, not below. Look, the truth is, it was too expensive for us to pay off those farmers to dig beneath their properties. So once your little ministry got the rights to that land, all we had to do was name a price. The ministry's a cheap whore compared with those hicks and their lawyers."

Osario looked to Isa for backup, but her head hung low. Isa had a colleague investigating the exact story Seth had just outlined. She'd gotten him fired before he could reveal the scandal, determined to keep her husband on track to becoming minister. Isa had known the truth, kept it from Osario like a prognosis. But now it was out in the open, and she couldn't bear to witness Osario's idealism being stripped away by the person he had once loved most.

Seth didn't know why and would never know why he decided to humiliate his brother. Perhaps Seth had seen through Osario's selflessness as egotism. Perhaps their past shoved its way back into him: Osario had stolen his birthday, had always made his life miserable—perhaps Seth divined that he would do so again. Osario had always been the favorite. But now Osario was no longer king of the universe. Now Seth was king. Seth had riches and adoration from those around him. And like a king, Seth was capable of brutality.

Predisposed to it. And there is no one to whom a king is more callous than the one who ruled before him.

Osario and Isa left without parting words or gestures. Osario drove them down the perfectly paved S's of Villa Real, so distraught and embarrassed he didn't notice the beat-up sedan was flying. Isa hadn't had the chance to announce she and Osario were to be married in three months. She had hoped the brothers could mend their relationship so that Osario could've had the best man he'd always wanted. In fact, that's why they had waited so long to finalize the wedding. And Isa would be out a maid of honor. The schism between the couples had yawned into a chasm. The brothers would not meet again until two years later, when the Ministry of the Environment would be suing RECOPE for a catastrophic oil spill, and Osario would look news cameras straight in the eye and proclaim Seth guilty. In front of their country, and for all the world to see.

Costa Rica is home to *sin*

and

bone

night

moon

unfortunate

death

and

nations

2011

It was a night of getting rid of enemies. On the television above the bar in a lonely cantina close to Escazú, Barack Obama addressed his own nation: America's greatest nemesis was finally dead. Osama bin Laden had faced a firing squad on his compound, ambushed by bullets faster than the sound of buildings falling. After his body was punched full of holes like a bus ticket, he was wrapped and tied in cloth and thrown out into the ocean. A *sea burial*, they called it. No one knew that a mummy could be buried in water. The confused bar-goers imagined American troopers standing with their feet on the waves with shovels, digging and tossing water and foam over their heads. Seth and Osario overheard the philosophical bar maiden say, *If the body is made of ashes and dust, ¿how can the sea be a proper burial? We came from earth, and that's the only place we can return to.* A patron interjected that demons like bin Laden don't deserve proper burials, and out broke an argument of inside jobs and American interventionism.

"You were there for that, ¿right, Seth?"

"I'm here in front of you."

"No, no. For the attacks. ¿You remember when we used to skip stones, and some would just plop in, sort of gentle? That's what those planes looked like hitting those towers."

"Oh. Yeah."

"¿In D.C.?"

"Yeah. Nieves and I could see the smoke from the Pentagon. We even heard the boom."

"¿And you turned on the TV?"

"Naturally. We heard it on the radio. They called it an accident at first."

"But it wasn't."

"No, of course not. The second the second plane hit the second tower, everyone knew."

"That it was planned."

"Yeah. Nieves was the first to figure it out. Even before the news anchors."

"And the people jumping."

"That was the worst part."

"They were on fire."

"Nieves couldn't watch the whole thing."

"No, neither could Isa. They act tough, but those two have pretty weak stomachs when it comes to tragedy."

"Nieves ran around the house. She climbed up to the apartment building's roof to watch the smoke from across the river."

"¿The river?"

"There was a river between us and the Pentagon. From the height of our building, you could see the smoke and its reflection in the water."

"Wow. Yeah, they finally killed the son of a bitch, then."

"I'm going to go get another round."

Seth stood up from the booth to get two more whiskies. He asked the bar maiden to water his down, while he got a double for Osario. He looked around as she stood on her toes to reach the Johnnie Walker Blue from the top shelf. There were few occupants tonight, and most of their attention was on the newscast. No one seemed to have recognized either of the brothers. Seth looked for any side glances or winces, but he was as incognito as a foreigner—he felt just like he did in D.C.: that he didn't belong. But here, at this bar, with what happened ten years ago, he was grateful to not belong.

"¿How is Nieves? ¿Did she end up opening a restaurant there?"

"No. We couldn't afford to find a suitable place or scrounge up the initial investment. Her father died, and we didn't really know anyone else, so there were no investors either. Even if we'd found one or two partners, she'd have forced them into silence. But Americans aren't like that. They always want a say. So she worked as a chef for a while at some fancy place in Dupont Circle."

"¿What kind of restaurant?"

"It didn't even know what it wanted to be. One week it was Asian fusion, the next you'd have thought you stepped into a French café. The couple who owned it were some sort of bipolar, I guess. Nieves couldn't handle it very long. It's not that she didn't know how to cook the food, she's just got a short fuse for wishy-washy people."

"¿She quit?"

"Oh yeah. Smashed the aquarium next to the host's podium too. There were Oscars and angelfish flipping all over the floor of the restaurant. Nieves joked that she'd turned the joint into a sushi bar."

"I'd forgotten she had a temper. Well, she didn't when we were kids, but I guess she grew it at some point."

"Yeah, probably from being with me for so long. I must have turned her into this cold snap. She can be a blizzard when she wants to be. But other times she's like a Christmas morning. All gentle, and pristine, and spectacular to wake up to."

"Isa is like that too. Sometimes I have to dodge her or a plate. You'd think she was always so sweet like she is on the news. That she smiles all the time and talks to people like she's interviewing them. At home she can be a nightmare, but like you said, she can also be a dream. Calm, and warm, and spectacular to wake up from."

"I guess those girls were made for us."

"Or, if we were to ask them, we were made for them."

Like all men who begin conversations about their wives, Seth and Osario switched it to their sons. Andrés and Horacio, cousins who'd never met, and whom Seth assumed would never meet.

"Andrés is already practicing for the track team," Seth gloated.

"¿At ten?"

"Yes, there's a team at the middle school he'll go to. I practice with him once a week at this track field close by. Sometimes I take him to the woods to run cross-country. I bring a towel with me because he always ends up tossing himself into creeks or ponds. But he's fast."

"Horacio has been playing fútbol. He's quite good."

"¿What position?"

"Goalie, actually. He's tall like I was at that age, and his arms are like wings."

"It sounds like they're both more athletic than we were."

"Well, when I was in school I played fútbol."

"¿For a team?"

"No, no. Just on one of those dirt-grass fields with my classmates."

"¿You went to a real school?"

"Yeah."

"¿Our parents let you go?"

"Yeah, they asked if I wanted to, and I said yes."

"Oh."

"Yeah. ¿What else does your son like?"

"He's good at math, and science, and anything you put in front of him, really. I mean, I help him with his homework, but he doesn't really need it, ¿you know? We check out books from the library, and he devours them. I ask him questions, and he knows the answers. He must get it from Nieves."

"Don't sell yourself short. When I got to school I used everything you taught me—I did well because of your lessons."

"That's good to hear."

"Yeah."

"¿And Horacio?"

"He's an asshole," Osario said, laughing. "I'm kidding, but only halfway. He takes after me in that way. He's only ten, but he's good at pranks already. He says he wants to record them and upload the videos to Facebook. I told him I'd wring his neck if our friends see Isa scream like a ghost."

"That would indeed be a sight."

"But he's smart, the little bastard. He skipped a grade last year. He's *already* playing on the middle school team."

"Oh," Seth said. He was surprised it had taken so long for Osario to one-up him. Osario had been camouflaging his nature this whole time, being pleasant, forcing pleasant conversation. Admitting his own faults, his family's. And even invoking sentimentality so Seth would lower his guard, so he could get in a swift jab. *My son is a year better than yours. He's not practicing* for *a team because he's already* on *one.*

Seth excused himself to the bathroom. Its floor was sticky, and it reeked. But Seth would've been suspicious if it had been clean. Like he was being set up. Seth pissed on the ground next to the urinal. Because of the raised grime, the urine pooled instead of streamed. Seth wanted someone to walk in and chastise him for the lack of tact and human decency. He wanted that person to snitch on him to the philosophical bar maiden who would burst in, pinch him by the ear, and throw him out. Maybe that would foil his plan. Part of him wanted his plan to be foiled because he couldn't stop himself anymore.

A man entered the bathroom. Someone Seth hadn't counted among the bar-goers. A nosy hallucination, or perhaps an old lush, just blown in. He must have been in his seventies, hair blond-turned-white beneath a baseball cap. An American, surely, with khakis and boat shoes. The man nodded cordially, and Seth bobbed his head, zipped up his pants, and washed his hands. As the air dryer roared, Seth glanced down at the pool of his own urine surrounding the feet of the unsuspecting man, who flashed him another nod before Seth left, returning to a new round of drinks that Osario had ordered.

"¿You take notice of the fucker who followed you into the bathroom?" Osario asked.

Seth nursed his fresh whisky. "¿The gringo?"

"The gringo."

"¿What about him?"

"Look at him," Osario said, his sweat glowing in the neon beer signs. Seth turned conspicuously to the older man who'd been at the urinal. He sat at the end of the bar, on the stool closest to the Elvira-themed pinball machine. From the lighting and this distance, Seth couldn't make out as many details as Osario seemed to want him to.

"There are thousands of gringos at bars in Escazú," Seth said. "And in Jacó, Tamarindo, Santa Ana, Puerto Viejo. They're everywhere. ¿What's so special about this one?"

"This one's from here. And he's stalking me."

Seth turned back to his brother, whose face had tensed into that of a man deeply afraid. "You have to start from the beginning," Seth said.

"There is no beginning with this fucker. Could be ten years now, or a hundred." Osario fixed his eyes on Seth's. "¿What do you remember about grandfather?"

"Not much."

"Don't lie. You had an extra four years with him."

"Well, he seemed to like me."

"He loved you."

"¿Do I detect a little jealousy?"

"Not at all. Someone had to."

"Hm. You're right. Okay, so I guess he loved me. I remember him being austere to Dad, amiable around Mom. Ola and he were friends."

"Ola . . . wow."

"Yeah."

"But ¿did he ever talk to you?"

"¿About what, Osario? You've lost me."

"His beliefs. Our heritage. About his family. His wife."

"¿What wife?"

"Apparently we had a grandmother, and she was German."

"¿How the hell do you know that? Dad was convinced grandfather yanked him out of an orphanage."

Osario pointed to the man sipping his beer. "When the fucker's not visiting my office, he's sending me photocopied articles. ¿Did you know Costa Rica had concentration camps during the war?"

"¿For Jews?"

"The opposite. They rounded up the Germans. And they threw our grandmother in." The seat beneath Seth shifted, as if locked into a track climbing to the top of a coaster. "Grandfather wrote all about it, for years. Wrote about Latin America trying to exterminate the white race."

"That sounds like—"

"Some Nazi shit, I know."

Seth hunched forward, making sure the American was completely in his blind spot, as if that would make him disappear from the world. "So that means that man is—"

"Either a Nazi, too, or some blackmailer. But I'm not in government anymore, so I don't care if our grandfather was a racist."

Seth threw back the rest of his Johnnie Walker; his eyes homed in on the ceiling fan, its years of yellow dust and grime. He heard a muffled call of his name, and he looked back down at Osario, whose moving mouth made no sound. Seth slammed his own glass down, which made no bang on the wooden table. The pinball machine didn't accompany its scintillating lights with rings or cheers. The bar had grown as quiet as a mortuary. Seth's grandfather, a—

"¿Mae, what's wrong with you? ¿Seth?"

Seth looked around. All the cantina-goers were looking back at them, called by his slammed glass, and decided to eavesdrop on a brotherly bar brawl. Osario leaned forward, staring at Seth as one does a precipice. "We should go. Let's find another joint."

Seth regained his equilibrium and smiled. "Yeah, I've got the perfect place in mind, little brother."

Osario stumbled out of the cantina while Seth paid their tab. He ordered a sealed bottle of expensive whisky and watched the barkeep leave to get it from the back. The American, staring at Seth from the other end of the bar, gave him a cordial nod. Gripping the neck of the bottle like one would a chicken's, Seth nodded back to the man and made his way out into the humid, humming night.

2011

Isa awoke with a splitting headache that quickly dissipated into a dull aching of her knees. Her body had the unique habit of transferring pain to its different parts, depending on usage or immediate importance. Pangs flowed around inside her like ocean tides carrying foam and pollution. Whether she was behind her anchor desk or her limbs formed an X on her bed, she was always in some sort of pain that would use her nerves like a highway. *Fibro-something*, the doctor said before she walked out to find a new one.

Isa snatched her mother's watch from the night table. Both hands pointed straight up in a diver's position before a plunge. Her iPhone, with its shattered screen, pieced together a stained glass *00:00*. No missed calls from Osario either. She double-checked the phone and nicked her thumb on the raised fiberglass crystals.

Sweat pooled in the indent between her carotid arteries, and when Isa sat up from the bed, it splashed in a waterfall down to her navel. She'd been completely naked waiting for Osario. Today was not a special date, so there was no way she could hold his tardiness against him. Their anniversary wasn't for three months and seventeen days. She'd just thought it'd be nice for her husband to come home from a hard day's work to his beautiful wife splayed nude and supple on their king-size. Isa took a sip from the champagne she'd set out; it had gone flat in her waiting, like the scented bathwater she'd drawn for them too. Isa had gone through all the trouble because she felt that she and her husband were drifting apart. That there was a widening gap between them filled with secrets, like biodegradable trash in a landfill. Secrets that would arguably disappear over time but in the moment were obvious, plentiful. Rotten.

Isa was positive Osario was having an affair, because so was she. With a sound guy, embarrassingly, who fumbled with her breasts every time he attached the mic to her lapel. It was loud gossip about the newsroom, but Isa didn't care. She had protection as the channel's most popular anchor. Osario must have been out with his mistress tonight—Isa had only a mild curiosity about whom it could possibly be. Maybe Osario's tennis instructor who didn't wear panties under her too-short skirt; one could smell her from the sidelines. Or Isa's best friend, Griselda, whose name she always thought ugly and said so once at a party in front of everybody. Isa's excuse was that she had been drunk, but it *was* a serious enough offense to justify fucking someone else's husband. Fair, Isa thought, with a shrug of her shoulders. But Osario's fling was most likely with their son's babysitter, a sixteen-year-old named Darling, whom Osario would surely call darling in bed. Men were so cliché. It was always the babysitter. Or, better yet, it was all three. Isa found herself contending with an army of other women, and she liked those odds. Isa had never backed down from a challenge, hence the performance tonight.

Isa made the bed, drained the tub, finished the bottle of champagne, checked on a sleeping Horacio, then made her way down to the pine-cabinet, marble-countered, stainless steel appliance kitchen, where she opened the fridge and cracked open two eggs that just yesterday had belonged to a mother leatherback turtle. The yolks had hardened just a bit, so she warmed them with her breath. These eggs were a delicacy if one added hot sauce and salt, which she did, because the guards, Thing 1 and Thing 2, had gone through the trouble of procuring them for her. Then Isa stepped through the sliding glass door onto the backyard lawn that overlooked Villa Real. Behind her, the mansion that had once belonged to Seth and Nieves radiated heat left over from the day and shone like a box containing all the world's chaos.

Isa tilted her head at a forty-five-degree angle to turn the crescent moon into a grin. The sound guy, Rafael, had the same kind of smile. Fake. In bed it became natural, almost, but still creepy. Isa didn't trust a man who smiled. She must have taken after her mother in that way. Nieves had inherited the family recipes, while Isa was gifted their mother's backbone like a hand-me-down: a bitterness that kept her upright, levelheaded. If she were being completely honest and self-aware (although she usually was—another endowment), this general dislike of men had served her well throughout her life. But most of all, in her career. She'd never been afraid of the station manager who propositioned her for sex or the weathermen who cornered her for lousy dates. They were answered with swift kicks to the balls or petitions to the Ministry of Labor on behalf of herself or co-workers. Those years left alone with her mother taught her self-reliance and moxie. *Punch first, kiss later* is what she always said. Those who bring forth mankind need not ask permission. Not ever. *They come from us, Isa. Never forget that.*

And Isa never did. She even instilled that mantra in her female interns, who had to dodge the grasping claws of producers, executives, and lowly guys from craft services. Isa equipped an entire generation of graduate students against the anchormen who swooped down upon them at every waking moment. She still received gifts from former junior staff who had moved on to CNN, Univision, or the BBC. Chocolates and flowers, soaps and essential oils, for her aching joints.

Back in the master bedroom, Isa checked her iPhone again for any missed calls from Osario. None. Just a text from Rafael asking what she was up to. Yeah, right, like she was going to drive in the middle of the night to that slum where he lived, and what? Lay like a starfish while he pumped and heaved by himself, watching the red numbers on the digital clock contort like limbs? That's what they looked like, she thought. Hands and arms displayed like hieroglyphs.

Walk like an Egyptian. Isa had always liked that song.

Costa Rica is home to

the American crocodile (Crocodylus acutus)

Crocodylus acutus

the American crocodile

2011

Ceiba, Aguacate, Guanacaste, Caimito, Marañón, Manguillo, Manzanillo, Peine de mono, Carambola, Achiote, Granadillo, Cedro, Lengua de vaca, Lengua de suegra, Colpachi, Manga larga, Hule, Palo de agua, Laurel, Zorrillo, Coralillo, Reina de la noche, Guachipelín, Poró, Higuerón, Jagua, Cacao, Jorco, Madero Negro, Manú Negro, Anonillo Negro, Quizarra Negro, Burío, Pilón, Algodoncillo, Guapinol, Cuajiniquil, Guabo Peludo, Guaba, Gallinazo, Jícaro, Chaperno, Costilla Danto, Mamón Chino, Balsa, Miguelario, Gavilán, Guayaba, Chan, Copal, Quiubra, Barrigón, Jobo, Huevo de toro, Danto plomillo, Vainillo, Manzana de agua, Aceituno, Yos, Almendro de playa, Roble Coral, Cortez Amarillo, Malinche, Canfín, Manteco, Plomo, Chancho, Chancho Blanco, Manú Blanco, Guácimo Blanco, Punta de lanza, Lagartillo, Yodo, Zapote.

Despite the darkness and their drunkenness, Seth and Osario vied to identify and recite every plant and tree they sped by on the way from the bar in Escazú to the Tárcoles River. It had become a game—instead of beers on the wall or Beetles as excuses to punch, the brothers called out the names of fragrant, towering flora and took sips from the top-shelf bottle in self-congratulation. It was as innocent as a competition between brothers could get.

Porrex and Ferrex, Romulus and Remus, Cain and Abel, Hodr and Baldur, Dingane and Shaka, Arjuna and Karna, Eteocles and Polynices, Genghis Khan and Behter, Atahualpa and Huáscar.

In their own game, so, too, were the tropical floras competing to identify and recite the two brothers as they sped past on their way to the Tárcoles River.

Route 27 was closed for twenty kilometers of construction. Seth grew frustrated but was also impressed the government would invest in bettering its roads. So instead of the direct route, the Audi jumped from Route 721 to 136, then 137. An hour-long drive became two, almost three. The more time that elapsed, the harder the Audi swerved, and the faster it raced, and the deeper it clawed into the asphalt. A jet-black jackal in the middle of the night. Besides the momentary outlines of leaves, all the world was dark. Even road signs and surface markings cowered from the car's darting eyes; they wanted nothing to do with what was about to happen. High above, indiscriminate stars crowded. The only truly discernible object in the whole universe to Seth was Osario's body carved out by the sound system's blue light. The radio played just above breathing volume, just high enough that Seth could ignore the sloshing bottle and his sloshing stomach. Osario shook awake from a quick nap.

"Mae, ¿where are we?" Osario smacked his lips.

"You'll see, Osario. I've got a surprise."

"¿A surprise? ¿From you? ¿What is it, our birthday?"

"You'll see. Trust me."

"¿Trust *you*? Forgive me for saying it, but I think I'd put more trust in a buzzard at the bottom of a gorge."

"Mae, shut up."

"My legs could be crushed under a boulder, and I could be wiping blood from my mouth, and the sun could be going down faster than a ball, and I'd still put more faith in the bird to do me a solid. Oh, come on, Seth. Don't get all quiet, I'm just fucking with you. I'm just saying, we've been driving for hours. If we were going anywhere, we would've gotten there by now."

"¿You want me to turn back?"

"No. No, no. I believe you. Let me have a cigarette at least. I don't care if it's a rental."

"Go ahead."

"And don't get all bipolar after, getting mad at me for filling this car up with smoke—"

"Just light it—"

"The seats are leather anyway, so you can just pat the smoke out—"

"Mae, I said just light it."

Osario fished out a burgundy Zippo from his breast pocket, his initials carved into the shiny metal: *OO*. "Jesus Christ, all right," he said after the click, the spark, and the return to his pocket. "Don't blow a blood vessel."

"And hand me one."

"Sure. ¿You feeling lucky?"

"¿What?"

"Mae, relax already. They're Lucky Strikes."

"Oh, yeah."

"¿What's got you on edge?"

"Nothing."

"¡Oh, shit! ¡Turn it up, Seth!"

Osario swatted Seth's hand away to turn the volume up himself. That Fleetwood Mac song from decades ago. The brothers, hypnotized again.

"Wow, ¿can you believe it? ¿You remember this song?"

"¿How could I forget it?"

"God, it was so good."

"Hit the note with me, Seth. Hypnotiiiiiiiiiiiized."

"I'm good."

"Aw, you're no fun. Hey, Seth, ¿where's the bottle? Let me get some. Jesus, it's more than halfway done and I feel like I'm the only one who's been drinking it. Here, have some."

"I'm driving, Osario."

"Aw ¿who cares? What, ¿a cop going to jump out of the dark?"

"Fine. Hand it over."

"¿Seth, you know what?"

"¿What, Osario?"

"I always thought Fleetwood Mac was better before Stevie. She ruined their sound. Before they were groovy, and cool, and mysterious, and then she just up and ruined it."

"I like Stevie. I like her voice."

"¿You know what else, Seth? It's funny, actually. I had a dream the other night."

"¿About what? ¿Flying over mountains?"

"No . . . I dreamt you cut me into pieces."

"¿What the fuck is that supposed to mean, Osario?"

"Mae, keep your eyes on the road. It's not supposed to mean anything. I had it last week, the night you called me. Out of the blue. And I woke up and forgot about it, and I just now remembered I had the dream. Relax. You know I never took any of that shit seriously."

"¿But I cut you into pieces?"

"That's what I remember."

"Osario, give me a cigarette."

"Here. I don't even remember with what, but it felt real."

"¿What did?"

"It hurt, Seth."

"Oh."

"¿You ever had a dream like that?"

"¿Like what? ¿One that felt real?"

"Yeah. It feels real, but I don't know, it also feels familiar. Like you're reliving—"

"¿Reliving what?"

"Jesus, Seth. I'm not sure. *Something.* Something you *got* to relive. You got to relive it so that you can resolve it, but you can only do it when you're not awake."

"Hm."

"¿So, you have had a dream like that?"

"I guess."

"¿What about?"

"I don't know, Osario. Lots of things. I feel like I've had to relive a lot of things."

"Oh, come on, lower your voice."

"I don't want to."

"Oh, now I know what this is really about. ¡Grow up, Seth! ¿Are you still sore about that whole thing?"

That Whole Thing.

That. Whole. Thing.

ThatWholeThingThatWholeThingThatWholeThing.

"Shit, Seth. ¡It happened ten years ago! It's older than our kids. It's ancient history."

Even though Osario *was* trying to downplay it, he was right, but not in the way he meant. It *was* ancient history. A fable in a fat, spatchcocked paperback, yellowing pages turned with indifference, read for a school project or out of sheer boredom. A book splayed on the floor like a sliced-open heart. Like one at the Oreamundo mansion years ago, because its shelf had been sold from under it.

WEIGHING OF THE HEART

2000

The morning of That Whole Thing began innocuously, with a sweet Salvadoran maid creeping into the hotel room, despite the Do Not Disturb sign hanging from the door handle like a lazy wind chime. Seth and Nieves jumped up, completely nude on the bed, and instead of chastising the maid, they asked her name (Gladys—pretty), what part of the country she was from (somewhere Seth had once visited), how long she had worked here at the Willard Hotel (fifteen years), and if she was treated well (not really). Gladys wasn't shocked by their nakedness but spoke shyly until they told her they were from Costa Rica, and she clapped her hands together and told them she'd always wanted to go. Like all Central Americans, they each bragged about their own country's beaches. White sands, palm trees like green feather dusters, vendors selling finger food by the surf. Seth and Nieves let her win, asked for extra towels, and handed her a hundred-dollar bill unscrupulously, of which she said she'd spend ten dollars on herself and the other ninety on her two children. We have just one, Seth and Nieves said. A newborn. Gladys wished them to have more, to birth a generation of generous people just like them. Generosity is a gene, she said. They all chuckled.

Seth and Nieves had left the baby, Andrés, back in Costa Rica for a week. Nieves needed a break from the three-month-old. Compounded with the stress of running her successful restaurant, she found motherhood to be an anxious commitment better handled in doses. Seth didn't mind either way—he loved the baby, of course, but most of all he wanted his wife happy. When Gladys the Salvadoran maid excused herself, he again began licking the valleys between her stretch marks, wanting to take advantage before they disappeared. Nieves giggled and recoiled at the tickle, but inched her abdomen closer to his lips, to his mouth, which wandered to a place that had been injured but was now healed and ready to be loved again.

Afterward they showered separately and dressed, packed their suitcases, and left another folded hundred on the pillow like a complimentary mint. Down in the lobby they thanked the concierge for a wonderful week as always. Before leaving the Willard, Seth found himself again on the plush armchair by the front-facing window, fabled to be where Abraham Lincoln sat, introspective and calm, before his inauguration. The Willard Hotel was in fact the Hotel of Presidents, and Seth sank deep into the cushion, wishing to join them. It was a pipe dream, he knew, but still a fantasy worth musing about.

Outside, autumn courted D.C. like a lover jealous of summer. Instead of flowers and sticky sun, it presented colorful leaves, a distinct and delicious morning chill, and cashmere overcoats neither Seth nor Nieves had use for back in Costa Rica. It had indeed been a wonderful week. D.C. provided them with time to disconnect and recharge, meet up with old friends, visit old monuments, and pay respects to Nieves's father, buried in an old cemetery close to Capitol Hill. At Dulles Airport a small private jet anticipated their arrival. They would make it back in Costa Rica by late afternoon.

A plane is akin to a time machine. Within the hurtling metal bird, one's reality is encapsulated, independent. Intense turmoil or joy might transpire tens of thousands of miles below, but within a plane, time is suspended to No Smoking signs, lukewarm meals, or the Mile High Club, in which Seth and Nieves renewed their membership. Only when the thick, fireproof tires of the plane scraped the runway, and the ladder was attached to the side like a prosthetic limb, did time resume, and that aforementioned turmoil flooded the tarmac, waiting for Seth.

A spate of protestors met the private jet at the runway, scores of people with simple clothing—tank tops, flip-flops, short shorts—balancing jugs and buckets on their shoulders, from which they began pouring brown contents under the feet of gun-drawn policemen in a tide. Seth and Nieves stared out of the circular plane window in horror and confusion. Who were these people? Why did they yell louder when they saw Seth's face appear? The hatch opened, and they were unsure who would barge in. In a reflex, both Seth and Nieves put their hands to her stomach. But it was Jade, Seth's vice director at RECOPE, holding a handkerchief to her face.

"We have to go, Señor Oreamundo. Right now," she shouted.

Seth was so terrified of the hollering mass he couldn't even hear what they were chanting. Jade hurried him along to a limousine while Nieves was escorted to another. The policemen pointed their guns at the crowd but knew if they shot, they'd be swallowed and dismembered.

"¿What's that smell?" Seth asked. He almost retched on the limousine's door.

"Get in, Señor Oreamundo. ¡Get in!"

The limousine sped away from the airport, and Seth hung his head down between his knees, contorting his face and blowing out of his nose, attempting to exorcise the stench. It was acrid, like shit and gasoline.

"Yes, you're right, Señor Oreamundo. You've always had a good nose."

"¿What do you mean, Jade? ¿Are you going to tell me what's going on?"

Jade became uncharacteristically silent. Across from him, she shrank and twiddled her thumbs. Seth saw that her usually shiny hair lay matted, heavy and oily. She hadn't slept.

"¿What is going on, Jade? Tell me."

"Seth," she said. "We're in deep this time."

"¡Spit it out!"

"There's been a leak."

"¿A leak? ¿Like a faucet?"

"No, Seth. A main broke in the Tárcoles River. We don't know exactly how many hundreds of thousands of liters, but the petroleum has been poisoning the water."

"¿What do you mean it's *been*? ¿How long has the main been broken?"

"A week."

"¡¿A week?!" Seth was shouting now. Like the protestors, bulging veins drew dark blue tributaries on his neck. "¿Are you inept, Jade? ¿When did you find out? ¿When were you going to inform me?"

"I couldn't reach you at the hotel, Seth. We found out yesterday morning when protestors stormed the municipality of Puntarenas. They vomited from ingesting the gasoline water and said silver fish floated belly-up all about the river. They threw stones at the closest refinery. Children are in the hospital, and the networks began coverage almost immediately. Sergio sent a crew to fix it, but the water level is too high to get to it. He shut off the valve leading to the main, but the damage is done."

"¿What?"

"Sir, the damage is done."

The damage to the river was indeed done, but for Seth, it was just beginning.

The day before Seth's plane touched down at Juan Santamaría International Airport, every network had caught wind of the oil spill, and their afternoon newscasts were scathing. Channels quickly created their own playlist of video clips (some borrowed from past international spills): children with mouthfuls of boils, gargantuan crocodiles drowning like dinosaurs in tar pits, egrets dyed black, shores dyed black, mangrove roots, women's feet, bellies of boats, fish and the hooks they were caught on, all dyed black. That night they placed the blame on RECOPE as a whole. The disorganization, its useless board of directors, and their questionable funding. It was only when Isa took over the story's reporting for her station that Seth's fate was truly sealed.

Well, to attribute That Whole Thing to her alone would have been unfair. An ambitious journalist can wield considerable power, yes, but hidden in offices and in private phone conversations, a separate group was planning Seth's downfall. In the reflection of that infernal river of oil, they saw an opportunity. The conspiracy was two-pronged and became entirely dependent on a single linchpin: Osario's betrayal of his older brother.

The morning the country saw the news reports, Isa arrived at the station to a heavy manila envelope addressed to her. She rushed over, having been called by her producer to lead the breaking midday broadcast. But when her intern handed her the envelope, she cleared her schedule. Its girth and weight frightened her at first (she'd heard of stations receiving letter bombs), but against her better judgment, Isa tore it open. What poured out like entrails were the last four years of RECOPE's tax returns, bank statements, write-offs, emails, faxes, and memos—all carrying Seth's signature. A believer might have misconstrued the evidence as a gift from God—the ammunition to take down Avarice and Evil—but Isa knew better. All over the documents were the fingerprints of the Devil, of someone hellbent on seeing Seth burn. A whistleblower who was well aware that a scandal of this magnitude would land Isa a promotion and Seth in prison.

At the same time that Isa was scouring the documents, Osario sat depressed at his desk in his corner office. The coffee he'd been served was burnt, and his new secretary arrived with a stack of memos that made her arms tremble. Too respectful to use his name, she addressed him as "Minister," which Osario had hated the past year. The title carried too much weight for someone with his sensibilities and morality, and he hadn't known that the position implied this much bureaucracy. He could no longer visit the forests he swore to protect and was instead strangled by a three-piece suit like a straitjacket in air-conditioned rooms. He grumbled at Styrofoam cups, which he'd tried to ban in his first month as minister, yet his secretaries served tar in them every day. He recycled tons of stacks of unnecessary correspondences, while everyone else tossed them in the bins next to their desks. "I'm the Minister of the Environment," Osario would whisper to the city outside his office window. "And I can't even get these idiots to recycle."

Edgar Zúñiga, the mayor of San José and the most powerful member of their political party, barged through the door with his arms extended, fingers stretched in triumph. He stood in the center of the room like a conquering general seeking counsel from his king. Osario, suddenly assaulted by Edgar's cologne, waved him in and asked him to close the door.

"Mayor," Osario said. "¿To what do I owe the pleasure?"

"Osario, kid, don't address me so formally. We're friends."

"I understand. ¿How can I help you, *friend*?"

"Surely you've heard about the spill."

"Yes, it's been playing on the news for hours. We've been busy getting a team together to investigate. I'm traveling to the Tárcoles basin in a few days to show my face because it's—"

"A disaster."

"Yes . . . an ecological disaster."

"Sure, sure. The environment. Sure. Say, Osario, ¿what if I told you Seth had something to do with it?"

"I don't follow, Edgar. ¿With the spill?"

"Now, I'm not saying he took a sledgehammer to the damn pipe. No, no. That's not what I mean. I mean, ¿what if I told you the state of that pipe raised red flags for years, and your brother ignored it?"

"I'd call you a liar."

"¿And why is that?"

"I mean, sure, Seth probably gets kickbacks from *somebody* to look the other way on things." Osario stared Edgar Zúñiga down, forcing down the memory of the dinner in Villa Real, Seth's smugness at his accusations. Instead, he focused on Edgar's money-green tie. Osario thought that if his neck got any fatter, his head would be pinched off like a ball of dough. "I know that. But Seth would never put anything natural in danger. You've met him; you know how that bastard talks about his plants."

"I thought you two haven't seen each other in years."

"You're wrong," Osario said. "We see each other at parties or events. And every time he talks to me about his goddamn plants."

"Well, from a dozen five-minute conversations, I'm sure you couldn't tell your brother has changed."

"But not in that way."

"Oh, Osario."

Their heated conversation was interrupted by Osario's secretary buzzing his intercom. Isa was on the other line, and it was urgent.

Edgar smiled. "Talk to your wife," he said. "Go home and work it out."

"¿What's that supposed to mean?"

"Nothing, kid. I'll be back tomorrow."

"Just finish what you're saying now."

"Trust me. I'll be back tomorrow."

Isa was waiting for Osario at the dining room table of their loft in Barrio Escalante. Isa began to speak, but the train passing in front of the apartment turned her into a badly dubbed movie. Documents from the manila folder rested on the table, compiled and organized by date—she wanted her husband to witness Seth's corruption chronologically. All night, Isa shoved papers in his face and recited them into his ears. All he could answer was "But he's my brother."

Edgar Zúñiga returned to Osario's office the next morning as he'd said he would. His tie had gone from money green to blood red.

documents for all the country to see. One would have thought she was speaking out of the goodness of her heart. An ethical, mordant tone. But she still remembered Seth embarrassing her husband at that dinner, and how he had abandoned Osario when they were children. In between scans of memos and tax documents, the network played footage of affected residents of the Tárcoles basin. They all said the same thing: *I cannot get the taste of diesel from ny tongue.* And from those mouths coated with irremovable oil, they decried ;eth's corruption.

The stench followed Seth everywhere that week as he tried to control ne damage. Even the scum from Seth's soap reeked of petroleum. Protestors umped outside Villa Real, their picket signs bobbing outside the private ommunity's gates (Thing 1 and Thing 2 giddy at the chance to shoot meone). At the glass facade of RECOPE's central office, citizens m the Tárcoles basin threw jugs of river water like window washers; ey were having it transported in pickup trucks, replenishing the hell o which Seth had been plunged. His reputation as tarnished as the er.

After RECOPE tallied more than four hundred thousand liters of crude released into the wild, Osario held a news conference by Orotina, a town e to the Tárcoles River. Diesel evaporated from the water's surface. The air awash in it. Reporters covered their mouths with bandannas as they raised microphones like pitchforks. Solemnly, Osario condemned his brother cly for the first time.

Based on mounting evidence," he said, "Seth Oreamundo has taken advanof his position and set Costa Rica's conservation efforts back fifty years. o his corruption and negligence, this basin and its environment will not r in my lifetime. His leadership has done irreparable damage to not only but this country's esteem. ¿How can we tout ourselves as a nation dedio the preservation of natural life with an ecological tragedy of this scale? I'm calling for Seth Oreamundo's immediate resignation and a full gation into his finances and the finances of RECOPE since he became ctor."

wind didn't dare blow, nor did anyone dare breathe.

hers betray brothers all the time. One might scam the other out of bucks, and the wronged brother might get him kicked out of a holiday hat sort of thing. The rivalry will go on for their entire lifetimes. Most

Osario spent the first few minutes speaking through his teeth. "¿\
you want from me, *friend*?"

"Well, me and the boys have been talking about you. The people
Young, handsome, a man with big ideas. Osario Oreamundo." Edga
his eyes and sharpened his grin. "President of the Republic."

Osario reacted as if he'd seen a tree felled. A both beautiful and
had just played out in front of him. "¿President?" he asked.

"Yes, kid. We've heard the rumors that you want the job. We kn
hints at parties."

"At parties." Osario laughed nervously. "Just there. And drunl

"Well, kid. That little joke could become reality."

"I can't say I haven't thought about it," Osario admitted. He
to Isa before, at dinner or in between lovemaking. He'd even
trees to whom he'd chained himself years ago. It had finally g
The universe answering a call. The mantra of manifesting.

"Of course you have," Edgar said. "There's just one little p

Osario looked up at Edgar, eyes widened by grief. Osario h
a gift, but the shivering child inside him knew that anythin
a price.

"We can't have a Minister of the Environment whose br
environment. There's no room for that kind of irony on the
cracks that Isa had left in Osario last night widened. "It's th

"But he's my brother."

"And he's standing in your way. He's standing in the
Osario. *You* must become justice."

"I can't sell him down the river."

Edgar almost laughed but stopped himself with a
We all know your plan for this country—we know ho
Change it for the better. We all know you want to *sav*
get you right there. There's no other way."

It was true. Between what his wife had revealed
had just offered, Osario saw no other way.

The protestors met Seth's plane at the tarmac bec
the evidence that same morning. The whole

brothers wake up just to get back at each other. It's a well-established, tedious affair. But the show really gets good when the scale is amplified. When those twenty dollars become twenty thousand, or instead of getting thrown out of a barbecue, one gets his brother exiled from a country. What Osario had just done, what he had just openly called for, was further than anyone thought he would go. Further than anyone thought he *could* go. And Isa and Edgar Zúñiga, separately but in perfect synchronicity, would push Osario to go even further.

An investigation was quickly mounted, spearheaded by the Ministry of Justice and Peace and the Ministry of Finance, both competing to see who could crucify Seth and his underlings first. Public scrutiny was only intensified by Osario's weekly commentary on a new segment hosted by Isa. It broke all ratings records, because never before had viewers seen sibling rivalry play out on prime time. Osario painted Seth as a callous villain, and Isa called for his just desserts. The country was watching a real-time, real-life telenovela. It even became interactive, with citizens phoning in with their own opinions about the scandal and the eventual trial. Some celebrated Osario's sacrifice, while others called him a traitor. Toward the end, a caller said that Good and Evil are born from the same womb.

Seth tried Osario's office many times to beg him to stop. In voicemails he apologized through tears, for which part he didn't exactly know. For everything, maybe. Seth wished for Osario to return his calls, list his infractions so he could lie prostrate in repentance. Still, though, Osario continued those newscasts, with Edgar's promise of the presidency driving him ever further. His birthright to be king.

Seth was found guilty of all charges. The mansion in Villa Real, their expensive cars and designer clothing, and Nieves's restaurant were all repossessed by the government. Seth spent the first half of 2001 in prison. His cellmates shoved his head into the shared toilet and cornered him in the showers. The guards, most of whom were denizens of the Tárcoles basin, ignored what they would admit was, if it were anyone else, overkill. Nieves and baby Andrés stayed with her mother, Gloria, who refused Isa's calls. She'd never seen such blatant, wicked ambition. Hunger for success was no excuse to strip a sister of her life.

In July, a colleague of Isa's was executed in front of his home in San Miguel, the first time a journalist had been murdered in Costa Rica. The first time its freedom of the press jeopardized. The reporter was investigating a Catholic priest turned radio host for rumors of embezzlement, and consequently punched full of holes. All the networks turned their attention from Seth and the oil spill to the Church's role in the assassination. With the spotlight distracted at long last, Edgar Zúñiga himself visited Seth at the prison with a proposition: leave Costa Rica forever.

"There's no use for you here," he said. "You'll only rot in this dump. And I'm sure your ass hurts." Edgar smiled.

"¿And my family?" Seth asked. It could have been the concrete walls or overcast day, but Seth was as gray as a headstone.

"Naturally they'll go with you. We'll give you a bit of cash and an apartment. This is your only way out. You can start over."

"¿What will I do?"

"You'll breathe fresh air again, Seth."

So Seth joined Nieves and Andrés on a surreptitious flight to D.C. (in his pockets were clippings of tropical plants from the mansion grounds). No one noticed Seth flee. He would fade into obscurity. His villainy devolved into myth, and like all legends, no one really cared about the details. Sometimes his story would come up in casual conversation over coffee, or between truck drivers stuck in traffic. And every conversation would end with *I wonder what ever happened to him.*

2011

Osario had fallen asleep by the time the Audi reached the shore of the Tárcoles River. His still-lit Lucky Strike had singed a hole in the leather seat, but Seth didn't care anymore. He eyed the whisky bottle, considered smashing it, gripping the neck like the hilt of a sword to plunge into the perfect artery. But Seth hadn't the stomach to dirty his hands. Even his seething hatred couldn't give him *that* much courage.

Studying his brother, Seth misinterpreted the position in which Osario slept for defenselessness. But it was one of guilt. A curled, implosive shame. What Seth didn't know and would never know was that Edgar Zúñiga had betrayed Osario just as Osario had betrayed Seth. After Edgar handed himself the presidential nomination that year, Osario knew he'd been manipulated. Of course their party would never have thrown a newbie onto the campaign trail, no matter how handsome, or young, or moralistic. Osario had done the Devil's bidding. The moment Seth's plane left for the United States, Edgar tossed Osario aside, leaving him in political purgatory.

What Seth did know—what he had found out through search engines and digitally scanned articles—was that the oil spill haunted Osario for his three terms as Minister of the Environment. Namely, the pollution had forced the American crocodile population farther from the riverbanks, past the delta and out to sea, where they ambushed gringo surfers and Costa Rican children collecting seashells. Under pressure from the tourism industry in his second term, Osario passed a decree to curb the crocodile population, allowing poachers to shoot on sight. It was condemned by the international conservation community, and he ended his tenure early, choosing instead to consult for petroleum companies throughout Central America forced to comply with new environmental regulations. It was lucrative enough for him to move himself, Isa, and Horacio to Villa Real and, out of some sort of sick nostalgia, into the mansion that was once Seth's. There was indeed money in oil.

Osario stirred awake like a larva. He smacked his lips out of thirst and rubbed his eyes of sand.

"Mae, ¿where are we?" he asked.

"Osario, let's make a bet."

This part of the Tárcoles wasn't as polluted as the rest. The current ran between a gait and a light jog, ideal for a swimmer. Large, volcanic boulders crowded banana trees painted white and luminescent by the moon, unnaturally bright for a crescent. Seth turned off the car and its headlights and could still see everything clearly. He counted the footprints following Osario to the edge of the river. Seth had bet his younger brother that he couldn't swim its breadth. And Osario, encouraged by the alcohol and deceptively slim extent across, accepted. He didn't care which river they had arrived at or what Seth had actually wagered. He didn't even bother taking off his clothes. The baser instinct of rivalry guided his limbs, and a fog of pettiness bloated his mind. Osario would best his brother again because he wanted to. He wanted nothing more than to see Seth's face contort in awe and humiliation. It would be as easy as swimming across a playful river. He'd have *paid* money for this opportunity.

On the opposite shore, hidden beneath the shade of palms through which the moonlight couldn't penetrate, twelve beasts sensed a disturbance in the river. One by one, they slipped into the gentle undertow. Quietly, without a splash. Courteous, so as not to distract either of the Oreamundo brothers from their thoughts.

When Osario made it halfway across, he turned over onto his back to float. He had underestimated the width and needed to rest. He closed his eyes and thought of Isa: naked on their bed, awaiting his return. All these months he'd clouded his love for her with other women—her best friend, his tennis instructor, the babysitter—but so often he noticed that Isa's clothes had gotten tighter, her hair longer, her breasts pushed up by new bras. The warm, languid current lapped at his erection. After this stupid bet he'd go home and make love to her. He just wanted to be inside her until he could release the frustration that had turned his constitution weak and malleable.

Reinvigorated, Osario turned over to butterfly stroke the rest of the river, but something nibbled at his foot.

A curious fish.

An affectionate reed.

A set of yearning teeth.

The Olympic facility with which Osario was skimming the river frightened Seth. His plan had been foiled. But stumbling to the edge of the muddy shore, Seth noticed twelve diamond necklaces snake their way to where Osario had stopped. Glittering, twisting chains of pure hunger. *It worked*, Seth thought. With a wild, gaping smile, Seth saw the finish line. *It actually worked.*

Seth laughed hysterically from the riverbank. Osario heard him.

"¡That's why Mom never liked you!" Osario sang into the night.

Seth touched the scar bright on his lip. "Maybe," he muttered. Then the splashing started.

From twelve different directions, twelve different crocodiles claimed twelve different parts of Osario like customers at a butcher shop. Sternum, sirloin, feet, chuck, thighs, tenderloin, love handles, buttocks, shank, lower jaw, Adam's apple. Every cut of Osario caught between snapping teeth the size and sharpness of splintered bone. Then the beasts began to roll. A troupe of synchronized swimmers. Using the friction of the murky water and their own body weight, they tore Osario into sizable, swallow-able pieces, dyeing the moonlit water a delicate shade of pink. It was over as quickly as it began, Seth the sole audience member at a spectacular, twice-in-a-lifetime show.

Seth backed away slowly from the bank of the Tárcoles River, his feet making loud sucking sounds in the mud. In a state of jubilant disbelief, he craned his head to the moon, then to the large, volcanic rocks, the rustling banana trees, and finally to the tar-black Audi, searching for *anyone* to share in the excitement. But in his intoxicating victory, Seth didn't notice a thirteenth beast inching toward him with a careful, lip-licking appetite.

In Costa Rica, the aggressiveness of the American crocodile eclipses that of all others in the Western Hemisphere.

THE NEW KINGDOM

2011–2018 C.E.

2018

Against a dreamy Amazonian sunset and splendid tropical flora, Jon Voight squints his beady eyes and tells a tale of mythic serpents to scare his fellow boat passengers. "They strike, wrap around you, hold you tighter than your true love," he says in an undisclosed Latin American accent. "And you get the privilege of hearing your bones break."

Horacio and Andrés sat on their best friend's couch watching the movie *Anaconda* for the first time. Xavier was already giggling like an idiot between blowing out clouds of thick smoke. It was his favorite film, but he didn't quote it like he usually would have. Instead, he mouthed the words as he rolled a new spliff. Andrés itched in his seat, checked his phone for his new girlfriend's Instagram DMs. They sent messages on every app—Instagram, Twitter, Snapchat—a series of memes and nudes that barely constituted conversation, but never texts. Horacio checked his Grindr notifications.

"I'm watching *Anaconda* with some friends," Horacio typed to *rawtopLoganCircle*. The yellow bubble reply: "I was in grad school when that movie came out."

"Are you guys going to pay attention or not?" Xavier huffed, sealing the paper with the tip of his tongue.

"Look, it's J.Lo," Horacio muttered to Andrés without lifting his eyes from the phone.

"She was so hot. Look at her ass."

"Can you believe she did *Selena* the same year this crap came out?"

"Hey, shut up, Horacio. My uncle directed this," Xavier snapped.

"I didn't know Peru had directors." Andrés winked.

"Yeah, and Nobel Prize–winning writers." Xavier spoke of his other uncle. "What have you Costa Ricans got? A soccer player who's always benched."

"Whatever, Xavier. Don't get mad. Andrés was just kidding."

"Yeah, dude. You got it."

"My bad," Xavier said. "Here, take a hit."

The three boys sank deeper into the white leather couches as a gargantuan snake terrorized Jennifer Lopez and her castmates: struck at, wrapped, and held tighter than their true loves. Privileged to hear their bones break. Admittedly, the special effects weren't bad for 1997—it was no *Jurassic Park*, but one could even argue it had better CGI than some of today's movies. Andrés slouched so hard his ass nearly left the sofa. He was so high he quickly forgot he had a phone and a face. Horacio was more conservative with his tokes and held the spliff like the pink cigarettes he bought at the tobacco shop on Connecticut Avenue, which infuriated all their friends. *Hold it like a joint, dude. Not like a fag.*

Xavier's family lived on a secluded street in Dupont Circle, just blocks from the Peruvian embassy, where his father worked as a diplomat. His mother was a famous architect, so the hundred-year-old town house's interior design had been featured in several lifestyle magazines. Horacio loved being here because it reminded him of the mansion in Villa Real condensed into two bedrooms, a living room with a fireplace and marble sculptures, a separate dining room and green-granite-countered kitchen, a rarely used basement, and the small, lush garden that led to the alley. Andrés was apathetic to the space itself. He didn't care about Victorian paintings or the original Barcelona chairs. He tolerated Xavier because he had good taste in music and the best weed connect out of their friend group.

Earlier that night the trio had been at a gathering in the woods over by the Naval Observatory. Rich kids from the Washington International School brought hookahs; truants from Wilson pills; and the geeks from School Without Walls a Bluetooth speaker, blasting Ethiopian jazz between passes of green apple shisha. Andrés flirted with the daughter of a Sudanese defense contractor, and Horacio with the son of a congressman (Republican). They would compare notes later in their bedroom. Pouring themselves vodka from a plastic handle, they wondered about tomorrow's AP Lit exam at GW's campus. If they'd get 3's like in last year's AP Comp. *Our moms will kill us*, they told Xavier, who was waiting for a kid to get back with forty dollars. *The future doesn't matter*, he answered. *All that matters is now.*

A girl, Betrina, got into a big argument with her boyfriend; their screams had broken up the party faster than a squad car. Horacio, Andrés, and Xavier climbed the knoll to Calvert Street, marveled at the moon-bathed mural of Marilyn Monroe, and crossed the bridge back toward Dupont. The fountain at the circle had just been turned on for the warming months, so the three soaked their feet, estimating how many pennies would be deposited this summer. How many desperate shlubs still collected pocket change, because how down bad did you have to be to make a wish in front of a Krispy Kreme? Xavier tossed a quarter and convinced them to watch *Anaconda* because his parents were at an art fundraiser and he didn't want to be alone in the house. Horacio and Andrés obliged, even if it meant breaking curfew and coming back stoned. As J.Lo caught the giant snake in a flimsy net, Andrés's iPhone dinged.

"My mom, Horacio. She wants us home."

"Okay. Tell her we'll finish the movie, then walk back."

The biblical serpent finished its rampage, and the credits played, and Xavier waited patiently for Horacio and Andrés to fawn over his family's cultural impact. Without much praise, the two boys made their way back home. They imagined Nieves and Isa sitting like cops by the door, ready to interrogate and whiff their clothes. Horacio and Andrés decided to take the long route home, north along Massachusetts Avenue, passing all the embassies lined up on either side like spectators at a parade. The Dominican Republic, Haiti, Kenya, Chad, Cameroon, Kyrgyzstan, Mexico.

"All the shithole countries," Andrés joked.

"Dude, shut up."

"I'm just kidding. Hell, if all of these are on the list, then you know Costa Rica's in the top ten."

"Andrés, you've never even been there."

"Yeah, but I know my mom's stories."

"She hates it for her own reasons. You can't judge a place without living there."

"Well, I trust my mother's judgment."

"Since when?"

"Since now. If you love it so much, why don't you go back, Horacio?"

"Andrés . . ."

"You're right, I'm sorry. Come here."

Andrés hugged Horacio apologetically in the early summer night air, pollen-laden and humid on their skin. Mosquitoes, emboldened by the prospect of balmy days, hovered about. Airborne phlebotomists tapping veins for samples. The two boys inhaled the scent of each other, the familiar undernotes of men they once knew. Andrés flexed his arm for Horacio to clutch gratefully, and they began walking again. Beneath the streetlamps, in the glow of the passing consulates, Horacio and Andrés looked eerily alike for cousins—their dark hair, easily tanned skin, green oases flecked in their brown eyes—and if one didn't know them well, they'd think the two were brothers. All these years together, they had become two halves of a broken, beautiful whole. Shattered by the absence of their fathers, then mended by motherlove and their own fraternal intimacy.

Seven years ago, when Seth and Osario had disappeared without a trace, Isa brought herself and Horacio to live in D.C. with Nieves and Andrés. These last seven years of occupying the same cramped, two-bedroom apartment, eating the same cooking, losing at the same video games and sports, befriending the same friends, and sharing the same mothers, Horacio and Andrés had become as close as brothers. Close in a way that Seth and Osario had never been. Had never been allowed to be.

EYELIDS OF MORNING

2011

Separately, Nieves and Isa accepted that their respective husbands were missing after a week of unanswered texts and distressed voicemails. They didn't think to call each other until months later. They initially saw no connection between Seth's and Osario's disappearances or that they both waited for their husbands in vain. A decade apart had split the sisters' perceptions of the universe, and more often than not, the other didn't exist in it. But even separated by so many miles, and borders, and memories, they reacted exactly the same.

Nieves googled the Shenandoah retreat where Seth said he'd gone. But when she called, they swore they had never heard of him. Besides, they weren't taking reservations until Memorial Day. Nieves called the West Virginia State Police, went down to file a report, waited in a cheap motel with a broken ice machine, and called the cell service provider to triangulate her husband. *That's only on TV*, the phone operator said. *This isn't* Law & Order, *you know.*

In Costa Rica, Isa burst into the office of a good friend at the Organismo de Investigación Judicial, a detective with questionable morals but undeniable results. She showed him the iPhone time stamps, begged him to find Osario, asked him to triangulate her husband with the help of the cell service provider. *That's only in the United States*, he said. *We don't have that kind of technology, you know.*

Both police departments arrived at the same conclusion: there was no trace of them. Normally, one would chalk this up to the ineptitude of law enforcement—little attention to detail, naps on the job, distractions by small-time dealers to fill quotas—but it was true. Seth had made sure to leave no trace of Osario and, in doing so, had left no trace of himself.

Nieves ran around D.C. visiting local bars and supermarkets, the Chipotle underneath the famous mural of Marilyn Monroe. No one had seen Seth in weeks. As a last resort, Nieves showed up at the Costa Rican embassy, where Ignacio was filing his nails and hitting on Darling, the receptionist. When Darling opened her mouth to speak, Ignacio cut her off, said he'd not seen Seth in over a decade, and that he wasn't to step foot on Costa Rican soil. After a dejected Nieves left, Ignacio snatched away Darling's visa and deported her. She had to give up her cat to an elderly neighbor who promised to take good care of it. The elderly neighbor eventually died and the cat became a stray.

Enough time went by that Osario's disappearance became a scandal in Costa Rica. Competing networks interviewed those familiar with Isa and Osario's marriage, painting her as the number one suspect—because if the husband goes missing, it's always the wife who dissolved his bones in acid. Isa's friend Griselda (whose name Isa had made fun of at a party) revealed she'd had an affair with him. So did the tennis instructor (with the too-short skirt), and the babysitter (men and their clichés). Isa couldn't go to the news station without being hounded by other reporters who contorted the situation to their liking, twisting her image like a worm caught at the end of a hook. The media fed upon her as so many years ago she'd fed upon Seth. Isa quit her job as anchor and threw her television out the window. It landed in the swimming pool with a fizzle of sparks and smoke.

After months of missing husbands, the sisters decided to call each other. First Nieves, who debated it over beers, then Isa, who missed the call but immediately returned it. They each thought the other might know something, that by some implausible chance their husbands had spoken to each other. But Seth was missing, Nieves said. Osario, too, Isa echoed. It was a curious, suspicious happenstance. But Osario hadn't mentioned any reunion to Isa, and Nieves repeated the ambassador's story. The two sisters were back to square one: their husbands had vanished into thin air.

They spoke every day for the next two months. Either chatting for a few minutes to ask for updates, or for hours on end about everything and nothing

at all. It works out that way: when one shares a vacuum with another, they will eventually fill that space for each other. There is no other choice because the gravity of loss is too great. Even from thousands of kilometers away, the sisters became inseparable again. And when their sons asked about their respective fathers, the bond between Nieves and Isa only strengthened. They needed to close the distance. Their husbands weren't coming back, and they needed to be together again.

Isa sold the mansion in Villa Real at a fraction of its value, packed up essential items, including the only inheritance her mother had left her—shotgun shells to be melted and molded into a necklace—and flew herself and Horacio to D.C. They moved into the Kalorama apartment, initially with the understanding that Nieves would help them find a proper place of their own to rebuild their lives. Isa marveled at Seth's splendid tropical flora that Nieves tended to as if the perfume would beckon him back. Nieves cooked every night, and Isa played sous-chef. The boys attempted to acclimate to each other, but it proved difficult at first. They bickered, wouldn't share their toys or video games. The sisters also attempted acclimating to each other; but that, too, proved difficult. Often they would pair off as if in a team-building exercise, the boys locked in one room, the sisters in the other. They reasoned that if one is stuck for enough time with someone they don't like, they would eventually find similarities and common ground. For the sisters, that activity became house hunting.

Isa was insistent that she had to find a place of her own. She couldn't keep mooching off her older sister. On their way to one apartment in Georgetown, Nieves confessed her dream of having a show on Food Network, so Isa suggested they go on *House Hunters* in the meantime. "You'll get exposure, right?" Isa asked sarcastically.

Nieves stopped the car at an intersection and threatened to throw Isa out. In her spontaneous fury she almost hit a white woman pushing an expensive stroller. Nieves and Isa began laughing at how ridiculous it was that they were reverting to girlhood. They'd known this process would be hard. It required patience, like waiting for a broken bone to mend. These moments stuck together in the sardine can of Nieves's Nissan or the confinement of the apartment helped them achieve it, just as a cast keeps that bone in place to fuse. The sisters calmed their laughter and wiped their eyes of it. The sedan was clotting M Street, and an impatient line of other cars honked

to move out of the way. Sororal breakthroughs were not to be had during rush hour.

The housing market wasn't kind to Isa, and because D.C. still limped from the recession, even her savings wouldn't last her more than a year, and the salary from a receptionist job she'd found couldn't cover even half of rent at market price. They didn't at first admit it to each other, but the sisters were thankful they wouldn't have to be apart. Even if there was a line for the apartment's only bathroom and their sons had yet to get along, they wouldn't have to be alone. So they built two bunk beds, one for the boys, the other for themselves, and gossiped in the dark as if at summer camp. Nieves feared heights, so she slept on the bottom; Isa liked to touch her fingers to the ceiling before falling asleep. The boys in their bedroom were the opposite. Andrés loved to grip the ladder rungs to descend, and Horacio could place his feet firmly on the ground for frequent midnight urinations.

Classmates taunted Andrés and Horacio that their mothers were lesbians. Parents at PTA meetings asked the sisters if Phase 1 was still open and if they wore matching Birkenstocks on purpose. Lipstick lesbians, wives corrected their husbands on car rides home from school fundraisers. And eyeing their children in the rearview mirror, they pleaded for them not to tease Horacio or Andrés. But asking kids to hold their tongues is like asking a volcano not to erupt; children hurling insults like molten rocks is as natural as it gets.

Horacio learned uppercuts faster than he learned English, because when the boys arrived home from school, and Nieves and Isa still slaved away in their office jobs, the boys watched hours of WWE reruns—even if these brawls were make-believe, Horacio and Andrés couldn't differentiate. They hid bruises from their mothers but were sure to make them shine on bullies' arms. And the thing about those particular bullies was that they followed an adult moral code (some Cosa Nostra thing they'd also learned from television), so Horacio and Andrés were never found out, never suspended, and never again taunted. Defending themselves brought the boys closer together. Battles with bullies, social studies projects, complaining about their mothers in the safety of bedtime fused them like that same broken bone. And eventually, they began to look like each other, act like each other. The necessary parts that Nieves and Isa couldn't provide, the boys provided for themselves.

Sometimes at night in their bedroom, when all the house was quiet, they wondered about their fathers. Seth's and Osario's whereabouts, or what each

boy could remember of them. They mused about which aspects of their fathers they'd inherited. If Andrés could raise a forest, or if Horacio would one day save the world. What they didn't inherit was their family's sins as their fathers had. They weren't cursed to repeat what fate demanded of them at the moment of their births.

Well, that wasn't entirely true.

They didn't have to repeat that *particular* destiny. There was another stalking the Oreamundos, one much rarer than what their fathers had enacted, but still as potent. However, the majority would fall on Horacio's shoulders. It was he who would eventually be forced to avenge his father. Seth's role in history wasn't yet over. Not by a long shot.

Fate was a cruel, playful thing.

HIS TONGUE WITH A CORD

2011

Seth thought he'd awoken in the Garden of Eden. He smelled clouds, their syrupy mist cutting through the room to which he had opened his eyes. Seth lifted his head from a soft pillow. After a momentary blindless, he saw an endless, familiar green beyond the sliding glass door. White, gossamer curtains danced like women's skirts. A humid chill raised bumps on his skin. All around him, a melody of rain informed him he might still be alive.

"You're up," a man's voice said.

"He's up," a woman's voice answered the man's.

Seth lifted his torso from the bed, and a white man and dark-skinned woman stood on either side of him, offering a glass of cool water, which he downed without pause.

"Don't drink it too fast or you'll throw up," the man said. He was in his seventies, hair blond-turned-white.

"I have the waste basket right here just in case he does, Max," the woman said. She was in her sixties, hair white-turned-lavender.

"¿Where am I?" Seth gasped.

"You're in our home," the woman said. "You're safe."

"¿Who are you?" Seth raised his voice.

"I'm Max," the man said. "This is my wife, Luzmilda. You're safe, Paulo."

"¿Paulo?" Seth said. "¿Who the fuck is Paulo?"

The husband and wife looked at each other, frowning.

"Maybe he's lost his memory," Luzmilda said.

"That would make sense. Amnesia accompanies these kinds of things."

"¿What kinds of things?" Seth asked, on the verge of tears.

"This is you, ¿right?" the man named Max asked, handing Seth an identification card: *Paulo Sebastián Torres-Minor. Age forty-four, one hundred and eighty-four centimeters, seventy-two kilos, eyes brown, hair brown.* "We found this in your pants pocket when we saved you."

Seth quickly realized he was still in Costa Rica. These people were addressing him by the false identity Ignacio the ambassador had created. Seth had woken back up to reality. An image of splashing and pink water flashed across his mind, and he stood to run.

"¡Please don't get up, Paulo!" Luzmilda yelled, but Seth lurched forward and tumbled to the floor, hitting his chin on the wood. "Oh, Jesus. Max, help me get him back into bed."

Seth wondered why he'd fallen. Perhaps the hard mattress had made his lower half go numb. He wiggled his toes. They all felt fine. Seth turned over onto his back and looked down to inspect. But what he saw was one leg. The right one. He studied the negative space where the left leg should have been. He screamed and scrambled backward on his elbows.

"¿What happened?" Seth shouted. "¿What did you all do to me?"

"Oh, child," Luzmilda said. "We saved you."

"We heard you," Max said as he and Luzmilda helped Seth back onto the bed. "From the riverbank. You were screaming bloody murder. We were visiting Luzmilda's cousin in Capulín. As we were saying good night, we all saw a fancy car turn from the main road onto a dirt one. *How strange*, Luzmilda's cousin commented. *It's heading toward the river. At this hour.* Luzmilda and I are curious creatures, so we decided to follow in our truck. But by the time we reached the clearing, we heard screaming, and in the moonlight we saw you being thrown around—"

"Like a doll," Luzmilda interrupted.

"Like a rag doll. You were in the jaws of a croc," Max said. "Scratching at the mud, trying to get away, but it was trying to pull you into the water. God, were you fighting. I had a crowbar in the back seat, so I grabbed it and ran to you. I hit that monster right between the eyes, and it let you go. But not before rolling to take that leg." Max pointed to the negative space, beginning from the end of the bed to Seth's mid-thigh.

"I tied you up with Max's belt," Luzmilda added. "So you wouldn't bleed out."

"You were unconscious by the time we brought you back here. There's a doctor down the road. We woke him, and he stitched you up."

"But why . . ." Seth began. The story hit him all at once. He hovered his palms over the missing leg, wanted to make sure it wasn't some sort of night terror—he still felt his toes wiggling. He must have been dreaming, but he dared not pinch the ghostly flesh. "¿Why didn't you take me to a hospital?" He was shouting again.

Max and Luzmilda exchanged glances. At first nervous, then confident. "We don't trust those government doctors," Max said.

"They're no good," Luzmilda corroborated. "The doctor down the road is an expert, a man of God. He worked as a surgeon in San José for many years. He's sewn up thousands of limbs. We trusted him to save you."

"He said it was a miracle you weren't in worse shape," Max said. "As lucky as anyone could be in an unlucky situation."

Luzmilda refilled Seth's water glass. She handed him a red pill and told him to swallow. They all sat in the tense silence as it took its effect on Seth. Luzmilda touched his forehead with a warm, wet towel, and Seth felt a dizzy weightlessness flow throughout his body. A long-forgotten, long-necessary sensation. Maybe it was the drug, or Luzmilda's small kindnesses and natural smile that calmed his anxiety. Maybe all of it. Max's reassuring tone and expressive blue eyes relaxed Seth. It was all unbelievable, nightmarish, but for the moment, looking at this couple who said they saved him from certain death, Seth relented. He slipped into a river of sleep.

Seth would sleep for weeks on end, but whenever he awoke, he couldn't close his eyes until Luzmilda forced him to take one of her pills. As his mind stumbled between glaring consciousness and deep sleep, he tried to piece together the parts of that night. Working backward and forward from the only moment that replayed clear as a movie screen: his laughter as Osario succumbed to the river; rolling and splashing, scales, and blood, and moonlight. Not many knew the sound of a brother crushed to death, twisted to death, drowned, and ribboned, and mauled to death. But projecting himself into events after that proved difficult. His brain must have shut off when the stray crocodile clamped onto his leg—foot first, or calf first; or maybe it jumped right up to the thigh and swallowed it whole. Seth couldn't remember its dancing. *Thrown around like a rag doll.* How quickly he was humiliated, he thought. Victory snatched away like a cheater's Olympic medal. What an unforgiving judge, the crocodile. Seth didn't even have time to savor the return to the throne before the impatient beast savored his flesh.

Seth had no choice but to form the memory according to Max and Luzmilda's account, inserting their testimony in order to move backward. But before the bet on the riverbank, everything swirled like the whisky had in his belly. A whirlpool of scenes from the drive: an argument, *That Whole Thing*; Fleetwood Mac; many cigarettes, *¿Are you feeling lucky?*; the catalog of flora they competed to name, as the plants must have named them; the sound system's blue light, starlight, the Audi's furious headlights in the middle of the night. Hours upon hours of undulating, insignificant details. Seth was stuck in infinite middle. He couldn't start his own movie. It rewound only so far. His frustration subsided only when Luzmilda arrived with the little red pill that glowed like a laser pointer in his palm.

Once a week, the doctor who'd saved Seth's life arrived to inspect the amputation and redress its bandages. Bronson towered a head over Max and mustn't have been more than a few years older than Seth. He used a crisp, veneering hair gel like out of the 1950s, and his brow was so prominent it turned his blue eyes brown. He lived fifteen minutes down the mountain, on a road he said would one day take his life. He'd had to dodge rockslides, mudslides, and even the Cegua once to make it to a patient's bedside. His Hippocratic oath included natural disasters and folkloric demons.

"And crocs, apparently," he chuckled, untangling Seth's bandage. "You're healing nicely. Two months and not an infection, even after you were in that creature's rotten jaws. Beats me what the hell you were doing by a river that time of night." He paused the dressing, awaiting Seth's explanation, but didn't receive an answer. Untroubled, Bronson resumed. "I fall asleep to *Apocalypse Now*, and suddenly Max and Luzmilda are dropping off a man, practically war-torn, on my doorstep."

"They said they trusted only you to help me. They said you were a—"

"A trauma surgeon. Fifteen years. In San Jose, California, and then in our patron saint here. I've detached, reattached, reincorporated, and exorcised the maladies of half the Central Valley."

"¿Was mine the worst you'd seen?"

"When they brought you to me, that leg looked like a flower." Bronson ignored Seth's question. "The white, broken bone and its brown inner marrow, the bright red muscle, the yellow fat and your pale skin—all wrapped around each other like petals. There was something artistic about it, I've got to admit. I've lost patients to semitrailers, backhoes, pit bulls, and exes, but never a croc. And the one that got you seemed to have been an expert. Snipped your artery like an orthopedic surgeon. This one." Bronson pressed his index finger to Seth's thigh. He felt his heartbeat in his phantom limb. "Yours wasn't the worst," he said, removing his gloves. "It was the best."

When Seth had resumed a normal sleep schedule, Luzmilda visited him a few times a day to provide food and coffee, the pills that calmed him, magazines, and the daily newspaper. Seth noticed some pages were always torn out, but he was too weak to put much thought into it. They were waiting for Seth's body to regain its strength so that they could teach him to walk again. Max had put a pair of crutches at the foot of the bed, and when Seth was ready to place them under his arms, they could begin his physical therapy.

When asked, *¿Paulo, do you have family?* Seth was cryptic. Nieves must have been going mad trying to find him, or maybe she'd prayed for it all these years and finally moved to Malibu like she'd always wanted. Sometimes he thought of Andrés, but he hated to admit that his son was the least of his worries. Sure, Seth loved him, but he was never truly meant to be a father. Or a brother, for that matter. Not even a son or a husband. He'd been born to be alone. A wolf, a blank slate of a man. This name, *Paulo*, suited him just fine. Paulo with a missing leg, a missing life. Seth's story, a chance to finally be rewritten. So he told Max and Luzmilda he was raised in Guanacaste, between Liberia and Playa Hermosa. His family hailed from Catalonia, like Don Pepe's. They escaped fascism in Franco's Spain and invested in palm oil. As a boy, he sought shade beneath trees as wide as buildings, his skin tanning from the oven-dry sun. He would bury himself in the sand in front of his family's beach house and learned English from gringos who sipped on mojitos at the next-door resort. It was a beautiful, normal adolescence. His parents had loved each other. His father was God-fearing but did not preach. Seth was the center of his universe because he was an only child. No younger brother born on his birthday. His mother had loved him and called him *my king*.

Over the next six months, Luzmilda took turns telling him her own stories, beginning a new chapter of her life when she visited Seth to massage the atrophy out of his body. Her ancestors were German, she said. Her parents had been Bavarian immigrants who owned coffee plantations by the Poás Volcano. "The government took everything from us," she said. "They snatched it all away when they declared war on Germany in '41. ¿Can you believe that? This insignificant stretch of forest declaring war on the great empire. My family had never heard anything so ridiculous. Luckily we avoided the concentration camp. We abandoned the plantation when we heard of our neighbors being taken away by the secret police. We ran and hid in the mountains." Luzmilda dabbed her forehead with a yellow handkerchief Max usually carried around in his pocket. As Luzmilda told her tale, Seth couldn't help but notice how dark her skin was, how tight her hair curled, how her lips, nose, and cheekbones betrayed this personal history. If Germany had been a nation in Central America, then, yes, the story checked out. But he did a good job of concealing his suspicion the more she spoke of her ancestry.

"The government was trying to exterminate the white race," she said as matter-of-factly as one says it's going to be a scorcher. *Exterminate the white race*—the bar in Escazú returned to Seth. The neon beer sign. Osario's anxiety. The bathroom floor of piss and grime. The man who'd walked in and flashed Seth a cordial nod. Seventies, hair blond-turned-white.

Max stepped into the room, angling a newspaper close to his chest. He wore a baseball cap and boat shoes. *It couldn't be*, Seth thought.

"Impossible," Seth muttered.

"¿What is it, dear?" Luzmilda sipped a sweating glass of orange juice.

Max lowered the newspaper to remove the cap and smooth back his hair. He stared at Seth over his spectacles, clean as mirrors. "You're talking his ear off, Luzmilda," Max grunted. "You're as aggressive as a croc. Let's let him rest."

"No, it interests me," Seth rebounded. A new static raised from the floorboards, and by the looks of it, it seemed to stand only Seth's hairs on end.

"How about," Max began, "we get Paulo walking again."

"I like that idea," Luzmilda said sweetly. "Get you up and at 'em," she said in perfect English. The static traveled up Seth's spine.

"I believe I'm ready," Seth said. He flung his leg over the side of the bed and received the crutches from Max. With his help and Luzmilda's, Seth lifted himself. The crutches dug into his armpits as he stumbled forward, his right leg atrophied from being so long unused. Like he was a baby taking its first few steps, Max and Luzmilda let Seth go, to get the hang of what would be this alternate reality. Through the bedroom doorway, the bungalow expanded into light-wood quarters—the living room of brown leather seating, a fireplace filled with flowers; the black-and-white tile kitchen floor and chrome appliances; a dark corridor leading to the master suite. The sliding glass door called Seth's attention, its gleam and the green horizon beyond it. As he limped, the mountains through the glass felt more and more familiar. The peaks themselves a memory, ridges well traversed in his mind, their emerald a jewel he'd once owned. Max walked past Seth to slide open the door, and there on the sunlit balcony, surrounded by crisp, inviting air, Seth looked out to the world he'd left six months ago. The bungalow hovered halfway up the mountain, and Seth looked below, following pews of coffee bushes leading down to a small valley. In its center, on a lush hill, stood a mansion: colonial style, a stone facade, its metal roof the shade of the forest. Each detail of the structure and its surroundings put themselves back together in a reluctant, disconcerting puzzle. Seth had played on those grounds. He'd snuck through its wooden doors, peered out of its windows, cowered in its shadows. There, nestled at the bottom of this mountain, was the Oreamundo mansion. Arrogant as a nightmare; inviting as one too.

"¿Where am I?" Seth murmured.

"You're home," Max said, resting his arms on the deck railing, and flashed Seth a cordial, fatherly nod.

Costa Rica is home to

One

witness

with two

mouths

2018

All the world glows green: jade, tattered wallpaper, mint-hued floorboards, Neo's face, painted sickly, like moss. "Do you believe in fate?" asks Morpheus. Cinematic thunder overhead. If one could see the lightning crack the sky in two, it, too, would be green.

"No," says Neo.

"Why not?" asks Morpheus.

"I don't like the idea that I'm not in control of my life."

Horacio stepped into *rawtopLoganCircle*'s row house. On the living room television, Morpheus offered Neo a red pill. *Freed from the Matrix. Freed from this simulation, this reality that is not a reality at all.*

The man pulled Horacio in without a greeting, helped him out of his skinny jeans and pulled his shirt over his head to fold on the plush, blue velvet love seat. They were tender, his motions and demeanor. Even though the man whose name Horacio didn't ask had yet to speak, Horacio felt serenaded, courted. Cared for. The man's nipples were pink, and freckles painted his skin as if from a flicked brush. The more Horacio studied the man's body—his muscles bulging from undressing, from picking up Horacio by his ass and carrying him to a large, disheveled bed—the more the man reminded him of artwork. A statue studied in art history class or marveled at in the National

Gallery. Zeus, or David himself, bronzed from a recent beach trip, who treated Horacio with the tenderness of a father.

"Call me Daddy," the man said. There was intimacy in a name that was not a name.

"Yes, sir."

"Good boy."

The man flipped Horacio over onto his stomach, grabbed his ass with both hands, and began kissing, then biting, then rubbing soft skin with stubble. It tickled. Horacio wondered how he tasted. What the man was tasting. If he liked it. He must have, because the man didn't stop until Horacio shivered from the cool drip of lube on the relaxed part of him, then was overcome by the addictive pain of being filled by another. Horacio wondered if the blade of a knife felt this good. He moaned into the pillow, but the man lifted the back of Horacio's head by his hair.

"Don't. I want to hear you, boy."

And like a good boy, Horacio mewled, begged, opened himself until all of the man fit inside him, and he wanted nothing more than to make the man a permanent part of himself. To walk around with him; to sit, and laugh, and sleep with this new, overwhelming addition. Horacio felt it pulse, felt milk pour from the man as if forced from a tube. Warm.

"Are you okay, boy?" the man asked.

"Yes, Daddy. I'm great."

Horacio turned over onto his back and rested his head on the man's pec.

"What's your name?"

Horacio wouldn't say.

"I'm Colin."

Horacio studied Colin's room, trying to guess his age by his belongings. In the closet, ajar, five suits hung in a neat line. A thick silver watch glinted, lonely in the center of the dresser next to a single cologne bottle. The only visible life in the bedroom was an orchid in full bloom, stark white. Colin had treated Horacio with the attentiveness and reverence one shows a rare flower. Horacio exhaled.

The Matrix played until Colin fell asleep. It was ten thirty on a Tuesday. At least fifty years old, Horacio said to himself, and sat up from the bed. He dressed.

The Oracle balances a green cigarette in her fingers, offering sage advice.

"Don't worry about the vase," she says to Neo, who steps back in confusion, knocking it over. A crash. Spilled green water and spilled green flowers.

"How did you know?" asks Neo.

Horacio let himself out.

The Oracle strikes a match, an enchanting, mischievous grin across her face. "What's really going to bake your noodle later on is: would you still have broken it if I hadn't said anything?"

Horacio blocked Colin on Grindr as he walked home.

He didn't know why Colin had asked his name. And Horacio didn't know why he had studied the room, the house, trying to get to know Colin from his material possessions. Why did he care? It was the anonymity Horacio had wanted, what they both said they wanted to begin with. Horacio didn't know why Colin had divulged his name. He broke their initial contract: to disregard that the other truly existed, so that henceforth they would exist only in thoughts and dreams of each other. Horacio touched the bark of trees as he strolled, stepping purposefully on ginkgo fruit, inhaling the shit-smell. He grazed dogwood flowers with an outstretched hand, the petals soft. Horacio felt something drip into his underwear. He was still carrying Colin inside him.

Andrés was surprised that his mother had been able to keep his father's plants alive after so long. He turned off the YouTube podcast he'd been half listening to and examined the splendid tropical flora in the dark. Horacio still wasn't home. Nieves and Isa had bickered about something or other for hours before conking out in their room, so Andrés didn't have to worry about covering for him. Andrés had only inaudible memories of what his father would call these plants—flashes of silent, jaw-stretching pronunciation, rounding of the lips, cold enthusiasm in the eyes. Andrés could google their genera if he wanted, but appreciating their leaves, their nighttime perfume, he'd rather name the plants himself, because a man's satisfaction comes from being the first to do things. He was his girlfriend's first lover, for example. They'd gotten nowhere past second base, but Andrés hoped that would change on prom night. A fantasy Horacio teased him about, because Horacio was obsessed with movies from the 1900s and their clichés. Andrés liked to think he was a pioneer in lovemaking, in plant naming. He worried that his girlfriend wouldn't go for his proposal once they got to the hotel room his buddies had booked, so he'd been seeking counsel from podcast hosts, loud men surrounded by scantily clad models. *Women are gold-diggers*, they asserted. *They only fuck men with money.* In anticipation, Andrés had gotten a job at the Chipotle beneath the mural of Marilyn Monroe on Calvert Street. He constructed burritos and rang up ornery customers who'd been skimped out on guacamole like his manager instructed. He was saving up for a new pair of pants and a wad of bills from which to flash from its pockets.

Andrés returned to his bedroom and resumed the podcast, the ranting interrupted by an unskippable ad for the November midterm elections: in concert, brown migrants tried to tear down Trump's fence, followed by a clip of a bald man—Mexican, from his accent—being sentenced to prison. "I killed cops," he bragged. "I will break out soon and kill more." His proud grin faded to text: DEMOCRATS LET HIM INTO OUR COUNTRY. "I will kill more soon." DEMOCRATS LET HIM STAY. More Fox News footage, this time of a Spanish-speaking man at the border. A white woman interpreted his declaration into the mic: "I wish to apply for a pardon. For my felony of attempted murder." WHO ELSE WOULD DEMOCRATS LET IN?

This was the first year Andrés would be able to vote, and the algorithm knew that. At first he complained of the incessant, unavoidable political ads to Horacio, who in turn connected Andrés's favorite podcasts to eventual fascist rhetoric. "They're targeting you because that shit you're subscribed to leads straight there." But Andrés wasn't a fascist, and his heart lit fire whenever Horacio or Xavier made fun of him, so he'd stopped mentioning it altogether. There were others with Andrés's experience on Reddit and 4chan, and he'd joined in their commiseration. The more alone he felt, the more the chatrooms embraced him like a homecoming.

The front door creaked open, and Horacio snuck into their bedroom. "Are they up?" he asked Andrés.

"No, they knocked out hours ago. Where were you?"

"Nowhere." Suddenly, the Grindr ping—the unmistakable strum of some obnoxious, homophobic instrument. "Fine," Horacio said. "I was out."

"You gotta be careful, dude."

"Oh, so I have to beware of gay men?"

"That's not what I meant."

Just as Andrés sought male guidance from his podcasts, Horacio found it in his hookups. It was fair, Andrés thought—they were both fatherless. He filled the vacuum within himself with advice from men with mics, while Horacio did so with affection from randos in dark alleyways or grimy basements.

“Now who’s full of movie clichés?” Horacio scoffed.

“I just don’t want you to get hurt,” Andrés said.

“And I don’t want you to get red-pilled.” Horacio shut off the light and splayed out on his bed across the room. Andrés turned over to face the wall, its polished paint reflecting the streetlamp light. Thunder cracked overhead, and all the world burned green.

THE FACE OF HIS GARMENT

2012

Seth sat on the ancient steps of the Oreamundo mansion. Situated on the bank of the great Tárcoles River, the house bathed like a maiden in the morning sun. By the water, Seth watched members of his family (those he knew, others he didn't) slicing open the stomachs of twelve crocodiles to retrieve the different parts of Osario they'd swallowed. On the sand softened by the receding surf, they puzzled his brother back together. Joints to their correct sockets, cleaved bones to their better halves. Seth's parents were there, and his grandfather, and the grandmother he'd never met, who had burned up in a furniture shop. Everyone repaired the jigsaw of his brother. Ola was the one to fasten the head. A pop, then lock, as if merely cracking the neck to relieve a bit of stiffness. The corpses of the twelve crocodiles washed back onto the water's surface, upturned bellies scooped out like canoes. Leaving Osario's put-back-together body on the shore, each member of Seth's family (those he knew, others he didn't) climbed into a different crocodilian cadaver and floated into the fog. Seth was left alone yet again, and he startled awake to the same mist-stained bungalow on the side of a mountain.

Luzmilda knew when Seth had had nightmares. She brought him the pills to swallow, whose dosage Bronson had increased slowly over the past year. Sometimes Seth saw in Luzmilda's eyes the coquettish glint of a predator. As if she forced down giddy hunger when he grew tired of his crutches or complained of perpetual aches. She asked if Seth was reliving the attack when he tossed so hard she would find him enveloped by the caul of the fitted sheet. One day, she asked who Osario was.

"That's the name you yell out," she said. "All night, you grunt it."

"No," Seth finally answered. "It's not a name. My parents are interred in an ossuary. In my dreams I visit their bones. And their bones are so white they frighten me."

"Imagine that," Luzmilda chuckled. "Being frightened by white. That's like being scared of light itself. Like cowering because you feel warmth and salvation. Perhaps you are afraid of being loved, Paulo. Perhaps you weren't as loved as you told us. But you're here now. Here with us, and we love you like a son."

"We lost our own son many years ago," Max said, walking into the room with a mug of coffee. "Killed by a Nicaraguan at a bar. Those monsters carry around machetes and chop through Costa Ricans as if we're sugarcane. Those savages think we're stalks."

"This is the first time you're mentioning him," Seth said.

"It is painful," Luzmilda said. "To lose a son, and to know there will never be justice for his death. The government let the murderer go, those bastards. The lawyers said our sweet son started that fight. Called him a 'dirty Nica' and swung."

"And good on him if that *were* true," Max reinforced his wife's statement. "They come here to kill, and rape, and leech off the money *we* give to the government for *us* and *ours*. Salvador was merely standing up for his country."

Both Max and Luzmilda looked to Seth for reassurance. "Yes," Seth said. "I'm sure he was a good man, standing up for his country."

"*Our* country," Max said.

"Our country," Seth repeated.

"Don't be afraid to say it," Luzmilda said. She handed Seth toast and a tube of guava jam. "One must never be afraid to speak the truth, ¿right, *Paulo*?" The glint in her eyes.

"Yes," Seth gulped.

"Paulo is our Salvador," Luzmilda said to Max.

Max didn't answer. He was staring into his coffee mug and breathing deeply.

"Your parents may be in an ossuary," Luzmilda continued, patting Seth on the shoulder. "But we aren't."

* * *

Over the past year, Seth's reasons for staying had changed as often as his bandages. Most obviously, his missing leg made him immobile. He'd still not mastered the crutches, and even if he could manage a quickened pace, Luzmilda in her sixty-odd years would catch right up. Max kept the truck in the garage, with its door that creaked as loud as an alarm, and Seth didn't know how many kilometers on foot through the jungle lay between himself and a hamlet or a narco's secret compound. Max and Luzmilda kept no telephone in the bungalow. Any business they had was handled by visiting or being visited. Those of the latter camp greeted Seth cheerfully when they arrived, but nothing more. Never once asking what he was doing here or who he was in relation to the couple, or even where his leg had gone. He'd acted nonchalant the few times he asked guests to take him into town—Orosi or Paraíso—for errand running, to which they answered, *Max and Luzmilda are taking good care of you.* At his wit's end, Seth pleaded to one woman like a maniac, and she burst out of the bungalow, her intended delivery of strawberries trailing behind like fat drops of blood. Even if Seth were to escape—smuggle himself into the truck bed while Max wasn't looking, or make a run for it over the mountain—what would he say to the Good Samaritan who found him? Any line of questioning, especially by an enthusiastic policeman, would eventually lead back to his true identity. The order of his exile, broken. Tracks leading back to his brother, butchered in the river. In no scenario did Seth see himself actually making it to a phone to call Ignacio at the embassy or Nieves back in D.C. He weighed the prospect of life in prison or a few more months here while Bronson fitted him for a prosthetic, and he overwhelmingly preferred the latter.

Besides the physical logistics that kept Seth trapped, he was saturated by equally endless mental and emotional obstacles. He didn't much mind being around Luzmilda. Liked her, even; her irresistible charm breaking through her jejune stories and obvious lies. Despite the pathology of her personality, she was affectionate. She'd taken the idea of *Paulo* and run with it. Treated Seth like the son they'd lost. Doted upon him as if he were a small, fragile child. She prepared any meal he craved, read gossip rags aloud in bed, kneaded the aches from his flesh, and groomed his hair, beard, and nails. The name *Paulo* had brought him into her good graces, and when she warbled it at dawn or whispered it before lights out, its two softened syllables rocked him like arms. Max, however, didn't join in his wife's tenderness. He was curt, cagey. But his coldness was not unlike a father's. Beneath the chill of his timbre resounded great respect. And at times Seth heard a swell of admiration. Perhaps, Seth thought, this is what it felt like to have parents. To be parented.

Then there was the mystery of his family's mansion. Down the slope from the bungalow was Seth's childhood home, winking like some jewel at the bottom of a box. Neither Max nor Luzmilda made mention of it, so nor would Seth, afraid of drawing attention to it. Attention to himself. On bright, moonlit nights when Seth was convinced his hosts were asleep, he'd hobble to the railing and scan the distant mansion's grounds for ghosts—his family's, his own. But only the wind frolicked through the leaves of coffee bushes. Through his phantom limb like fear.

"¿How long have they been here?" Seth asked Bronson one day in late July, sitting in a new wheelchair. He felt like a broken arm in a sling.

"Since 2005, I think," the doctor said. "¿How does it feel?"

"Fine," Seth lied. "¿And they bought this house?"

"No, Max and Luzmilda built it. Test the wheels. Sometimes these new ones can get stuck, rub together, and start a fire. Nothing a little WD-40 can't fix." Bronson kept his attention on the spokes and tires. "They built this house after they bought the mansion down the mountain."

Seth froze in his testing of the chair. The wheels squeaked, so the doctor approached, his breath keen on the back of Seth's neck. "¿They built a house after they bought a mansion?" Seth asked.

"I don't understand it either. Max treats the place like an antique. ¿You know that one piece of furniture your mother never let you touch? ¿Like your grubby little hands would make it fall apart? You didn't hear it from me, but Max locks himself inside that place for hours on end. If I'm down the road, taking a piss or chatting with a neighbor, I see him pry open that ancient gate and drive up to that corpse of stone. I can't tell if he treats it like a clubhouse or a mausoleum. I asked one time offhandedly if it had belonged to his family. He said no, just someone whom he respected."

"¿Who'd he buy it from?"

"The Orea-somethings. I never met them, but the neighbors say they were a weird couple whose gossip stretched as far back as the last century. Some say they had political connections, but no one knows for sure. Most of the neighbors moved to the area in the late '90s, and I've only been here since '02, after

California. That family had apparently spent one hundred years alone there. Like that book."

"¿What happened to the couple?" His parents.

"Oh, they died. That's why the house was sold. They'd lost the rights to the land in the '80s to the coffee companies, who parceled it off. Illy, Folgers, Maxwell—¿don't those sound like greedy relatives? Max nabbed the property from the last exporter holding out for a buyer because the bushes weren't bearing fruit. ¿See that ocean of plants? Barren as a hedge garden. I heard these mountains used to smell like breakfast. Now it's just dirt and the perfume when the rain hits it. Fine with me, though." Bronson pushed Seth back and forth in the chair like a wheelbarrow. "My doctor says I need to lay off the caffeine," he chuckled. "¿How does that feel?"

Seth nodded and motioned for his crutches. He lifted himself from the wheelchair, slid open the glass door, and wobbled onto the deck.

"¿Need some fresh air, huh?" Bronson said, wiping his hands.

Seth peered down at the Oreamundo mansion, delicate fog coating it like gauze. "¿When did you say you could fit me for a prosthetic, Doctor?"

"Soon," Bronson answered. He packed up his bag and slammed the truck door behind him, waving a single, respectful palm at Seth before he pulled off down the serpentine mud-gravel road.

THE DOORS OF HIS FACE

2013

They named Max after his father. In a city of glass close to the border with Mexico, he was born into a camp which, throughout his early childhood, he assumed had been constructed to make kids concentrate in school. Beyond the bakery's alluring, delicious hand, the stink of spinach hung in the air, and dawn's clouds were green, fibrous, and veiny. Max grew up with other classmates' rumors that a statue of Popeye the Sailor Man stood firmly on dry land, though he'd never see it. He lived with his parents in a cottage in the camp's center, the German section, with its baked German goods served in the German-decorated mess hall. On the outskirts of the camp were the Japanese, with the Italians' neighborhood a barrier between the two forced-together nations. Max's parents slept in one bedroom, while Max dreamed in another, about what lurked beyond the walls—the monsters who had plopped them here or the angels who would pluck them to safety. Despite his German lessons, the adults spoke Spanish. Within the walls, those here were German, but beyond the Gulf, his parents were Central and South American. Born on this land, Max had the unique advantage of being North American. He even had papers to prove it. His parents' papers, however, had been shredded in front of their faces.

A year before he was born, his father, Max Sr., had been living comfortably in Costa Rica, working in the government; Ava, his mother, enjoyed a debutante's privilege in Peru. However, *their* parents' homeland across the Atlantic had outgrown its borders like a forest: a natural perennial process, because there was nothing more beautiful than German woods. Max Jr. imagined his grandparents' nation beleaguered by odious lumberjacks, hacked at for merely spreading beyond its own tree line once or twice. This meant that the men, women, and children of German descent were either forced into camps back home or tossed onto steamships like rats, smuggled into a place called New Orleans, where their documents were shredded in front of their faces. Stripped of their nationality, they were transported here to Texas. Max Sr. and Ava met one afternoon at the camp's theater, where Japanese girls were putting on a play. Sitting next to each other by chance, they commented to each other on the beauty of the performance, and afterward, Max Sr. invited Ava to an evening pastry. It was a spark not unlike in the movies: a quick marriage, an even quicker conception, and in 1942, Max Jr. arrived by stork, he was told. Sometimes he dreamed of that benevolent bird.

His family wasn't let go until three years after the Second Great War ended, their hosts the victors. His parents couldn't decide whether to go back to Costa Rica or Peru, so they settled on New York City, where his father could easily find work as an engineer. But no one would hire a German, especially a Spanish-speaking one, and the consulate lay as bare as a haunted house. With no other choice, Max Sr. became a garbageman, and Ava a night maid. His parents argued over money, and over secrets they huffed and hissed in Spanish. Subjects from back home, Max Jr. assumed, pretending to read comic books as they fought. Several times, his mother mentioned papers—documents, newspapers, letters. Texts that angered her. Max would hear the slam of his father's metal-leather trunk. One day when his parents' shifts overlapped, Max snuck into their closet and jimmied open the trunk with a nail, then rummaged through stacks of papers—the documents, newspapers, and letters. There were memos headed with an odd acronym—NSDAP—addressed to or signed by his father, as well as official-looking forms belonging to the Costa Rican government. Beneath the bureaucracy lay stacks of newspapers, all from one periodical called *El Cartaginés*. Max flipped through years of them. Beneath the newsprint were neat stacks of bundled envelopes. Unsealed, unsent letters, all addressed to someone named Otilio Oreamundo. The author of the newspaper's weekly column, he realized. *Alemanes*, a word he recognized. And *Campos de concentración*. For years, this Otilio reported on German camps in Costa Rica.

"He was a great friend of mine," Max Sr. said in the doorway. "Whom I always believed would do the right thing. He understood what your mother is reluctant to admit: the world wishes to exterminate us. Society sees your blue eyes and wants to pluck them out, wants to uproot your beautiful blond locks from your scalp. He was my confidant, you see," his father said, bending down to dig through the stack. From the bottom of the trunk he exhumed dozens of photographs—some featuring himself and Otilio Oreamundo, dapper in pressed suits, posing in front of different buildings of his father's design, constructed, he said, with Otilio's invaluable help. But there was one structure that bore no humans in its frame. It looked like an ancient temple in the middle of a jungle. *A discovery?* Max Jr. asked. No, it was a shrine from his father's mind. An offering to a man that should have won. "I wish to see him again," his father said. "Otilio. To thank him for his great work, for his companionship and inspiring words. Perhaps I will before I die."

Ava discovered them hovering over the trunk that day and kicked Max Sr. out of the house. She burned its contents, an effigy of the man named Otilio Oreamundo. Max's father moved to a mold-laced, roach-infested apartment in deep Brooklyn and died of esophageal cancer when Max Jr. was twelve. Alone in a hospital bed because his mother didn't even tell her son his father was sick. After the small, underwhelming funeral, Max Jr. arrived home and rummaged beneath his mattress. He removed a photograph he'd smuggled from the trunk, bent down the middle: his father on the left of the crease, and Otilio Oreamundo on its right.

"When I was old enough, I moved here to Costa Rica," Max said. "Tracking down Otilio was difficult; everyone I asked said he'd become a recluse after losing the election in '48. Where to, no one would say. No bribes or begging brought me any closer. I'd arrived at a dead end. In the meantime, I started a shipping business, importing appliances from the U.S., and on weekends I scoured this whole country for the temple my father had built. If I couldn't find Otilio, I might as well claim my birthright. Even when I met and married Luzmilda, I traversed every forest from Guanacaste to Limón. You wouldn't believe the things I saw in between—marijuana farms, vicuña ranches, poaching facilities for jaguars and monkeys, and even an orgy of macaws on the clay side of a mountain. Salvador was born, but I didn't let that stop me. Then, one day in August of '81, I drove past a horde of palmers and decided to ask if they'd happened to see a temple in the middle of the forest. There was a woman holding a baby who pointed me in the direction from which they'd come. She didn't know how to describe the path up to it but said I'd know it when I saw it. I've learned in my life that you have to believe in people with blind faith, so I cut the motor and continued on foot—I trusted my feet more than I did my truck. After about a half hour, I saw two men dismount their horses and hack their way through the underbrush. The one with the machete was older, his hair and mustache white. About a hundred meters behind, I followed onto the trail the old man had cleared and emerged on the other side to lush knolls and overgrown footpaths. I couldn't believe my eyes. At the top of that hill stood the building from my father's photographs. Magnificent, more impressive and intimidating than any skyscraper that hurt my neck growing up. I fell to my knees, and I swear to God, I outstretched my arms. I wanted to embrace this temple, call out my father's name. When I came to, I noticed that the younger man was actually a boy. He studied the temple's pyramid and the crocodile atop it before stepping inside. I had no idea who they were, so I went to the left wing and slid through a hole a tree branch had punched through the facade. I waited behind a trunk, watching the old man and the boy weave between obelisks of sunlight, catching only bits and pieces of their conversation over the crunch of glass and echo of stone. From where I stood, it sounded like a tour. Then the man left and before the boy could turn to fix his eyes on me, I hid, shadow-quick. When I heard his footsteps leave, I followed down the corridor, and from the entrance I saw him: Otilio Oreamundo, standing exactly where you're standing right now."

Seth balanced on the weather-worn steps before the doorway of the temple, through which the stink of rot and rock blew out with Max's every revelation.

"And the boy was standing where I am. I would have shouted to them, but I was too stunned to speak."

"¿How did you know it was Otilio?" Seth asked, resituating a crutch beneath his armpit.

"Every year I imagined what age and gravity would do to the face I saw in my father's picture. And adding up those four decades, Otilio looked exactly as I'd predicted. Not a hair out of place, or wrinkle unwrinkled."

"¿Did you get a good look at the boy?"

"No. His back was turned to me the whole time. But I assumed it to be his grandson. For years, I thought it could be Osario."

"Thought," Seth repeated. The crocodile atop the pyramid yawned from an exhausting, familiar hunger.

"*I do not know why men want power*," Max said, excavating Otilio's words from Seth's memory. "I remember clearly now. He asked: ¿Why do you want power, *Seth*?"

Seth's phantom limb kicked to run. "¿The whole time?" Seth sighed. Again a gust of stone-stink.

"No, I can't pretend that I knew from the beginning. When I followed Osario to the bar that night, I couldn't have fathomed it might have been you he was talking to. Impossible, I thought, because the Seth Oreamundo I knew about disappeared. Putrefying in a prison cell or banished somewhere. ¿Where were you all those years?"

"D.C."

"Imagine that."

"And you followed us."

"All the way to the river."

"¿And Luzmilda?"

"She really was at her cousin's in Capulín. It's true that she applied the tourniquet when I showed up with you, unconscious in my truck bed. She rode next to you the whole way back, in fact. But she didn't witness you on the riverbank. After you tossed your brother in."

"¿Who does she think I am?"

"We'll let her see the man named Paulo. Since our Salvador was murdered, she's fallen into a hundred different depressions, every single one unique as a flower in a field. But I'm allergic," Max said coolly. "I'm not one to sulk. After my father died, I did something about it. And after I watched Osario and my plans get torn to shreds, I did something about that too."

"¿Why did you want my brother?" Seth paused for another deep breath from the temple. "¿What do you want with me?"

"My father loved your grandfather," Max said, passing Seth down two stairs. The back of his head looked appetizing, bludgeon-able. "They had unfinished business. ¿See that number above you? The year the revolution began. The new world order our enemies extinguished. Until now. We are torchbearers, lighting the way through the cave of this putrid society. You will come to the same conclusion as your grandfather, as I came to my father's. It's our destiny, Seth. This temple is living proof of that."

Max descended the stairs at a younger man's pace, skipping one or two steps just for the fun of it. Today, his white hair burned blond. His beard, arm fuzz, eyebrows, the shade of a lion's mane. In the sunlight, Seth's body hair, too, resembled the coat of another animal. His spirit had been relieved of a strange weight. Yet something smaller, rounder, and dense started a drumbeat within him. An organ, inherited, that could flex like an arm, supply blood like a heart. And like a desperate lung or a gluttonous throat, it would begin to crave.

Costa Rica is home to

its own myth

2018

The night Horacio and Andrés graduated high school, Horacio attended his first orgy. One ceremony took place late morning, while the other started at seven that evening. *Class of '18.*

Neither Horacio nor Andrés was particularly excited about walking across the stage, shaking the principal's hand, or holding their diploma up like a torch—their generation didn't believe in these kinds of rituals. This was all for the parents. Nieves and Isa cheered idiotically from the front row when their sons' names were called. Nieves wore a herringbone suit (her forehead glistened, and sweat curved around her lips), but Isa had actually paid attention to the weather forecast and wore a chartreuse linen dress. Their sons had done it. They had completed this part of their lives and were on a path to success, each having gotten into NYU. They would pack up, head out, and move into dorms in the fall. They would fulfill their own destinies.

It took weeks for Horacio to convince Andrés of New York last year, after he fished the first season of *The Real World* out of a bargain bin. The city's snow-lined streets, moody artists, and undeniable style invited his imagination into a horizonless world where liberation curled around every corner, and he and Andrés could be whomever they wanted as long as they were together. Andrés fought it initially—he wanted a state school. Tailgates, fraternities, a life of red Solo cups and football games. He didn't care about bands or clubbing, and he hated the idea of not being able to see the sky. To win him over, Horacio forced him to watch *Taxi Driver*, *Do the Right Thing*, and *The Godfather*, the latter of which did the trick. Andrés couldn't see himself ever becoming a mobster, but the idea of an underworld where different rules applied excited him. He liked knowing that there were people who existed outside the system, who took matters into their own hands.

While Nieves and Isa flooded the auditorium with noise and jubilation, each sister was trapped in her own mind with the prospect of being alone with the other after the boys moved to Manhattan. They'd been inseparable as girls, apart as teenagers, together again as women, then That Whole Thing dug a furious chasm between them. Seven years reunited now, but with their sons as crutches. If left unaccompanied, they didn't know if their relationship could stand on its own.

Nieves and Isa took their boys to Haydee's to celebrate. To everyone on the street, to the staff and the owner herself (whom everyone swore was a vampire), they bragged and scrolled through graduation photos, pictures of their acceptance letters and financial aid offers. The two sisters made a fuss and ordered more pitchers of margaritas, and the two boys sunk deeper into their seats, embarrassed. They couldn't wait to move and use the excuse that their dorms had no space for their mothers to stay. Isa asked Horacio why he wasn't eating much, and he said his stomach hurt. Nerves, his mother said. *That's all right. We'll take some dishes to go.* She smiled, and tousled his gelled hair.

Horacio and Andrés spent that afternoon in Xavier's backyard, puffing on a hookah, exhaling thick, blueberry clouds. The summer between high school and college was finally here—freedom was what the boys had agreed upon. House parties, drives to the Shenandoah, sneaking into bars and maybe a club or two. Oh, the magic of the next three months in the sweet stagnancy of academic purgatory. Nothing would matter; they could do whatever they wanted. The three graduates blew smoke rings, relit the coals like experts, and divined what summer would hold for them. The joy of boys left to their own devices.

Inspired by their afternoon conversation, Horacio decided to push his limits. He answered a Craigslist invite to an orgy that night. Before the store-bought enema and scalding shower, Horacio studied his body in the mirror. He sucked in his abs and counted his ribs. He tapped his collar bones; they answered with a hollow sound. He grabbed his ass with both hands, bounced the perfect mixture of muscle and fat. Horacio thought back to the man who mistakenly revealed his name, and the way that man with a name had looked at him. That's the way they'll all look at me, Horacio fantasized. That's the only way he wanted men to look at him. He didn't mind being an object if it meant becoming a talisman to be worshipped.

The Uber was uncharacteristically early (Horacio met the driver three blocks from their apartment building) and uncharacteristically speedy (no traffic on the Fourteenth Street Bridge into Virginia), so Horacio arrived ten minutes before the actual start of the party and was greeted by the skeptical host, who asked for Horacio's ID. *Legal.*

He treated Horacio to a beer from the white fridge, which he sipped slowly and deliberately. Seven o'clock came, and men of all ages and body types flooded in, standing on the periphery of the cerulean gym mats set up carefully on the floor. Horacio eyed a few men, and they eyed him back. When the host had finished reciting the house rules—conditions, consent, condoms—he invited everyone to strip. They did so, except for Horacio, who was suddenly surrounded by more nakedness than he had ever seen in his life, and he realized the hollow sound his collarbones had answered with earlier was fear. Horacio could get down only to his underwear as the orgy began. Everyone else paired up while he stood with his back to the wall. In front of him an ocean of testosterone overflowed, a chorus of sounds he'd only ever heard in porn. The men now a writhing mass, like earthworms in a rainstorm. Horacio smelled clay and silicone, sweat from the disturbed gym mats and ripe bodies. He quickly realized his limit had been reached the moment he walked through the door. Horacio had underestimated freedom.

The exit lay beyond the men, on the opposite side of the apartment. Horacio had almost figured out the logistics of his escape when a man walked in, very late. He stripped bare, opened the fridge for a beer, and stood next to Horacio. He introduced himself.

"Carlos." He smiled, his breath pungent with cigarette smoke and Listerine meant to mask it.

Horacio could feel Carlos studying his anxiety. He felt foolish. *What did you think was going to happen at an orgy?* Horacio imagined him saying. But Carlos asked him, in Spanish, if he wanted to go make out. Horacio looked up because he recognized the accent. A Costa Rican, here at an orgy in Crystal City. Horacio agreed, and they walked to the center of the squirming, moaning sea, and kissed. Tenderly at first, then the Costa Rican man named Carlos coaxed Horacio's tongue out of his mouth with his own, massaged his back, then his ass. Horacio felt weak. Even in Carlos's grip, he thought he'd fall over.

"Let's get out of here," Carlos said as if he'd read Horacio's angst like a neon billboard, and tousled his hair. "This place is a little loud. Let's go get a cup of coffee."

They dressed in the foyer, and Carlos called them an Uber to Dupont Circle to grab lattes down the street from Carlos's hotel. At one of the semicircular benches, a woman in a head wrap played an original song on her guitar. A homeless, shoeless man danced cha-cha to the melody that was clearly not a cha-cha. Horacio and Carlos sat at the lip of the fountain, facing each other, and commented on the beauty of the evening.

"¿So, you're from Costa Rica I take it?" Horacio asked.

"I am. And judging from your ass, so are you."

"Born in San José, lived there until I was ten."

"¿What made you move here?"

Horacio sipped his coffee to avoid the question. He slipped off his shoes, dipped his feet in the water, and grabbed a wish with his toes. "My mother" was all Horacio said. "¿What are you doing here?"

"Visiting friends," Carlos answered. "I'm here until tomorrow, then I start grad school."

"¿In San José?"

"Yes. ¿Do you ever go back?"

"No. My mother doesn't talk about it much."

"You should. If you come back, I'll show you around. I'll take you to the volcanoes and the beach, and we can fuck all night." Carlos grinned.

"I've always wanted to go back. I'd do anything to go back."

"Well, ¿what's stopping you, Horacio?"

Horacio stared into Carlos's black eyes. He was much taller, so Horacio's neck cramped a little. Beneath his tight, white shirt, Carlos had a body that belonged in magazines. What was stopping him? Now that the most handsome man he'd ever kissed was asking—inviting him, even—what was it that intimidated him? *Everything*, Horacio wanted to say. *Everything is stopping me.*

"Nothing," Horacio said. "I guess nothing is really stopping me."

The sun marched groggily off to bed, and the humid air cooled; the refreshing fountain mist coated Horacio's legs with goose bumps. It wasn't yet midnight curfew, so he went back with Carlos to his hotel. They shared a cocktail at the dimly lit bar—a mezcal drink with gold glitter. "Our shit will be worth money," Carlos laughed.

Carlos's room was large, with a clear view of the circle. Cars honked and tried to pass one another. Restaurants closed, unplugged their string lights, folded chairs. Horacio and Carlos both stripped down, but they didn't have sex. Instead, Carlos sat on the comfortable armchair and Horacio straddled him, cowgirl. Horacio's dick rested on Carlos's abs, and he could feel Carlos's tip underneath him. They talked about their days, their schools, a bit about their families. Carlos spoke of his father, but Horacio didn't. When the topic arose, Horacio interjected Nieves into the conversation. He had two mothers instead. She was stricter than Isa: harsher, but caring.

"So, ¿they're sisters?" Carlos asked.

"Yeah, but everyone thinks they're lesbians. People think Andrés and I are twins and that our moms adopted us from another country."

Carlos's parents were both psychiatrists in San Pedro. "I'm certifiably crazy," Carlos said. "Anyone within earshot of a psychiatrist is mentally ill. Especially their kids."

Horacio laughed sincerely at all of Carlos's jokes. He was funny. This beautiful man could make him laugh and had even saved him from his first orgy.

"I did save you, ¿didn't I? I guess that makes me your Prince Charming."

"¿Does that make me Cinderella?"

"I don't know. ¿What happens to you at midnight?"

Again they kissed, and again they both grew excited at the touch of the other. Horacio didn't know if it was the lust he felt for Carlos or the Spanish they spoke to each other that made him feel as if he were home again. Within Carlos, Horacio felt the cool breath of the valley, the humming cloud forests and rumbling mountainsides of his youth. Again Carlos invited him to visit, and at the final moment, when they had exchanged WhatsApp numbers and a last kiss in the hotel lobby, Horacio agreed.

"I'll even pay for your plane ticket, so you know I'm serious," Carlos said. "I'll make you fall in love with me."

IRON AS STRAW

2016

Now-barren coffee bushes fought back marauding secondary growth in a decades-long war between industry and naturalism. Rainforest reclaimed the crops as the revolution unshackles the working class. From Ola's footsteps into the dense coppice grew white turmeric flowers, and from the bush Gilberto had watched burn sprouted a holy jacaranda, which just last year had bloomed, purple as smashed shells. The concrete walkways to the roastery and to the storage shed had been swallowed by the green throat of the trees; managerial dwellings, drying shacks, and the decaffeination facility all lay disassembled by vines; and the hundreds of specimens in Otilio's greenhouse had broken free of their prison—or rather, had incorporated its metal framework into their new definition of liberation. The only manicured section of the grounds now was the driveway to the mansion's impressive threshold. Hammocks littered the wraparound porch, empty as fishnets. Patio furniture dropped arms and legs like vestigial limbs. Inside, beyond the giant mahogany door—praying to stay on its hinges for another year—the foyer walls shimmered with sconces, paintings, and mounted porcelain vases. The mansion had only one floor, so there was no grand staircase, but its ceilings reached as high as a church's, vaults pocked with the nests of perennial birds. The marble floors, still as cool and smooth as ice, led down a number of different corridors: to bedrooms, bathrooms, the parlor, one to the kitchen and down to its adjacent larder, and one that ended abruptly at a concrete wall painted emerald green. The half of the mansion Gilberto demolished, including Otilio's room and the smells that lingered.

Max's monthly meetings took place in the library, where long ago, hundreds of books sat in mountains on the floor, because their cases had been sold right out from under them. Shelves now floated on the walls, relieving space for chairs, side tables, and a showroom's worth of floor lamps. In the center of the room sat a Victorian billiard table, its four bronzed metal legs malleated into a quartet of pouncing lions. And above the fireplace's green marble mantel hung a human-size oil painting of two men: a rendition of Max's creased photograph of his father and Otilio Oreamundo. Colorized with deep, royal hues (in a John Singer Sargent style Max didn't ask for but ended up really liking), these two adversaries had been limned as comrades, as Max and Seth had by meeting-goers who had loosely organized under a name Max had found in a railway engineering book in the Oreamundo library: the Garroteros.

A brakeman once had many important jobs on a locomotive. He'd been a jack-of-all-trades, and if he didn't fall to his death, he could have mastered them all. Primarily, as the name suggested, a garrotero was expected to apply the brakes in case of a speeding train—the last line of defense against, say, crashing into another, or tumbling off a cliff. He was also tasked with being aware of the axles burning from the train going too fast, gaining too much progress at one time. And lastly, to the brakeman's great pleasure, he was entrusted with sniffing out freeloaders, and he could hurl that vagrant from the steaming machine with impunity. Such were the responsibilities of the brakeman, who thought himself a vanguard: a protector of contents, passengers, and all that they meant. Max's so-called Garroteros convinced themselves that Costa Rica was a runaway train. The government had been too liberal these past decades. Too lenient on immigration and neoliberalism, and now the axles had caught fire. The country hurtling toward ruin.

The first few years of these meetings in the Oreamundo mansion had resembled soirées, sometimes group therapy sessions. Alcohol was served, then coffee and semisweet pastries. White men and women—Costa Rican and gringo alike—traveled from all parts of Cartago and the greater metropolitan area by personal invite or word of mouth. In these meetings, high-spirited chatter eventually turned to insistent complaints—about this or that, families and jobs, or the lack thereof. And as even more time passed, these gripes underwent ugly transformations into blame: companies had not relieved one of his employment, for example, but it had, in fact, been *stolen*. By whom? By Nicaraguans was the popular conclusion. And who ran these companies? Well, the Chinese, the Garroteros surmised. Costa Rica was being invaded by these forces, from the North and from the East. By barbarians and the Orient, who took business from Costa Ricans, and their own government representatives allowed it—no, *encouraged* it.

Max welcomed the Garroteros' proliferation. While the name still fit slack, with enough time it could be tailored to whatever he wanted. The organization's membership had reached the physical limit of the Oreamundo library by 2016, because Costa Rica was a large train and needed many hands to hit the brakes and halt this monstrosity that liberals called progress—how else would they all survive? Personal anecdotes fed discussions, but, with Max's steady captainship, there was always a political undertow below the choppy surface of their frustration. Never in the first years did anyone call for violence. Everyone was merely flexing these newfound ideas, becoming used to them and their potential. Max and Luzmilda recounted their son's demise. Men claimed to have been swindled by Chinese shop owners. Women had survived the shame of Nicaraguans' catcalling. Younger members eventually joined, showing their seniors articles scoured across the internet: machete attacks, sons and daughters converted to the gay and lesbian agenda, the Chinese government infiltrating the public sector, buying up kilometers of real estate. *They're taking over. But perhaps it's not too late.*

For as much time as he could manage, Seth stayed quiet in these meetings he was forced to attend. Max seemed to be allowing him to acclimate, as if the rhetoric were warm, inviting water, but Seth's heart found it thick and disgusting as sludge. He scoffed under his breath, picked apart petty arguments and racist rhetoric in fantasized debate. Sometimes, though, he would step back, outside of himself, and the meetings would play out as if from a simulation, a matrix only he—or Max—could see: Seth's brain had retained its software from his time as a politician, and what he detected was potential. It was when Max instated a monthly fee (which the constituents paid gladly) that Seth realized Max had assembled a herd of sheep—white as wool, braying—whose nascent hatred could be exploited for whatever purpose, which Seth tried to predict with every passing forum. Max was as effective as Gilberto had been so many years before; the Oreamundo mansion had traded in evangelicals for

Nazis—though there were *plenty* of Nazi evangelicals in the Garroteros, the most fervent and generous to the cause.

Luzmilda still addressed Seth as Paulo, as did the rest of the group. *¿What's your opinion, Paulo? ¿Aren't you outraged? ¿Whose side are you on?* Besides the obsession to include him, the members treated Seth with unbelievable kindness. If his arms ached from the crutches, they helped him to Max's truck to return to the bungalow. If his leg cramped, women and men alike massaged it. He was waited on hand and foot, tended to like a king who'd not yet realized he was next in line for the throne. Only Max knew Seth's true identity, and living as another man was becoming more difficult to resist. It took years, but eventually Seth began to answer to the name *Paulo* without second guessing, even if sometimes he grew tired of it. Many days he wanted to cry, *¡Here I am!*

To everyone's disbelief, he would shout, *I was found on the banks of a river in Genesis. Son of Adam and Eve, brother of the murderous Cain, and Abel slain by his hand. I am Abel's replacement. From his blood I rose, congealed into this thing you see before you. This is my name and has always been my name. I know not who this Paulo is. That is not what God bestowed upon me.* But when these confessions threatened to overtake him, Luzmilda's hand would appear, soft as María Cielos's had never been. He regained himself as the person these people wanted him to be. The beating organ within Seth feasted on this strange adoration as the brain mistakes a drug for happiness. It took longer than anyone expected, but Seth had lost his impulse to flee completely.

"¿I thought your mother burned these along with everything else in your father's trunk?" Seth grabbed a newspaper from a stack on the billiards table. Issues of *El Cartaginés*, from June 1942 to the date the Great War ended.

"¿You remember Laura? ¿The woman with straight black hair and the green eyes that twitch? She works for the archives in the National Library. Brought me every paper that featured your grandfather's column."

"Even librarians have joined." Seth ran his sarcasm over the newsprint.

"And lawyers, and union reps, syndics, councilors, deputies, and the mayor of Tucurrique. Our message is everywhere, even in *your* realm."

Seth felt a top button tighten, and a tie loop around his neck, noose-taut. His shoulders itched for a suit, his feet—phantom and physical—for dark leather wing tips. *His realm.*

"And your grandfather's," Max said. He stared somberly at the stack, Seth's trembling hand upon it. "¿What was he like?"

"Stern," Seth began. "Quiet, but with that confidence that frightens lesser men. Like my father. Gilberto was hesitant around my grandfather, and since Otilio took me under his wing, he was hesitant around me too. My grandfather taught me everything—how to argue like a lawyer, sow plants like a farmer; we rode horseback all around these mountains and dove into every book you see around you. He showed me the world before I even knew that such an idea existed. If he hadn't been in my life, I wouldn't have known there was anything beyond these walls. You could have told me the rest of the earth was one giant, manless block of green, and I'd have believed you. But Otilio always challenged me. He opened the horizons of my mind and pushed me to meet them, like a ship rushing to touch sunset. But . . ." Seth paused, flipping through time, both in his memory and in the newspapers, following along as the rhetoric of Otilio's columns grew more radical. Seth mouthed the words he was reading with deep sadness, as he had his grandfather's name over his sarcophagus. ". . . he contained a darkness within him. Something that hurt him always, like a bullet too dangerous to remove. Sometimes I felt that a ghost was talking to me, doting upon me. I could never shake the inkling that he'd transitioned into my life from a previous one, that he'd been someone else before I met him. That shadow self frightened me."

"That darkness was his rejection of the world that wished to hurt those he loved," Max said, pouring himself a drink. Dusk chilled the air, and he tossed three logs into the fireplace. Orange brushed over the portrait of Otilio and Max Sr. "Same as my father. Light creates shadows, which means love creates hatred. Otilio's love forged his odium for the system that sought to exterminate your grandmother. ¿Don't you see? The same society snatched my son away and let his assassin roam free. It's all a part of their plan—dilute us with miscegenation, trim us down with genocide. Your grandfather came to that conclusion, and perhaps that's why he banished himself here to this plantation—to nurture and protect his heirs while he set them on the path to save the rest of us. His love for you is proof of that. That's why my father's stories sent me here—to find you. It's fate, ¿don't you think?"

Seth's organ hammered against his chest, pulsed and raced throughout his phantom limb.

"Convene with him," Max said, lowering his head, angled enough to be considered a bow. "His words are more powerful than mine."

The great door of the library creaked shut. Seth wanted to toss the newspapers into the fireplace. Wanted to set this whole place ablaze, with himself and Max inside. But the hands that had guided Seth as a child had typed these words. Did the same eyes that saw the good in Seth truly envision the world like this? Had his grandfather's heart really believed in what Max said? How could the man who loved Seth be wrong? Not even Otilio's shadow self had ever lied to him. It was when Seth read the words in his grandfather's voice that they began to fall into place. Their intention shifted to that of love, of truth. Seth sat with his back to the stone wall, replaying his own political career with this new lens. Seth had pushed Costa Ricans from their homes for foreign interests, facilitated land-taking for Chinese companies that offered better prices on oil. He'd allowed bureaucrats to line their pockets with inflated budgets for Nicaraguan aliens. Seth was no better than the government that kidnapped Otilio's wife. The further Seth got in the years of his grandfather's column, the more Otilio's voice chastised him—how disappointing to raise a traitor rather than an heir. Seth had bought into the same system that had imprisoned his grandmother, that had imprisoned *him*, then cast him out like jetsam. By the time Seth got to Otilio's final column in 1945, Seth had corrected his own past, reworked it like a puzzle assembled wrong, because it had been missing important pieces. Hours later, the borders of his understanding had been recontextualized by his grandfather's words. There was only one way forward now. To the new world order, to the throne.

Far off from the Oreamundo plantation, beyond the canopies and peaks daubed dawn pink, atop the pyramidal temple Max's father had built, its crocodile yawned awake, preparing to devour the rising sun.

BRASS AS ROTTEN WOOD

2017

A family of four Nicas wants to cross the San Juan River from Nicaragua into Costa Rica (illegally, of course). The father is up first: he swims across, touches wet feet on dry land, and yells, "¡I'm Costa Rican now! ¡I'm Tico!" The mother, with great difficulty, manages to make it, too, and leaps with joy: "¡I'm Costa Rican now! ¡I'm Tica!" Next is the older sister, who crosses and declares the same: "¡I'm Costa Rican now! ¡I'm Tica!" Having watched his whole family succeed, the young son, excited, dives into the river, but begins to drown, and implores his family for help. The worried women plead to the father, "He can't save himself, ¡I don't think he's playing around!" But the father answers, "¿So what? Let the son of a bitch drown. ¡Technically he's still a Nica!"

Luzmilda's cousin, Pedro Augustín, laughed too hard at his own joke in the darkness of the minivan. Outside, the night pulsed with leftover Christmas cheer. Weekly feasts and bull runs would visit towns named after saints for the next three months, halting finally for the observation of Lent. Those who'd drunk themselves into stupors would imbibe no longer, and womanizers would again pay attention to their wives, if only for forty days.

When the echo of Pedro Augustín's chuckles dissipated, he, the three men in the back seats, and Seth on the passenger's side breathed shallow, audible breaths through their mouths. Beyond the tinted glass, crowds passed by in huge shadows.

"I didn't find that funny," Cristiano said. "Those Nicas got here and probably applied for government assistance."

"And the daughter is probably a dyke," Cristiano's brother Paul added.

"It's a joke," Javier sighed. "Stupidity apparently runs in your family," he said to them.

"¿Oh yeah?" Cristiano tensed his face. "¿Aren't you Nicaraguan? ¿What runs in *your* family?"

"Take that back," Javier growled.

"That's why you're so mad." Paul grinned. "A hit dog hollers."

"Those were probably his parents and his sister," Pedro Augustín said from the driver's seat. "I guess the son didn't actually drown. He's sitting right here with us. ¿Do you want a towel to dry off?"

"All of you shut up," Seth said. He eyed everyone through the rearview mirror. His voice had regained its politician's intensity, and the four other men sat still as tombstones. Seth lit a cigarette and squinted through the smoke and the windshield, searching for smaller groups of Nicaraguans. He looked down at his prosthetic, its gold shimmering in the streetlamp light.

The day after Seth had left the Oreamundo library, having scanned his grandfather's newspapers, Bronson arrived to fit Seth for a prosthetic. The good doctor had it fashioned quickly, and with great ceremony Max and Luzmilda bestowed it upon Seth like a weapon of legend. Excalibur as a limb. Over the past year, he'd become used to its precarity: sometimes he lurched forward or felt as if he stood perpetually on an incline. But he'd underestimated the confidence it would return to him. Whole again, he could finally stand on his own for the Garroteros' public forums and lead the more secret meetings of officials loyal to the cause. Brakemen had infiltrated several corners of the Costa Rican government—from small cantons to medium-size municipalities; whole local police and fire departments had signed on; and they'd even netted high-ranking federal appointees who were too young to remember the scandal of Seth Oreamundo. Seth hoped once this grassroots movement took hold, congressmen would come flocking. But so far, individuals with any sort of legislative potential existed on the margins. With Max's blessing, Seth was positioning himself as the movement's leader and eventually, if everything went according to plan, the candidate of a new political party.

"That Trump was good for banning terrorists from his country," Cristiano said.

"I wish our president had the balls to do that," Paul chimed in.

"Instead he's trying to legalize homosexuality." Javier gritted his teeth. He'd thrown his son to the curb when he found out the types of bars he frequented. "This country is uncontrollable, and we need a man like Trump to do something about it."

"The United States for gringos, and Costa Rica for Costa Ricans," Pedro Augustín said. "We have to get *them* out."

Seth sat between the four brutes tonight because certain members of the Garroteros had been getting sloppy. The recent election in the United States had awakened new appetites among their ranks, the most dangerous one being that for violence. With America great again, the more radical constituents of the Garroteros called for Costa Rica's return to its former glory, which meant the expulsion of every Nicaraguan within its borders. Seth thought it a fine idea. He wished to see the government finally take the side of its own people. However, he explained, success would be a legislative long game. But impatient outbursts continued in monthly meetings, with a growing number of members demanding immediate action. Palpable results. Seth looked to the movement he was inheriting from Max and found it to be a pressure cooker of meatheads and hicks. Before the Garroteros could splinter, Seth and Max decided to let its more radical factions blow off steam. An intimidation campaign to control their appetites. Under strict instruction and the cover of darkness, masked groups of Garroteros were allowed to swoop into Nicaraguan communities to frighten, harass, and threaten. It had worked so far: authorities were still oblivious to the Garroteros' existence, and its extremist constituents quieted down, sated. But earlier this month a city block on the outskirts of San José had been razed to ashes. A dozen houses of wood and scrap metal set ablaze, the news channels covering a dozen Nicaraguan families watching on in horror. Seth traced the match back to Luzmilda's cousin, Pedro Augustín, who joked in the driver's seat and asked Seth for a cigarette. Seth chaperoned the men tonight in hopes of curbing whatever hankering hadn't been satisfied by the fire.

The crowds dispersed, partygoers flocking to neon bars. The men studied the sidewalks for stragglers. And there, in the emptiness of the February street, a Nicaraguan of about twenty-five staggered out of an apartment building. Alone.

"Let's go," Pedro Augustín said, gripping the door handle.

"We decided on a group," Seth growled. "Not an individual."

"*You* decided," he answered. "We didn't ask for a babysitter."

"Your cousin decided."

"¿Luzmilda?" Pedro Augustín laughed. "This was her idea, Paulo." He eyed the rearview mirror. "¿About as old as Salvador, right?"

Javier's reflection nodded. Seth realized what was about to happen. He lifted his left arm to slam onto the car horn, but Cristiano caught his wrist and twisted it behind the seat. Another arm appeared around his neck, the elbow cradling his jaw, pushing hard against his throat.

"¿What did you think we were doing, Paulo?" Cristiano whispered. "¿What do you think *you've* been doing this whole time?"

"Stop until he gets somewhere darker," Javier commanded. The accusation of his Nicaraguan heritage meant he would hit hardest. Pedro Augustín's foot lifted from the brake and the blue-black van stalked the man. When they'd passed the last streetlamp, the only light coming from weak stars and the distant glow of beer signs, Pedro Augustín cut the motor, yanked on a ski mask, and left the car first. The night was thick and black as molasses and, to the four men who left Seth alone and stunned in the van, just as sweet. Masks on, the brothers Cristiano and Paul gripped crowbars, and Javier cracked his knuckles. Skin to skin, bone to bone. Reconnection before the final severing. Seth noticed Pedro Augustín stood farther back and walked slower than the others. He was a coward, as those with the loudest mouths usually are.

"¡Nica!" Javier yelled, his voice cracked and violent. A tree felled by lightning in his mouth. The young Nicaraguan turned around and smiled. He'd only ever known friends to emerge from the dark.

"¡Compas!" he shouted. "¡Happy Candlemas, compas! We pray to the Baby Jesus tonight." The man's jubilance froze the four men. It was indeed a night of importance, the fortieth day after Jesus's birth. "¡He was purified today!" the man continued. "Our Virgin took him to the temple to present to our Lord."

A stone soared past the young man's face like a turtledove.

Seth swung the car door open and stumbled onto the cool asphalt.

"Compas," the Nicaraguan man muttered. "¿What is . . . ?"

Javier swung first, breaking his index finger and the Nicaraguan's jaw in the same fluid motion. The young man had broken that jaw before, a fall from a tree as a child, and his favorite grandmother nursed him back to health. Seth struggled to his feet and tried to sprint. The brothers swung their crowbars, aimed expertly at crackable bone. Yesterday the young man prescribed his girlfriend breathing techniques to ease her anxiety. Seth's prosthetic wobbled, grated bone; the ground shifted beneath him. He watched from ten meters away as Pedro Augustín finally joined in when the Nicaraguan lay barely conscious, and kicked the softest parts of him. The young man had recently joined a local gym, and he had befriended his trainer and her sister who taught Pilates.

The scene wasn't as loud as the men expected. Yes, bones snapped, but only momentarily, while the rest of the flesh hadn't made a peep. Unsatisfied, Javier balanced the heavy stone that had initiated tonight's rites high above his head. Before Seth could scream for him to stop, Javier let it slip from his fingers to the man's upturned face, as if allowing God to do the honors. That indeed made a sound, and all five men flinched.

They left the young Nicaraguan there in the middle of the road, cushioned by the molasses of the night. Javier, invigorated by having killed what he'd always wanted to kill within himself, ignored his fractured hand and drove them back. No one spoke. They couldn't open their mouths without the reflex to vomit. Seth's hands trembled all the way up the mountain. *¿What do you think you've been doing this whole time?* Seth couldn't fathom that anyone would have gone this far. Invasion, extermination, replacement—language Seth thought one kept locked and safe inside the mind, not to be enunciated by rock-clutching hands. Rhetoric was a play to be studied, not staged. But Seth's sermons to the Garroteros had been acted out tonight—every sinew of anger he'd tugged at, all the fear he'd exploited, the solutions he'd proposed: performed by knuckle, and metal, and stone. And just as he'd started it, he had done nothing to stop it.

When the men arrived back at the bungalow, they each went to their own quarters and adjacent cabins, except for Seth, who marched straight into Max and Luzmilda's bedroom. They were sitting up reading books like the old, happily married couple they were.

"I'm proud of you," Luzmilda said before Seth could speak. "This is the first step."

"Come to us, Paulo." Max uttered that name for the first time. Seth lost his will to fight. He limped over to their bed, removed his prosthetic, lay his heavy body between theirs, and fell into an unbearably deep sleep.

2018

Horacio couldn't get Carlos out of his head. He tried his best to play coy, refusing to send a WhatsApp message until Carlos did first. That's what Sophia Loren or Ava Gardner would have done—put her iPhone on vibrate, smoke a cigarette on the roof, forget the man's whole existence until he reminded her of it. But Horacio was neither of those starlets, so he checked his phone every few minutes and masturbated to the memory of Carlos saving him from his first orgy.

After an epic failure on prom night, Andrés's girlfriend broke up with him, so he quit his job at Chipotle. Free again, he spent all his time with Horacio, who was grateful for the distraction. Their first night reunited, they went to Montrose Park with rich friends who were about to leave for their annual European summer vacation. The gang shared cognac, overjoyed on the moonlit playground. Horacio played on the swing set as he had when he was a kid, determined to go over the bar; Andrés lay on the rubbery ground, shirtless for no reason. A golden retriever appeared and weaved through the group. Their friend Claudia ran her fingers, her arms, and then her face across its fur. The owners, an older white couple, emerged from the shadows.

"We're not cops, kids," the man said. He sported a gray Harvard tee.

"Who's got a light?" the woman asked. Andrés, drunk, passed her his lighter, and the woman sparked up a joint. She sported a brown Brown sweatshirt.

Horacio stopped his swinging to observe the chatty couple, ex-hippies turned corporate consultants. They still believed in love and liberation, they promised, but they had always wanted a place in Georgetown. *You sell out for one of these town houses. Trust us, kids.*

Horacio and Andrés stumbled home after midnight. In their room, Horacio lay next to Andrés and picked gravel from his back. He ran his fingers over the red-pink depressions, a braille only he could read. For the next week, they rinsed and repeated the summer ritual, wandering Northwest at all hours. Lunch at Kramers bookstore, a tour of the Church of Scientology, dancing at the drum circle, hollering in the echo chamber at the Canadian embassy, splurges at vintage stores, record stores, and liquor stores. Muggy nights at the Cliff, on the forbidden Starbucks roof in Georgetown, and in the glow of lamppost lights at Malcolm X, Kalorama, and Rock Creek.

Isa and Nieves studied Horacio with growing concern. Two undercover agents in broad daylight. Even Andrés couldn't ignore it: Horacio wouldn't stop checking his phone. The flashing screen spotlighted his face at family dinners or at crosswalks on their way to meet Xavier, and especially in the late-night hours of their bedroom. That blink of light and Horacio's immediate scowl became the week's main topic until Isa finally broached it on a Sunday night.

"Baby," she said, serving Horacio roasted vegetables. "You have to tell us why you keep looking at your phone like that."

"Like what?" Horacio said defensively.

"What are you waiting for?" Nieves asked after a sip of wine.

"Yeah, dude," Andrés said. "You're acting weird as fuck."

"Language," Nieves said. Again a sip. An insistent dip of her head.

"Who are you guys, detectives Stabler and Benson?" he said to his mothers. Horacio looked at Andrés. "Munch."

"Fuck you, dude," Andrés laughed. "At least let me be Ice-T."

"The point still stands, baby," Isa said. "What's going on with you? Please tell us."

"It's not that big of a deal."

"So then tell us," Nieves said.

"He's waiting for a guy." Andrés snapped his fingers. "Duh."

"Andrés, shut up; you're supposed to be on my side."

"Maybe if you would've told me I would've told these two to lay off."

Nieves slapped the back of Andrés's neck.

"What'd you do that for?" Andrés flinched.

"I don't know," Nieves laughed. "Seemed like the right reaction."

"Who's the guy?" Isa asked.

"Where'd you meet him?" Nieves said. Two sips this time.

Horacio sat in this interrogation scene with the anxiety of a culprit. But he didn't know where his guilt came from. Privacy, perhaps, but he was usually open about these things with his mother. Isa knew she couldn't stop him from hooking up with men (though she had no idea of their ages) and stuffed his wallet with condoms. Perhaps because he'd met the man at an orgy. Something that had scandalized him would surely scandalize them. Judgment or laughter, Horacio didn't want to receive any of it.

"Let's go to Costa Rica," Horacio blurted out.

Isa spat her food, both cartoonishly and with sincere disgust. Nieves and Andrés looked at her as if she'd retched all her insides onto the plate.

"¿What the hell are you talking about?" Isa switched without realizing.

Andrés knew very little, so he checked out of the conversation. Nieves slammed her wineglass on the table. She repeated Isa. Both sisters' veins bulged from their necks. Blue, bright.

"I want to go back," Horacio said. Andrés regained his attention. "¿Why can't we go back?"

"You know what this means to your mother," Nieves said. "You know how she feels."

"¿But *why*?" Horacio lifted himself, gripped the tablecloth. Isa straightened her hand, and Nieves prepared to stop whatever her sister was considering.

"Calm down, dude," Andrés said. "It's your dad, dummy."

Everyone looked at Andrés. Melancholy painted their faces.

"Our dads," he corrected himself. "You got to put two and two together, Einstein."

Horacio lowered himself back into the chair. He apologized, ashamed of his outburst. His tantrum. "I guess I'm not as grown-up as I think I am," he said.

"It's not your fault," Isa said. "It's hard when your home turns into a graveyard. Costa Rica is nothing but pain and ghosts for us."

"Maybe when you're older," Nieves said, determined to be fair about it.

"Let's clean the table and go get ice cream," Isa said.

"It's nice out," Nieves added. She scraped leftover food from every plate onto her own. "Everyone, get two scoops so I can try them all."

Horacio sat on the toilet with a stomachache, rocking back and forth in frustration. The ice cream had unsettled his stomach, and his mother's denial had unsettled his heart. All these years in D.C., she'd acted as though not mentioning his father proved that he'd never existed. She called Costa Rica a graveyard, but Horacio wondered if she'd even found his father's body. If she'd interred him while Horacio was at school one day or packing for their move here. Considering how cagey she acted around the subject, Horacio couldn't rule out her tiptoeing into a funeral parlor to cremate him herself. And all this time with Andrés had gradually buried Horacio's memories of his father, as Andrés had of his own. But sometimes Horacio would remember the IMAX theater in Escazú, his father's excitement for their weekly movie: his marvel at its gargantuan screen and the worlds into which it transported them. He'd been in spaceships with his father, on dinosaur-infested islands, deep below the ocean, in stuffy American courtrooms. Horacio wished to return to that theater and back home to Villa Real.

Dry, lavender bolts coruscated over the National Cathedral. Between thunderclaps, Horacio heard Andrés watching a Vice documentary about Krokodil, a Russian opiate that turned the skin to scutes. Horacio's iPhone pinged, muffled by the distant lightning. A WhatsApp message.

"My Prince," the message from Carlos read.

"There you are," Horacio wrote back.

"I'm back home, sorry I haven't texted. Been with my mother and aunts. They're well and they send their hellos."

"¿You told them about me?"

"Of course. I told you I was serious, and that's why I'm telling everyone else too."

Horacio locked the phone for a few minutes. His stomach gurgled.

"I bought you a ticket," a new message read. "Eight, Thursday morning, direct."

NOR THE HABERGEON

2018

Seth and the other Garroteros traveled to the city of Cartago in three separate cars, stuffed like sardines in rolling cans, while Seth mulled over the plans agreed upon by himself, Max, and Luzmilda. They would be meeting with sympathizers from secret WhatsApp groups and the followers recruited on Facebook pages, which Seth was sure were full of moles, so he'd had Javier meticulously scan and expel any members who didn't contribute to the discourse. He didn't want cops to suss out their plan. The capital's law enforcement was not yet on their side—a different priority for a different future in which the Garroteros had conscripted enough commoners to storm the congressional hall and seize control of the Costa Rican government. To stop the proverbial train before it careened off a cliff.

To date, the Garroteros and their proxy pages had accumulated 127,000 followers. Out of that number, Max predicted two hundred would arrive for their planned counterprotest of the annual Pride parade. Before settling on the parade, Seth and Max had gone back and forth for weeks, deciding which type of rally to hold, for which reasons it would publicly stand, and the level of aggression they would permit their members. Max, goaded by Luzmilda, sitting at his side as counsel, pushed for an anti-Nicaraguan march, to be held at La Merced, a park where Nicaraguan refugees gathered to receive food and provisions from local churches. This was a main topic in the Facebook pages and chats: Costa Rican nationalists regarded the park as a tumor, and without recourse or consequence the Nicaraguans would metastasize and swallow San José. To many members and to Luzmilda, it was a dire prognosis, and the Garroteros were the only chance of salvation. Chemotherapy with the cutting edge of patriotism.

For the sake of the Garroteros' political future, Seth found that option too divisive. A fifth of Costa Rica's population was now Nicaraguan. That was a million people, Seth said. A million cousins who worked odd jobs and neighbors who borrowed sugar and greeted each other at Sunday masses. Of course, that type of rally could eventually be held, but not now. The Garroteros had to test the waters, see if they had garnered real, physical support. They needed an immediate target, a smaller group, relatively powerless and still unpopular to the general public. Max agreed. *The faggots and their flags.* The Pride parade was less than a decade old, with no more of a turnout than a fútbol game. *Queers can't fight back. You hit one on the street and they run the other way. Sissies are just that: sissies.*

And so it was decided, and the forces of the Garroteros would gather soon. Besides the members Max led from the Oreamundo mansion, there had sprouted loosely organized splinter groups in almost every canton. Battalions, they called themselves. Each battalion had local leaders with no real power within the organization. Said leaders held their own monthly meetings at bars or in churches after services. And each battalion pushed the issues affecting their respective province: fishermen from Puntarenas, truck drivers from Heredia, businessmen from San José. The Garroteros now had the advantage of grassroots support from every sector and class, gentry and rubes alike. Easily gathered in one web of nationalism, xenophobia, and homophobia. A holy trinity as good as the Father, the Son, and the Holy Spirit.

Seth and his personal guard arrived at a small hotel in the center of Cartago. Javier, who had confessed on the drive that he wished to meet his son on what he called "the battlefield," surveyed the march's organizing social media page for updates. He checked the sponsors of the parade—private banks, cell service providers, multinational fast-food chains—and he urged the Facebook groups to boycott every single company, no matter how low their interest rates, how fast their internet, or how unbelievably delicious their burgers. Pedro Augustín checked the members into the quaint inn where they would set up their home base. Seth went straight to his quarters and marveled at the cleanliness of the room, like that hotel in Limón from so many years ago. That midnight he had awoken and crept into a park, to the center of a moaning forest, and crawled to the foot of a man who kissed his seed from Seth's lips.

"Paulo," Pedro Augustín interrupted Seth's memory. He made himself comfortable on Seth's bed.

"Hm."

"¿Nervous?"

Pedro Augustín had tried for a year to gauge Seth's mental state after the attack on the young Nicaraguan. He wouldn't stop asking Seth questions about it, sifting through Seth's answers, or lack thereof, to present later to Luzmilda. They had all expected to see a news report, the OIJ declaring an investigation, but nothing. No coverage or even a scrolling banner at the bottom of the screen. No one cared. It had gone better than anyone had expected. But Seth knew they all still dreamt of the stone, heard the crunch when all was quiet in the night.

"No," Seth said. "I'm not nervous at all. Come back when most of the members are here."

At six, Seth was to greet a conservative evangelical coterie with years of experience protesting the Pride parade. Its members were vocal in the group chats and had readily volunteered to impart their knowledge. Every year, they skulked on the sidelines of the parade with signs and a megaphone, screeching out scripture and threats. And every year they danced their dance, allegedly gaining favor from God as one would guarantee rain from the sky. A blessing if they condemned enough homosexuals and harassed drag queens on floats. The first few years they were pelted with empty red cups, or their megaphones disabled by Super Soakers. Men made out in front of them, allies argued futilely. This group loved it; they lapped up the epithets and anger. But gradually the queer procession took them for granted, having realized the bile was harmless.

Santiago, the leader of the group, had grown concerned that the word of God was falling upon deaf ears. Seth assured him in tonight's meeting that sinners' ears would perk up this time. Santiago's followers nodded jubilant heads. Their mission was no longer to be fought in vain. They were still the vanguard, and now the Garroteros were their cavalry.

Whenever Seth led these meetings, he felt teeth tightening around his phantom limb. A sensation that wouldn't let go. It tried to whip him back and forth in his chair, gave him vertigo as he spoke. Santiago was to procure dozens more signs for Seth's reinforcements, and he promised Seth over seventy heads at the protest. Seth imagined they'd be a fervent faction, but ultimately too pacifistic. As useful as extras on a movie set. Seth needed main players, ones perfect for the television cameras.

Those players Seth found the next night in Heredia on a lush property with rows of ornamental plants. The owner, an American expat and war veteran named Tom, met them at the gate and led them to the back of the house, where a dozen Costa Ricans and the expat's wife lounged on a porch, chatting away the afternoon.

"My buddy lost his leg in Afghanistan," Tom said, looking at Seth.

Seth squinted his eyes, wished his cane sheathed a sword.

"He relearned how to walk too. Now he runs marathons. You ever run a marathon?"

Seth didn't answer. He faced the group and went into his pitch, offering them organizational support if they promised to attend the protest. Tom cut Seth off many times to volunteer reconnaissance, data analyst friends, and alleged connections to the CIA. He was trying to position himself and his battalion as those with superior expertise. As if Seth's group needed *them*. Seth did not fight Tom; he let Tom say his piece until he ran out of breath. Seth handled the meeting calmly but with an increasing rancor emanating from just below the surface of the conversation. The slits in Seth's eyes reflected Tom, like a fool who was coming to the edge of a river for a closer look.

Cristiano and Paul smiled. The Costa Ricans shifted in their seats. Tom's wife tapped him on the shoulder. Everyone wanted him to shut up.

Tom finished, and Seth let the silence simmer. "Look," Seth said finally. "We aren't fucking around. I don't give a shit about your buddy and his missing leg. Even if you had connections, the CIA is dead. They must have blown some of your brains out in Iraq if that's the way you're going to talk to me. We're done here."

Seth stood in a fluid motion without the help of his cane. All eyes stared at him in disbelief.

"No, no," Tom backtracked. "No, I'm so sorry to have offended you. Please, sit, Paulo."

Tom's group had just witnessed their alpha bested, and Tom's wife backed away from him and rested against a wall with a face of soft disgust, fiddling with her wedding ring. Seth addressed Tom's group again, continued his pitch uninterrupted this time. They turned out to be a battalion of ex-cons, including a cop who had served time but still kept his badge. He'd murdered a prostitute in a drug bust, but because she was trans, he got off easy. "Scot-free," Tom said, smiling, trying to get back into Seth's good graces.

"The police are all friends," the cop said. "They'll be on our side, because they all hate fags as much as we do."

Successful and satisfied, Seth and his group excused themselves and drove back to the quaint Cartago inn. The Garroteros were growing stronger, all thanks to him. The shaky foundation on which the organization had been built was solidifying, and the prospect of a political party was finally coming into view. It became clear to Seth that RECOPE had never been the goal, but a path leading to this moment. He wondered if everything before had conspired to get him here—his brother, the exile, the phantom limb that flexed—as if he were meant for this all along.

¿Why do you want power, Seth? his grandfather had asked. For this sensation, he realized. The euphoria of fate that has driven men, both lesser and greater than Seth, for millennia. An almost alchemical concoction of power and adoration, whose rim he'd merely licked before, but from which he now planned to drink his fill.

Costa Rica is home

until

the very end

2018

Carlos picked Horacio up at Juan Santamaría at three in the afternoon. The airport hadn't changed much since Seth arrived for the last time seven years ago. The duty-free overflowed with the same artisan souvenirs: wooden croaking toads, Boruca masks, delicate landscapes painted on feathers, Imperial beer paraphernalia, woven bags. Passing through Immigration, the only thing Horacio was worried about was if his mother or Nieves had called Interpol. But he was eighteen—only a child could be stopped and held for being rebellious, for boarding a plane and arriving in the country his family swore to never return to. Horacio passed through the final checkpoint, an adult, a master of his own destiny, allowed to forge his own path: to walk outside, past insistent cabbies offering deals, to the curb where his lover leaned against his car, taking quick drags from a cigarette with an even, toothy smile. The taxi drivers stopped when Carlos kissed Horacio. All the airport seemed to go silent, except for the thunder of a plane taking off. They kissed with their eyes open, to observe the beauty of the other and to keep their peripheral vision alert. Only when they finally let go, and Carlos loaded Horacio's bag into his buffed, charcoal BMW, did the passengers resume searching for their names on flimsy, swaying papers, boarding their buses, off to beaches and rainforests, dental appointments and brothels in the capital.

"¿How was the trip?" Carlos asked as he turned to exit onto the highway.

"Not bad." Horacio smiled. All of this excited him. Even the small, affectionate curiosities set his heart into rapid beats. He felt like a refugee, risking his life for love. *Like one of those old movies*, he wanted to say. Horacio wished for the world to go black-and-white for a while, or maybe even Technicolor, to saturate the green of the passing treetops, the blue, endless sky, and Carlos's turquoise-rimmed glasses he wore only for driving. "But they only gave us peanuts."

"Then let's get some food in you, prince."

Again, the tachycardia of infatuation.

"¿Where do you want to go?" Carlos asked.

"You tell me," Horacio said. "You're the top, you decide."

"But I bow to you, my prince," Carlos said. He switched gears, swerved in between cars to come out ahead. "All around we'll see fast-food signs. You can choose from them. Or, rather," he said, "let's go to Barrio Escalante. There's a whole strip of restaurants we can try."

But they didn't make it to lunch—Carlos drove them straight to his apartment in the neighborhood of Los Yoses. He unloaded Horacio's bags, wouldn't let him lift a finger, not even to take off his own clothes in the apartment's threshold. Carlos didn't force Horacio to shower, or even clean out.

"I don't care about that stuff," Carlos said. "Everything about your body is beautiful, whatever happens. Nothing will turn me off."

They went three rounds; Horacio thanked God his body cooperated, that he'd put on extra layers of deodorant and brushed his teeth in the airplane bathroom. Even though his stomach grumbled, it was all going perfectly. The more Carlos called him prince, the more Horacio believed he was in a fairy tale. *Princess*, he secretly wanted Carlos to say, but who could be dampened by semantics when serenaded by a handsome man?

At six in the evening they showered together; Carlos washed Horacio's hair and body, and Horacio his. They towel dried, stayed naked for a while smoking and planning the week's agenda. Carlos would take them all around the country: an observatory lodge overlooking the Arenal volcano, to his family's beachfront hostel in Limón, and to Playa Hermosa, Tamarindo, and Coco in Guanacaste. They were to leave early tomorrow.

"*Now* let's get some food in you." Carlos smiled.

"I want a beer," Horacio said. "And a burger."

"Then that's what you'll get."

When they reached the door, Carlos patted Horacio's ass. "Keep my babies in there all night," he said, and, like a gentleman, let Horacio walk out first.

Horacio had no idea how Carlos managed to cram an entire country into a week. The highways and side roads brought Horacio back to trips with his father and mother as a child—journeys to five-star resorts and hotels nestled in cloud forests. The asphalt hadn't changed, but the trees had grown stronger; cliffs had fallen, made mud by rain, taking houses with them; waterfalls still dove in ancient contest. Carlos chewed fruity gum and sucked his teeth when other drivers managed to jump ahead of the BMW. He was a competitive driver, didn't care if he overtook a school bus or trucks balancing livestock. Horacio asked where they were every few kilometers, pointed out green signs with white writing of names he was sure he remembered, even if he didn't really. Carlos handled Horacio's curiosity more affectionately than his father had. Didn't anger at every *¿Are we there yet?* Instead, Carlos held Horacio's hand, clutched it to the gearshift. *It's like we're both driving. We have to teach you how to drive eventually.*

Their final destination was Arenal, the volcano now ten years defunct—shut down like a factory, dormant as a beast.

"At night, it used to throw flaming rocks like cherries," Carlos said. "Whole embers flicked from a cigarette, tumbling down the peak. Now it's just waiting."

"¿Waiting for what?" Horacio unpacked their clothes, piled folded shirts and shorts into the fragrant dresser of their cabin adjacent the lodge.

"I don't know," Carlos mused. "Maybe for someone to disturb it. Or it'll wake up from a dream with a revelation, and we'll all crane our heads to listen. Arenal will awake with wisdom."

Horacio sat on the toilet to pee and left the door open so that he could still hear Carlos's theories. "Or," Carlos began, walking into the bathroom to check his eyebrows. "That's hot," he interrupted himself.

"¿What?" Horacio said.

"You sitting down like that. Anyway, maybe Arenal will erupt and kill us all." He laughed. "¿Wouldn't that be something?"

That night they ordered mojitos and waded in the Jacuzzi close to their cabin, across a single-file suspension bridge. They stripped, letting all parts of themselves be poached by the bubbling water. They ran back naked to the room and fucked. Showered, and fucked. Fell asleep, awoke, and fucked.

The next morning Carlos scheduled a nature hike, then a trip on horseback through the hills. Around ten they lounged on the sundeck facing the volcano. Clouds crowded the peak and, by the afternoon, dispersed like swatted insects. A glasswing butterfly landed and died in Horacio's coffee. He snapped a picture of the caffeinated carnage on his iPhone, the poor creature delicate on the glossy, brown surface. Carlos asked if he would post any photos of them on Instagram, and if so, to make sure to tag him and adorn the post with affectionate emojis. But Horacio answered that he'd wait until tonight to curate a boastful, sappy photo dump. He was lying, because he didn't want any digital evidence that he was here in Costa Rica, didn't want to give away his exact location so that Isa, Nieves, and Andrés could track him down like an international criminal. Horacio didn't want Carlos charged with kidnapping, so he put away his phone, fished out the butterfly corpse, and nonchalantly recommended they get massages at the spa.

"Coming right up." Carlos winked.

Carlos had delivered on his promise to make Horacio fall in love with him that week. From butterfly gardens to brisk, misty forests, Carlos used Costa Rica itself as a romantic gesture, presenting the country to Horacio like a bouquet. Horacio had never eaten so much food or had so much sex in his life. It was as if Carlos had appeared out of thin air with the sole mission of courting him.

Two nights before Horacio was to board the plane back to D.C., Carlos took him to a friend's house party in Los Yoses. They dressed in the apartment, gelled their hair, and walked the kilometer to Casa Mango, a ten-member house of queers and artists who'd come to the capital to make it big. There lived a guitarist from Golfito who had run away from his pigheaded father's farm; a ballerina with steel soles and a dark sense of humor; three painters whose artwork fought for space on the walls. The owner, a young man named Daniel with cat-green eyes and a wide, angular face, welcomed Carlos with a hug and a spliff.

"We've got edibles in the kitchen," he said. "Coconut moonshine in the tub. And Carlotta the Spaniard is selling hot dogs—but between us, they're not that great."

Daniel took notice of Horacio, examined him for a few moments. The black lights turned his smile purple. "¿Who. Are. *You*?"

I am myself, Horacio wanted to say.

"This is *him*," Carlos said, pointing his lips to Horacio.

"I thought so." Daniel took consecutive tokes from his joint, held in the smoke, and blew it theatrically out into the air.

"He thinks he's the caterpillar from *Alice in Wonderland*," Carlos said.

"*How doth the little crocodile improve his shining tail, and pour the waters of the Nile on every golden scale. How cheerfully he seems to grin, how neatly spreads his claws, and welcomes little fishes in with gently smiling jaws.*"

"We'll never get him to stop," Carlos chuckled.

"Go on inside," Daniel said. "Debauchery awaits."

The two-story house smelled of fruit and tobacco, pungent alcohol and sweat. There was an open mic in the living room, an orgy in the bedroom next to the only bathroom. The visual artists had segregated themselves to the balcony, the humanitarian queers to the kitchen, and all about, Carlos buzzed, Horacio tagging along to smile, and hug, and smoke, and drink. Carlos pointed to a man in a linen shirt and cargo shorts.

"He's a congressman."

"¿Here?"

"Of course. Sometimes a house party is the only place you can truly be yourself."

After working the room, Horacio and Carlos landed on Carlos's group of closest friends, who were arguing over whether the Ministry of Culture was actually investing in new artists or if it was just keeping aging, uninventive hacks in positions of undeserved influence and esteem.

"Absolutely not," Gustavo said. He was the son of bankers, had gotten an art degree in New York City. As a side project he opened a jazz venue downtown, in a million-dollar home once owned by French aristocracy. "They haven't featured artists under the age of fifty since this century began."

"This millennium," their friend Alberto added.

"We're trying our best," Carina chimed in, shooting exasperated glares at everyone. She'd been working at the ministry a year now, was trying to change it from the inside.

"Impossible," Carlos said. "It has to be dismantled, like all systems."

"¿Oh yeah?" Carina said. "We'll all be on the street. There'd never be another gallery in San José. Like I said, there are some of us on the inside who care."

"¿Is this him?" Alberto, who was taller than even Carlos, studied Horacio with the face of *How old is this kid?*

"It is," Carlos said.

"He's been talking about you an awful lot." Carina grabbed Horacio's chin in a motherly inspection of his face. "You are as beautiful as Carlos said."

"He is," Gustavo said. His mustache defied gravity in cursive.

"Bring him with us," Alberto said. "Tomorrow."

"¿What's tomorrow?" Horacio asked.

"The parade, silly." Carina stood on her tiptoes to whisper to Alberto, covered with her hand where mouth met ear.

"Pride," Carlos said. "Let's do it. ¿Have you ever been to one?"

"In D.C.," Horacio said proudly. "Twice."

"Oh, a veteran." Gustavo smirked.

"It'll be fun," Carina said. "There will be a whole group of us, a battalion of queers."

"With rainbow uniforms." Carlos grinned. "Let's do it, prince."

"¿Prince?" Gustavo said.

"¿Like the book?" Alberto said.

"The Little Prince," Carina said. "Sent from another planet to ours."

"To learn your secrets." Horacio smiled mischievously.

"He can keep up," Carina said. "I like him."

"So do I," Carlos said. "¿What do you say?"

"¿Do I have to wear clothes?"

"Never."

Horacio had actually only ever been to one Pride: last year's D.C. Youth Pride, held at an embassy by Malcolm X Park (re-rechristened Meridian Hill when the gentrifiers moved in). Horacio dragged Andrés and Xavier with him, the three pacing the patterned-concrete walkways, passing a joint between them like priests toting a censer of holy smoke. The weekly drum circle rattled and pulsed in the air, added an urgency to their stroll like a '70s movie soundtrack. As they approached the embassy, the air grew denser with Axe and petroleum jelly. Friendly white ladies welcomed them in and let them pass into a courtyard filled with D.C.'s gay youth. Horacio's lilac crop top caught everyone's attention, and without warning his brother and best friend, he jumped to the center of the dance floor to emulate what he'd seen in voguing videos on YouTube. He wasn't very good, admittedly, but the other kids, those who'd created their own ballrooms on the steps at Gallery Place or in their lunchrooms, hyped his style, stiff and awkward as it was. Andrés and Xavier waded on the sidelines, swallowed whole crackers and cheap cheddar squares, not participating as respectfully as possible. For that day they'd be allies—whatever that meant.

"How come there's no straight pride parade?" Xavier joked.

"Shut the fuck up," Andrés said. "Let them have their space."

"Don't say that again." Horacio smiled, catching his breath and wiping his exposed belly of sweat. "These kids will beat your ass."

"I know, I know, I was kidding, Jesus."

"They're painting people over there," Horacio said.

"Oh, God, please don't say—"

"Come on, Andrés, for me."

"Just don't take any fucking pictures. I can't have this shit all over Instagram. What would Diana say?"

"You've known her for three weeks, dude," Horacio said. "And you've only seen her in person twice."

"That's not the point," Andrés said. He looked to Xavier for backup, but he was entranced by a thick girl with spiky pink hair and a large septum piercing. *Matadors' capes are pink. Olé.*

"So, you can't get caught with your faggot brother?" Horacio scoffed.

"That's not what I said. Xavier, man, pay attention."

"No, dude. That was fucked-up," Xavier said robotically, hypnotized by the bull-girl.

"Now I know how you really feel," Horacio said. "I want to go."

"Bro, come on. I'm sorry. I didn't mean it that way. You *know* that. Why else would I be here?"

"Then take a picture with me, with all of these rainbows and queers in the background."

"Xavier, take my fucking iPhone and put it on portrait mode."

"Smile." Xavier smiled.

"Better yet," Andrés said, "let's do a selfie so your dumb ass can get in the shot, Xavier. If I gotta have documentation, so do you."

The boys took their selfie, and Horacio led Andrés and Xavier to the center of the dance floor to let loose. Madonna, Chaka, Britney, Cher, Selena, Whitney, Christina, Rihanna, Beyoncé, Gaga, Ariana, and Janet all chaperoned the youth pride celebration like the apostles. Divas at the last supper. In ecstasy, the gay kids, the trans kids, and the little lesbians and their girlfriends vibrated and celebrated, forgot that they couldn't be themselves at home, or had no home at all, or sold their bodies on K Street, or had yet to release themselves from the proverbial closet. It was a divine spectacle. An apotheosis.

Carlos's neighborhood awoke to the brawl of two cats on a tin roof. Dawn light reflected in their predator's eyes. Hisses, and growls, and high-pitched cries; rumbling, and crashing, and the distinct hush of claws into fur; vehemently locked in combat, so evenly matched, and the exact same color. Gray, striped, with yellow irises.

"Let them duke it out," Carlos said, scratching the back of his head, fixing sleep's stubborn cowlick. "The neighbors don't even know if they're real. It's all the time with those two. Little apparitions at dawn."

"I've never seen anything like that before," Horacio said.

"Nature's weird here. Both real and unreal at the same time. Beasts are always fighting themselves. Say, ¿what time is it?"

"Seven."

"Not bad. Turn over, prince, onto your stomach."

"It's too early."

"It's never too early. I'll make us coffee after."

Horacio and Carlos made love for the first time. This past week, even as Carlos had been courting, and wooing, and serenading Horacio with gifts, and vacations, and affection, Horacio hadn't yet convinced himself what he felt was love; he'd yet to tear away the layers protecting the softest parts of himself. The chain mail and armor forged by feelings of abandonment. Osario's disappearance hadn't left a hole in Horacio's heart, but a scar across it. Carlos had slowly undressed that protection like a bandage, and looked upon the wound without disgust or fear, and instead kissed it.

Carlos finished inside Horacio, rubbed his belly, and left to make coffee from a French press, talking to Horacio from the kitchen, as if Horacio could hear around corners. Horacio lay on his stomach and reached for his phone. Another missed call from his mother. Two more from Nieves. Instagram, Snapchat, and Facebook notifications from Andrés. Just another twenty-four hours until Horacio would see them again, try his best to explain, dodge the ceramic plates his mother could so expertly hurl. He'd apologize. But he'd *needed* to do this, he would underscore. They *had* to understand. Even if the ghost of his father had had the chance to find him in the dark and follow him all the way back to D.C., Osario hadn't manifested or yanked his feet while he slept next to Carlos. Horacio had been left untouched by the past. Instead, he forged a new future, dispelled the improbability that a man could love him. Surely they could understand that. Or perhaps that's why Isa and Nieves would reproach him. They more than understood it. They'd lived it, and lost it, and knew, without the slightest doubt in their motherly hearts, that it would happen to Horacio too.

"Prince," Carlos shouted. "¿Do you want toast?"

"Yes," Horacio answered. He sighed and lifted himself from the bed. "¿What time are we meeting your friends?"

"Noon. Alberto, Carina, and everyone will be waiting at the Paseo Colón."

"Okay, ¿and what do I wear?"

"Something sexy. ¿You brought something sexy, right? If not, you can rummage through my closet. I've got something in there.

"It's special this year." Carlos spoke quieter now that Horacio was in the kitchen. "¿Almond milk?"

"Sure. ¿Why is it special?"

"They're going to pass a gay marriage law this year."

"That's wonderful."

"It is. Now we can get married whenever we want."

Horacio looked down into the coffee, black and slick as oil. Carlos was so good at this, knocking Horacio off balance and righting him in the same motion, like a friend on a curb who grabs onto your shoulders to push, but pulls you back just in time. *Saved your life.*

You made ossuaries out of those crocodiles, Big Brother. It took a month for them to digest all the bones. My bones. Whittled them down with acid into sharp things, then dull things, and finally into a soup of marrow. But you made one into your own ossuary, ¿didn't you? Idiot. You didn't even see it crawling out of the river. With my last breath I should've hollered out, ¡Payback comes faster when you're not paying attention! That's exactly what I should have said, but I had another thing's teeth in my mouth.

If Isa would have known what you did, I'm sure she would have scoured the river for my pieces, tried to put me back together just to spite you. Isa the necromancer. Say, if women can bring life into this world, ¿do you think they can bring it back? I bet they could if they really put their minds to it. I say *that Isa would have brought me back, ¿but who am I kidding? She probably wanted me dead anyway. Or if she didn't want it, she was apathetic to the idea. Nothing worse than a wife's apathy. But you know that well, Big Brother. I know that Nieves lives up to her name.*

Oh man, ¿and what of our sons? ¿What will they do without us? I could have been proud of Horacio if I'd had a little more time. Sure, I knew he was going to grow up to be a fag, but maybe if I had another decade to get used to the idea . . . I've seen what's inside your head, Big Brother. I know now that it runs in the family. No, no, don't misunderstand, there's nothing inherently wrong with it—it's nature, ¿right? Fate. No way around it, I guess. No use fighting it.

Even though we tried to, ¿didn't we, Seth? Man, we tried to fight. Destiny always wins, though. Always, always, always.

I wonder if Mom and Dad really knew what was going on. If they'd ever resisted Grandfather's strings. Yeah, they had their roles in us, but then they croaked. You weren't even there when it happened—but what could you do about it; you were in D.C. You couldn't come back even if you'd wanted to. They were slammed right into the family vault, like closing a filing cabinet. Together, next to Grandfather. Atop the blank spaces that bear our names. It didn't even happen tragically either. They just stopped breathing at the same time. Peacefully, like Grandfather. Like Ola in that forest. I guess I'm the only one in our whole family who didn't go out with a final, tranquil sigh. No, you had me suck in water and bone. Speaking of bone.

It took a whole month for them to break me down, Big Brother. Osario, the king, shit out into the Tárcoles River. Imagine that. ¿And you were king for what? ¿Thirty seconds? How drunk you must have been on that momentary royalty, the nostalgia of being ruler again. You had four years without me, sure, then a fleeting half minute after. Long live the king.

¿Now you're what? ¿A vassal to those two? A lowly errand boy. A shell of a king, conquered by nature, chewed up and spit out into what you are now. Weak. Lame. Tragic. That's it: you're tragic, Big Brother. To think I fell to you. Dethroned by you. Erased from history, denied my myth. Call me bitter, but I have the right to be. But don't misunderstand: I came out the winner. Yes, I'm dead, but so are you—only you're forced to walk around still, a restless spirit doing others' bidding.

Sure, I suffered the pain of death, Seth, but it's you who's stuck in hell.

HIS BREATH KINDLETH COALS

2018

The capital awoke to fabric. Flags of all kinds, all factions, all political and social beliefs flapped from poles and floats, billowed from shoulders and storefronts. To wave a flag was to choose a side. Many didn't know they had awoken to war. Others had counted on it. Flags to the latter were for battles, not celebrations: to wrap around the dead, not the living. A doting breeze cooled the sunburned asphalt of the main avenue and sidewalks, blew so steadily that flags saluted in perfect right angles, as if they'd been starched into place. In four hours, the parade would begin. Drag queens' sequin gowns shimmered, each diva preparing a lip-sync on her respective float. Muscular men in leather choreographed hip gyrations, lesbians in crop tops filled water guns. Beaded necklaces of as many colors as the flags would be hurled to cheering parade-goers, necks like bottles at a county fair. The parade would act like an atomic nucleus, attracting people like electrons bouncing around to the beat. Vibrating in such jubilance, even the most conservative passersby would want to join in, just to see what all the fuss was about.

In the sparse, shell-white hotel room, Seth attached his prosthetic while watching the morning show on Canal 7. Four women and a gay man sat at a round table like Arthurian knights, clucking and recounting fabulous pregnancies: how big their bellies got, how any viewer could google the photos if they wanted. It was absurdist theater, Seth thought. All that chatting, at that speed, while saying absolutely nothing at all. But unlike Beckett, it was boring. Seth was sure that housewives cramped their fingers dialing the number on the screen, wanting for forty seconds to hear their voice on the television, dreaming that one day they'd become interesting enough to sit at that table of mid-morning knights, gibbering the entire day away.

Seth brushed his teeth, shined his cane with a cloth, pulled on his pair of indigo Levi's, buttoned up his sky-blue button-up, examined his scruff, decided not to shave, and threw a few punches at the air for practice. He'd dreamt of Osario but had no memory of exactly what. Not his brother's face, or his voice: just the soft, faint perfume of the river. That hint of petroleum, grainy silt, and fresh mangrove leaves in the current. How unsettlingly similar the smell of death and life. It penetrated the hotel sheets, primed the walls, saturated the pages of the Bible in the drawer. Seth showered again to rid his skin of sweat's sulfur, the diesel fumes from the cracked window. How unsettlingly similar the smell of earth and hell.

"Paulo," Pedro Augustín said after knocking. "It's time to go. We'll be late. The fire can't start without the spark."

The boom of war drums greeted Seth's group at La Plaza de la Democracia in downtown San José. Even from two kilometers away Seth's group felt the parade in their chests. Never had the world heard a battle begin so cheerfully. Seth rolled up his sleeves. The sun stung his skin, needles tucked in the rays. He wanted to wear his sunglasses, but he would need to look every man in the eye. All the different battalions, with their own interests and goals, wouldn't cohere without his leadership. In the slits of Seth's eyes, they would all fall in line. This was necessary to prove to not only Max and Luzmilda but the world that their movement was organized. Most important of all, they needed to convince the country that the Garroteros were a force to be reckoned with.

All the factions were to arrive there by eleven, but by eleven thirty, no one but Seth's group occupied the plaza. Strutting pigeons' coos became taunting giggles. Seth, Pedro Augustín, the brothers Paul and Cristiano, and Javier, who clutched his phone like a rock, paced back and forth, dreading the WhatsApp message from Max and Luzmilda as to why the Facebook livestream hadn't started. The plan had been to broadcast the rally, yell slogans into the sky, convince viewers that they weren't alone, that it wasn't shameful to join the Garroteros—because how bad could it be if there were *that* many people joining the cause? The five men twiddled their thumbs, drafted messages to the battalion heads, and smoked two packs between them. But at noon on the dot, as if broken loose by a storm, a river of flags flooded the streets on all sides of the plaza. Truck drivers, cabdrivers, Uber drivers, fishermen, domestic workers, pulpería owners, a priest here and there, farmers, waiters, baristas, restaurateurs, car washers, window washers, fed-up government employees, and the pensioned, the unemployed, and the underemployed rushed into the plaza in rumbling waves. Their advance shook the concrete. The taunting pigeons and other birds flew into the air at drastic angles, dodging the vibrating canopy of flags.

Seth had seen all these iterations of the Costa Rican flag before on the internet, but never flying proudly in person. They all did the same thing: replaced the seal with the appropriate political symbol. By far the most common, the swastika, slicing into the white, red, and blue of the fabric. Tom the American expat wore the Confederate flag as a cape. He stood like William Walker, readying his conquest of Central America to annex and introduce into the Union as slave states. But there was one flag that stood out, one so egregious it made even Javier wince. Several members of Tom's group flew the Costa Rican flag with a Rottweiler's face at the center. A reference, of course, to a young, undocumented Nicaraguan man mauled to death by two rottweilers a decade before as police, paramedics, and witnesses stood idly by, listening to the screams and snarls without the slightest intention of helping. Seth's group had seen the flag before on the social media pages, the rottweiler hailed as *The Savior of Costa Rica*. An irony, they all knew—being scandalized by a beast who carried out the same violence they had. But, Seth wondered, how would it feel to have his face sewn into a flag?

The river stopped, congealed into a lake of blood surrounding Seth's group, rippling with every gust of wind. Cheers resounded, crashing into each other in an unintelligible cacophony.

"Javier, now," Seth said. "Start recording."

Pedro Augustín removed an airhorn from his messenger bag. He covered one ear, held it high above his head, and the sudden blare quieted the crowd. Flapping filled the silence, competing only with the surging joy of the distant Pride parade. The brothers helped Seth onto a concrete bench that he used as a podium. Pedro Augustín handed him a bullhorn, and with a quick politician's smile, Seth addressed the mass of no fewer than four hundred.

"Brothers," he said. "And sisters. I see the pain in your faces. The anger in your hearts. But what is most clear to me is the pride in your flags."

The crowd cheered.

Seth held up his hand.

The crowd quieted.

"Costa Rica is a runaway train. The government has let liberalism run unchecked. Every day illegals wriggle past the borders into the gutters and slither out to rob, and rape, and collect the same benefits denied to its citizens. Us."

Ovation, battle cries.

"And every day we careen closer to moral ruin. This government allows fornication and entertains the idea of two men marrying and even adopting children. The values that raised us no longer exist in Costa Rica—we are a country turned on its head. Down is up, wrong is right." Seth paused, released his finger from the bullhorn to gulp. "And death is life.

"We are the Garroteros, brothers and sisters. We are here to stop this before it's too late. We are the saviors of Costa Rica. You, my friends, are the saviors of the homeland.

"Today is a seed," Seth said into Javier's camera phone. "A seed that will grow into change. Today we fight for the soul of Costa Rica. Today we fight against its transformation into Sodom and Gomorrah. Our country will not fall into the hands of pedophiles and predators. We won't let our children be converted to sin. We must act as the shield of God and rally against the rot of our society. ¿Are you with me?"

For the first time, the audience's cheers erupted loud enough to drown out the gaiety of the distant parade. Seth had won them over. Endless waves of applause. Seth felt loved. Respected, whole again. The brothers helped Seth down, and rally-goers formed a line to shake his hand. This was what Seth had always wanted. The path he'd taken didn't matter. It had led him here, to this very moment. He was finally a beloved leader. He had finally surpassed Osario.

Long live the king.

Everyone heard them coming. From the east marched the cantillating river of crimson flags, flooding, and pushing, and separating the festive parade-goers from their friends, as if Moses himself had turned the sea red and parted it in the same spell. The invading crowd chanted loud enough to drown out the EDM from a passing float, quieting the queens who lip-synced to a Whitney Houston remix. *I want to dance with somebody.*

We are the change, the protestors chanted. *¡We are the saviors of Costa Rica!*

Horacio and Carlos were buying bottles of water when they heard the shouting. Carlos's friends waited outside the pulpería, passing around a rainbow Hula-Hoop and dancing.

"¿What the hell is that?" Horacio asked. The discordant, competing rhythms tensed his muscles.

"I have no idea," Carlos said. "Let's find Alberto and them. Come on."

"They showed up out of nowhere," Carina whispered to Horacio and Carlos on the sidewalk. Perhaps if they were quiet and still, the protestors would pass them by.

"Look at the flags," Gustavo said. "Shit, mae, ¡look at the flags!"

Swastikas flew like weapons on the breeze, menacing, hurtling into the parade. Horacio recognized Confederate flags peppering the bastardized Costa Rican ones. Carlos and his friends stepped back, trying to camouflage into the wall of the corner store.

"Faggots," Gustavo said. "They're saying *faggots*."

"Jesus Christ," Carina whispered. "¿Where did they come from?"

The crowd wore fútbol jerseys, the bright vermilion of the national team. They squawked and flapped fabric, curled their fingers into talons. Horacio and Carlos's group watched this protest of scarlet macaws invade the march, hurtling over the barricades into the parade, pushing everyone out with their absonant song. A terrifying hymn of hatred and bile. To the trained ear, a dirge. An uncontrollable, biting anger overtook Horacio.

"¡Nazis!" Horacio screamed. His voice quieted the closest part of the river; the protestors stopped and stared.

"Horacio, shut the fuck up," Carlos said. He grabbed Horacio by the arm to yank him to run, but Horacio pulled it away.

"You Nazi pieces of shit," Horacio said. He stood completely straight, puffed out his chest.

"¡Horacio!" Carlos yelled.

"Your little gringo boyfriend is going to get us killed," Alberto said. "We have to get out of here."

"¡Come on, Horacio!"

"I'm not going anywhere," Horacio said. "I didn't take you for a coward. Come on, back me up."

A circle had begun to form around Horacio—one half the parade-goers behind him, the other half protestors opposite him. He stood like a gladiator awaiting an opponent to dare approach. Horacio turned to Carlos.

"Kiss me," he said.

"You're insane."

"I never told you I wasn't. Come on, just do it."

Carlos looked back to his friends. "Fine," he said to Horacio. Then Carlos kissed Horacio like he'd kissed him the first time, in the center of that writhing floor of naked men. The verges of ecstasy and certain death were surprisingly similar. For the briefest moment, Horacio and Carlos forgot where they were, electrified by the other. The protestors, just as Horacio had planned, jeered and marched toward the lovers. In an equal and opposite reaction, the phalanx of parade-goers stepped forward, closing ranks, preparing for battle.

Rather than spearhead the march, Seth and his group stayed toward the front middle. He delivered orders with the bullhorn—one flank here, another there, to spread out and displace until it was only his protestors. Seth still needed to decide the next steps, examining the situation in order to escalate or merely overwhelm with sheer numbers. Today didn't *have* to get violent. It was better that it didn't. The Garroteros had to play an organization that didn't lower itself to violence. At least, not against civilians. This demonstration was to disperse, not destroy. But Seth heard a commotion from the right flank, close to a pulpería with a red awning and beer signs. He had the brothers Cristiano and Paul clear a path for him. There stood a young boy, no older than eighteen, shouting against his crowd, with a herd of queers behind him. There was something undoubtedly familiar about his face—Seth couldn't pinpoint exactly what, but it shot chills through his muscles. Bright bolts in a blizzard; a rattling of his cane against his prosthetic through his jeans. Again the sensation of teeth digging, tearing, enjoying.

Epithets of all kinds flew into the air, as many as there were mouths hurling them. It was beginning to get ugly. *¡Nazis! ¡Faggots! ¡Fascists! ¡Communists! ¡Hypocrites! ¡Degenerates! ¡Xenophobes! ¡Dykes! ¡Racists! ¡Trannies! ¡Homophobes! ¡Abominations!* So on, and so on, and so on.

Seth's protestors condensed, and marchers from the floats and parade crowded the barricade—too thin a barrier to prevent a skirmish. All around Seth, his people brandished knives and bottles, mouths stuffed with cloth. Disorder overtook the crowd, and Seth yelled for Javier to cut the livestream. Instead, other protestors unsheathed their phones and held them above their heads, high as the flags, high as the rising, sun-hot anger. Seth shoved his way to the very front and locked eyes with the boy. He felt as if all the world's volume had turned off. The boy smiled mischievously—a smirk of having seen right through him.

A shell of a king, conquered by nature, chewed up and spit out into what you are now.

In the overwhelming silence, Seth's heart demanded that he murder the boy for the look on his face, but his mind considered two options: rally his crowd to hold back, to let them shout and jeer all they wanted—the Garroteros wouldn't be intimidated by jabbering cross-dressers—or with the bullhorn, he could ignite the situation. But a battle was becoming increasingly unwise, as policemen approached from the south, only heightening the tension in both groups. Seth smelled gasoline from Molotov cocktails. He felt water on his face from the marchers' neon plastic guns. There he was again, at the bank of the Tárcoles River. And there Osario was, staring back at him from the boy's face. Seth gripped his cane, but it was Pedro Augustín who would spark the skirmish. He descended upon the opposing crowd of marchers, tackling a girl. They both fell to the ground, and everyone stared in disbelief, deciding what to do. It was when Pedro Augustín slammed a fist down onto the teenager's face that it all erupted, descended into blood and chaos.

There was running, both toward and away; screams, curses, cries to stop, roars to go on; the music of metal, the crush of plastic, the shatter of glass, the flap of fabric and flame. Seth had fallen to the ground, and when he looked up, the pulpería was on fire. The boy who'd started this was gone. The brothers Cristiano and Paul helped Seth up, and Javier led them to a side street. Since they carried no flags and no hint of red in their clothing, the stampede of policemen rushed by. Sirens filled the afternoon, and the billowing black smoke from the corner store blinded combatants, scattering them in fits of violent coughing.

Everyone's phones rang, but no one answered. Seth's iPhone vibrated with Max's name, Pedro Augustín's with Luzmilda's. They'd seen the Facebook livestream, watched the pitched Molotov cocktails in either horror or excitement—it had either been a disaster or was all according to plan. Seth looked around at his lieutenants' sweaty, soot-coated faces. They gritted their teeth, failure ice chips in their mouths.

"We need to save this," Pedro Augustín panted.

"¿How?" Seth asked.

"Get back on the livestream, tell everyone to disperse."

"Say it's their fault," Javier coughed. "That we were peaceful, and they were the ones who started it."

"That's our only option," Pedro Augustín said. "We can't be silent or it'll all go to hell."

"Fine," Seth said, rolling down his sleeves, fixing his hair, wiping his face with a handkerchief from Javier's pocket.

"Let's find a nice house with a bench, a fountain, or rosebushes," Pedro Augustín said. "You have to look presidential."

They found a mansion with an extravagant garden a few blocks away. Clean plaster acted as the perfect backdrop, the scarlet roses complementing Seth's white skin and blue shirt perfectly. He himself became a flag, a symbol. The brothers gripped their phones, Cristiano posting to Facebook, Paul to Instagram. Pedro Augustín became a newsroom producer. "Go, Seth," he said. "Now."

"Compañeros," Seth began. "Many of you might have seen videos of what has transpired, and many will misconstrue what exactly happened. How it actually began. I've just escaped with my life. Our peaceful protestors were attacked by miscreants and psychopaths. We were merely exercising our God-given right to manifest. The only pride these people showed was that of anarchy, of discord and the dismemberment of our society. We are all victims." Seth paused dramatically. He sighed and lowered his head.

"We are all victims of these people, addicted to debauchery and violence. Yes," he said, "we are spiritual warriors against their menace. However, we must fight another day. I ask that my people who were peacefully protesting disperse. Let those criminals kill each other. We must save ourselves to save our country."

Pedro Augustín looked down at his phone and held it to his ear. Seth stared into his eyes. Pedro Augustín gave a thumbs-up, and Seth looked confidently back into the phone cameras. "Thank you," he said. "And God bless us all."

"Your little prince from another planet almost got us killed."

Carina's straw sunhat fell as she hunched over in exhaustion. Gustavo lay spread out like a starfish on the asphalt in the middle of a side street. They'd all run away from the parade without pause for at least a kilometer. Zigzagged the whole way, past startled yuppies walking poodles, grandmothers juggling fruit, and traffic signs bent like fallen trees. Alberto jogged every morning, so he was the only one still with breath; he scrolled frantically through his phone, reliving the bedlam. It wasn't yet over, because they still heard cries and saw smoke undulate into the sky, as if made of fabric too. A group of police officers sprinted past without acknowledging them.

"I'm surprised they're not carrying machine guns," Gustavo coughed.

"They only brandish them in grocery stores," Alberto said. "They care more about pilfered toothpaste than they do about us."

"They're probably joining in," Carina added. Her sunhat rested on the ground as if hiding a surprise underneath.

"Yeah, I'm sure they'll get a few licks in and blame it on those Nazis," Alberto said.

"You almost got us killed," Carina growled at Horacio. He sat on the hood of a burgundy Toyota, wiping his forehead with both forearms.

Carlos stood. A strap of his tank top had been ripped, and both his knees bled. "Lay off him, Carina. I'm serious."

"Whatever," she said, and left to walk a lap of the side street.

Carlos approached Horacio, placed his hands on Horacio's thighs and leaned in. "She's right. ¿What the hell got into you?"

"I don't know," Horacio answered, suddenly embarrassed, scolded like a misbehaving child. "Something told me it wasn't right: what they were saying, what they were going to do."

"I really thought you were mature for your age," Carlos said coolly. "But I guess you're still a kid."

Horacio's heart would have broken in that moment if not for the coursing adrenaline. His surroundings still pulsed like a mirage, so Carlos's words didn't register with the intensity he'd intended them to. Horacio felt as if he'd just ingested shrooms or been bit by a venomous animal. The world swayed, and so did he. Carlos swayed, even though he stood still, indignant.

"I don't feel well," Horacio said.

"Here, drink water." Carlos handed him the crushed bottle. He cradled Horacio's head to his chest. "I didn't think I'd end up dying for you," he said. "But I think I would have."

"Romeo and Juliet," Gustavo scoffed. "Jesus Christ, look."

Horacio and Carlos turned to Gustavo's grave expression and his trembling finger pointed in the direction of Seth's approaching group. They'd dusted themselves off, looked as normal as a team of buddies on their way to watch a game. An undetectable pack of predators.

Seth recognized the others immediately. The unmistakable gaggle of queers who had started it all. That boy, the rebellious look in his eyes, smug, as if his body were steel and Seth's jelly. Horacio, he heard one of them call him. *Horacio*, Seth repeated, as if hearing an echo, one that radiated from deep within his cavernous heart. The closer Seth and his group approached, the clearer Osario's features became. That boy carried his brother's eyes and his nephew's name. *It couldn't be*, Seth thought. *Impossible.*

"Look what we found," Pedro Augustín yelled. The brothers Cristiano and Paul cracked their knuckles and Javier slicked his hair back with sweat. They were preparing something without Seth's permission, and Seth knew that even if he ordered them to stand down, they wouldn't. This day had left them bloodthirsty. Carnivorous, cannibalistic. In place of their bodies stood beasts of prey—winged, fanged, taloned, barbed, cloaked in desperation. The kids closed in, readied their fists too.

"I thought they would have run by now," Javier laughed. "They made this generation of queers tougher."

"¡Your father!" one of them shouted; the rest giggled. At first Seth had seen fear in them, but now these kids were defiant, waiting for his group to make the first move.

"It's unavoidable," Seth muttered. He inhaled the bloodlust, stared deep into Horacio's eyes, knowing that the impossible had truly become possible. Fate, as it were, was unavoidable. "Leave the little one to me," Seth said.

Seth's gang descended upon Horacio's, Pedro Augustín going straight for the girl, who ran around a car to avoid him. Javier lunged at the one named Carlos, and they writhed around like expert wrestlers, tore skin on the gravel and asphalt. Knees into ribs, elbows into cheeks, jaws, and temples. The brothers took on the rest, while the boy, Horacio, still sat on the hood of the burgundy Toyota, calm and steady as a snake. The cool, indifferent confidence of his brother. Seth didn't have to speak, didn't have to ask his father's name. Seth knew. He'd never been surer of anything in his life, and he swung his cane like a weapon of legend.

Horacio dodged, and Seth gave chase, ignoring the pain his prosthetic caused, the metal digging past muscle into bone. It wasn't designed for so much movement, such anger, but Seth felt as if his phantom limb had been resurrected for this final act. This final erasure, the extinction of his brother and his enduring bloodline. The final dispelling of Seth's eternal punishment. After a full block Seth cornered Horacio, snatched him by his shirt collar, slammed him into a gutter, and wrapped his calloused hands around his throat. From the boy emanated the memory of that infernal river of oil. The smoke from the candles on his fourth birthday. The coffee, and the concrete, and the whisky from that night. Horacio gasped for air, and with each inhale, Seth's thumbs pressed deeper into his neck, digging for artery and trachea, massaging the life out of him. For just a millisecond, Seth felt something hard, something sharp to his head before all the world went black.

Horacio had reached for a stone as large as his fist. Before he lost consciousness, he swung its jagged, dense edge into the attacking man's temple, the impact enough to immediately release his grip. The man slouched over sideways, and Horacio pushed him off. He coughed life back into himself, curled in pain as his surroundings returned in waves of hot color. His own crying startled him, and when it felt as if his throat had reinflated, he sat up and rested his back against the bumper of a parked car. Panting, he studied the man for signs of life. Readied himself for another sprint in case he awoke, but the man didn't move. Not when Horacio got to his feet, or when he vomited, or when Carlos finally found him, shoulder dislocated and lip twice its own size. Not when Carina kicked the man in the stomach or when Gustavo put two fingers to his jugular. Not even when the paramedics and police arrived to interrogate and file reports.

"It's biblical, ¿no?" one policewoman commented to another. They shared a coffee and traded a pen to jot down notes, periodically shooing away nosy neighbors. "Getting stoned in the twenty-first century. Like something out of a book."

Costa Rica is

Costa Rica

A PATH TO SHINE AFTER HIM

2018

Nieves and Andrés studied the white sheet, its many human ridges. Snow-capped mountains of nose, and chest, and foot. They waited for the detective to return from the bathroom. It was freezing, this morgue. A hypothermia-inducing chill exacerbated by their anxiety. Nieves tried to hold Andrés, but he shook her off and walked to the end of the table, where a tag hung from a big toe like on a present beneath a Christmas tree.

After a week of desperate visits to Horacio's many haunts in D.C., led by Andrés, whom Isa and Nieves used like a bloodhound, they received a WhatsApp call from Carlos. He explained who he was, how Horacio had lost his phone in a skirmish, and what exactly happened at the Pride parade a few hours earlier. They needed to come, he begged. Horacio was all right, but they needed to be on the next flight to Costa Rica.

It was eight hours of excruciating maternal purgatory, both Isa and Nieves either silent or weeping on Andrés's shoulder until they arrived at Juan Santamaría, where Gustavo came to pick them up. "He's safe," he said. "But he's shaken. We can piece it together for you when we get to the police station."

Horacio had spent the day at the precinct, repeating his story between sips of tea and bouts of coughing. Fingerprints burned into his neck, clear and dark enough that the officers could have used them as identification. His eyes glowed so red that it startled Isa when she came running into the station, as if her son had transformed into an enraged beast. But instead, he wailed, and no one in the room could figure out how he could still summon that much breath. Instead of forcing Horacio to speak further, the detective read his statement aloud in a rote, indifferent voice. The boy hadn't died, so there was no use in exerting the energy to sound empathetic. Isa cried, and so did Nieves, but Andrés remained stoic, interlocked his fingers with Horacio's, who sat with his head hung so low his chin rested on his chest. They'd found the attacking man's cédula in his pocket. It said Paulo, but the man's prints and eventual dental X-rays contradicted that. Horacio had killed a man with two names, two lives. A double homicide, a lingering cop joked, who was promptly fired.

Nieves and Andrés hovered over the shrouded body, the fabric so sheer Nieves saw a familiar pattern of chest hair poking through like weeds. Isa and Horacio had stayed in the waiting room because Isa had sensed that it was less her business than her sister's. The forensic pathologist swiped the sheet off like a magician, and in the half second it took to reveal the corpse, Nieves thought there'd be nothing there. Just air, or perhaps a rabbit with a winking nose. But Seth was unmistakable. Haggard, as if he'd been in hell all these years. With only one leg, gnarled and overused. There her husband was, the man she'd loved. Who'd disappeared seven years ago, whom she'd dreamt of but never told anyone. Whose splendid tropical plants she'd kept alive all this time. In order to move forward, she'd hated his memory, had constructed a version of him to reproach and stab when no one was looking. But here he lay, more horrible than she could have ever imagined.

"It's him," Andrés said softly. "My father."

The detective wouldn't believe a minor and looked to Nieves for confirmation. "Yes," she mumbled. "Seth Oreamundo. My husband."

"Good," the detective said, and motioned for the pathologist to again drape the body. Again the cordillera of human features. The ridges of Seth's nose, and chest, and foot. And in the corner of Nieves's eye as she left the morgue, Seth's phantom limb held up the fabric too.

"It's really him," Nieves said to Isa. "After all this time, this is where he ends up." Her tone had changed mid-sentence, transforming in an almost alchemical process from despair to loathing: a clawing, ancient wrath the moment she looked down at Horacio and his bruised face. *He* had murdered her husband. The love of her life, even if she was never truly convinced of it. Death erased the parts of Seth Nieves hadn't known, the parts of him that had frightened her, that had kept a packed suitcase beneath her side of the bed. Her grief and sudden resentment rewrote every memory, and now Seth had been a perfect husband, an attentive father, and that suitcase beneath the bed had been packed in preparation for a cruise. A getaway because they loved each other. But now her husband was spread out like a slab on a table, a stele with scars that looked like writing. A code, a language only she could decipher. Horacio had done this to him. To Andrés, to her. Nieves would have lunged at him if not for Isa wrapping her arms around her, whispering that they'd get through this together.

The press figured it out quickly. An old colleague of Isa's spearheaded the headlines, the hours-long segments and ruthless investigation. The news channels worked more efficiently than the police, as was usually the case. High-ranking members of the Garroteros were hauled off in handcuffs. The brothers Cristiano and Paul snatched from a bar, Javier in his stained-brown briefs from a girlfriend's house, and Pedro Augustín after a televised police chase (he sobbed and begged for his mother when they slammed him onto the hood of his pickup). But even the most decorated detectives of the OIJ couldn't find Max or Luzmilda. Vanished. Their compound was raided, documents and logs confiscated and scoured. The provincial station heads of the Garroteros were brought in for questioning, many charged with acts of terrorism, others with attempted murder. Government prosecutors swung down the gavel with Olympian force, because what was more embarrassing for such a peaceful nation than to house an organized cult of Nazis?

Leaked photos of Seth's autopsy made it onto front pages. Rags, gossip columns, and respected newspapers plastered with his pale, stiff face. They spun his story every which way, the entire country debating his motives, and whereabouts, and means. Some called him an exiled prince, while others christened him the god of destruction. A mythical beast within a mortal whose only living purpose had been dismantling society. He'd been here all this time, a man by another name, but with the same rotten heart.

A week into the news stories, a journalist connected the date of Seth's counterfeit cédula with Osario's disappearance. Ignacio the ambassador was summoned back to Costa Rica and, under oath, testified before the cameras that he had indeed helped Seth sneak back into the country—he hadn't asked

Seth's reasons because they'd been old friends. Never could he have imagined that Seth was capable of *that*. But then again, he wouldn't put it past him. *Ask anyone about his eyes*, he said. *Anyone who'd looked into them would agree with me.* Ignacio was sacked, jailed for fraud, for abuse of power, and hit with a charge to commit a hate crime that didn't stick.

Isa, Nieves, Horacio, and Andrés tried their best to avoid the news, the papers, and the rumors. But the scandal swallowed them, transported them into a new, stark, inhospitable universe populated by assaulting reporters, gossipers at the supermarket, and citizens who skirted their eyes in disgust. Carlos no longer answered Horacio's messages. When Horacio went to Los Yoses to find him, his friends ignored him—Gustavo scoffed, while Carina spit at the ground before he could step closer. Alberto was the only one who would speak to him. *He doesn't want anything to do with you. Anything to do with your family.*

The relentless young reporter who had connected the dates of Seth's return to Costa Rica and Osario's disappearance had once been Isa's intern. Since childhood, he'd been smitten by both her face and her journalistic moxie. As a teen, he'd watched her segment with Osario during Seth's trial over the oil spill in the Tárcoles River. He fantasized about her, and when he enrolled in the university, his cousin pulled a few strings and he became Isa's assistant, fetching coffee and cigarettes, becoming her verbal punching bag; but he didn't mind one bit. The proximity to the love of his life overshadowed menial tasks or Isa's inventive forms of abuse.

Since Isa left Costa Rica, he'd had a rough go at the journalism business: wrote ten-cent articles in the backs of rags or went months without work. But when a buddy showed him Seth's autopsy photos, the reporter started to dig. A grave robber, in a way. He followed the trail of Seth's fake cédula to an overdue bill for a black Audi rental that had never been returned. He remembered the precise date Osario went missing (he'd comforted Isa that day). The week overlapped. He studied the autopsy photograph and noticed the scars around Seth's half-missing left leg: teeth-marks. When he brought the evidence to the biology department at the university, a distinguished professor and zoologist confirmed that the marks came from an American crocodile. *I've seen it a dozen times*, the professor said. *Colleagues of mine, and stupid gringos who approach the river. Those clean incisions are a dead giveaway.*

A journalist's instinct is as powerful as hunger, and as reliable too. The young reporter scoured old newspapers in the national library and found an archived article about Gilberto's Baptism in 1983. The location: Capulín in the Tárcoles River basin. The reporter traveled to the hamlet and for two days he interviewed locals, whose profound memories recognized the picture of Seth he held in his hand. Butchers confirmed that he'd indeed been there seven years ago, buying chicken bits with crisp dollars. Why, they'd had no idea, and still didn't. But he was already piecing together a brilliant puzzle, its completion his ascension to greatness. And perhaps Isa's good graces. Because what woman wouldn't fall in love with the man solving the mystery of her missing husband?

The young reporter knocked on the doors of shacks, was directed to stay on ratty porches while he questioned. One kind woman invited him in for coffee, excited to have some company, her children gone to college, her husband out fishing. The reporter removed the photographs of Seth and Osario from his bag, put them on the table as if the woman were a medium who could summon them back from the dead. And after a minute of dramatic humming, the woman walked over to a plastic desk to retrieve a burgundy Zippo.

OO, it read.

"¿Where did you find this?" the young reporter asked, cradling the lighter, inspecting its value in the light.

"My husband," she said. "He takes to the river at dawn. I miss him all day, but he's a good provider, always comes back with a great catch: fresh, still squirming—mostly snappers, which is why my house smells so delicious. Anyway, sometimes he uses a fine net—so fine it even catches tadpoles—and one day, however many years ago, he scooped this up along with some muck and a license plate. Double *O*," she said. "I assumed whomever it belonged to was a secret agent. Like Bond."

She waited patiently for the young reporter to complete the line, *James Bond*, but he was busy clicking open the lighter and turning its wheel. A spark, an eye-blue flame.

"Still works," the woman said. "¿Amazing, isn't it? It mustn't have been in the river very long."

"Try to remember," the young reporter insisted. "The date. The exact day he found this in his net."

"May," she said, staring up at her tin ceiling. A gecko hunted gnats, scratched its dainty claws on the metal. "Or June."

"¿Are you sure?"

"I think so. It was a little before Father's Day because I remember remarking that the river gave him a gift. That it was generous enough because we were too poor to give him anything so elegant ourselves." The woman paused her thought, gripped onto the word *poor* as if she'd caught a delicious trout in her hands. "¿Do you want that lighter? I can leave it to you for, oh, let's say, one hundred thousand."

The young reporter considered it. The price was half his rent. But he approached the situation as if he were being swindled at a souvenir market. An inevitability. This was no trinket. This little wine-colored Zippo was an artifact of a destiny fulfilled.

Horacio stirred in Isa's arms. In her sleep, deepened by fibromyalgia medications, she swaddled her son, interlocking her hands like a safety belt. She'd spent the week dreaming of car crashes, so every night she held Horacio tighter, just in case. The Airbnb yawned, light leaking through the cracked window, birds chirping in a soft alarm. Horacio was the only one awake. He unbuckled his mother's fingers and made his way into the kitchen, scooped cheap coffee into the cheap percolator, and waited at the counter. He wouldn't dare leave in case reporters had spent the night outside the gate like lampposts, cameras ready to flash, and snap, and invade. Weeks of this: curtains drawn, dark as doors, sneaking out only to buy groceries or cigarettes with sunglasses and baseball caps on. To protect their identities from being blasted on the news.

Horacio drew the curtains just enough for the morning to shine onto the percolator, to study his reflection. The red in his eyes was almost gone, the purple ribbon around his throat splotched yellow, sickly. In another few days the only remnants of the Pride parade would be in his memory. His uncle Seth's grizzly frame pressing down on him with unimaginable force. The warm, jagged rock in his own fist. The percolator whistled. He poured himself a mug and turned on the television, muted. The news began, and there was Osario's face, on the screen like a hung painting even if another news story was playing. His father haunted traffic accidents, a symphony at the National Theater, cooking and fashion segments. Every morning, the channels dedicated half an hour to the speculative tragedy: expert herpetologists described crocodilian behavior, how quickly a gullet could dissolve splintered bone. The young investigative reporter recounted his journalistic journey throughout the Tárcoles basin, new testimony gathered like eggs, all starting with a little Zippo branded *OO*: Osario Oreamundo. Yesterday that reporter announced a book deal—he would spend the rest of his life documenting the Oreamundo family down to its final member. He would investigate and interview his way to the truth: why Seth had thrown his brother into a river of crocodiles and why Seth had been reborn a radical terrorist. Isa had gone about smashing everyone's cellphones, and Nieves let her. Horacio and Andrés didn't fight Isa's hammer. They knew it was the only way. They knew they'd spend the rest of their lives running from the truth that even they, deep down, wanted explained.

The two bedroom doors clicked open, and Horacio shut off the television. He prepared three mugs and forced a smile when Isa, Nieves, and Andrés filed in. No one spoke. Andrés lifted his foot to remove a piece of fiberglass from his sole. He flicked it across the room. Nieves scowled at nothing in particular. Her mug trembled in her hands, and she drew the curtains defiantly and walked out onto the veranda. Isa kissed the back of Horacio's head, parted his hair to inspect the scab from the concrete she'd told him not to scratch. Some of it flaked off into her coffee, but she drank it anyway.

Andrés left to join Nieves.

"What do you want to do today?" Isa asked Horacio.

"What *can* we do?" he answered.

"We can take our chances out in the world. Anything, baby. I have to get out of here, even if we have to mow down a dozen paparazzi to find some peace."

"Should we ask them to join us?"

"I think we all need space. We've got cabin fever, and the outside world isn't helping."

"Okay," Horacio said. "I'll grab my things and meet you in the car." Horacio downed his coffee, grabbed a windbreaker and his green Ray-Bans. He peeked through the glass at the veranda, where Nieves and Andrés were in inaudible conversation. Anger parted their lips, stiffened their shoulders and jaws, clenched their whole bodies.

Isa sped the silver Honda out of the driveway without seeing if the automatic gate closed behind them. It didn't matter because Nieves would murder any slippery reporter wanting the full scoop. Horacio flipped through the radio channels: the dribble of breaking news; Radio 2's American nonsense; static, and static, and more static. Isa was driving with such concentration Horacio didn't speak. He waded in the pool of his own mind. Thoughts of Carlos, what he might be doing on a Monday morning. What they might be doing together if none of this had ever happened. Horacio grew hard and hid his erection with the windbreaker. It wouldn't let up for an hour, the car's motor down winding mountain roads and the warm, licking sun enough to keep it going until Isa pulled into a rest stop named after a saint.

Horacio and Isa were quick. Bought ginger ales and yuca chips, keeping their heads low through the aisles and at the checkout counter. Back in the car they chugged and munched, then pulled off like a bullet back onto the roadway. Sometime later, along Route 127, leaf-green signs that read CAPULÍN grew like rare trees. Horacio eyed Isa because he recognized that name from the broadcasts. He opened his mouth to ask but stopped when he noticed the way her hands gripped the steering wheel—if it were made of anything other than metal, it would have crumpled in between her fingers. They pulled into a hamlet, drove past butcher shops and bars, and two competing churches stuck in a Mexican standoff on opposite sides of a plaza. Locals ignored the Honda, let it pass without a second thought.

Suddenly, on a dry stretch of a busy street, Isa swerved the car into the mouth of a dirt road but stopped, intimidated by the green of its continuation. Ancient trees cat-cradled in a giant archway, seemingly endless till the eye came to a brown, triangular speck. Over the gravel echoed the inside of a shell. Rushing, lapping, the give-and-take against a riverbank.

"Mom?" Horacio whispered. The turn signal clicked its teeth impatiently. Half the car still hung out in the middle of the road. Southbound traffic honked, and drivers left their cars to curse. Horacio waved his hand at a man approaching to tap the window; he threw up his arms, shook his head, and returned to his chrome tanker truck. Horacio didn't wish to break his mother's spell. She was quiet, hawk-focused, as if in a virtual reality where the car raced and jumped over mountains. In her eyes he saw her plans as she imagined them: the squirm of rubber on the gravel; the water, its stink and muck; the infinite scenarios of what had happened between the brothers; the who-did-what-and-why; and the eventual, throat-burning shout at the river. "Mom," Horacio repeated. "It's okay. It's over."

Isa exhaled exaggeratedly, then trembled her hair, checked the rearview mirror, and lurched the car forward to turn around in a dangerous and expert U, flinging pebbles at windshields and her smile at all who were inconvenienced. "Where should we go?" Isa asked.

"Let's get some proper food," Horacio said. "Something I've never tried."

"I'm in the mood for a vigorón." Isa grinned. "Like my mother used to make."

Horacio and Isa returned at four o'clock, sun-kissed and sunburned, respectively. The Airbnb radiated with Nieves's cooking, and Andrés was setting out plates on the false wood veneer of the long dinner table. Horacio washed his hands and sat opposite Nieves, who served herself last and ate her food with disconcerting apathy. Horacio eyed Andrés, who hadn't showered. His foot tapped on the linoleum floor. A restless leg. Isa, too, approached her plate with indifference. The room grew cold, and Nieves finally spoke.

"We're leaving tomorrow."

Isa sighed relief. "That's a great idea," she said. "We can all pack our bags tonight."

"I said *we*." Nieves motioned her head to Andrés without letting down her glare at Isa.

"I don't understand," Isa said.

"Well, you better catch up, sis."

Nieves's body parts tensed into straight lines. She dug her fingernails into the table. Andrés was still, head down.

"Why would we separate, Nieves?"

Nieves fixed her gaze from Isa to Horacio. He saw himself in her eyes. Wide, distorted.

"You can't be serious," Isa said.

"As a heart attack."

"I don't believe you."

"Believe it," Nieves said. "I won't sit across from this little murderer any longer."

Nieves motioned to stand but so did Isa.

"What did you just call him?"

"You heard me."

"Say it again. Sound it out before I break your jaw."

As in all their fights—ridiculous and bloodcurdling alike—the sisters lost sight of anything and everything around them. Andrés lifted himself from the table and motioned for Horacio to follow. They climbed into the silver Honda and sped out onto the late afternoon road. Andrés rolled down his driver's-side window. The wind whipped his black hoodie's drawstrings and his overgrown hair. Horacio studied his jaw, tensed, and the five-o'clock shadow that didn't look too bad on him. He leaned the passenger's seat back, lying down for the rest of the ride to stare through the sunroof at the clouds, long and bright as turmeric stains.

After an hour on the 127, past the familiar green signs that read CAPULÍN, and through the hamlet of butcher shops and bars, Andrés swerved the car into the mouth of the dirt road that had frozen Isa like a judgment. Dusk dyed the archway of trees the darkest shade of green Horacio had ever seen. Breaking through the brake, the car lurched onto a miry bank, the tires complaining and growling in the slop. Andrés cut the motor. He unbuckled his seat belt and left the car. Horacio watched him walk toward the water. He, too, left the car and didn't bother closing the door behind him. The sun was long gone from this angle; its leftover rays reflected off the bellies of distant clouds, pregnant with rain and bolts. Andrés sat on a dry, neglected log; Horacio, at its other end. A quiet seesaw of cousins turned brothers, looking on at the rushing, tenebrous river. At the vibrant life it provided and the bitter ghosts it made.

"How do we escape it?" Andrés asked, more to the water than to Horacio.

"Together," Horacio whispered.

"What if we can't?" Andrés ripped a strip of bark and flung it. "My mom's not gonna lay off."

"She won't. And I don't think my mother will either."

"She's got it stuck in her head . . ."

"Maybe in New York we can . . ."

"She never even liked my dad . . ."

"We don't have to go back *every* summer . . ."

"And here he was, standing in this fucking mud." Andrés's voice broke Horacio's train of thought. The dorms, their classes, the liberation of the city all melted away.

"What the fuck was he doing before he was on that table, Horacio? Seven years gone, going out of his mind. He was already a maniac. A goddamn loony. You know he took me to the zoo before he disappeared? Took me to see the crocodiles."

Andrés shouted the last word at the river, goading it for the specimen Seth had hunted all those years ago. "He stared at the glass, into the monsters' eyes, and whispered to them. Talked to them like I'm talking to you. Is that in me,

Horacio? Is he in me? I'm probably standing right where he was. And your dad . . ."

Andrés's thought slipped into the river.

"You did the world a favor. I've heard about bad blood, how it spoils the moment you're born and the rest of your life you bleed vinegar. What if I have that blood, Horacio? Sometimes I feel so alone I want to burn the whole world down. You can be in the room next to me, and my mom can be in the kitchen, but I know you all don't want me there. Like, if you had the choice, I'd disappear. And I want to take a match to the whole thing. Starting with my dad's stupid plants," he laughed, wiping his eyes with his sleeves. "What do I do if I have that blood? How can we escape if my father's always there?"

Horacio couldn't answer. Andrés grew silent. A calm, decision-making quiet. He removed his black hoodie and started toward the river. But he didn't stop where Horacio thought he would. He kept going. Horacio shouted from the log, but Andrés didn't answer and didn't stop walking. It was when his feet touched the water's edge that Horacio shot forward, shoes sucked and snatched by the mud. He made it barefoot and winded by the time Andrés had surrendered, waist-deep, to the current and whatever lurked beneath. Horacio wrestled him away from the river, onto the bank, Andrés fighting and howling to return to its inviting, stinking murk. Horacio flipped Andrés onto his back, pinning his shoulders down with both hands. The sweat from his chin fell to join the tears on Andrés's cheeks. If there was anything Horacio could say in this moment, he couldn't. Andrés stopped kicking and gazed up at Horacio, who didn't lift his body. Andrés pushed his head forward. Horacio lowered his. A slow, determined grief broke their geometry, closing the space between their chests. Cradled by night's cold-blooded blanket, sinking into the silt, the boys, stripped of everything but a past that would far outlive them, looked into their reflections in each other's eyes. Andrés opened his mouth. Horacio opened his.

In the darkness, an overflow. The desperate, primal urge of the body to revert to water, to return to the place it's welcome; to revisit the infinite histories within itself that glister like a school of silvery fish. Hunger slunk and snaked away into the river, back to where it had hatched. Where the future is but an appetite, and fate a shivered heart to be weighed upon the tongue.

"¡Hey, wait for me!"

"¡Hurry up, Osario!"

"¡Wait by that tree, Seth! We're far enough away from those things."

"Catch your breath."

"It's caught."

"¿Can you believe it?"

"I can't."

"¿Do you think everyone in the house will believe us?"

"Not a chance."

"We almost died."

"Don't be dramatic, Seth. The monsters weren't even paying attention to us."

"Nieves and them wouldn't have run if we weren't in any danger."

"¿Did you see the size of those things?"

"That's what I'm saying."

"I guess they could have swallowed us . . ."

"Or torn us apart . . ."

"Maybe you're right, Seth."

"I'm always right."

"Yeah, sure. You think because Grandfather reads to you, you know it all."

"That's not why, Osario."

"¿Then why?"

"Because I'm older."

"Because you got lucky, Seth."

"¿Do you want to be the older brother?"

"I'd be a better big brother than you. I'd actually give you a hug on your birthday."

"It is my birthday."

"You know what I mean. Our birthday. I'd slap your back and tell you, 'Happy birthday, Little Brother. I'm so grateful you were born. We get to share the world together. ¿Aren't we lucky our mother chose the same day to love us?' That's what I'd say."

"Hm."

"And we'd be glad together. And I'd protect you."

"¿From the crab?"

"The snake."

"I would have protected you, Osario."

"Maybe."

"I would have. Sit with me."

"I don't want to."

"Come on."

"Fine."

"You don't know what it's like, Osario. Being the oldest. Sometimes I can't handle the pressure. I have to be a man all the time, and you get to be a boy still. I have to be strong even though I want to curl up into a ball."

"Drama queen."

"I'm serious."

"I know."

"Father can't stand me, and Mother doesn't even want to be in the same room as me."

"That's not true . . . Okay, fine, maybe that's true. But they still love you, Seth."

"Not like they love you."

"If I was older, I'd make them love you. I'd throw them down on the ground and say, 'Hey, you, love Seth just as much as you do everyone else. He's good. He's a man even when he doesn't want to be. He's my brother and that's enough.' Hey, don't cry."

"I'm not."

"Maybe I can be the big brother for a while."

"It doesn't work like that."

"Well, maybe we can have a do-over, then. You'll be born on my birthday and we'll always share a cake and they'll make it half and half because I don't like chocolate. And they'll sing to both of us, and we'll grow up and get married and celebrate all the time with our families. It doesn't have to be here. We can run far away. It'll be a new life and we can make it how we want. I'll be there to protect you whenever you need it. I'll be strong when you can't."

"We'll have to wait. We can't have a do-over until this is done."

"That makes it more exciting, Seth. It'll be so great. You'll see."

"It's getting dark. Let's get back."

"¿Do we have to?"

"Yeah, before those monsters change their minds."

"But you'll protect me, ¿right?"

"Yeah, Little Brother. Now, come on, we have to go."

ACKNOWLEDGMENTS

Back in 2015, I wrote a short story about brothers and crocodiles between making crepes in Costa Rica. When I sent it off into the wilderness, *Cardinal Sins* journal at Saginaw Valley State University scooped it up from the muck and gave it life. If Submittable is natural selection, then I owe those editors all the thanks in the world for setting this novel on its path to evolution and completion. Long live independent and university journals.

Ten years later, Amber Oliver read that story turned manuscript and said yes. What a gift to have had you as my editor to decipher the scattered hieroglyphs of my mind. Thank you from the bottom of my heart. I extend eternal gratitude to Mo and the team at Bloomsbury, you expert crocodile wranglers, you.

Thank you to my agent, Erin Harris, for staring into the deep, dark maw of the future and trudging forward without fear. Never fear.

Thank you, Deise Nishimura, for recounting what happened between you and that Amazonian croc; your harrowing journey of survival and grace. Seth wouldn't have been able to finish his story without yours.

Thank you to Ingrid Rojas Contreras, Tin House, and my 2019 cohort for treating these first pages with generosity and respect.

Thank you to all my readers and listeners throughout the years, especially those who helped me crack the code time and time again. Jenn, Zefyr, Vanessa, Tara, Meaghan, Jessica, Isle, Diana.

I couldn't have done it without the love of my friends, my family, and especially my sister—who deserves her own Nobel Prize for the hours of having to listen to me yap about this goddamn book—and my grandmother, the culprit for my incessant need to story-tell.

I honor the spiritual protectors of the river, who lurk beneath our dreams to ensure we do not pollute its flow with our greed, our unfortunate hubris. May we keep the waters of this earth clean and allow life to continue without our thirsty intervention.